1

CLAWS

I sprang onto the picket fence, gauging the trajectory like those old American baseball holos we'd seen in school, back before the empire and its pastime collapsed, of course.

The pungent smell of the Conalds' dog hit me, but he wasn't anywhere in their big yard. Must be in their two-story mansion. What did a dog do all day? Despite being wolfish—and an unusually wild animote at that—I hadn't the slightest idea. Actually, domesticating pets at all was weird, but the Conalds were good people, I guess.

I dove for the ball but came up shy as it clattered to the ground alongside Mr. C's rusty e-bike. He'd let me ride it once. It'd be nice not to have to walk everywhere, but would take Mom months at the center to afford something like *that*. At least we didn't hit it or break a window, again...

My spine tingled as I reached for the ball. There was a faint *crunch*.

Bruce appeared from around back, staring me down, the fifty-kilo mutt baring his teeth as he crouched. Jeez. I took a step back, unsure how to react—it was always strange between us half-human animotes and animals. Was it jealousy? My claws shot out as I stood taller to scare the dog off. The wind turned, and a whiff of flowers and feces hit me.

Bruce froze and time slowed. Without warning, he dropped his shoulder and charged, muscled body bounding toward me as he built up to killing speed, his uncomplicated eyes burning with primal anger.

Crap. I ran for the fence. I was fast, he was faster.

At the last second, I spun and snarled, flashing my fangs. He skidded, whimpering, and slammed through the white fence, bolting down the dirt road.

Shoot. Should I follow? It might make things worse. I ran to Mr. C's porch and hammered on the painted door. Nothing.

The window didn't help, only my disheveled reflection: bags under dark silver eyes and even my hair—short with flecks of silver, black and brown—looked messy. Forgot to shave too, dark stubble covered my pointed cheeks and chin. Oh well. Mr. C wouldn't mind. Another knock. No luck.

Now what? "Pavel? Toras?" I yelled. They must have taken off when the dog appeared. Crap. Tapping my wristband, I opened a virtual screen, fingers flying through the air as I fired a quick message to Mr. C explaining what happened.

I headed in the direction Bruce had run, but stopped. After what happened at Ms. Ivey's, I knew I should grab Mom. She'd have a fit otherwise. I sprinted home.

Three minutes later, our two-room hovel came into sight. The door was ajar, good old Elly at the kitchen table, calling Vovi from the sound of it. Elly's blue eyes focused on two glimmering holographic screens floating in front of her.

Mom was out back, bent over her newest pet project; a tangle of sweet potatoes along the 3D-printed wall. Her jet black hair was in a bun, furry arms sweating. Being wolfish, we didn't eat many vegetables, but "It's cheaper if you grow it," as she liked to say. Unless you lived in the cities... but for bottom-dwellers like us, that would never happen.

I told her everything.

She dropped the roots and whipped around, brown eyes thrashing me as mine sought cover in the dirt beneath my feet. "Not again."

"It wasn't my fault," I said before she got going.

She stood, her eyes blistering. "It's never *your fault!*"

After getting the facts straight, we headed out. It was a chilly autumn day, but a beautiful one, colorful leaves dancing in the wind. Mom took a deep, calming breath, looking around our well-kept little yard as mist rose from her lips. "Did Roge see what happened before you left? I hope you didn't leave a mess and not say anything, Raek Mekorian. That's not how I—"

"No, I tried..." I cut in. I explained everything again which seemed to placate her, somewhat.

Dread built as we walked the dusty road, past sporadic huts and shacks. A handful of furry neighbors were out, enjoying the weather or on video calls as they gardened or gossiped, but we hurried past. Mom was on a mission, which was never good.

As we got closer, Mr. C's slimy, wet musk assaulted my extra sharp nose. He must be back. I should have waited...

Mom's expression darkened with each passing meter as she ran callused hands through her sweaty hair. Not a good sign.

Mr. C appeared, his pale-green-tinted skinscales standing out against the backdrop of the enormous two-bedroom house. He was tall and bald, with emerald eyes, a pointed nose, and his signature ultra-warm red jacket.

Mom put on her best smile. "Roge, I am really sorry. Whatever the boy's done, we'll make it right."

"I know, Preta. You wolfish are good about honor," he replied. "I got your message, Raek. What happened?"

Both adults turned to me and I fidgeted. "We were all playing down the street..." I pointed for effect. I'd been through this enough to know details and sincerity went a long way. "I didn't mean to scare him or hurt him, I swear. Dogs don't do well with *our* kind."

We all shared a knowing look. It happened all the time with us animotes—descendants of those ill-advised initial genetic experiments—and unenhanced animals. It was innocent at first, a gene here, a mutation there. But it was never enough. You'd think reptilian genes for regeneration or canine ones for metabolism could only help, right? Talk about unintended consequences... Eventually, there were dozens of types of animotes and the -ish thing stuck, hence "wolfish."

Mr. C pulled up a virtual screen with several areas highlighted and pushed it to my school-issued wristband. "Bruce has run away before. I'm sure Raek will find him." He patted me on the shoulder. "Be glad you're not a cold-blooded old fart like me, it's going to be cold tonight."

That would suck. I turned to leave.

"Don't make me regret this, Raek Mekorian!" Mom yelled before I'd gone far.

"Yes, Mom," I answered without looking back, rolling my eyes. She always had to have the last word...

"I'm sorry," she said as I took off. "Kids, you know?"

"Don't be too hard on the boy. Remember the things we used to...."

By the time I reached the crumbling mass graves at the edge of town—about two hundred meters out and not the place to dilly-dally —my sharp ears could no longer hear what they were saying. Odd, must be windier than usual. Skirting the creepy memorial, I shivered, avoiding the place like, well—like the plague it once was before it changed *everything*.

* * *

Where was he? It'd been almost an hour.

Crash.

Something was out there, in the murky forest. The fur on the back of my arms and neck shot up, an electric shock stabbing my spine. My heart raced and the wolf in me smelled blood, feces and fowl too.

I found Bruce, what was left of him that is, the moon casting an eerie glow on his limp body. Insects stirred and wings fluttered as I crept into the clearing. It was surrounded by billowing pines and hefty oaks, making it near impossible to see into the wood or distinguish much beyond the sappy butterscotch of the trees.

The dog's scruffy hind leg was broken and missing from the joint down. Warm blood dripped from the wound.

Ugh. I knelt next to him, but his side wasn't much better. Gashes several centimeters deep ran the length of his torso; sticky blood matted his fur. Was that bone? Jeez! What did this? The claws were sharp and narrow, wicked long too. Wait, there were six of them. Six? No way. I'd never seen the six-clawed beast before—no one had, as far as I knew—only heard tell. This was *definitely* experimental!

Holy crap. My chest thundered. It wasn't safe here. But the dog's pulse... If Bruce was alive, I had to save him, at least try... It was my fault he'd escaped. I retracted my claws, as far as they'd go, and put my fingers under his jaw, holding my breath. Come on, Bruce, come on!

No pulse, nothing. Pressing harder and harder, my fingers went numb, desperate to find a pulse. Damnit, Bruce. My claws scraped his clammy skin as his body cooled.

Standing, my knees buckled, body shaking. I hadn't realized how scared I was, or how dark it had gotten. Without wolfish eyes, I wouldn't have been able to see anything. Even so, everything beyond thirty meters was black.

My fur tingled and gut twitched. Something was approaching. *Crunch*. A twig broke. A loud *THUD*.

I sprinted all the way home—all thirty minutes—not stopping until the door was slammed shut and locked behind me.

Mom jumped up from our little kitchen table, rattled. Her brown eyes were wide with startled fear bordering on anger, her wiry body tense.

Bent over, panting, hands on my knees, I let out a deep breath. Another. My heart was exploding in my chest, lungs about to burst. What was I thinking? Alone, at night...

Bleary-eyed, his dark hair disheveled, my brother Vynce opened the flimsy door of our joint sleeping room, careful not to wake Elly. "What happened to you?" he joked—like always—to hide his unease as he shifted from side-to-side. "You see a ghost, or a cop?"

"Is everything okay, baby?" Worry lines creased Mom's normally confident face at the mention of the corrupt police force. She wrapped the ratty light blue bathrobe tighter and crossed the makeshift living room in an instant. "Did you find—"

"Bruce is dead!" I burst out. "Something killed him."

"Hold on, what happened?" Her eyes narrowed as her furry face darkened. "Are you okay? Where's the dog?"

"I told you, he's dead." Jeez, I was shaking. Covered in goosebumps, I replayed the scene in my head. For once, my fur wasn't warm enough. "In the forest. Whatever it was ripped his leg clean off and sliced open his side. Six claw marks. Six!"

"My god!" She covered her mouth, and her claws shot out involuntarily. A raw, animal fear I'd never seen flickered across her face as she threw her arms around me. "Are you okay, baby?"

No, not even close.

"Awesome!" Vynce flashed his fangs, and put his arm around me. "Did you see—"

"Shut up, Vynce!" Mom barked. "Go back to bed. No, on second thought, go get Mr. C. Tell him what happened. Put on your jacket and bring your wristband. Ping me when you get there."

He grumbled, scratching his 'tough guy' beard as he slumped away.

"Now, Raek, tell me everything."

After I'd finished, Mom sighed. I couldn't believe she'd stayed quiet the entire time. That was a bad sign. It also meant she believed me, which was good. I got mixed up in stuff a lot, even once with a pair of emulate elites after she'd pulled me from soccer to focus on school—damned immortals. She didn't always believe me, didn't realize I was in the wrong place at the wrong time.

Ten minutes later, the door flew open. It was Vynce, Mr. C on his heels, his wiry body rigid. Here we go...

"Where's Bruce? What happened?" Even in a thick black jacket and denims, Mr. C looked cold, scared, and angry, his hair rumpled, emerald eyes flashing. "Raek?"

"Raek was telling me what happened, Roge," Mom said, hands on her bony hips. "Sounds like Bruce was attacked."

The odd-shaped flaky skinscales along Mr. C's neck flashed burnt crimson, then back to normal. You'd miss it if you blinked. But I'd seen it. I was positive. My stomach tightened. This was all *my* fault. If I hadn't jumped the fence...

"I am so sorry, Mr. C," I sputtered. "I was too scared to carry him back. I... It was dark. There was blood everywhere."

"It is okay, Raek." He gritted his teeth. "You did the right thing. I'd never risk a boy's life for a mutt. Your brother tells me there were claw marks. Six of 'em. Are you sure?"

I flinched. Of course I'm sure. "I can take you back there if you want. Do you think it's—"

"Shhh! Let's not speculate until we know more." He gave me a serious look that stopped me dead. "Wouldn't want to start a panic. I'll be back at first light. You, Raek, and you, Vynce." He looked at us and his face hardened. "I am going to need your help. Raek has some of the sharpest eyes and ears in town. I'll grab Merck and his son Roderik in case there's trouble. They're bearish boys, brutes in a fight."

Made sense he'd bring his Resistance buddy. It took a special breed to stand up to the vicious Global Democratic Republic, or GDR as we liked to call the BS world government. We'd had two executed in town almost a year to the day.

With that, he said goodnight and headed out.

Sleep? How could anyone think of sleep at a time like this? Vynce and I were wired and stayed up late, hushed whispers and dark tales.

2

ADVENTURE

Bam. *Bam. BAM.*

What was that? Had the elites decided to eradicate us at last? I launched from bed, sneaking a glance in the living room.

Vynce looked up from the couch, laughing. "Kevo's an idiot! Stupid junkie plugged into the Neuroweb and forgot to activate his sound fields." At least there were only a few worthless VR users in our town.

Calm down, Raek, it was a dream...

From the other room, Vynce laughed again. Typical Vynce, always relaxed and joking. Why couldn't I be more like that? Instead, here I was, terrified, close to pissing myself, and we hadn't even left.

A knock. Mr. C opened the door and let himself in. He wore a rugged brown jacket and hand-me-down denims, a massive hunting knife on his hip, and, along his back, a thirty cal. A rubbed raw blade was tucked into his black hiking boots.

A second later, Mr. Ilt and Roderik stepped through the doorway. Both wore leather vests over their thick bearish fur, massive hand-made crossbows over their shoulders and a pistol at each hip. Mr. Ilt had a machete as well... Dang, I should have gotten ready earlier.

Mr. Ilt's right arm was bare from the forearm down, a tiny seam below his elbow. It was a prosthetic, a good one too. How the heck could he afford *that?*

"One second!" Vynce checked himself in our one mirror and shoved things into a bag.

Mom and Elly came out of our one bedroom, making things even more crowded.

"Morning, Preta," Mr. C said with a smile. "Didn't mean to wake you."

"It's fine, Roge. Wanted to see the boys off." She looked at us, her face cast in iron, and subjected Vynce and I to 'the stare.' "You two take care of each other. And listen to what Roge and Mr. Ilt say." Her eyes burned my forehead until I looked down. "They are in charge, no exceptions. I'll see you boys home for supper. And be careful." She pulled us close, hugging each in turn. "You never know what could happen," she added with uncharacteristic apprehension.

We escaped the cramped house and before I knew it, we'd reached the edge of the woods and drew our weapons. Everyone turned to me and Mr. Ilt said, "Lead the way, Raek."

"Give me a chance to get my bearings." I sniffed, staring at the trees. It was a lot different during the day and the forest must be dozens of square kilometers. My nose wasn't *that* good. But I couldn't let them down.

Why was this so—Wait! I recognize this stump. I tripped on it last night. Closing my eyes, I turned. "Here. This way!" I flew down the path before someone yelled, and had to pause to let the others catch up.

An hour later, we walked into the still clearing. "This is it," I whispered as if my voice might bring the beast back. But where was Bruce? Running to the spot where he had lain, I sniffed. What happened? "He was here. See the blood on the grass?"

Mr. C and Mr. Ilt tiptoed over and knelt beside me.

"Bastard came back, I guess," Mr. C said, eyes clouded, face drawn.

From off to the side, Roderik said, "There's something over here! Looks like drag marks."

Sure enough, specks of crimson littered the ground, the grass flattened in the most unnatural way. The huge dog had been dragged. What could do that?

Mr. Ilt patted his son's shoulder. "Boys, stay sharp. It might be nearby."

We all froze, our eyes flicking to the foreboding trees. Was it out there?

"I don't hear anything," I said, more to myself than anyone else. Everyone knew my ears were some of the best in town, and didn't comment as I led on.

Thirty minutes later, we found the body, the rotting scent growing stronger and more sickening with every step. We cleared the undergrowth and saw Bruce, what was left of him at least.

Everyone recoiled and Mr. C let out a gasp, his face contorting. It was awful. Half the hindquarters and a large portion of the torso were gone. Flies buzzed everywhere, making it impossible to think straight.

No one dared mention the six claw marks.

For once, my nose let me down. We couldn't find a trail. No footprints, no scents, nada.

After a while, Mr. Ilt said we should head home.

Roderik tried to protest, but his dad said, "Some battles aren't worth fighting. Besides, there's enough pain and suffering for us animotes as it is. No point getting killed out here and making things easier for the elites." He gave Mr. C a knowing look.

Mr. C nodded. "We may not have a vote, but we have numbers. One day things will be better." His voice trailed off, a distant, sad look in his eyes I'd seen many times before, one all animotes knew too well: frustration, sadness, a scarce hope.

Heading back, my mind wandered. It had been like this since The Experiments. At least that's what people said. In those days, humanity was united—not as a civilization—but as a species at least. All the races could even breed together! I couldn't wrap my head around that.

Something made me jump, and I clutched my knife. It had been Grandpa's before those drunk cynetic cyborgs blasted him. He died a few years back, a rough patch between animotes and the GDR. I was too little to remember him.

"I know, sir. I thought, I could learn it on my own and try to apply, convince 'em. You know?" Pavel said in an excited voice.

"No, I don't know," the inspector replied icily. The man's hard eyes narrowed further. "Can you spell it out for me? Which part of the law did you think you could convince 'em to break?"

"Um, well, I didn't—"

"I think what Pavel is trying to say, sir," Ms. Hetly cut in, "is that he has big dreams and wants to contribute to society. Right, Pavel?"

"Yes, ma'am. Yes, sir. That's—that's what I meant." Pavel looked away, flushing.

"I don't buy it. Remember your place." The enhancer sneered. "You're dismissed, all of you. Get out!" He turned to Ms. Hetly. "Not you, Pelly. You stay here with me."

His voice gave me chills as we rushed for the door.

4

AUTUMN

UTUMN WAS MY FAVORITE season, but it always ended too soon. This autumn was no different, except for the attack. The months flew by, but people were on edge. Even good old Mr. Trew seemed stressed. Elephantish, I've heard. But it's hard to tell. A lot of folks are like that, their human DNA is dominant. But if you see someone on the street without a fancy evosuit, they're animote. We could never afford that kind of awesome tech. I'd seen holograms of elite kids messing around: the suits absorb impact, prevent burns, even stop a knife.

They weren't faked either. I checked. That was a big problem for a while, before The Experiments. Scientists researched AI back in those days. The Bioplague changed all that. When the GDR formed, it clamped down on AI research. Said it was for our protection, but it was about power. AI could change everything. They didn't want that.

We even had to watch *Terminator* in school. All. Six. Of. Them.

Mom's voice shattered my sleep. "Wake up, Raek! It's time for school!"

Had I been dreaming? Crap, I fell asleep. I'd wanted to practice more warehousing examples before today's test.

There was a knock at the front door. By this time, I was dressed and ready.

"It's Pavel!" Mom yelled. "Did you study for manufacturing?"

Crap. "Yes, Mom," I lied, not making eye contact as I slipped out the door.

Pavel was waiting on our dinky doorstep, anxious to leave. The weather was beautiful with a rich red sunrise and warm breeze.

"Ready, princess?" He elbowed me in the ribs and earned a jab for his snark as we hurried to avoid being late.

At school, something felt off. A crowd of parents milled about the entrance, talking to a group of restless teachers. Gloomy, nervous energy hung over the place.

We heard snippets of conversation. "What's all the commotion..."

"Have you seen..."

"Police?"

Pavel and I looked at each other.

Ah, Professor Fitz. If anyone could tell us what was going on, it would be him.

"Professor Fitz, Professor Fitz!" I ducked through the crowd and dodged a huge bearish dad to get to him, grabbing his arm.

Professor Fitz looked terrible, heavy bags under his dark eyes that reminded me of a Neurowebber. From the looks of it, he hadn't slept. His beard was unkempt, his hair disheveled, and even his signature microfiber shirt had wrinkles.

"Professor Fitz, what's going on?"

"Raek, Pavel, I'm glad you two are okay," he said, tone grave. "There's been an attack. By the elites, Merie Mram. She was a year or two younger than you boys. She was found dead. It looks like elites, the cynetics."

I gasped. Merie? Vovi's sister? Vovi was always at our house. Jeez, little Merie...

"You boys should go home. We don't need anyone else getting hurt. School is canceled today. I'll see you tomorrow, unless the search takes longer."

He stepped closer, giving each of us a glare Mom would be proud of. "And don't even think about it, Raek. You either, Pavel. This is a job for adults."

Actually, it was a job for the police, but they could care less.

His eyes narrowed further. "I don't want to see either of you in those woods. Got it?"

"Yes, sir," we said automatically.

"Linus, get over here!" someone shouted.

"I have to go, boys, and so do you. Go home, and stay home." With that, he turned in the direction of the caller and disappeared into the crowd.

Elly tapped me on the shoulder and I jumped. For a second, I thought she was Vynce—they had the same eyes and nose, plus her hair was back in a bun. "Jeez, sis, a little warning would be nice."

"Thank goodness I found you, Raek," she said, talking fast, her voice high. "Have you heard? We need to go home. *Now!* Oh, Pavel," she added, noticing him. He turned bright red. Pavel was even more embarrassed around girls than me, especially Elly—not that they'd ever be able to have kids or a future, him, owlish, and her, wolfish.

"Let's stick together, Raek, and find Vynce. Pavel, you can walk with us. Come on." With that, she turned and scanned the crowd.

* * *

We got home fine, but it took longer than usual. We were excited and nervous, and must have checked over our shoulders a dozen times. It had been a long time since anything like this had happened.

Accidents and occasional run-ins were one thing, but murder—cold-blooded murder—didn't happen often. Even with the mixing in the cities, violence was rare thanks to extreme punishment. Out here though, there was nothing. Kiag was a small animote town, one of thousands. We knew everyone.

Outsiders were another story, hothead cynetics and emulates in particular. They'd grab a maglev, zoom a hundred or more kilometers and be here in thirty minutes or less to bother our women without consequence. At least that's what parents said when they thought we weren't listening.

I was deep in thought when Vynce punched me in the shoulder. "You listening, dude? What do you think?"

He must have been standing there all along. "I think we should help find Merie's killers," I said. "Those bastards can't get away with this."

Elly appeared in the doorway. Crap. "Shh." If Elly heard, she'd rat us out.

"I want in," she said, as if reading Vynce's twin mind and knowing we were up to no good. "Merie is Vovi's sister, and I want in. Vovi too. Tonight?" She scratched her button nose and twirled her golden-brown curls—her nervous tell.

No way. My jaw dropped. Vynce looked just as shocked.

"Yeah, tonight," I answered for both of us. It felt good to be the impulsive daring one for a change. And Elly always looked out for me.

We talked timing before looking at each other. No one said a word. If we got caught, we'd be dead. Mom would kill us. She was a tornado when she went off, destroying everything in her path.

The afternoon dragged on. I couldn't concentrate on my Political Theory homework. I should have done it last night, but forgot. Then again, it was propaganda BS, at least that's what Vynce said. He'd heard that from one of his friend's dads.

Mom called dinner. Sweet potato soup, again. Ugh. If we were mouseish, it wouldn't be a problem, but the bland, earthy aroma was embedded in our biofabbed walls after countless nights of the taste-less medley. Always potatoes or soup or veggies, the cheap stuff. Meat was a rarity. In a world where half the population had cheap, high quality, lab-grown meat, you'd think we could afford some too. And we could, if it wasn't for the town tariffs. Plus a hunting permit was out of the question, way too expensive, and Mom wouldn't risk much poaching.

During dinner, Mom gave us the spiel—the *be careful and don't do anything stupid* spiel—as we stared into our orangey, day-old soup. Somehow, I kept a straight face.

After eating, Mom left with the leftovers and we put our heads together before Elly went to make cocoa.

"Wow, cynetics. It's happening," Vynce murmured once she was out of earshot.

"I know. We probably won't find 'em though." I hoped we didn't. They must have gone home...

His eyes lit up. "We might though, we'd be heroes."

I didn't care about being a hero. "I just want to stop those guys, those pigs."

A noise. I was supposed to be keeping lookout. I didn't smell anything but sprinted outside to be sure.

It was dark out, pitch black. The Moon was a sliver of itself in the night sky. The cold night air gave me a rush, fur on the back of my neck rising as the wolf in me readied itself.

Mom took forever paying her condolences. They weren't close, but that's how Mom was. She helped everyone.

Fifteen minutes later, I headed in. Elly was at the table, two virtual screens open, typing fast. She was smart, always had been. Not much of an outdoorsy girl, but boy did she love her books, the exact opposite of her rebellious twin. While Vynce hated school, Elly had read all thirty physical books in the three closest libraries, even though they were boring governmental ones.

Two hours to kill. What could I do? I had to burn this nervous energy in the pit of my stomach.

The web. I hopped on our family's one computer. It was an old clunker, 2050s or 2060s at best, and couldn't handle the VR Neuroweb. Probably a good thing, might be too tempting.

Blinking twice and raising my eyebrows, it verified my secure sign in and decrypted my account.

What was I looking for?

"Show me the news." Nine glowing screens appeared filling my view. The story at the top right caught my eye and expanded, others floating to the side.

Animote Rebels Involved in Firefight with DNS.

Interesting. Did they have video?

'This is Grahme Yipel reporting live from Faelig. Today, the Department of National Security (DNS) raided the apartment of a group of known animote terrorists. While details are sketchy, officials report the terrorists were targeting several large schools and hospitals. The damage would have been catastrophic.'

The camera panned to a small apartment filled with munitions and explosives, even a couple bulky anti-aircraft guns. 'An anonymous tip allowed officers to apprehend the suspects before the attack. We won't be seeing these traitors any time soon, other than the execution... And we have a short message from Minister Fury himself.'

It cut to a lofty wood-paneled office, a statuesque hard-eyed man with charismatic intensity sitting at a mahogany desk. He radiated power and there was something familiar about his abyss-black eyes. It gave me the creeps.

He stood, now even more imposing. 'Remember, helping or harboring possible fugitives is a capital crime punishable by death. If you see or hear anything suspicious, contact your local DNS office. It is our job to keep you safe.' His icy stare engulfed the camera and Grahme jumped back in, signing off after a foreboding silence.

I was skeptical of reports like these. We'd seen enough banned dystopian films—thanks to Mr. C—and read enough contraband sci-fi to know propaganda, violence, and government control went hand in hand. Either way, most of the story was bogus. The rebels—at least how they'd always been described to me—would never hurt kids. Bombing a school, no way. Sure, children might be injured blowing up government buildings or a police station, but a school? I didn't buy it.

That led to a rabbit hole.

Vynce tapped my shoulder, scaring the daylights out of me. "I'm ready, I'm ready." I gave him an angry look to hide my fright and took a few deep breaths. That was one thing about a real computer versus a band connection; the sound field. Somehow, focused sound waves shielded you from all but the loudest of outside noises. Great for concentration and flow.

He smirked and nudged me in the ribs. "Good. Hope you put your big boy panties on."

I rolled my eyes. He liked to play tough, but I could take him. That was new. Before I'd turned sixteen, I'd been a lot smaller. Vynce had always won when we brawled. But I'd gained ten centimeters and five or ten kilos the last twelve months. Now we were both about 185, although he was a dork and would stand on his tiptoes to say he was taller.

Everything was ready. Plates were cleaned, dishes washed, and Vynce had stopped watching his Zone Five reality show—some survival thing elites loved where animotes competed for a job in Caen.

I listened for Mom's rhythmic breathing. She was out cold. "We're good. Let's go."

We headed out.

It felt like the night I'd found Bruce and I had a bad feeling about this. "Where's Vovi?" I asked.

"We're meeting by the school," Elly said. "She thought it would be safer, behind the old field."

Smart. Wooded enough to avoid attention but not so thick with pines we couldn't find each other.

We took one last look at each other before setting off, creeping down the winding, unplanned street. It was quiet, dead quiet. No one was out and all but a few homes were dark. It was one of *those* nights. No one wanted to be out.

Toward town, things picked up, adults coming back from a long day searching. A noise made me jump into the bushes, pulling Elly and Vynce with me. Thirty seconds later, Mr. Ilt and Professor Fitz's voices appeared, walking back from the Black Forest.

"...makes me so mad!" Mr. Ilt barked. "Those bastards, how'd we not find 'em? Think they took a lev back already?"

"Patience, Merck, we'll get 'em. I'm as angry as you. We all are. It could have been anyone. We'll give 'em what they deserve. Besides, maglevs only come once a day."

Professor Fitz's voice shocked me, got me excited too. Was my Science History teacher a secret badass? Wouldn't have guessed that. They passed us and he said, "So, we covered the northeast up to the Furnace, and Roge and Frank checked the northwest beyond the crypt.

I heard someone did most of the southeast. Just leaves the southwest for tomorrow, and making sure they don't backtrack."

They agreed to meet at sun up and headed off in opposite directions.

I'd been so intent listening, I hadn't noticed the other adults leave. All at once, we were alone.

"Ready guys?" I asked.

We were, sort of... but it was getting cold on the frozen earth anyway, so we hurried off.

At the field, a *snap* pulled me from my reverie. It was Vovi, I could smell her. Reptiles had an interesting scent, a bit scaly... wet... I don't know, like snake's skin? She was here, somewhere.

She activated her band's field beam, illuminating the clearing and signaling us. We did the same, and all checked again to make sure we'd deactivated GPS. Didn't need Mom finding out.

Vovi was bundled in three fluffy layers, and her face had an eerie greenish glint in the light. "I was worried you wouldn't come."

"What are friends for?" Elly hugged the short girl. "Besides, it's not like we're going to catch 'em, just find 'em so the adults can, right? That's not so bad," she added, as if trying to convince herself.

"We should get going," I said.

Vynce nodded, and told Vovi what we'd overheard. "They didn't search the southwest yet," he said. "We should start there."

"And stick together," I added.

Walking to the start of the forest, I couldn't shake the feeling this was an awful idea. I pushed the thought to the back of my mind. "Keep your light fields off until we're further in," I said. "Someone might notice otherwise."

"We should have weapons out too," Elly said in a hushed voice, her eyes jumping at every little noise. "You never know."

We grabbed our knives while the girls unhooked staves for a few practice swings. Everyone looked as terrified as I felt, but no one said anything.

Once we'd worked out the jitters, we set out.

We'd been walking ten or fifteen minutes when there was a *crash*. I didn't jump this time, but the girls did. After we recovered, we looked at each other as if to say *are we really doing this?* When we didn't hear or smell anything, we continued, but not before spreading out to cover more ground. The wind howled an eerie *whooshing*. My stomach was in knots. My gut sensed danger.

What were we doing?

5

A BRIGHT LIGHT

"Vynce?" I turned. Nothing. No lights, nobody. It was graveyard silent.

Crap! What happened? Did the cynetics get them? My mind raced. How had I gotten lost?

Once I'd calmed, it hit me. I was so focused, I'd gotten distracted. We must have wandered apart. And the forest grew darker and more sinister with each passing step.

There was a huge fallen tree maybe five minutes back—three meters in diameter, hundreds of meters long. It was old. Maybe they'd went left while I'd gone right. That made sense, right? I retraced my steps, searching the ground.

A dark, ominous fear set in, growing more terrible with each passing minute. Cold sweat broke out on the back of my neck and I had to clench the knife in my hand to keep from shaking.

A yell. It sounded like Elly, or maybe Vovi. Where? I ran, heart pounding.

"Ahhh!" she yelled again, sounding more animal than human.

Elly? I tripped over a moss-covered log, stumbling before regaining my balance, and pushing my legs harder.

"Help!" someone cried. A muffled *thud*. Silence.

Elly was in trouble, I knew it. Shit. Something was wrong. Fear and anger boiled inside of me. Where was she?

A gap in the trees revealed two mysterious figures illuminated by creepy moonlight. They were bent over something and as the wind changed, I smelled her.

There was a body on the ground, a bloodstained face. It was Elly. The figure touched her. They'd killed my sister and were going to... I was going to be sick.

Something inside me broke. I exploded. Everything was red, a nexus of pain and hate. I stabbed the first. He shrieked in surprise and rage, eyes ballooning as his cries split the still night.

Grabbing his throat, I lifted him into the air, crushing, squeezing, ripping—doing everything in my power to kill him. My fingers tore through his reinforced skin. My hand tingled, glowing. What the—?

A burst of light shot out, like a flash or a laser. His head disappeared, obliterated by the blast, blood congealing in a burnt crisp.

The other cynetic who'd been attacking my sister turned, pale face filled with horror, his mouth aghast. Something in my eye registered a message firing away. What was that? Like an AR headset, but inside me. Throwing myself at the second cynetic, my fist connected with his gooey left eye. Again and again and again. I punched and stabbed and clawed until I collapsed, crying and exhausted, on the pine-strewn floor.

Darkness.

When I regained consciousness, I remembered Elly. She was lying there where I'd last seen her. No... I put my shaking fingers under her clammy jaw. There had to be a pulse.

I tried and tried but couldn't feel anything. The overlay thing happened again—blue numbers showing her body temperature and heart rate. The heartbeat said zero. She wasn't breathing. Come on, Elly. Mouth to mouth... I tried CPR.

No... The tears came.

Clenching my fist, I tried the electricity thing again. I had to save her, *anything*. It didn't work. Nothing happened. I failed. Was she really gone?

I collapsed, and retched raw pain, stomach burning.

When I rose, I noticed the bodies littered around me. There was blood everywhere, my clothes, my hands, everything.

What did I do? I shivered. How did I kill a cynetic? That's, that's not possible... It didn't make sense. That blast, I'd seen holos... Cynetics could do that. But not me, I was an animote. I was wolfish... Like Mom and Vynce and Elly.

No, Elly! Words died on my lips. My sister... I should check her pulse again. It was pointless, she was dead. But I had to be sure. I had to.

She'd done everything for me...

My body shook. Nothing. I was going to be sick again.

I should go home, find Vynce and Vovi, make sure they are okay. And Mom. How was I going to tell Mom?

I ran. Faster and faster, faster than ever. The trees and scenery whipped past. I didn't notice or care, rage and grief driving me.

When I got home, Mom and Vynce were sitting outside with bags under their bloodshot eyes.

"Raek, baby!" Mom launched from her chair, eyes frantic. "Where were you? I was so worried." Her arms crushed me. "Vynce told me everything. You idiots. I told you not to." She looked around, eyes filled with rabid fear softening to relief. "Elly? Where is Elly?" She grabbed my shoulders, shaking me. "Where is my Elly? Wasn't she with you? Tell me she was with you?" Mom was quivering, barely holding herself together.

"Mom, I'm sorry." I couldn't get the words out. What could I say? "It's all my fault. Elly, Elly's dead. I couldn't save her." I swallowed hard, fighting back tears.

"Dead? What do you mean *dead*?" She noticed the blood on my hands, recoiling.

Miserable, I nodded, not saying a word.

A shrieking, blood-curling wail escaped her lips. She collapsed, sobbing. I stood there, shocked. Tears came.

Ms. Ivey peeked her tiny head out the window, saw Mom on the ground and sprinted over. My old English teacher never moved so fast. "What happened?" She bent to check on Mom. "Is everything okay?"

I blacked out.

6

ON THE HUNT

"Shhhh." A faint scraping. My arms, my legs, everything felt funny, a strange, inescapable heaviness.

Mom's voice. "Doc, is he going to be okay? What happened?"

"He'll be fine. He just..." The words faded away.

It was so comfy, so warm and cozy. My eyes opened a second later. I was in bed, but in the living room, and Mom was passed out in her favorite chair. Vynce was asleep on the couch in the corner, bundled tight as the brown wool blanket rose and fell.

Tapping my head to wake myself, the AR overlay thing happened again. I jumped out of bed, clenching my fists. My body, my clothes, everything, was drenched in sweat. There were numbers above Vynce, electric blue readouts of body temperature and heart rate, like I had superpowers. I almost choked.

This is just a dream, this is just a dream. A few deep breaths. I should do the mindfulness thing Grandma had taught me. If anything could awaken me from this nightmare, it was that... Maybe I was dreaming. I'd wake up and Elly would be here.

Everything would be fine.

After what felt like hours, I opened my eyes. Please... The clock on the wall said it'd been five minutes. Shit. They were all still here. I was still here. Except no Elly. Nothing changed. Another surge of pain.

The weird numbers were still there too, floating above their faces. I tapped the side of my head and the displays disappeared. That was good to know, as long as no one else could see them. Shoot, what if they could? I'd be shot.

In the corner, Vynce stirred, blinking as he let out a yawn. "Raek!" He jumped, mouth agape. "Are you okay? You passed out. What happened?" he added, lowering his voice when he realized Mom was asleep.

"Where's Elly? Where is she?"

He winced. "You don't remember?"

So, it was true. The bloody knife twisted in my gut. Pure guilt.

Vynce nodded, wincing, and told me everything.

Mom opened her eyes, noticed me, and leapt from her seat, her eyes wide. "Baby, you're okay. I was so worried." She flung herself at me. "Three days. Three days! What happened? Come here."

She pulled me tight. It felt so good. I cried.

Wait... "You're saying I have been out for three days?"

Mom clenched her fists, sinewy arms bunching up. "What happened out there, baby? It looked like a warzone!"

"I don't remember," I lied, not making eye contact. "They attacked Elly and I exploded. I don't remember. Somehow they died, and I collapsed."

Despite gentle eyes, she raised an eyebrow. "Okay. Maybe you'll remember later. I'm sure some of the adults will want to talk to you. I hope not the DNS. We'll do our best to make sure that doesn't happen. Attacking cynetics and all..." She lost her resolve and stifled a sob.

We all grimaced. The penalty for violence against superiors was your dominant hand, no questions asked. For murder, it was death.

"They said something about a message," I blurted out. Should I tell her? "Before he died, the cynetic, he said he pinged someone."

"No!" Mom gasped as a shockwave rippled through her. "So, someone might know what happened." She placed both hands around my head and cupped my ears, looking me in the eyes. "Are you sure you don't remember *anything* else, baby?"

I shook my head, torn. She'd be terrified of me... "No, nothing."

"Vynce, Raek... we never had this conversation. Raek, get your clothes, enough for a few days, and put them in your bag. Bring a mat, a blanket, and I'll pack some dried food. Maybe I'm overreacting."

She took a deep breath. "In case, hide that bag somewhere, not in town. Don't tell me where, don't tell anyone. If anything happens, anything at all, I want you to go there and hide out. It'd only be a few days. Got it?"

I shook my head. "No way. What about you guys? I'm staying! This is my—"

"Damnit!" she barked. "No, you're not. We'll be fine. We always are."

Holy crap. And she didn't even know about the blaster yet.

What had I gotten myself into?

* * *

The next few days passed in a blur, adults coming to offer condolences, cards, and sympathy. Lots of tears and hugs. Rumors too. A few tried questioning me. One or two got angry and started yelling. Mom kicked them out, dragging offenders to the door with an intensity none dared protest.

By day three, I was cooped up, by day five, losing my mind. I was meant to roam and hunt and be free. I told Mom I was going for a hike and maybe hunting if I saw anything. We needed the food, so she caved.

"Fine, but stay south of the village. And don't go into that forest, boy! You got it?"

A nod.

"I'm serious, Raek!" She gave me a look I'd never forget. "I can't lose two of my babies."

I hurried out the door, bag on my back. Freedom. The wind at my back, the rustling of leaves... I lost myself, lost track of time. I chased the scent of a rogue buck for a while, a twenty pointer by his hooves. The thought of meat, of juicy, non-plant-based steak for the winter drove me farther.

At last, I found the poor guy. I wasn't the first. A pack of wolves or wild dogs had caught it, tearing flesh from the bones and leaving behind a bloody carcass. It wasn't worth carrying home, the good parts were gone. Plus it was getting dark.

Time to head back. I'd been out all day, and while it was fun, pained darkness haunted me. I thought about Elly, about what was happening to me, about everything. Images of her bloodied face assaulted me. Stabbing guilt.

Gunfire snapped me out of it. That's odd. Why would someone hunt so close to town? Maybe a wild dog roamed a little too close, or stole one of Mr. Leot's few chickens.

Something wasn't right. The streets were dead silent and empty. Was that blaster exhaust? The burnt acid stench of charred skin torched my nostrils.

I turned onto to our street and the smell was stronger, nauseously so. The door to Ms. Ivey's house was ajar and I ran over. She'd know what was going on.

Ms. Ivey was tied to a chair in the middle of the room, red hot heating strips and burns covering her arms and legs. Her head was gone, blood everywhere. She was unrecognizable, except for the Moon-shaped birthmark on her right hand. Ugh... Who'd done this?

Sick to my stomach, I backed out. Don't touch anything. I'd seen crime holos. Fingerprints, fragments of skin, hair, bone... My DNA shouldn't be anywhere near this.

Someone was watching me, I could feel it.

I spun and a tall, black-clad officer with narrow blue eyes stood on the path, eyeing me. He looked to Ms. Ivey, and back to me without a reaction. My gut told me he was an emulate, I don't know why. What was an immortal doing *here*, the house of a simple teacher? Had he killed her? Why?

"Excuse me, sir." Walking toward him, I bent my head in an intentional timidness. "Can I help you?"

His mouth opened, confused. "Well, I… we're investigating two missing cynetics." He reached for his hip holster.

I didn't hesitate, striking like lightning, fist pummeling his chin before surprise even registered. Landing on him, my claws ripped at his eyes, fists pounding his head and chest. Power coursed through me. If I didn't kill him, I was dead.

He pulled a blaster and aimed for my head. He fired, but I dodged it and horror appeared on his face, mouth hanging open. He fired again but my left hand pinned his arm to the ground.

The man was bleeding everywhere at this point, some blue pseudo-organic mixture. Even his body's mechanized skeleton and inhuman strength couldn't stop me. He was losing and he knew it.

I had to finish the fight before more officers showed. Ripping a brick from Ms. Ivey's path, I brought it smashing onto his forehead.

His components and memory chips exploded everywhere, blue goo gushed over the sidewalk. It was over.

The surrogate body spasmed twice and stopped. He—or it, or *whatever* he was—was dead.

Wait, what had I done? Shaking, I stood. The shock should have been crippling, or at least slowed me. Instead, I felt calm and relaxed, despite the tremors.

Our window was dark and the place was deserted.

Where were they? Mom had said to run. I did.

It was light out when I reached the edge of the forest. I was lucky, no cops or townsfolk along the way. Everyone must be hiding. But what was going on?

Despite sprinting, I was far from winded. Blood pumped through my veins, power like I've never felt before. In a small clearing, I shimmied a tree, and pulled the bag from my back. Thank you, Mom.

A few sips from my canteen to quench my thirst. Now what?

It got dark fast. A wolf howled and it hit me: I was an outlaw. What was I going to do? The DNS would find the body and know something happened. Things would get worse.

And Ms. Ivey, that was all *my* fault. She died being questioned and tortured. The burn marks on her arms and legs were seared into my mind, her headless miserable body. Ugh.

And where were Mom and Vynce? Were they okay?

There were three possibilities where they could be: home, our old campsite west of town, or captured. As long as it wasn't the third. I had to go see for myself.

It took three gut-wrenching hours of sneaking to reach our street, three-to-four times longer than usual. But no one saw or followed me. Approaching from the back, I scurried through the Ivey's and Lonet's yards and hopped the ugly mini fence into ours. Everything was dark and deserted. Not a good sign.

I crept to the window. The place was a mess. Tables and chairs were tossed about and glass shards blanketed everything. Even a few caved walls, like a bomb went off.

Were they okay?

Out of the corner of my eye, movement. A hand clapped my shoulder.

7

HOME IS WHERE THE HEART IS

W ithout thinking, I dove and came up two meters away, knife in hand. I was ready to fight for my life... How do I use this damn blaster?

The figure flicked a staff and sent my knife clattering to the ground.

"What are you doing, Raek?"

What the—? "Professor Fitz? What are you doing?"

"The same as you," he whispered. "Trying to find out what happened."

"But, why are you here?" Something didn't add up.

"I was waiting for you. Knew you'd be back."

I was suspicious now, angry. "Why?"

"Shhh." He grabbed my shoulders and pulled my face to within inches of his bitter coffee breath. "Want to live? Want to see your family again? If you do, be quiet and follow me. We haven't got much time."

"But what about—"

"That can wait. We need to get out of here. See the shadow in the corner, over by your couch?" He pointed. "That's an enhancer from the DNS. He's been here all night, waiting for you. There are two more like him and another team of cynetics on call five minutes away. We have to go, now!"

A team of cynetics, for me? "Okay. But where?"

"The last place they'd expect."

8

TRUST

"School? You can't be serious," I said, as we rounded the corner and the outline of the rundown schoolhouse came into focus.

"What kid would hide in a school? Or willingly go?"

He had a point. Reaching into his pocket, he pulled out a large old key ring, some ten-odd bronze and silver keys jangling as he did.

"You have a keyring?" My mouth fell into a lopsided grin. Was he serious?

He smiled. "Of course. They can't track the low tech stuff."

Again, he had a point. Who was this guy?

Once we were in, we closed the door and descended steep concrete steps to the half-finished storage basement. Even with lights on, the space was small, damp, and not well lit, just three low tech bulbs, one flickering. If he wanted to kill me and dispose of the body, this was the perfect place.

"Why were you at my house? What were you doing? How'd you know about those goons?" I asked, voice rising. "And why don't you use a band? *Who* the heck are you?"

He smiled. "That's a lot of questions, son. I'll start with the big ones." He cleared his throat. "Why was I at your house? Like I said, I was waiting. I knew you were in trouble. Your next question: Why'd you need my help? I don't have a good answer, other than I've lived an interesting life, made a lot of friends, and more than my fair share of enemies. I've been in your shoes before. We'll leave it at that. What was your next question?"

"The DNS?"

"Simple," he replied. "I came after I heard what happened. You're a smart kid. I wouldn't be able to find you unless you wanted to be found. But you'd want to see your family. I'm friends with Ms. Qin, two houses over. She's visiting her sister so I let myself in, turned off the lights and hid. Half an hour later, twelve DNS broke into your house and searched the place."

Twelve? Holy cow.

"An hour after, nine of 'em left. That leaves three." He must have seen the pain in my eyes because he added, "I don't know what happened to your family."

I said nothing.

"For the smartband, I already answered that. Prefer anonymity. And as for who I am, I'm your Science History teacher."

Thump, thump! Feet clattered and there was a rustle of leaves. Had they found us already?

"Stay down, Raek!" Professor Fitz commanded. Scowling, he rose to his knees and crawled to one of the dirty glass windows with a view outside. Careful to not make a peep, he peered out.

SLAM.

My heart skipped a beat.

9

FLUSHING

"I'll be damned." He chuckled. "Never thought they'd come here."

"What? Who?"

"Students." He shook his head with a smile. "Don't they know there's no school when cops are tearing apart their town."

I shuffled over to look. Basketball. It'd been forever since I played.

Why was Fitz helping me? Something told me I could trust him... "So, what's our plan? How do we find my family?"

"I don't have a plan," Fitz answered. "Only to get you out of here and keep you safe. For now, we need to forget about your family. Hopefully they got away."

Forget about them? I couldn't, but now wasn't the time. "What about the rebels, the Resistance? They could help."

"I wouldn't be so sure," he replied. "They've had their share of leaks. Some want to take advantage of you. The first mixed-breed human... imagine the implications, breaking the GDR's propaganda."

Even the Resistance? "Are you saying they can't help me? Am I better off alone?" Fear gripped me. Alone...

"You're not alone, I'm here with you." His huge hand squeezed my shoulder. "I won't abandon you, son." There was deep-seated pain in his eyes as he said it. "We should go inland, away from the towns and big cities, somewhere levs don't go. The further we are from the DNS and the rebels, the better."

"You'll come with me?" I felt pathetic saying it, but I *needed* him.

He smiled. "Yes. We should go tonight, though. The longer we wait, the riskier it is. And son," he added, expression softening, "you'll need to tell me what *actually* happened in the forest eventually. Okay?"

I nodded. Could I really leave? At least I wouldn't be alone.

An hour later, Professor Fitz said we should get some sleep. He went to his classroom and returned with two, quarter centimeter thick sleeping pads and a tough brown backpack. Setting the bag on the floor, he spread the blue mats—some nano-layered pressure-distrib-uting deal for a "lighter-than-air sleep"—a meter apart. "That one's yours." He pointed where I was sitting.

"I could never afford this," I stammered.

"It's yours, consider it a gift." He paused. "Let's see, sun will start to set in…" he checked his watch. *Wow*, a watch? "Five hours. Gives us four hours to sleep and an hour to get ready."

Rummaging through his bag, he grabbed a pistol-shaped gray device. "Oh, I forgot about this!"

"What's that?"

He flipped a switch and pointed it toward me. "A connectivity sensor." He sounded like a teacher as he moved it up and down my body. "Senses full-spectrum radiation to make sure we're not emitting any trackable digital signatures."

It beeped, twice.

"Shit!" he said. "Your band, quick, take it off!"

What why? He snatched my wrist. "Raek, they can track that. They probably know you're here. Why didn't I think of that earlier? Hurry."

My fingers slipped as I ripped at the band and he said, "Quick, the bathroom. Flush it. We have to hope it goes through the pipes and still sends a signal."

I sprinted upstairs and into the bathroom, past the smaller stall doors and to the 'mega-toilet' as we called it. Myrtha had quite the rear end. The extra flush power would help here. Throwing the band in, I made a peace sign. The toilet registered a number two flush and swirling water vortexed downward, filling the bowl. My band disappeared into the bottomless pit.

Stay down, stay down... That would be awful, grabbing it out of that sinkhole to try again.

After a minute, it was gone for good. Phew. I raced back, taking the steps two at a time. Professor Fitz was at the window.

"Shhh... Quiet, Raek. Cops."

I hurried over. Sure enough, ten cops huddled by the entrance. One was off to the side, waving busy hands and talking to a holo. It was hard to make out what they were saying because a VTOL took off somewhere nearby. They weren't the quietest but had pretty much replaced all other aircraft since they could take off or land anywhere, hence the name, VTOL—vertical takeoff and landing.

I'd never seen a real VTOL, only holos of military ones laying waste to whole towns.

The holographic officer threw up his hands. Something was happening. A map appeared.

Fitz tapped my shoulder. "We need to go, son. Now!" We ran upstairs to the other side of the building. Officers there too.

A VTOL landed and Fitz reached into his bag, grabbing two blasters.

"Know how to use these?" he asked.

I shook my head. He clicked a few buttons and handed it to me. Holy crap, a blaster... "Press your finger here. Good, now it's locked to you. Here's the trigger. Point and shoot. Follow my lead. Shoot anyone that comes in."

We continued down the hallway, guns in hand, until a blast shook the building. "That will be the front door," he murmured. "Hurry. We'll hide in my classroom."

Boots clattered on the stairs. "Spread out!" someone yelled. "Remember, boys, capture if you can, kill if you must. This kid doesn't make it out!"

Kill...?

A flurry of, "Sir, yes, sir!"

Professor Fitz looked at me. "Raek, are you a cynetic?"

"Yeah. I think so." But how'd he know?

"Good, that will help." He inched his door open and we slipped in. "You should be able to handle a few, right?"

Um… I flushed. "I'm not sure how to activate things. Last time, I got lucky."

He swallowed hard. "Oh!" Gritting his teeth, he turned over his desk and arranged it in the corner. "Your sleeping mat!"

I threw it to him. He draped it over the table. "These aren't only comfy, they absorb impact too. Do the same thing, far corner."

I imitated him, but with a thud. Shoot, did they hear that?

"When they come in, open fire. They might throw micronades or something bigger. Stay calm and keep shooting."

Something bigger? "Okay."

The noises were louder now, a weighty echo pounding the halls. They'd covered most of the school already. We were running out of time.

"Any other tricks up your sleeve?" I asked. He had to have something…

"Afraid not. We'll have to—"

A scraping outside the door.

We exchanged a glance. This was it. At least we'd go out with a bang.

Sorry, Mom.

A handle creaked.

10

DARKNESS, LIGHT AND GRAVITY

I held my breath, eyes fixed on the door. It didn't budge. It must have been the one across the hall.

"All clear!" someone yelled.

Ours was the last door left. This was it!

A siren blared. The officers froze.

"What was that?" a voice yelled.

"Heck if I know," another replied, voice thick with an accent I didn't recognize.

Down the hall, a yell. "Shit, boys, you hear that? Commander's saying the kid escaped. They're tracking him now." A chuckle. "Idiot ain't realized we can track his band. He's headed south toward the reservoir."

The VTOL took off, roaring away.

"What're you ladies waiting for?" an angry voice bellowed. "You hear me?"

"Yes, sir!" There were sounds of scrambling chaos as they ran to the waiting vehicles, loud boots fading in the distance.

After what felt like ages, we both let out a breath. Had we made it?

Fitz was pale. "That was too close. You okay?"

Too shocked to speak, I nodded.

We sat in silence, waiting for them to come back. I couldn't believe it. Were they really gone?

"This doesn't change anything," Professor Fitz said at last. "We need to leave, the sooner the better. So, you're cynetic?" He laughed, shaking his head. "I should have known."

"I didn't even know myself. Found out a few days ago, and I'm still not sure," I added. "I'm wolfish, how could I be cynetic?"

"For now, let's focus on surviving."

"Professor Fitz," I blurted out, voicing the question I'd been ignoring, "am I a freak?"

"No, son, you're not a freak. I have no idea what you are. You're different, you're special. But you're *not* a freak." He put his hand on my shoulder. "I don't know what you are, but you're hope, hope that one day we can reunify the subspecies."

Whatever that means... for some reason, it made me feel better.

"Since we're going to be spending a lot of time together and almost died, you should call me Fitz. Everyone does. I'm not your professor anymore. We won't be coming back."

We won't? What about Mom and Vynce?

"We were lucky once," he said. "It won't happen again. I'll try to keep you safe, but you never know."

We left as dusk settled, winter days becoming short.

He pushed a brisk pace, muscular legs whooshing in his black trainers, gray shoes gliding along the dirt path. Once we made it to the woods, I relaxed a bit. The woods were my element.

After an hour, I couldn't see jack. How could he?

I asked.

"Spectraglasses." He tapped the wiry metallic frames.

How'd I missed those earlier? I felt a twinge of jealousy. "Infrared?"

"Zoom, too. You can try these when we stop for the night."

We'd been going for maybe ten silent minutes when I got a bad feeling. "Something doesn't feel right."

"I know," he replied in a hushed whisper. "Something or someone's been following us."

"There's a turn next to that big tree, not the Solstice one." I motioned with my head and outlined a plan. "On the count of three."

At three, he sped off, and I fell back, pretending to pee. It took two minutes to make it to the tree but Fitz wasn't in the branches. Where was he?

Turning the corner, I tensed, breathing shallow, ready for an attack. Any. Second. Now. Any second...

After five minutes, I turned. Where was Fitz? What happened?

Crash.

A bright light filled the wood.

11

SMOKING GUN

I ran toward the noise. It was off the trail a ways. Bushes and thorns tore at me as I panicked. It was too late.

The smell of burnt wood wafted through the air. A blaster? "Raek, is that you? Help!" Fitz called.

Shoot. My mind went into overdrive. The DNS had captured Fitz. How many...

A growing fire flickered, and I smelled, mmm. What was that? My stomach was playing tricks on me. No... Was that roast boar?

What was going on? Bandits?

Fitz sat cross-legged, stoking a fire, smiling as a thick slab of juicy meat cooked on the makeshift spit. It smelled delicious. "Raek, that you? You can come out now. It was a test."

I crept through the trees and stepped into the otherwise empty clearing. "What's going on? Where's the DNS? What happened?"

"Calm down, son." He smiled. "It was just a test. You passed."

When I didn't say anything, he added, "You have to be paranoid to survive now. Everyone's looking for you. You don't know who you can trust, not even me. Now come here, help me with this boar."

"No!" I spat. Prick. "Why'd you do that? I could've killed you."

"But you didn't." He gave me a serious look and held my stare.

"You stayed level-headed, investigated, and were ready for anything. You even made a good plan."

But still... "And the person following us?"

"A deer, probably used to humans feeding it and wanted to stay close. I brought the boar from school," he added.

"You're sure it is safe?" There could still be something out there.

He nodded. He'd set up perimeter sensors.

Idiot. I should punch him.

He bribed me with the lenses, and, by the time I'd finished with the glasses, the hog was perfect: a blood-red rare. Mom never hit the mark.

"Those lenses," Fitz said once we'd finished eating, "are just some of what your eyes are capable of once you get your SmartCore running. Known a few cynetics in my day," he added when he saw my surprise.

I sighed. "It doesn't always work. If I tap here," I touched my right temple, "sometimes it activates, and other times, it doesn't." I could hear the frustration in my voice. None of it made sense.

"We'll figure it out." He patted me on the back. "Hang in there."

A half-hearted nod. And somehow, I had to find my family.

We slept most of the day, using the packs to block the sun from our eyes. I slept better on that tiny pad than I'd ever slept on our ratty mattress at home. Vynce rolled a lot and Mom snored. How were they doing? Where were they? Were they okay?

Guilt gripped me. It had been twelve hours since I'd thought about them. My own family, and I was leaving them behind. What son, what brother, what *person* does that? I had to find them.

"We made good time last night," Fitz said, saving me from myself for the time being. "In a day or two, we'll be outside the danger zone. I doubt they'll use many drones or VTOLs this far out."

"You've seen a drone? In real life, I mean, not in the holos?"

"I have." A mischievous look crossed his face, an epic story in the glint of his eyes. "Let's say drones and I have a difficult relationship. They've caused me a few headaches. To be fair, I've shot down a couple. Guess we're even."

So that's where he'd gotten his money. "Did you sell them?"

He shook his head. "Too risky. DNS monitor back channels, don't want anyone having *that* kind of power…" Which led to a rambling story about AI and some dystopian surveillance sci-fi he'd read once.

Freaky stuff. If it was true, if companies and governments could watch you everywhere… At least we didn't have that. I shuddered. There'd be no rebels, no freedom, no life. It was hard to wrap my head around.

A bird cawed, pulling me back to thinking about drones and searching the skies. If they had weaponized drones, what chance did we have? I'd seen dark web holos, crowds of animotes gunned down, bombs left and right.

We continued for hours, alone with our thoughts. What was he thinking about? He'd had a life, by all appearances a good one, and he threw it all away… for me. I felt bad.

And Elly… She'd be here if it wasn't for me. I should have been there, or not let us get separated in the first place. Fitz interrupted my guilt like calling on me in class. "While we've got time, how much do you know about the cities, about the different subspecies?"

Enough. "I had a project in Political Theory a ways back, Mr. Cadvin's class, before he disappeared," I added. "We studied non-governmental textbooks, banned stuff: the megacities that fell apart during the Bioplague—Singapore, Paris, New York…. They're dead zones now." I outlined everything I knew of how animote labor helped them recover.

"And cynetics, I'm not sure what their tech can do. Obviously, built-in blasters." I lifted my arm for emphasis. "And I've heard they, I mean we—" The weirdness of it made me uncomfortable "—We have reinforced skin and bones too. Continuous connectivity, enhanced vision." I paused, thinking. "That's it."

Fitz gave me a studious stare before breezing over enhancers and emulates, which triggered the image of the officer's gushing blue blood. At least he'd get to reboot in a new surrogate body. Was that still murder?

"Not half bad." He quizzed me about the GDR and DNS, and the founding of the New America Government as we passed a weird tree formation, its massive trunk split into three vertical limbs like an inverted tripod. He noticed my eyes wandering.

"Raek!" he stepped in front of me and locked eyes. "This isn't school, I'm not your teacher. There won't be a test at the end. This is your life we're talking about. I need you to focus." He grabbed my shoulders. "Trust me, the small things are the difference between life and death." His eyes moistened.

"Sorry," I mumbled.

"Don't be sorry, be alive. Animotes everywhere need you. There's *never* been a mixed-species human. Do you know what that means?" His eyes flashed, but the anger faded from his voice.

My stomach growled. Fitz must have heard it. "We should stop here, find cover before it gets light. I'll work on camp."

"I'll get firewood."

Twenty minutes later, I'd loaded as much as I could carry, my third and final load.

Ambling back, a lone wolf appeared, watching me. He—I think it was a he—was huge. Gray matted fur covered him, tints of white and black speckling his snout and backside. The legs were raw power. Combined with razor-sharp teeth and crushing bite strength, he was a killing machine.

"Was it you that howled that day?" His eyes were dark as night. "Were you warning me?" I paused as he sniffed the air, holding my gaze. "If only you could understand me. I don't want any trouble. I'm like you, an outcast, a hunter. I live for the chase. But now, I'm the one being hunted. Guess you know about that." I sighed.

Fitz said something in the distance and I turned. When I looked back, the wolf was gone, a ghost disappearing into the night.

Dumping the firewood, I strode up to Fitz. "Where are we headed?"

"Old Canada, used to be called Toronto but these days people call it Lhalas." He smiled. "Look at a map, anything that's left has a new name."

"What's in Lhalas?" It was one of the few remaining megacities, more than two million people... mind-boggling.

Fitz's eyes twinkled an annoying glow. "We're going to see an old friend."

I'd learned better than to ask. He'd tell me, or he wouldn't. That's just how he was.

It was strange to think I was leaving Kiag, the place I'd lived my whole life, all my friends and family, neighbors, memories. Kiag's too small to find on most maps, but it was home for me. It was Old America, our history classes covered that much. I wasn't sure which of the fifty-two little countries in the American empire it was though. It was weird to think about so many governments. Who was in charge? Who told everyone what to do? I had trouble wrapping my head around it, let alone hundreds of other nations around the world.

"Get some sleep, we'll need it." Fitz laid down, twisted his shoulder, and closed his eyes, already asleep.

But me, I was wired. I wanted to figure out this darn SmartCore thing. Maybe it was like a computer. Sitting cross-legged by the fire, I tried voice commands. "Activate," "On," "Turn On," "Begin," "Start," "Reboot," "Restart." Ten whole minutes of nothing. "Damnit!" I jumped up, kicked a nearby tree, and stomped my throbbing foot. How do I do this?

The foghorn snores ended as Fitz sprang out of bed, eyes wide. "What's happening?" he snapped, more alert than I'd expect.

"Nothing." I looked away, ashamed I'd let it get to me. "It's my freaking SmartCore. I can't make it work."

"Go to sleep, son. We have a long day tomorrow." With that, he rolled over and was asleep again in seconds. Cue the bagpipes.

Taking a deep breath, I sat shaking. I could almost hear Grandma's knuckled voice telling me to meditate. It couldn't hurt. Sitting by the dwindling fire, I closed my eyes and focused on my breathing. Thoughts bounced, but I let them drift away into the abyss.

Who knows how much time passed. After an eternity, *something* happened, like resetting a computer or a secondary operating system. I felt… *different*, like my brain could move in a new dimension. I had access to something that wasn't there before, and stepped in.

A command center filled of knobs and gauges and screens appeared. A glowing interface to my right caught my eye. I touched it and felt my arms again. It was strange. I didn't 'feel' them per se, I *felt* them, *knew* them—their activity level, output, maximum capacity. Flexing my fingers, similar insights popped into my subconscious. The power in my hands, the sharpness of my claws, even the growth of my fur.

I was scared, but even more intrigued. Pulling back, I was in the command center again. The new sensations remained in my arms and hands, on the edge of my awareness.

A helmet looking thing sat in the center of the room, like the old astronaut ones from the space race. One small step for communism, one giant leap for mankind. This felt like that.

I slid it over my head, and when it touched, another shift. My body disappeared. Everything was gone, even my arms. I was consciousness, nothing more. No interfaces or joysticks, monitors or gauges; just black empty abyss.

Something like feelings emerged. The light, the feeling—*whatever* it was—grew larger, brighter. The empty landscape expanded.

One glowing field was interesting, different and yet *familiar*. It felt foreign.

As it grew, my understanding grew with it. For the heck of it, I touched the brightness.

My body was ripped through a vortex.

12

HUNTED AND HUNTING

"What happened, Raek? Are you okay?"

I opened my eyes. "Jeez, Raek, don't scare me like that." Fitz stood there, shaking me.

Squinting, I adjusted to the harsh light. "Where am I?"

"You're here, Raek. What are you talking about? I went to bed and... You must have been sitting there for hours."

"Hours? That can't be. I was meditating and..." My jaw dropped. No way... "Was that real?"

"Was what real?" he asked.

"That. All of it. The command center, the helmet, everything."

He draped a blanket over me and I pulled it tighter, describing what happened, which according to him, sounded like a cynetic's SmartCore. I guess that made sense...

We set off a little after 21:00. It was plenty dark, and, as usual, Fitz set the pace. I followed. After walking in silence a while, I stopped. "You said you wanted to teach me things... Like what?"

"There's a lot you need to learn, son. History, culture, politics, combat."

"Combat?" Was he serious?

He nodded. "Hand-to-hand combat and military strategy."

"I can handle myself!" Fighting at least made sense, but military strategy... I didn't plan on going to war.

He spun, kicking the back of my knee. I collapsed.

"You always have to be ready." He helped me to my feet. "You never know when you might run into trouble."

"That was a cheap shot," I said through gritted teeth.

He smiled. "It was. Think the DNS will play fair? In fact, if it is life or death, I don't want you to play fair. I want you to survive. Got it? So, show me what you got."

Was this another joke? "You want to fight? Now?"

"Yeah, hit me. Pretend I'm the DNS officer that took your mom away."

What? My fists balled. "You said you didn't know what happened."

"I lied." His eyes sparkled, a knowing smile crossing his face. "Had to get you out of there."

"You bastard." I took a step toward him. "We need to go back. I'm going back."

"I won't let you. Besides, they're probably dead by now." He shrugged as if it was nothing.

Dead? "Screw you." I leapt at him, claws out, teeth bared.

He backpedaled, smiling and shifting his weight, hands at his sides.

"You're pretty confident, old man!"

He said nothing, waiting. Charging, I swung. He swatted my hand as if it was nothing, flipped me over his arm. My face slammed into the dirt.

Standing, I dusted myself off, face stinging.

I stepped closer. "You did that on purpose, didn't you?"

"I did," he said with a slight grin. "I don't know what happened to—"

I sprang, fist flying toward his face. He dodged it and dropped me with a knee to the stomach. Ugh. Hitting the ground hard, I clenched my gut. I was going to be sick.

He laughed. "I did tell you not to fight fair, didn't I?"

"You did." I chuckled despite the pain.

"Sorry, Raek. What I said about your family, it was wrong of me." He sounded sincere. He was a hard guy to hate. "To be honest, I doubt they made it, but if they did, you're no good to them now. You need training. You're a cynetic, yes, and have certain powers and strengths, but you'll be up against millions of cynetics."

And I had no idea how to use my powers.

We walked on in a heavy silence after that, until Fitz stopped in a small clearing. "Let's make camp."

After assembling the tent, we popped nutrient shots and laid the micro pads. I was exhausted and ready to sleep when there was a crash. We looked at each other.

"What was that?"

Pointing, I held my finger to my lips. On the far edge of the clearing, a swarm of birds squawked as they took to the sky. "Whatever it was," I said. "It came from over there."

We snuck back into the forest, putting out our campfire and covering our tracks. Probably nothing, but we had to check.

We got closer and heard voices, men. Four or five of them.

"You think he came this way, Major?" one asked.

"Nah, Lieutenant, I don't know that," a southern voice drawled. "Only know my orders. And you know yours, Lieutenant. We're to search the northwest perimeter of the woods for 'em and report back."

"Yes, sir," the lieutenant responded. Hesitating, he added, "I was wondering, sir, what's an animote section doing looking for an animote, sir?"

"Following orders!" the major snapped. "This wolf bastard killed his own sister and murdered his neighbor. What kind of person, animote or otherwise, does that, you think? He's an outlaw, a villain, a murderer. Now, get your sorry asses up and spread out. I want a perimeter on our location and preliminary reports from each of you in a quarter-hour."

"Sir, yes, sir!" their voices echoed.

We retreated, careful not to make a sound. Once we were out of range, I whispered, "What are they talking about? It's a bunch of lies!" I wasn't a monster...

"They're soldiers, Raek. The GDR lied about what happened to turn animotes against you. They don't know about me yet," he added. "Anyway, it doesn't matter. We need to get out of here. They can't know we've been here."

A noise. "They're coming, Fitz. We need to go, now!"

He finished one last sweep of the campsite, and we sprinted through grassier parts of the clearing to avoid leaving footprints. I swung the bag on my back. "Where to?"

He took a deep breath and looked back. "They don't know we're here, we need to keep it that way. They're searching about three hundred square kilometers with checkpoints at logical positions. That's how I'd do it," he added, outlining the basic math.

Was he in the army at some point?

"They'll have people stationed at nearby towns and cities looking for outsiders," he said. "That means we'll be roughing it for a while, son. Might take longer to reach Lhalas than I thought."

"Shhh. I see 'em. By that tree." I pointed.

"Your eyes must be better than mine, can't see a darn thing."

Wait. How'd I do that? I concentrated on making the image larger. Nothing. Slowing my breathing, I tried again. It worked and the pair came into focus. "There's two of 'em. They're looking around the camp. Wait, they're pointing toward town. Crap! He has goggles. Get down."

We hit the ground with a *thud* as they swung the goggles, searching the path to the town before hitting the treeline itself.

One of the soldiers reached down. "Shoot, he found something. He grabbed it and waved to his buddy. We're screwed." What did I miss? "He's reaching to his mouth." He was going to signal his team.

At the last minute, he opened his mouth and tossed something inside. Jeez. A giddy laugh escaped me. "It's a berry," I said at last. "He found a berry and ate it."

"Let's hope he doesn't find more."

Both soldiers snapped up. The berry guy tapped his helmet, stiffening. Without warning, the pair jogged back the way they'd come, packs swinging on their camouflaged backs.

"We should get a few hours of sleep," Fitz said. "We might not have the chance for a while."

To be safe, we hiked a kilometer west and into the woods a good way. There was a secluded grove, thick brush and trees lining its sides. We set our packs on the thin layer of pine straw. It felt great to sit.

After unrolling our mats, we fell asleep at once.

13

THE SPIDER

I was in the middle of a strange dream with a cyborg, Calter Fury, and my invisible father when something in my subconscious pulled me awake. A spike of adrenaline shot through me.

Alert at once, I checked the clearing, listening to hundreds of wild critters welcoming me to their wonderful home.

Some instinct—I'm not sure what—told me to turn. I did, eyes shifting to infrared like the lenses had. I blinked twice. Nothing happened.

A small boy came into view, walking alone with a large walking stick, a small brown knife at his hip. He smelled strange, an odd mixture of woody moss and spicy curry, and seemed relaxed, immersed in the world around him.

A squirrel in the trees behind me startled the boy and his eyes flicked to me, expression equal parts interest and terror. He was young, no more than nine or ten, with light brown hair covering his arms and face. A dark ponytail protruded from his orange cap.

I blinked and this time, my vision returned to normal.

"Hey, what's your name?" I asked. "Mine's Ra—" I stopped myself. "Raj."

"I'm Kelep." A big smile plastered his carefree face. "Want to play swords?" He lifted his stick with a grin, in case I didn't know what he meant.

I didn't and was tired. "Want to sit with us?" What was this kid doing here?

He shrugged. "Sure, why not? We can spar later."

I kicked Fitz. "Hey, man," I said, careful not to use his name. "Look who I found. This is Kelep."

Fitz cracked his eyes and noticed Kelep. Yawning, he said, "Nice to meet you, Kelep. My name's Brol. Are you from around here? Live in town?"

Kelep nodded. "My father's a trader. Brings goods and devices from the cities to towns and villages in the area. He wants me to take over the business when I'm older," he added proudly, standing straighter. "He got back yesterday. Restocking for a big trip this weekend. Headed to the city, to Itany, I think. He proceeded to tell us all about it.

Fitz and I looked at each other as Kelep looked away. I could tell we were both thinking the same thing. The question was, would it work?

After chatting a while, hearing about school, the town, and what his father did for a living, I thought my plan could work. When the kid had to pee, Fitz and I stood to stretch.

"Think it'll work?" I whispered.

"It is not that simple," he said. "He could be a spy for the government, many traders are. In exchange for rumors and information, they're granted special trading rights, something all traders want. That could—" His voice changed. "Hey, Kelep, find anything interesting? You were gone a while."

"Just a funny looking spider." Reaching into his pocket he pulled something out. "See."

It was jet black with a glossy gleam, small, distinct red markings on its back. I froze. Shit. "Kelep, hold still. That's a Northern Black Widow, they're extremely dangerous. Don't move."

His eyes flared. "A what?"

"Shhh. Don't talk, don't even breathe." I inched toward him, looking around as I did. Fitz caught my eye and handed me a stick, as if reading my mind.

By now I was less than a meter away, focused, not moving a muscle. A deep breath, another. I knew what I had to do, the question was, could I do it before the spider struck.

Northern Black Widows were one of the most poisonous animals alive, its venom fifteen times deadlier than a rattlesnake. I'd never seen one in the wild, only nature docs. The boy wouldn't stand a chance, even a two hundred kilogram man wouldn't.

I'd only have one chance.

My muscles surged, tension building as my pupils dilated on the boy's hand.

Lunging forward, I swung. Time slowed as I saw the arc of the stick before it happened. A last second correction and the branch blasted the spider's torso, sending it flying into the woods.

Shocked relief slowly flooded Kelep's and Fitz's faces. Kelep blinked several times, quivering.

"Oooohhhhh, wwwooowwww!" he sputtered at last, "Ttth-haannnkk yyoouu, Raajj. II tthink you saved my life."

"Are you okay, Kelep? Why are you talking like that?" Did it bite him? I grabbed his hand to check. "Why are you talking so slow, stuttering?"

"What, no!" He pulled back, his eyes wide. "It didn't bite me. I'm fine."

"What are you talking about, Raj?" Fitz big eyes were worried. "I heard him fine." You did?

Wait, the stick, the swing, the slow down... was that my Smart-Core? It had to be. Had my reaction time increased? Weird. I'd ask Fitz later. "So, you're okay?"

"Yeah, thanks to you." Kelep looked at his band with a start. Must have gotten a buzz or something. "Guys, I have to go! I'm supposed to be home by 17:00 for dinner."

"It was nice meeting you, Kelep," Fitz said. "We'll be here a few days if you ever want to come and play again. Oh, and Kelep," Fitz added. "Your dad will be super proud when he hears about the Black

Widow and how brave you were. We'll be here in case he doesn't believe you."

He thanked us and left. I turned to Fitz. He had a grin on his face.

"What was that about?" I asked.

"The boy's father's headed to Itany this weekend. You saved his boy's life. If he has any sense of honor, he'll want to return the favor. We'll help him unload his wares and be on our way. I figure we have pretty good odds."

Fitz was one sly cat. Why didn't I think of that?

"Great thinking on the fly, *Raj,*" he added as an afterthought.

I don't know why, but him saying that made me feel better than anything we'd done so far. Escaping the DNS, killing the cynetics, saving the boy... something about the way Fitz said it made him feel like the father I'd never had. Almost...

Mom never talked about my dad. He must have traveled a lot. Maybe only visited Mom when he was in town, maybe he had women everywhere he went. I didn't know, and I didn't care. He was dead to me.

Fitz yawned. "I'm going to grab some shuteye while the sun's up. You should too, or try your SmartCore again. See what you find." He rolled over and was out within seconds.

How could *that* guy do it? Wait, 'that guy?' Not three days ago, he was Professor Fitz, my Science History teacher. And now he was 'that guy,' a friend, and like a father to me. I choked up and closed my eyes.

Darkness.

14

UNLEASHED

Time stood still and I found myself back in the SmartCore, the control room. So many interfaces and moving parts... I walked to the corner and stepped on a silver pad. What's this for?

A tingling shot through my feet and spread through me, sparks of electricity setting me on fire. My skin glowed, tiny points appearing every centimeter, every tenth of a centimeter, smaller still, until a mesh grid covered me. What was happening?

A bone-rattling chill. The next instant a searing hot pain. It ended.

The glowing dots faded and my body became *just* my body again. What the hell was that?

Opening my eyes, I was back in the forest. Around me, trees grew to the sun and birds sang. Fitz slept like an angel by the fire.

My eyes darted, frantic. I *needed* food. I needed meat. *Now.*

Grabbing my blaster, I set off, unable to think straight. An all-consuming hunger overpowered any semblance of rational thought.

My senses were hyper-alert. Something was happening inside me.

I caught the scent of deer and changed directions, heading southeast, deeper into the forest. Leaves crackled. He was two hundred meters away, grazing. In my wild state, I charged him. Once he realized what was happening, it was too late.

I sprang, claws slashing, as I landed on his powerful back and clamped its neck, ripping its throat with my fangs. There was never any question. My teeth tore into him, blood drenching my lips. I ate the venison raw. It was glorious, the drive overwhelming, and I gorged at least two kilos.

I sliced what I could of the remainder, slung the animal over my shoulder, and headed for camp. Passing a chilly stream, I rinsed my face and beard so Fitz wouldn't think me a savage.

A fire was going as I rounded the bend. "So, that's where you went," he remarked. "Thought so, but you shouldn't run off."

"I was starving." I didn't plan on elaborating. "You want some or not?" He must be starving too.

We got a spit going and draped the meat over the fire. It was getting toasty, a perfect rare, when we heard the *crunch* of leaves.

Not again. We grabbed our knives.

Tapping my temple, thermals appeared. Two figures approached from the right, one large, the other small.

"Get behind that tree." I pointed.

He rose, fading into the darkness.

Kelep and his father stepped into the clearing. Kelep's father was a tall, muscular man with a strong jawline, thick black hair, and the dark eyes of someone who wasn't to be trifled with. He wore jeans, thick leather boots, and a bright vest. A hunter?

"Perfect timing," I said as they got closer. "We've got dinner on the fire, a fresh kill. Have you eaten?"

He shook his head. "You must be Raj." He held out his hand. "I'm Abe, Kelep's father. Wanted to thank you for what ya did for my son."

Fitz emerged from the woods. "Had to take a leak, sorry. What'd I miss?"

"I was thanking Raj for protecting my son. He's your boy?"

"It all happened so fast." I shrugged. It wasn't like I could tell him the truth. "Kelep reacted well. You've done good with the lad."

Abe grinned from ear to ear as we squatted around the fire, slicing a couple of fine cuts and making small talk.

"I hear you're going to Itany?" I said once Abe had finished.

"Heard right. Got me a big shipment and need to make sure it's delivered on time." His eyes narrowed. "One of my mates quit a month back, got working papers for the big city. Been looking for help since. Don't know who he ratted on for an opportunity like that." He shook his head. "Least it wasn't me," he added. "How'd one of ya like to do the run with me?"

"What about both of us?" Fitz asked. "We need to get to Itany, get my wife from the in-laws. Could use a lift and would be happy to help in exchange for a ride."

"Free labor?" Abe laughed. "I'm a trader, I'll take that any day." He told us to meet him Saturday at sun up at a warehouse north of town. After finalizing plans, they excused themselves; Kelep had homework he'd forgotten to finish.

The next two days were nothing special. With plenty of meat and water nearby, we weren't worried about anything other than getting ready. Somehow Fitz started telling stories about his childhood.

He'd grown up further west, but wouldn't say where. From what I could gather, they'd been poor and he had a younger brother, but his mother died giving birth. When he realized what he'd been saying, he changed the subject.

The next morning we talked backup plans. What if something went wrong? Where would we meet? What if the DNS came? He grilled me for hours, and at the end, we were exhausted.

A brief walk and a hearty dinner, and we slept the rest of the day.

After packing our belongings and cleaning camp Saturday morning, we set off, both anxious to get there *before* encountering cops.

The reddish-brown barn came into view an hour later, an enormous big rig outside. It could have swallowed our place whole. People used to drive those things?

"Hey, Abe!" Fitz shouted when we reached the front. "We're here."

There was a rattle from inside the barn. "One sec!" he yelled.

He emerged a minute later with a thin silver wristband, spouting specs with a salesman's ease and a greedy smile. "Only trader in the region with access to these babies. Rich buggers will eat 'em up." He had us load those up first, "In case we have any trouble with bandits."

After thirty minutes of mindless lifting, a horn blared. I jumped, hand flying to my knife. What was that?

"Come on, boys!" Abe laughed. "It is time to get this show on the road."

"You scared the crap out of me," I told him once we'd piled into the front seat.

"She's got a mighty fine horn, doesn't she? Wakes other truckers the hell up." He smiled. "That's not all she does." He tapped a small nondescript knob. "You might not hear it, but she's a multi-frequency jammer for dealing with drones or vehicles taking too much interest in my truck. Throws their navigation for a loop. Two crashed not twenty meters away and never knew what hit 'em."

"By the way, where you coming from?" Fitz asked.

"Willows, 'bout halfway between here and The Brooks." He turned from the road. "The Brooks used to be a hopping place I hear, Big Apple they called it. City got crushed. Pa used to tell me stories. The Fall sounded terrible, madness. They teach ya bout that, boy?"

Did he think I was an idiot? "Yeah, they do. Not a lot, but some."

"Gotta tell ya something." His eyes were still off the road, which seemed like an awful idea. He wasn't the smartest cookie. "I ain't a huge lover of the GDR, but they did okay considering how bad things were. Imagine folks doing that genetics stuff, unnatural that is."

I was thinking of a reply when a drone appeared. Not a good sign. "We got company." I pointed. "Should we hit the horn?"

"Not yet," Abe replied. "Let's see what the little guy does."

A few minutes later, it was gone. "What'd I tell ya. Not a big deal." He grinned. "Got any brothers or sisters, Raj?"

"Nope, just me."

"That's a shame. Nothin's more important than family; family and business that is." He smiled. "My Pa taught me to be a trader: nego-tiate deals and bargains, where to sell, who to talk to, that kinda thing. My brother wasn't interested, always getting in trouble. Joined the army, no surprise there. Stationed overseas, I think. Something about keeping the peace, problems on the Continent. I should call him, it's been a while since—"

Abe's head exploded, words dying on his lips. Holy crap! Blood splattered everywhere, spraying me. The wheel slipped from his hand, spinning as the truck turned. We jackknifed, flipping, once, twice.

SLAM.

Everything went black.

15

PITSTOP

An amplified voice boomed everywhere at once. "STAY WHERE YOU ARE! HANDS WHERE WE CAN SEE THEM. WE HAVE YOU SURROUNDED. OUR SHOOTERS HAVE YOU IN THEIR SIGHTS. "

Disoriented, I opened my eyes. The windows of the truck were shattered, the big rig lying on its side. Fitz was awake, peering out the door, rubbing his head.

Where were we?

The cruiser doors opened and armed officers piled out, blasters leveled at us. Red dots appearing on our chests.

Stay calm, Raek. We put our hands up. My cybernetics wouldn't help here, not if there were other cynetics in those vehicles. We were screwed.

As long as they didn't kill Fitz. There was enough blood on my hands.

Officers advanced on the rig, guns drawn, unblinking.

"TOSS YOUR WEAPONS AND COME OUT WITH YOUR HANDS UP. ANY FUNNY BUSINESS AND THEY WON'T BE ABLE TO ID YOUR BODIES, YOU'LL HAVE SO MANY BLASTERS UP YOUR ASS!"

We flung the blasters out.

"We get it. We're coming. Don't shoot!" Fitz yelled. "Don't let them take you alive," he whispered as he ducked out.

There were six officers, two in front, four behind. Three had blasters, three didn't. So, at least three cynetics with built-in blasters of their own. Outnumbered and outgunned. At least it couldn't get much worse.

"We're law-abiding citizens." Fitz stumbled to his feet. "What's the meaning of this?"

One of the black-clad officers stepped forward. He was a small slim fellow, unarmed except a pair of curved knives. I'd bet money he was cynetic. Size was irrelevant—he could be strong as an ox and nimble as a snake—his mechatronic muscles and superhuman reactions made him a formidable opponent. And I had no idea what I was doing...

He sneered, pitch black eyes an abyss of suffering and pain. "Cut the crap. Raek here has been a naughty boy. Don't move your hands, kid. We know you're semi-cynetic, *freak*. The nerds back at HQ are excited about you. Half cynetic, half animote... they're *dying* to open you up and see how you tick." He smirked.

Open me up? Swallowing hard, I fought to control my emotions. Don't let him get to you. "And, Professor Fitz," he said icily. "What brings you here? Aiding and abetting a half-breed traitor to the state, sounds like capital crimes."

He raised his palm, pointing it at Fitz's head. "How'd the boy get his cybernetics?"

Fitz shook his head but stayed cool. "Beats me."

"Liar."

Not Fitz too. I took a step forward. "He doesn't know and I don't either."

"Bullshit. You're going to tell me or your friend dies!" the cynetic hissed.

"I don't—"

"Wrong answer." His palm illuminated. He fired.

No... Fitz's right ear evaporated before my eyes. "You'll have to work on your aim," Fitz coughed as blood gushed from the wound.

The cynetic scowled, his eyes narrowing. "Lucky for you, I'm just the deliverer. Search them, boys. Find *everything*. You know what'll happen if you miss anything." He turned to the officers behind him. "Torch their bags and car. No sense leaving anything to chance."

Tasers hit me and spasms wracked my body. Once I couldn't fight it any longer, I collapsed to the ground, peeing myself in the process, until the pain subsided.

"Sorry about that," the cynetic said with a mocking grin I'd have wiped off if I wasn't writhing. "Standard procedure and all. Besides, it's only a ten-hour ride to headquarters. You don't mind sitting in your own piss, right?" A few officers joined in laughing.

"Name's Thorn, by the way. In case you want a name with the face. Pleasure to meet you." His lips curled into a predatory smile. "Hurry up, load them in the cars. Separate them. We don't need any funny business."

He turned and swaggered back to his car with a confidence that made me sick.

It took another ten minutes to finish their invasive search and burn our gear. Everything we owned, up in flames, just like that.

So much for our luck improving. At least Fitz's ear stopped gushing. Was he okay?

Stepping toward the car, I had an epiphany. If I was cynetic, I could access the web. In the five steps before being shoved into the cruiser, I posted in three separate radical forums asking for help.

-

Help, I'm an Animote-Cynetic hybrid, REALLY!
Wolfish w/ cybernetics
Captured by DNS/GDR
Username: @nightstalker1
Password: howlsatthemoon
My internal GPS is on!!!

-

No one would see it. And if they did, they wouldn't believe me. How could they? They wouldn't be able to help either. Still, it felt better than doing nothing.

Maybe the fact I existed, a mixed-breed... maybe there were others. Maybe there was hope, maybe.

An officer jabbed my finger with a micro-needle. A small prick.

Everything spun.

16

AN APPLE A DAY

I awoke feeling weird. My head was—I don't know… off.
   The door opened.

Stay calm. Think, Raek. Look around, what do you see? It was an operating room. Everything was pristine and white: the walls, the floors, the table. Crap, the table. Why was I strapped to a table? No windows, two swivel chairs, a camera above me. To my right was a drawer filled with scalpels, saws, and all manner of horrible looking tools.

No! I strained my arms and legs, desperate to get out, but tiny red restraints dug into my hands and feet. Ah, that was tight.

What was going on? My heart pounded. What Thorn had said? *"The nerds back at headquarters, they're excited to open you up…"*

Someone whistled an eerie tune in the echoey hallway. It made my skin crawl. There was a voice, but I couldn't make out the words—my ears weren't working right.

A small, slimy blob of a man walked in. He was hideous. So short, grossly overweight, and completely bald, a face covered in boils. He smiled at me, his tiny black eyes alight with excitement. "Our patient finally decided to wake up, Dr. P."

Behind him walked—if possible—someone equally as ugly. It was tall and gaunt, skinny beyond any degree of health or youthfulness. And its skin was worse still, so pale and thin, almost translucent— veins and bones practically poking out of the decaying body.

I couldn't tell if it was a man or a woman until I saw the hands. They were massive, much too big to be a woman's, with long, smooth fingers and manicured nails. "It would appear so, Dr. R. It's time to get to work." He smiled toothily at me, hideous, perfect, pearly whites making me ill.

"Raek, my boy, you've been given a gift. It's our job to under-stand that *gift*, to cut it out of you." The fat man's eyes were fanati-cal, stretched to the absolute limit of his revolting face. "We're to peer into your soul, open your genome, and find what makes you tick. Ready for a little fun?" A tiny giggle escaped his disgusting lips.

Before I could respond, he grabbed a blade from the dressing table and stabbed my hand.

I screamed as spasms gripped me. Tears came.

"How did you get the nanoSTEMs?" Dr. P asked, voice rising. "Were you going to the Resistance? Did Lyam tell you where their headquarters is?"

Sobbing, I closed my eyes. "I don't know. I don't, I swear." My nerves were on fire, pain blinding.

Stay calm. No luck. Piercing agony brought me back to hell. "I don't know!" I screamed. My SmartCore downregulated the pain until his partner hacked off my big toe with one efficient swipe that sent my nerves ablaze.

I passed out on the third toe. It was more than I could bear. Before everything went black, it hit me. I'd never walk again.

I came to in time to hear, "Got to take a trip to the little boys' room. Don't miss me." Another disgusting giggle, and the door thudded shut.

"Raek, we need to hurry!" The skinny one unclasped the restraints binding my feet.

What? My eyes opened, widening. "What are you doing?"

"My name's Robiert, I'm undercover with Rebel intelligence,

spying on the GDR's research programs. I'm on your side. We need to get you out of here! You may be our side's last chance."

He handed me crutches, and I stood speechless. What was he saying? It wasn't possible, was it?

He unhooked my shaking hands.

"Did Harding tell you where to go? Where the new Resistance headquarters is? I need to get out of here too, my cover is blown after this."

"No. Why?" Wait, who's Harding?

"Follow me!" The sickly man locked the door Dr. R had gone through and opened another. "Down here, come on." He hurried deeper underground, feet echoing in the tiny stairwell as I struggled after him. Where were we going?

The echo. Something about it was *off*. My ears again... they'd been acting up since the officer injected me. Come on, Raek, focus. I shook my head to clear the fog.

At the landing, he had another series of questions.

Something wasn't right. If there were sound sensors in this hallway, talking made no sense. The things he was asking—it hit me. My ears, my eyes, my senses... everything was off. You can't model consciousness, can't know *exactly* how someone experiences life.

This was a simulation, it *had* to be. A virtual world.

Really?

Closing my eyes, I concentrated on my breath. Please be right...

"Raek, hurry! Raek? What are you—Where's the new headquarters? Raek?"

I blocked him out, blocked everything and went deeper and deeper. He stabbed me twice. Still, I fought, pain searing. Everything disappeared and I signaled my SmartCore to wake up.

A shockwave rippled through me.

There was light.

17

THE BUS

The smooth micro-fibers of the seat, the rhythmic bumps of the road—I was still in the car. We must be driving to Caen, to HQ. My eyes stayed shut.

At least we still had time. I flexed my hands and wiggled my toes. They were there, and they worked! It was a simulation, just virtual reality. Holy crap! I wanted to cry.

That was unreal. No wonder junkies got hooked.

Keeping my eyes closed, I slowed my breathing. They couldn't know I'd awoken. It was the one advantage I had.

I was in the backseat, the middle, I think. Two officers from the smell of it.

"How much longer, Stev?" the whiner in the front asked. His name was Wilk from what I'd gathered.

"City's pretty big, busy at this hour." The driver paused, thinking. "Thirty, forty minutes, not more." Thirty minutes… that's it?

"Good, I'm starving. Babysitting isn't a bad gig after what we heard about this kid. But heck, you'd think they'd feed us or sumthin'. How's the wife by the way?"

The car stopped, and so did my heart. Were we there, *already*? No, he'd said thirty minutes.

"Gotta love traffic," Wilk complained. "That them in front of us?"

"I'll be damned, it is. Roll your window." A brief electric *whirr* and a blast of fresh air and noise. "Fancy seeing you here."

"Stev, Wilk… how's it going fellas," a deep voice from outside boomed over the din. "How was the drive?"

"Uneventful," Wilk said. "Kid's been asleep, plugged into the sim the whole time. Hope they're getting good intel. Wouldn't want to be him, right? What 'bout you?"

"Same. Tigerish scum's out cold."

Fitz. He was right there… And he was alive.

Now what? I didn't have a plan but I didn't have time. This was my last chance.

Leaping forward, I blasted the driver in the face, taking his head off before firing at Wilk. At point-blank range, he never stood a chance. My targeting acquired the two officers in the vehicle next to us. A multi-burst shot. The first blew the window. The next two hit the officers within milliseconds. Blood splattered their bioleather seats.

Instinct told me all threats were neutralized, but I was on high alert, panicking and wired. Were they dead?

I tried the handle. The doors were locked. Leaning, I kicked it off the hinges and slammed through the ultralight steel door.

Adrenaline flowing, I dove over to the other cruiser. There were bikes, buses, and scooters everywhere. A large circle of onlookers had formed on the sidewalk, several commentating like they were filming. Were they armed?

Fitz was sprawled in the back seat, breathing labored. The doors were locked. I smashed the glass, praying no one fired. Shards flew, but I didn't bother to duck. Grabbing Fitz's limp arm through the gaping hole, I dragged him to the side, his stump of an ear ripping open once more.

Sirens blared and people screamed as I lifted him out. Shit. Tossing him over my shoulder, I ran, warm blood dripping down me.

The city was big, unbelievably, unthinkably, unimaginably big. Buildings stretched to the sky in all directions. I'd never seen more than a two-story hovel, except in the movies. *Unreal.*

Flying across the busy sidewalk, sounds and smells assaulted me: flowers, burnt rubber, yelling, sweat...

After four blocks, a small red bus pulled up and a brown haired girl in gray leaned out. "You the hybrid? That you they're after?"

What? I looked at her and continued to run.

"It's you. You posted on Animote Power?" she snapped.

Oh! I stopped. She had big brown ears and light fluffy fur covered her hands and cheeks.

"Chimpish?" I asked.

She nodded. "Get in before the DNS show up and take you and your friend to the Basement." Where?

The sirens were getting louder, and a VTOL took off somewhere in the distance. Did I have a choice?

I climbed in, twisting sideways to make Fitz fit.

"Step on it, Jame!" the girl yelled. "What you waiting for?"

A small man with a greenish tint and scaly skin was at the wheel. He wore a blue hoodie pulled low, his green eyes snatching a glance at Fitz and I as we passed. He floored it and I dropped Fitz into a seat, collapsing beside him.

Where were the VTOLs? We zipped through chaotic streets as sirens faded.

"*Quite* a stunt you pulled there." The girl had come to sit across from us. She was pretty—in an unconventional way—dangerous brown eyes, full lips, and a spunky smile to match her sporty physique. "You're lucky. That's the busiest intersection in town. Anywhere else and they'd have arrived sooner. We wouldn't be having this conversation."

"Who are you? Why are you helping us?" Turning, I readied my blaster, lining up the shot. I hoped I wouldn't need it.

"Name's Zedda." She stuck out her hand. "We're helping cause you asked."

"And because you're rare," Jame added from upfront. "The Cause needs you."

"Cause?" I gave her a questioning look.

She rolled her eyes. "Animote freedom. We're fighting for equality, to end the Troubles."

Made sense. "Rebels?" Fitz had warned me about these guys.

"That's what the government calls us, or terrorists." She shook her head. "We think of ourselves as freedom fighters, fighting for the rights of animotes everywhere, and to overthrow the government."

That didn't sound so bad. "Whoever you are, thanks. I had no idea what I was going to do."

"Yeah, I got that." She laughed. "You did okay, taking out two cynetics and two enhancers."

"Two and two?" I asked.

"The decals on their cruisers. Besides, partners are always same species. DNS doesn't mix 'em, wants to avoid conflict."

Wait, was this another sim? I closed my eyes, concentrating.

"I know what you're thinking," Zedda interrupted. "This isn't a simulation. Check your eyes, check your ears. Always have something *only* you know about."

I opened my eyes and focused. She was right. Everything felt normal, no *off* feeling. Satisfied, I said, "Where are we headed?"

"A safe place. Can't tell ya, at least not yet," she added. "Security, we gotta change cars a few times." At this point, I was beyond caring.

* * *

We screeched to a stop and my eyes bolted open. Weird, no bus. We must have switched to this delivery van at some point. I didn't remember and that worried me.

We were inside an abandoned warehouse of some kind: high ceilings, gray sheet metal walls, no windows. Could be underground for all I knew. The lighting was artificial, the ground, concrete, and a constant weak echo.

How'd I let myself fall asleep? What was I thinking?

GPS? No luck. Like the simulated surgery, this place had jammers, but my other senses checked out. I wasn't dreaming, this wasn't VR.

All that happened in the blink of an eye—a hundred milliseconds or less—as my eyes opened.

Zedda was looking at me. "We're here. Grab your friend and let's go."

Fitz was still out? Must have been wicked sedatives. It had been twelve hours according to my SmartCore.

What if he was going through a torture sim? I punched his arm to wake him. No reaction, not even a groan. Not a good sign.

Bending, I tossed him over my shoulder and squeezed through the door.

Zedda interrupted my train of thought, "Welcome to The Initiative." She smiled. "It's not much, but it is all we got. Ashlo, Henk, get over here. Search him. Raek, meet Ashlo and Henk. They're brothers, vets of the cause. Been with us for years, ever since their dad died."

Two man-shaped mountains appeared from a hallway off the main entrance, each two meters and pushing a hundred kilos. Round black eyes, thick, matted brown fur, powerful arms and legs: bearish. Dark beards and battle-tested noses rounded out the look, and apart from a few centimeters difference, I couldn't tell them apart.

"I'm Ashlo," the taller one said.

"I'm Henk," the second added.

"I'm Raek. Nice to meet you."

"We gotta search you," the first said.

"Standard operating procedure," Henk added.

"You're part cynetic?" Ashlo gave me a skeptical look.

I nodded.

"We'll use this." He pulled out an ominous rod.

I must have winced because Henk added, "You won't feel a thing. Checking for bugs—"

"And weapons," Ashlo finished. "Anything metal or biofabbed out of the ordinary. Hold out your arms—"

"Spread the legs too," Henk commanded. "Got to ask you a few questions."

I did as I was told, but not before priming my blasters in case. They were big, but I could probably take them.

Ashlo passed the rod over my arms, legs, and abdomen while Henk hooked polymetal sensors to my head, arms, and chest, and quizzed me on everything from where I was born to my family origins. Once satisfied, he said, "Looks like you're clean."

"Same here." Henk held a cup. "Spit into this."

"What for?" DNA was a whole nother can of worms.

Henk's face hardened. "DNA test. Gotta make sure you are—"

"What you say you are," Ashlo finished.

Ashlo laughed. "We're messing with you, dude. You're all clear. We don't need your DNA. It's obvious you're cynetic and you're wolfish. Welcome to The Initiative." He grasped my hand and gave it a firm shake.

"Thanks," I murmured. Finishing each other's sentences... talk about a crappy sense of humor. "You had me going there." I peeled off the sticky devices and handed them back to Henk.

"We've been working on that," Henk said. "No one can tell us apart, figured we'd have some fun with it." He shook my hand as well. "It's an honor to meet you, Raek."

Zedda reappeared. When'd she leave?

"Your room's over here." She led the way toward the far corner. "They do that to everyone, big goofy idiots. They're harmless, well except in a fight," she added with a hard stare. "They'll rip your face off. Stone cold killers, the both of them. Other than that, they're teddy bears."

Was that a threat? Neither of us said anything. I'd have to watch my back.

"Wait, where's Fitz?"

"What? Who?" She gave me a look. "Oh, your friend. I had Ashlo carry him to the medical ward to get checked out. End of this hall, on the left. He'll be out a bit longer, but we can go see him if you want. He's in good hands."

"No, that's okay. Can you show me around, get a feel for the place?" Always prepared, just in case.

She shrugged. "Suit yourself. This is your room." She opened the door. "It isn't much, but it's a little privacy."

The layout was similar to old cubicle offices at the turn of the century, temporary dividers creating isolated solitude.

And she wasn't kidding, it was small: two meters by three, maybe a hair more. The concrete floor had a simple blue mat. Everything about the place screamed underappreciated and underfunded. Made sense. When fighting the government, fundraising was tough and frills, irrelevant. I could respect that.

"It's perfect," I said. "Thanks."

"Laundry is where you came in and the mess is toward the middle. Upstairs has more sleeping quarters, and the fitness room, far side." She pointed.

It was a lot to take in. I saved it all for later.

My stomach rumbled. "You said there was a mess hall." Sounded pretty good about now. I'd kill for a good steak.

"Follow me."

We walked a few minutes, weaving this way and that, passing many empty sleeping quarters and a few interested faces. Twice, people came to stare.

Stopping in the middle of a hall, Zedda knocked on a cell door. "Hey, Paer! Come here, I've got someone I want you to meet."

Zedda whispered, "Agtha's one of the oldest and most experienced members of The Initiative. Been fighting the GDR since the start of The Troubles. She was there during The Experiments, remembers the Fall. She's kind of our oracle, our good luck charm. Everyone calls her by her last name: Paer."

Cue the fairy godmother: wizened, kooky, with a hunched back and all.

The door opened and a wiry woman with short, caramel hair, a square face, and the eyes of an intellectual emerged. Wow, was I off... A raw energy permeated her, it was contagious. According to Zedda, she must be seventy, *at least*, closer to eighty. She looked thirty-five and fiery.

Paer stuck out a furry hand. "I'm Agtha, good to meet you."

"Paer, this is Raek, the hybrid that posted on the forums. He's legit. Wanted you to meet him."

She nodded. "See you around." With that, she stepped back into her quarters, closing the door.

"She can be frosty at first," Zedda explained. "It's not you, she's like that with everyone. Takes a while to warm up. She's lost so many friends in this fight, it's hard for her with new people."

Imagine, decades of undercover fighting...

"That's why I wanted you to meet her. She's rough, but critical to our operation and on the Council of Elders." She must have noticed my confusion because she said, "Our group of elected leaders. Holds a lot of weight, given her experience. Plus, she's an *animal* in the gym and the field. The Initiative's the only family she has."

Family... " Zedda, can you help me with something?"

She pursed her lips. "Maybe. What's up?"

I told her about my family.

"And you want to find out what happened?" she asked.

I nodded. "I'd appreciate it. If it wouldn't be too much to ask," I added, feeling the beginnings of hope.

She smiled. "Sure." In a more serious tone, she added, "You might not like what I find."

They were okay, they had to be...

A delicious aroma hit me. "Smells good."

"Well, it's food," Zedda said with a gag. "Avoid the meatloaf. Anti re-cooks it and re-serves it over and over. Anti's the cook by the way, or at least the one who cooks," she added with a grim grin.

"You hungry?"

She shook her head. "I need to take care of some stuff, operational updates and such. I'll find you later." Turning to walk away, she added, "Watch your back, Raek. I trust everyone here, but only so far. We have new recruits all the time, you never know. There's a bounty on your head, a *big* one."

She left, leaving me to think about what she'd said.

The mess was empty when I entered, except for a chubby black-haired man singing to himself as he worked away in the huge, well-equipped kitchen. Must be Anti.

"When the moon hits your eye like a big pizza pie, that's amore!"

The *thump* of the door made him jump and send a pan clattering. "I didn't hear you come in." He turned red as his marinara and studied me closer. "I don't think you've met Anti. Are you new? I'm Anti." He walked out of the semi-divided kitchen and offered a gloved hand. "I'm the *official* head chef of this mess, and I'm at your service. Today's special, a savory spaghetti with me grandma's signature meaty marinara. You hungry?"

I was starving and said as much.

"Help yourself. Anti's got to get back to dinner prep. A larger than usual crew tonight." He smiled. "Rice and beans with a side of meatloaf for over three hundred. Need anything, let Anti know." He left, humming away.

I grabbed a seat at one of the many long wooden tables and was on my second helping when Ashlo and Henk came in. A wave. They lumbered over after loading up.

"Can be a bit intimidating, all this, I mean." Henk motioned around us.

"It's huge. How many people live here?"

"Ranges from about 120 up to 200-300. Tomorrow will be a big day, lot of folks coming in," Henk added. "Average is about one-fifty."

That's it? "The whole resistance?" No wonder they hadn't made more progress...

Henk chuckled. "Not even close. There are a bunch of cells around the world, and smaller grassroots movements in most towns."

Ashlo scowled. "Should be more. We outnumber elites but *we're* the repressed 'minorities.' How's that possible? How's that okay?" He shook his head in disgust.

"That's why people like us need to start the movement, the pushers. Once we get it going, there will be followers. You'll see."

"I hope you're right," Ashlo murmured. "As long as the hippies don't get their way."

"Hippies?" I asked. "Why?" What did this have to do with hippies?
Henk nodded. "Heard of Martin Luther King, Jr.? Gandhi?"

"Of course I know Gandhi," I added, louder than I'd intended.

Ashlo rolled his eyes. "His whole thing was a peaceful protest. Sitting in squares, civil disobedience… that kind of thing."

"What's wrong with that?" I asked.

"It doesn't work!" Henk growled. "The elites don't give a shit about us."

"What Henk means," Ashlo cut in, "is since The Experiments and subspecies divide, elites feel justified in their position. In Luther's era, in Gandhi's time, people were the same, intrinsically equal. That's why slavery was abolished, democracy thrived, and everyone could vote. But today, they say: 'Should we give pigs and cows the right to vote?' That's how they view *us*…"

"But is war the answer?" I said. "Isn't there another way?"

"You mean a sit-in, a demonstration?" Ashlo replied.

I nodded. "Yeah. If we banded together—"

"Two groups tried it, one in Zone Three and one west of here. It wasn't pretty." Henk gritted his teeth. "Several hundred gunned down in each. Rumor is, Minister of Security Fury ordered the DNS to open fire on protesters that wouldn't disband." He sighed, we all did.

I felt their hopelessness. They were on edge, they needed something. They needed a miracle.

They needed hope.

18

HITTING THE DECK

After eating, I went to the infirmary. The door opened to a state of the art medical ward complete with propped beds, IV racks, and a freckled nurse at a spotless desk in the far corner, beady brown eyes eyeing me. "What can I do for you?"

She listened and led me past an inverted imaging array into another room. "He's in there."

Sure enough, Fitz was asleep on a gurney, wireless sensors hooked to his arms, chest and forehead. "Is he okay?" He looked horrible.

She nodded and checked her band. "Sorry. Another patient, allergies…" She hurried off, leaving us alone.

He wasn't moving and that worried me. *How* was he still asleep? It had been *fifteen* hours. He should be awake by now. I should wake him up, right?

Another group raced in carrying a red-faced woman as I closed the door. Everything fell silent. I leaned over him. "Fitz? Fitz." Nothing.

After a series of hard slaps didn't help, I grabbed a small cup from the dispenser, filled it in the sink and dumped it on him.

He rocketed upward, eyes wide, sensors squawking.

"No!" he screamed. "Not again!"

Our eyes met and horror crept into his gaunt face as he paled, recoiling. His biomarkers skyrocketed, beeping. "Not him, not Raek! I won't fall for this again. I don't know where they are." He touched his ruined ear.

Jeez. "Fitz, it's me. It's Raek."

He launched himself at me, massive shoulder slamming my face and sending us flying into the wall. We fell, hard, and he sprang on top of me, using his weight to pin my arms.

"Fitz!" I shouted. "What are you doing? It's me! This isn't a sim, this isn't virtual."

He pounded me, fists raining down. "Where did we meet that night?"

What was he talking about? Shit.

"Where?" he roared, eyes half-mad. "The night you disappeared."

Um... "Behind our house." What did that have to do with anything?

His voice weakened and the punches slowed. "And where did we hide in the school when the DNS came?"

"In the basement, but we went to your room." That's what he was doing. "We barricaded ourselves behind desks and used micro mats as blast absorbers. Is that good enough? There were officers inside my house that night, three of 'em. Waiting for me. You saved my life. Fitz?"

He collapsed, sobbing onto the floor, an inhuman gasping laugh escaping his shivering lips. Jeez.

"Raek, you have no idea how glad I am to see you. I thought, I thought I might never get out of there." He looked me dead in the eyes, a serious expression on his face. "You have no idea how bad the food is."

I couldn't help but smile. "That's the Fitz I know. It isn't much better here, but there's food."

He didn't want to talk about it and I couldn't blame him. It was bad enough for me, and he was under twice as long.

"You're right, I'm starving. But where are we?" he gestured around us. "And are you okay? What happened?"

Heck if I know. I told him everything, including my simulated torture and escape. He listened, focused, never once interrupting.

"So, this is the new rebel headquarters," he remarked when I finished. "Must mean we're near Caen. Right under their noses." The beginnings of a smile. "You mentioned food?"

"I'll show you around. Let's find Zedda." We exited the medical ward with little more than a look of shock and a few quick exams from the nurse.

After that, the day passed in a blur. At eight p.m., we found our way back to bed and I passed out the moment I hit the mat.

When I awoke, my SmartCore told me it was 6:00 a.m. Ugh... The lack of windows and natural light was unnerving.

There were a decent number of early risers when I swung my door open and weights smashed above. Might be just what I needed.

Jogging upstairs, people stirred, the occasional early morning romp.

Halfway down the hall, a figure emerged. Bending to clear the low doorway, out stepped a tall, athletic beauty. She wore simple crimson and blue fitted pants, her skin an ornate golden brown pattern. She was intoxicating.

"Hey," I said, unable to help myself. My pulse ramped. What was it about pretty girls?

She gave me a funny look, warm eyes inspecting me. "You're new here, aren't you? You must be Raek."

I nodded, confused and on edge, despite her good looks. "You know my name?"

"Zedda told me. I'm Lilia." She offered a manicured hand, a stark contrast to her powerful grip. "Pleased to meet you, Raek."

I shook it, not too hard I hoped. "Pleasure's all mine."

"How do you like it here? Are you getting settled?" She seemed genuine.

"I am. It's good, a bit overwhelming, but good. You talked to Zedda about me?"

"For our meeting tonight. I'm on the Council," she added. "Going to train?"

I nodded, grinning like a fool. Get it together, Raek.

She checked her band. "It was nice to meet you, but I need to run." She hurried in the other direction as I continued down the hall, unable to get her out of my head.

The hallway ended in a big metal door with a *Do or die!* sign on it. Intense bunch. But in war, it *was* do or die. I guess it made sense to practice with a similar intensity.

The door opened to pounding music—Metallica 2pointAI, banned now—and a familiar sweaty blast. I downregulated my nose—something I'd learned by accident in a weird dream—and after a second, could breathe again.

Ashlo and Henk were sparring in the far corner and I headed over.

On the way were hulking guys and gals squatting heavy weights, athletes on rings and bars, and a small girl with sim goggles blasting imaginary targets. They'd pulled out all the stops.

When I reached the brothers, Ashlo and Henk were locked in a heated struggle, a small crowd gathered around, grimacing in excitement.

Ashlo—the bigger of the two—had his brother pinned to the floor, massive arm tight around Henk's bulging throat. "Tap, come on." His face contorted in a panting smile as he applied more pressure but Henk kept fighting.

Henk's eyes were closing when he sprang into motion, blasting off the red mat and flipping forward. The crowd gasped, going silent.

Ashlo's face smashed the mat and Henk twisted from the choke, spinning his brother into an armbar, legs squeezing Ashlo's vulnerable shoulder.

It hurt to watch.

"Tap, Ashlo. Don't make me break it."

"Screw you, Henk! I'm not tapping." Ashlo gritted his teeth. "I don't tap..."

"Cut it out, the both of you!" came a loud, commanding voice. "The fight's over! We have more important issues. Henk, your brother's arm, now!"

Paer strode over. "You idiots aren't going to break *another* arm or leg. You're too damn important. Get off that mat and get yourselves dressed. Lilia was looking for you."

"Yes, ma'am!" they snapped, jumping from the mat and jogging to the showers, tails between their legs.

Wow. Paer was a powerhouse. She headed toward me. "They'll want to talk to you downstairs as well. We have a meeting at 10:00 every Monday, you need to be there."

"Thanks for the heads up."

"Want to spar?" She gave me a funny look, challenging yet playful.

"Me? Spar with you?" I took a step back.

"What, am I too old to spar?" Her eyes flashed.

"No, no, I meant—"

"Good, let's spar."

We suited up in protective headgear and light gloves, and stepped onto the soft circular mat.

"For rules, anything goes except the eyes and groin." She gave me a look, sizing me up, or mocking me, I wasn't sure.

Everyone was watching. Damn it. Talk about a first impression, kicking some old lady's butt. How'd she talk me into this?

We squared up, circling. Her footwork was outstanding. Mine wasn't half bad—Mom made us have lessons when we were younger—but Paer moved with impossible grace and precision.

"You know I have cybernetics?" I asked. "I don't want to hurt you—"

"Kid," she said with a smirk. "If you hurt me, I'll bake you cookies." The crowd roared and I flushed. I was trying to be nice, lady.

Moving inward, I threw a few feeler jabs but she dodged them with a smile.

As I lined up a combo, she faked and her right fist sledgehammered my stomach before I realized what happened.

Ugh... Dropping my arm to cover my body, her left clobbered my face. I stumbled, struggling to stay upright. My reaction time had to be twice as fast as hers, yet she was crushing me. What was going on? I'd underestimated her. "Well played."

She gave an innocent smile before she swept my leg and pounced, elbow crashing into my jaw as she landed. Her knee slammed my abdomen, knocking the wind out of me.

Struggling to defend myself, I remembered something Mom said once, "Wolves don't attack, baby, they kill."

Spinning my hips, I knocked her off and launched upward, creating space. As I landed, I put all my force into an uppercut, impaling her jaw. She dropped like a rock, out cold before she hit the floor.

Stunned silence, no one said a word.

Someone clapped. Others joined in. Soon I was swept up in high fives. I did it, I'd won, somehow... Next time I might not be so lucky.

Paer blinked, bleary-eyed. "Wh—where are we? What happened?"

Offering a hand, I helped her to her feet, her pupils dilating at last. "You're an amazing fighter, Paer. You knew what I'd do and how I'd react before I did."

"I want a rematch one of these days," she said through gritted teeth.

"How about one better?" I asked. She'd be the perfect tutor and Fitz hadn't taught me much yet. "Would you teach me?"

"Too busy, kid. Can't." She shook her head, face set in a hard line. Dang... "But thanks for asking, makes an old lady feel appreciated."

Someone called her over and she disappeared as Zedda came over to congratulate me. I tried to downplay it but she'd have none of it.

"I've never seen her lose, not once. Rumor is it's been years, some tigerish guy, I think. You'll have to ask Ashlo or Henk. They're more interested in that stuff."

Tigerish, mhm? No way...

"I'll see you at the meeting." She smiled. "First, I need to get some climbing in." She headed for the rock wall in the far corner. Chimpish, I laughed to myself. Our little animalish tendencies.

After showering, I went looking for Fitz.

When I got to his room, he was chatting with an older brunette I hadn't met. She had kind eyes, a warm posture, and petite hands that kept up with her whirlwind mouth. Fitz waved me over. "Raek, this is Fenni. She was sharing all the good gossip, you wouldn't believe some of the things... Fenni, meet Raek."

She smiled and after a quick hello, continued, "Like I was saying, sounds like the raids were successful. There's a meeting tonight, 18:00. Sounds like a big deal. Targets were high profile government buildings, I think."

"Really? "I didn't see anything on the web or forums. The elite web either."

She nodded. "That's normal. Our successful missions usually get swept under the rug." She wagged a finger. "Command and control 101. Never let the enemy appear strong, successful or human. It goes something like this: we attack some GDR building or assassinate a corrupt leader and it's either not reported, or labeled an accident: gas leak, bad heart, car accident… you get the picture."

She paused, basking in the attention. "*But* anytime we fail or something goes wrong, it's *everywhere*." She rolled her eyes. "Terrorist plot to blow up a hospital, thwarted. Rebels kill four innocent kids before being gunned down by *heroic* DNS officers…." Another eye roll. "It's always something like that. And no, we don't target hospitals, children, or innocents."

Fitz said, "It's true. Been like this for years."

"We always kind of thought so, at least our family… But you never know." I paused. "Guess that's the point. But don't people post footage? Shouldn't there be hundreds or thousands of videos and holos and articles?" The more I thought about it, the less sense it made.

She chuckled, Fitz too. "You ain't seen the data centers have you, honey? Who do you think employs the best developers and hackers, even some simple AI? The GDR spends the bulk of its monitoring budget on cyber, I'd bet."

Talk turned to the day's plans, and I told Fitz about the meeting. "We've got an hour to kill but—"

A funny, knowing grin on his face stopped me. "What? What is it?"

"It's nothing. I'm surprised, that's all," he mused. "Lilia, haven't heard that name in years."

"You know her? How?" Was she *that* old? Darn.

"Long story. We ran in similar crowds."

I was about to respond but thought better of it. Fenni was eyeing both of us and seemed loose-lipped. "I'm gonna grab some coffee from the mess, want some?"

"I could use some caffeine. Give me a sec." We said our goodbyes, and, after Fenni left, I gave Fitz a questioning look. "Later," he murmured.

We made it to the mess and fresh brewed coffee and savory biscuits hit me. Fitz perked up and I used this as the perfect excuse to ask about Lilia. "So, you know Lilia?"

"I do. Another life."

"Were you guys, well, lovers?" I fought to keep my face a mask.

"What? No." His brow furrowed. "What makes you say that?"

"You're avoiding the topic," I said, not wanting him to realize I was jealous.

He told me they'd been early members of the Resistance together, gone on a fair number of missions...

"But why'd you leave?" I asked.

"Differences of opinion," he said without elaborating.

I was sick of the guessing games and narrowed my eyes.

"To be honest," he said. "I'd had enough. I was tired of fighting, tired of trying to break the system. I wanted to build a better future for animotes, for all of us. That's why I became a teacher, I wasn't lying when I said that. Education is the key to opportunity. It's the thing I never had. I wanted to change that," he said at last.

Someone yelled my name.

It was Jame, the guy who drove the bus with Zedda and saved us.

"Hey, Jame!" I said over the noise. "Space for two more?"

"For a mixed-breed magic man... Move over, Bret, Othie."

I looked down, uncomfortable with the special treatment. The two scooted to make space which made me feel even worse.

"You didn't have to do that," I said.

"I didn't have to." Jame smiled. "I wanted to. Bret and Othie are great, but they're a bit dull," he whispered. "Besides, I've been meaning to talk to you."

You have? I introduced him to Fitz. "So, what's up?"

"Wanted to make sure you were getting the hang of things, feeling at home. Stuff like that."

"Yeah. Everyone's been super welcoming. Are they always so friendly?" Seemed out of character for an underground movement.

"Well, you are a living legend!" Jame exclaimed. "An animote-cynetic hybrid, that's never happened, like *ever!* You're a symbol of hope, man."

"What are you talking about? I'm a kid, an ordinary guy."

"Tell that to *them.*" Jame pointed two tables over.

Sure enough, they all looked away. They'd been talking about me...

"I'm not some hero, I'm not a savior!" My voice rose, breaking the din. "I don't know what I am." Other than a freak. "I'm an outcast I guess..."

"Not anymore, buddy." Jame clapped my arm, a big grin on his boyish face. "They got big plans for you, the Council that is." They do?

I didn't like this much attention. Not. At. All.

"You're all anyone's talking about." He snapped his fingers. "By the way, is it true you knocked out the old lady, you beat Paer?"

I shrugged. "Lucky punch. She should have won the fight."

Fitz raised an eyebrow but said nothing.

"I knew it." Jame signaled one of the guys at the other table. "Hey, Drue, get over here!"

A tall muscular guy headed over, long golden curls and a thick, blond beard covering his cheeks and chin. "I heard, Jame. I know. Congrats, Raek." He tapped his silver band twice. "Twenty creds?"

Jame nodded, tapping his smartband. He held it to Drue's with a grin as continuous biometrics verified their identities to make the process fast and secure. Wow, twenty, Mom would kill me if I gambled away so much. My stomach panged. I missed her. Were they okay?

Jame beamed. "I told you. Never bet against my friend Raek." He patted me on the back.

"Look at that!" Fitz exclaimed. "I lost track of time. It was nice meeting you two, but we have to run."

We hustled to the entranceway and were lucky Zedda found us because I had no idea where to go.

"There you two are. I've been looking everywhere for you. Come on." She hurried along the far side which was all new to me. "Offices and meeting rooms are on this side of the building," she explained.

We reached a large official-looking door. Rather than a fabbed cubicle, these rooms appeared permanent, built when the building was, and adapted to the layout today.

She knocked twice and opened the door. I took a deep breath, no idea what to expect.

19

OLD FRIENDS

At the center of the small whitewashed windowless space was a mahogany table, nine seats around it, six of which were full. The three chairs nearest the door were empty. At least these were cushioned, a stark contrast to the spartan efficiency of everything else.

We tried to be quiet but everyone stopped to stare. "Sorry we're late," I mumbled.

"Don't worry," Lilia replied with a sympathetic smile. She was seated at the far side in what appeared to be a prominent position. "Come in, take a seat. Make yourselves at home." She gestured to the open seats.

I was the youngest in the room, a year or two younger than Zedda, and at least ten younger than anyone else.

"Ladies and gentlemen of the Council," Zedda announced. "I give you Raek Mekorian and Linus Fitz."

Several eyebrows jumped as a few Council members gave Fitz curious glances.

"Linus, eh?" Paer said at last, breaking the awkward silence. "That what you're going by these days, Lyam?"

Fitz smiled. "Why, Agtha, still so direct after all these years? By the way, you're looking lovely, darling. Fiery as always."

"Till I die, Lyam, till I die. You know that."

"I do." There was a twinkle in his eyes.

What was going on? I was so lost. Fitz knew Paer? And Lilia? And Linus wasn't his real name, it was Lyam. My head spun, and they hadn't even asked me anything yet.

"It's good to have you back, Lyam," Lilia said. "The Resistance lost a great fighter and leader when you left. We understand, what happened and all," she added. "Still, it is good to see you and have you back."

I kicked Fitz under the table to let him know I was on to him. As soon as we left, I'd confront him.

"So, your name isn't Linus?" Zedda asked.

Thank you, Zedda!

"Depends on who you ask," Fitz replied with his usual nonchalance. "What'd you want to see us about?" He looked to each Council member in turn as he said it.

"Raek, the boy," the older man next to Lilia said. He had brown hair, big blue eyes, and a powerful frame, arms and face covered in dark clover spots. "Let's save the reunion for another time. We have things to discuss. But as Raek is new and some of us don't know Lyam, let's introduce ourselves." He paused, eyeing me. "Raek, it is nice to meet you, son. My name's Hrun and I'm the president of the Initiative and oversee the Council. I help the seven of us come to an agreement, even when we'd prefer to argue," he added with an ironic smile that didn't quite reach his eyes.

Lilia introduced herself as well. Second in command, not bad.

The pale blond man to Lilia's right waved a large manicured hand. "My name's Mico and I represent the Old Europe contingent of the Initiative. I manage our missions and hubs on the continent including old Britain, Ireland, and, of course, Scotland."

"Good idea, Mico!" Hrun added. "We should say where we're from. As Lilia and I are responsible for overseeing all ops, neither of us have a specific regional focus. She's based out of Caen, and I've come in from Zone Three. I bounce between our Asian hubs."

"Raek and I have met," Paer said when it was her turn. She gave me a smile, no hint of the competitiveness earlier. "And, Lyam," her eyes sparkled, "well, we go way back. I'm responsible for Zone One ops and overall strategy."

"Raek, Lyam, it's a pleasure to meet both of you. I'm Ganla and Zone Two's my territory." The olive-faced woman next to Paer flashed a sharp smile and raised pencil-perfect eyebrows. She was pretty, and radiated energy. "I add a bit of Latin fire to this lot and while it's too cold up here, it was worth the trek."

Fitz was next and my ears perked up. "Most of you know me as Lyam, but for the past ten years, I've gone by Linus Fitzgerald, teaching in a small town northeast of here, Kiag. Raek was a student of mine, Science History. I'll let him tell you the rest."

He turned to me and I took a deep breath. "Thanks. My name's Raek, most of you know that. You also know about my *condition*. I have no idea how it happened. Do you want me to talk about that now, or do you have specific questions?"

"Whatever you're comfortable with, Raek." Lilia's encouraging smile and creamy voice reminded me of home.

I relaxed. Thank you Lilia. "Where to begin? I guess the beginning's as good a place as any." I told them about my life, my family, that I'd never known my father. I described our town, my senses, hunting in the woods... everything. The six-clawed beast, the incident with Vovi, and about Elly. By the end, I was drained and slumped in my chair.

Hrun cleared his throat. "Quite the story you have there, Raek. I'm sorry to hear about your sister," he added, his voice a touch softer than before. "Don't give up on your family. We'll see what we can dig up."

"Be careful," Fitz said. "If DNS knew he were here, they'd redouble their efforts to find him. It's better they think he's hiding somewhere in the woods."

Hrun nodded. "For the time being, nothing about this boy leaves the building, not a peep." He looked at each of us, face a determined chisel. "*Understood?* We'll emphasize that at the meeting tonight." He gave Lilia a sharp look.

"I don't know." Lilia's eyes flashed fire. "We're running out of time. We can't continue like this forever. Isn't it delaying the inevitable?"

"What do you mean, running out of time? This is my life we're talking about," I said, harsher than I intended. "I want a say in what happens."

"Times have been tough," Hrun replied. "We've been losing ground for years. The government ups taxation and enforcement budgets every year, making it harder and harder for us to operate. Every day they intercept more and more of our comms. Every week officers and volunteers are killed in their raids and—"

"You all know what this could mean," Lilia cut in, her voice electric. "An animote-cynetic hybrid, it invalidates their propaganda. We could have equality, we could have peace… heck, we could even rule!" She paused, a slight smile crossing her face.

"We outnumber them. The ability to breed with cynetics, or to cybernetically advance existing animotes," she continued. "What happens when we have our powers plus theirs? We need the people, we need the towns. Without them, we know what happens…"

There were nods and sighs all around. There was a practiced feel to what she said. They'd had this discussion before.

"We don't have to decide anything now," Paer said with a finality that closed the topic. Phew. "We've gotten to know each other and said things we wanted and needed to say. Let's give this two days to settle and consider what we talked about." She stood. "Now if you'll excuse me, I'm starving. I heard Anti is serving something new today, not that nasty-as-nails meatloaf he's famous for. I'd prefer to get it while it's hot."

"Thank you everyone for coming. And thank you, Raek, and Lyam, for being here," Hrun added. "Agtha's right, this meeting is adjourned. See you all tonight."

Everyone filed out, everyone except Fitz and me.

"Interesting," I said once the heavy door had closed.

"Yes and no." He pursed his lips. "They've been having that debate since I left. The question is always timing, and peace versus war. We've always been divided."

Oh, nice of you to tell me now... "That why you left?"

He nodded. "Among other things." Such as...

"Why does it take so long? It's been decades of fighting."

"Sometimes," Fitz—or Lyam... Fitz I decided—said, "there is no right choice, no good solution. Sometimes all the brainstorming in the world isn't enough."

Huh? I raised an eyebrow.

"Part of the Initiative," he said, "the part that changed the name to the Initiative, believe people are inherently good. They think it's possible to reunite mankind and create an equal society for all. Because of that, they push for peace. The bombings, the attacks... these hurt their cause." He sighed.

"Then we have folks like Lilia, people who've had everything taken by the GDR. They want revenge. They've always been the stronger of the two sides, hence where we are today. They want war, they want rebellion. And most of all, they want *you*."

"Me?" I looked up, startled. "What do they want with me?"

"They've been searching for something to unite animotes for ages. They *never* expected someone like you, a hybrid human. You're better than they could have hoped, proof the subspecies could co-exist, even breed. You could be a rallying cry. They want you to spark a revolution."

I opened my mouth and closed it again. Me? "Don't I get a say? I don't want millions, or tens of millions to die because of me."

Fitz grimaced. "I'll do everything I can to prevent *that* from happening, to let you choose. I didn't want to come here, remember." His eyes hardened. "I wanted to go to Lhalas until you were ready."

"And now?"

"We wait and see. In the meantime, how about some food?" He licked his lips, carefree smile emerging once more.

How could he be so relaxed? Seeing my expression, he added, "Tonight, after the meeting when we know more, we'll talk. Okay?"

I guess... My stomach grumbled. "Fine, let's eat." At the door, I stopped. "Why didn't you tell me your name, your real name?"

"I had to disappear. That's a story for another day. My name has a lot of baggage and heartache. I chose a new one, simple as that."

"So, what do I call you?" I asked.

He smirked. "I'll leave *that* to you."

20

HOPE

The mess was wild when we got there, fifty loud, hungry fighters jockeying over Anti's latest creation. It smelled wonderful, and I was salivating. After the bald tank of a man in front of me got his steak, and a fair bit of sauce, it was my turn. I *filled* my plate, sampling the Tyson Cargill flavor-injected biobison as I walked on. A delivery truck had crashed and somebody filled their Benz with the fantastic cargo. Talk about a win.

Paer was in the corner by herself, plate empty. I headed over. "It's good, isn't it? Mind if we join?"

"I don't do much meat, almost never. But it's the best darn thing Anti's ever made!" She laughed, *actually* laughed. "Not a high bar mind you, but—Oh, Lyam."

"Agtha." Fitz tucked his long legs under the bench. "It's been a long time."

"It has. Too long."

They knew each other well. Had they been lovers? Maybe she was the reason he'd left.

Paer broke the awkward silence. "How have you been?"

"I've been good, at least until all this. Life was quiet, relaxed. I was teaching." He popped another bloody bit of steak into his mouth. "What's the split these days? Still an impasse?"

Paer motioned her head at me. "Lyam, you know I can't—"

"Don't give me that crap, Agtha." Fitz lowered his voice. "You owe me. You—" He swallowed and paused. "You owe me."

She sighed. "We're four-to-three in favor. Lilia, Mico, Ganla and Obowe all want war while Hrun, Zedda and I aren't sure." She motioned to me again. "*He* tips the scale in their favor."

Fitz brow furrowed. "If it's four-to-three, why isn't there more of a push?"

"There is. Things have been escalating since Lilia took the number two spot two years back. Hrun's tried to keep his hand on the dial, slow things down. Still hopes rational minds will prevail, but I doubt it. Looks bad."

I couldn't wait any longer. "I don't get it. What's wrong with war? Isn't the whole point to break out from under the GDR? Isn't war the only option?" Henk and Ashlo thought so and I was inclined to agree.

"It's good, *if* we win," Fitz replied. "But, what if we don't? And what happens if we do? Conquered people don't like to be subjugated. If anything, we'd flip the existing power dynamic. Sure, it's better for us, but it's not stable or sustainable in the long run."

Oh... "So, short term versus long term thinking," I said.

"That's a good summary. Any ideas on timeframes, Ag?" Fitz asked. "And would it work?"

She shrugged. "We're not sure. Sims show *at best* forty percent chance of success, but they're also just simulations." She looked at me. "Without you, our odds drop to five percent. There's a lot riding on a symbol of hope, on *you*. And to be honest, it gets worse every day, like Hrun said. The GDR's preparing. Our chances will never be better, at least not if things continue how they are," she added.

We all looked down at our food.

A crowd enveloped me in a claustrophobic wave as we left.

"Raek?"

"That's him..."

"Is it true?"

A girl grabbed my hand, another touching my furry ears. Three guys offered high fives. Everyone stared, everyone wanted answers. It was overwhelming. A million variations.

* * *

The day passed in a blur after that. Forty percent versus five. No wonder everyone was interested in me. How could I make a seven hundred percent difference? Me? Me!

What were they hoping for? Victory would take a miracle, and I was still a kid. I was sixteen. Weren't there adults that could lead or do something? There must be someone else, anyone else... Why me?

These thoughts and more raced through my head all day, a sea of uncertainty threatening to drown me. I had to find somewhere to hide, to think.

Sneaking upstairs, I headed toward the fitness area. If any rooms were empty, it would be those closest to the constant thudding weights.

Since talking with Fitz and Paer, I noticed people watching me everywhere I went. Had I missed it earlier? Jame was right.

The constant stream of attention was awful. And I'd been surrounded four times. How was I doing, did I have cybernetics, was I actually wolfish?...

Ugh... Leave me alone.

Picking a door, I knocked. Nothing. Another knock. Silence. Phew. I opened the door and jumped in. Freedom!

Locking the door, I took a deep breath and sank to the floor. I crossed my legs to get comfortable. What was I going to do? If I'd learned anything these last days, it was that meditation was the ultimate escape. I cleared my mind, letting the chaos of the past few days slip away as the entire universe shrank to the space of my thoughts. My body disappeared soon after, and after who knows how long, I found myself in my SmartCore's command center.

It was filled with equipment and devices. Too much, too overwhelming. I relaxed further, drifting deeper into nothingness as everything dissolved into clouds of light and dark. All at once, something clicked. I *felt* it in my bones, at one with my body.

Returning to my wakened state, I couldn't find words to describe it. It was like understanding, like being shown the light, remembering something you'd once known and never truly forgotten.

It was getting dark when I emerged from my refuge, 17:45. The meeting started soon.

Taking the stairs two at a time, I made my way toward the entrance, passing tons of new faces. It was bigger than I'd expected.

By the time I saw the elevated podium, I was surrounded by hundreds of clamoring bodies. We were cramped, nervous and energetic. Everyone was curious what was happening.

Where was Fitz? At least alone I guess I'd attract less attention. I pulled my hood over my face. The last thing I needed was another scene, and this way, I'd see people's unfiltered reactions.

The lights above us dimmed and others illuminated the podium where Lilia, Hrun, and several serious-looking folks I didn't recognize were standing.

Hrun stepped forward. "Thank you all for coming!" he boomed, his voice amplified through the air. "Can everyone hear me?"

There were a lot of nods and grumbled assents.

"Good. We wanted to share some exciting news and talk about the future of the Initiative." He waited for the jitters of the crowd to die. "As many of you heard," he continued, "we had two successful ops within the past week. The first took out a VTOL factory a few hours north of Caen, a major blow to the DSR's supply chain. Their Rapid Response Units, RRUs, account for a third of our casualties. This should cut their global VTOL production *at least* ten percent, and we plan to target more in the coming months." He paused, sipping water and hacking. "I'll let Lilia tell you about the second op," he finished in a raspy voice as he rubbed his chest, coughing twice.

Lilia strode forward and grasped the podium confidently. "The second attack was more political in nature. You're aware of the recent attacks on women in our towns and villages. Wives and daughters assaulted in record numbers by male elites and left for dead." My fists balled and heart hammered for war as my mind drifted to Elly, that night... "This cannot stand!" She slammed her fist on the podium, her eyes blazing. "This. Will. Not. Stand!"

There was a hush among the crowd as everyone held their breath. My skin tingled as pain, guilt, and anger swirled.

Teams had captured several offenders, forcing confessions and allowing the victim's fathers to enact revenge, filming the whole thing. They'd uploaded videos to the web—and the elite web—and dumped the bodies around the city to "issue a warning," as Lilia said, "that our daughters are not to be messed with."

"This is *our* time, my friends," she said. "A time for animotes, time for freedom." She threw back her head, silky hair tumbling as she thrust her fist into the air. "Freedom, freedom, freedom!" Her voice hit earth-shattering levels.

The chants grew louder and louder as more and more joined in. Soon, fists flew everywhere, the chorus deafening.

Lilia signaled for silence and it quieted. "That's not all. Today we stand in the midst of a miracle. The impossible. Today, we have hope."

My stomach flipped. Don't do it, don't do it...

She smiled. "As some of you may have heard, we received a call for help yesterday. We weren't sure whether it was a hoax or a trap. It seemed *too* good to be true, but I am here to tell you, the world is changing. Raek, come here."

I closed my eyes, squeezing them shut, but a light appeared, illuminating me. Shoot. Careful to avoid eye contact with anyone, I made my way to the front.

As I reached Lilia, she shouted, "How many of you have been bullied or mistreated because you're an animote, called an animal, a savage, or beaten down by society? How many?"

An excited, angry chorus.

She introduced me with all the drama of a blockbuster holo, putting her arm around me. "Tonight I give you the first mixed-breed hybrid in human history. I give you *our future!*" She lifted my hand into the air and the crowd roared.

She was an excellent speaker. If I wasn't terrified, I'd have been impressed. Instead, she motioned me to the podium, intending me to speak. Crap.

I shuffled forward, hands in my pockets. What should I say?

"Um, hi. My name's Raek, and it's true, I'm wolfish. But I'm cynetic too." They were *all* staring... "I don't know what happened to me or how I got this way. I only know what I am, not where I've come from." I shrugged and tried to smile. "I'm no one special. I'm a guy, like any of you. I, I don't have anything else to say."

Lilia rushed forward, clapping and saving me. "Raek Mekorian, ladies and gentlemen. Give our *hero* a hand!"

Hero? Uh-oh! That didn't sound good.

Where the heck was Fitz? My world spun, stomach flipping. What was going on? People clapped, cheered, and screamed... the energy was electrifying. I wanted to disappear.

The crowd rushed forward, arms outstretched. People patted me on the back, yelling.

Surrounded. Shit. It was all too much.

21

TROUBLEMAKER

When I came to, everything was white and orderly, lights raking my eyes. The medical ward again, probes on my arms and legs, a pulsing red heartbeat on a virtual screen floating above my bed.

"I was wondering when you'd wake up."

What? I looked around, groggy, eyes half open.

Fitz stood from his chair in the corner and walked over. "How you feeling?"

"Like crap." Ugh. "How did I get here?"

"You remember what happened, the meeting and all?"

How could I not? I nodded, grimacing.

"You passed out. All the commotion and attention. It must have overwhelmed you."

"Where were you?" I looked at him and remembered why I'd been alone. "I couldn't find you."

"I'll tell you the truth about the space race later, okay?" he said, his tone turning businesslike.

The space race? I was about to ask when Lilia came in. Fitz caught my eye as he turned to leave. Something told me to hold my tongue.

"How's he doing?" she whispered. "Is he okay?"

"He'll be fine. Doctors say it was shock. They're giving him fluids and monitoring his vitals, but he's fine."

"I see. I came by to apologize for not giving him a heads up about what we were planning."

"That was planned?" Fitz exclaimed.

"Well, more or less." She looked away. "It wasn't set in stone, but I felt the moment, the energy... Didn't you? It was perfect. It was the *right* time."

"Perfect for who?" Fitz snapped.

"You know as well as I do, Lyam, why this matters. You've sacrificed more than most."

He has?

"He's a boy, Lilia!" he hissed. "Remember that."

"You think I don't? You think this isn't hard for me too?" She was getting louder, but Fitz was blocking her view.

"You know what I think, but now's not the time. I need to go."

"I'll tell him you came by if he wakes," she said as he left.

I kept my eyes closed another five minutes. What was that about?

After what felt long enough to be convincing, I opened my eyes a crack. Feigning sleepiness, I looked around, avoiding Lilia before doing a double take.

"What, what happened?" I croaked. "Where am I?"

"Everything's fine, Raek. You're in the medical ward. You had a little fall, that's all." Her voice was soft as she held my hand. "The excitement of last night shocked you."

I let my jaw drop. "Is Fitz here, I mean Lyam?"

"Not since I got here," she lied. "I've been here an hour, maybe he was here earlier." A forced-looking optimistic smile crossed her beautiful face.

Something was *definitely* up. I needed to find Fitz and find out what he'd wanted to tell me. "I'm thirsty. Do you have water?"

"I'll ring the nurse and have her bring you something nice. How does that sound?"

"Thanks, Lilia." I did my best dopey smile. "You're nice, you know that. Pretty too. I'm glad you're here." I opened my mouth in mock surprise. "Uhhhhh, I didn't mean to say that... the medicine."

"It's okay, Raek." She smiled at me.

Lilia hung around another half hour or so, talking to me, telling jokes and asking about life as I gnawed salty jerky. If I hadn't known better, I'd have fallen for it.

As it was, I was lost and confused. I fell asleep not knowing what to do or who to trust.

A light tap on my arm jolted me as a hand clamped hard over my mouth.

Alarm bells exploded in my head.

This was it.

22

WAKE UP

Rocketing out of the bed, I threw both my arms at my attacker. I wasn't going down without a fight.

"It's me, shhh," Fitz whispered. "Relax, Raek. We needed to talk and don't have much time."

My fist stopped seconds before trainwrecking his jaw. "Fitz?" What? "What are you doing here?"

"Shhh!" he whispered again. "We don't have much time. Hrun's dead. It was made to look like a heart attack but I think he was poisoned. Everything's accelerated. Lilia's in charge and the timing is too perfect. I think she planned it. I think she killed him!"

My legs caved and I sank to the bed. "What? She was here earlier. I heard what she said. She lied, told me she hadn't seen you."

"That doesn't sound good. Are you dressed? Can you walk?"

"I'm fine. These darn nurses won't let me leave."

"Did you not hear what I said?" He grabbed my shoulders. "Lilia's in charge now. She wants war at any cost. She'll use you as a figurehead, even if that means a martyr." He looked me dead in the eyes. "Is that what you want?"

"Well, no. But if it is what we need..."

He shook his head. "It isn't safe here now. I can't protect you. You need time to learn your cybernetics. We need to think." He gritted his teeth. This was the first I'd seen him scared, burning eyes two steps from full-on panic.

Footsteps. We both froze.

Who was that?

A nurse appeared. "What are you doing here at this time of night, Lyam?" Her voice echoed through the empty ward.

"Darthie, you're still here?" Fitz smiled. "I'm glad Raek's in good hands. Couldn't sleep. Too much excitement from last night. I wanted to check on him. When I got here, he was awake."

"The boy needs his sleep, Lyam. It's good to see you." Her eyes narrowed. "I'm going to have to ask you to leave."

Fitz stood. "Take good care of him for me."

She walked him to the door. "You always were a troublemaker, Lyam," she muttered as they rounded the corner. "It's good to have you back."

A wave of exhaustion hit me. I was out cold before they'd exited the ward.

23

ALWAYS PREPARED

I awoke feeling great and ready to get out of there. After a debate with the nurses, they agreed to release me.

Where was Fitz? We had to talk. My mind raced as I hurried through the crowded halls toward his room, ignoring the looks and waves as I passed. I didn't have time for small talk.

Before I'd gone far, I bumped into a weary-eyed Zedda. "How ya feeling, hero?" she teased before turning serious. "Sorry about what happened. None of us knew she was going to do that."

"Yeah, well... it's okay." I gave her what I hoped was a reassuring smile. She was actually quite pretty in her own way. How I'd miss that? "What's been going on? They wouldn't let me leave..."

"You mean you haven't heard about Hrun?" She gaped.

I shook my head. Maybe she'd have more details. "I mean, I heard something. Fitz mentioned—"

"He had a heart attack at the podium. He was in the medical ward before you. He... they couldn't save him." She swallowed hard, biting her lip. "No one expected it. He wasn't young, but he wasn't old either. It's horrible."

Jeez... "Who's in charge now?"

"The whole Council, but in reality, the position falls to Lilia. She's not happy, mind you. Said she prefers the VP role, but if the Initiative needs her, she'll step up." She paused. "Tough, huh? I wouldn't want that kind of responsibility, *especially* not now."

"Me neither." I shook my head, studying her face. She seemed to be telling the truth.

"By the way, I did some digging, called in some favors." A pained expression clouded her face. "Your family. I didn't find anything. I'm sorry."

They were all dead, weren't they? I closed my eyes and fought back tears. "Thanks." I couldn't bring myself to say more. An uncomfortable silence descended.

Wait, Fitz... "Sorry, Zedda, I need to find Fitz. Wanted to thank him for coming to see me and stealing food from the mess. Best leftover bison meat ever," I added with a fake smile.

"Okay... Get better." She gave me a girlish smile and clapped my shoulder, her hand lingering a moment.

I headed for Fitz's sleeping quarters but he wasn't there, so I tried the mess. No luck.

Maybe he was training. I sprinted upstairs, pretending not to notice the onlookers.

He wasn't in the fitness area. Had something happened? Had Lilia caught him?

Speaking of, Lilia and Paer were sparring on the mat. Without thinking, I waved and they signaled me over. That was stupid. Now I was trapped, unable to leave without being rude and making Lilia more suspicious. Where was Fitz?

"How ya feeling, kid?" Paer asked as I got closer. "No round two today, I think. Give it a week or so."

I nodded absentmindedly, not paying attention. "I've been better, but I'm also feeling much better."

Lilia looked concerned. "Have you eaten anything? You look beat."

"Only what the nurse brought me yesterday. That's a good idea." I had my out. "I'm going to grab a bite to eat. When's the next Council meeting? Do you guys want Fitz and I there?"

"There's an emergency meeting at noon to discuss what happens next. Hrun's passing was so sudden." Lilia sighed, shaking her head. "The funeral's not until tomorrow, but we need to keep things running smooth. He'll be missed."

She told me to drop by around one and I turned to go.

"Raek," Paer said, "tell Lyam I want a rematch with him too."

"I will," I answered.

Running, I took the stairs two at a time. Had something happened? The main entrance inched open and a figure slid through: Fitz.

"Where have you been?" I asked. "I've been looking everywhere for you."

"I'm sorry, son. Last night after I left you, I had to find out what was going on. Wanted to get the lay of the land and see if my contacts knew anything. Spent the night meeting old friends around the city, finding out who we could trust and if any could help us."

"Would have been nice of you to tell me."

His eyes darted around. "Shhh! It isn't safe here. We need to find somewhere to talk."

"I know the perfect place." I led him to the abandoned sleeping quarters and we both slipped in.

"It's worse than we thought," he said. "I talked to some people. They said now's the worst time for war. The towns are feeling more scared than angry, and the rebels are weaker than they think. The betting houses in Zone Three are in on the action. The line fluctuates between forty-five-to-one and fifty-to-one for the government. It doesn't look good."

"And that's why they want me."

"Exactly! They need a spark, something to light the fire in animotes everywhere. The videos Lilia talked about didn't do it. Ten thousand views before the government pulled them. Now they're gone, and not coming back. And there's the other thing they didn't tell us." He paused. "The GDR's considering increased enforcement in the towns. They're worried about violence and plan to deploy cleanup squads in every town: small armed units to intimidate and end uprisings before they begin."

"The army's big enough?" That must be tens of thousands of soldiers...

Fitz laughed a pained laugh. "They can do anything. It's the government we're talking about. Their resources are limitless." He shook his head. "Plus they control the money supply."

"What if now's our last chance?" I could hear the desperation in my voice.

"There's no such thing as a last chance, son. Unless you give up or die, you haven't lost. Besides, it's suicide to stay. I don't trust Lilia."

"Okay, we'll do it," I said after a moment. "We'll go. But when? By the way, Lilia and Paer said they want us at the end of the Council meeting at 13:00."

He stroked his beard. "Interesting. That'll tell us a lot. Let's plan to leave tonight. I think we have to. Make things ready. Steal as much food as you can, enough to fill a pack. I'll make other preparations. And Raek." He grabbed me and pulled me closer. "Take this."

Reaching into his bag, he pulled out a piece of paper and scribbled something. "Memorize it. It's the name and address of an old friend I'd trust with my life. Just in case," he added. "Quick, let's go before anyone notices we're missing."

He left, leaving me alone with my thoughts.

On the run, again. I'd been getting comfortable here. Would life ever be the same? I doubted it.

What was this paper?

Lars - 1104b Heartlow Drive.

24

DECISIONS

The rest of the morning was spent getting ready. I needed a bag to carry everything. I missed my burned pack. It had been a Winter Solstice present from Mom, my only that year. Painful memories stirred. Mom... But she'd say to "Pull yourself together." I tried. I'd do it for her.

I had what I was wearing, not much else. I needed thicker clothes if we were going to be on foot.

The laundry room was empty. That was a good sign.

I hurried down the rows of washers and dryers, pausing at each.

A jacket, perfect. The door opened as I grabbed it. It was Henk.

"Doing laundry?" he asked.

"It's that time of week." He moved closer and I closed the dryer with my foot, tapping the start button while his back was turned. Phew, close one. "Good. Should be done in an hour," I said, loud enough for him to hear. "Henk, can I ask you a question?"

"Shoot."

"Do we have any spare gear, uniforms or anything? Maybe a lost and found? The cops burned our bags so I don't have much."

"Zedda didn't show you when she gave you the tour?" He laughed, shaking his head. "Give me a second to flip this and I'll show you." He walked to the machine I'd just closed, and opened it. "Laundry neighbors," he remarked as I looked away. Something like that.

He messed with the load, took a few things out, and closed the door again. "Let's go."

We walked out the door and Henk said, "I've been meaning to ask you, what's Lyam like? He must be pretty cool."

"What?"

"I mean, the guys a living legend." There was a boyish envy in his voice I wouldn't have expected.

I stopped. "What are you talking about?"

"Lyam, Lyam Harding." His eyes widened. "You don't know *who* he is?"

"Not really." What else didn't I know?

He snickered. "Man, he was one of the originals. He assassinated the old Minister of Security, Boris Yarin, went on more successful missions than anyone—except Paer—and rescued Lilia from prison." He shook his head. "But his wife was killed in that failed op."

My jaw dropped. "Fitz was married? Are we talking about my Science History teacher?"

Henk laughed, patting me on the back. "He's a lot more than a teacher, bud."

My mind was reeling. Why hadn't he told me? He'd hidden his *entire* past from me. He was my best friend, and I barely knew the guy.

"We're here." Henk opened a small unmarked door, distracting me from Fitz's deception.

We stepped into a room fit to burst: walls lined with layers of shirts, shoes, pants and more, a dizzying array of colors and patterns, even camo.

"This is a goldmine, Henk." Vynce would have loved this. "Where'd we get it all?"

"You accumulate a lot of junk in forty years. Whenever we raid someplace valuable, we grab the good stuff before we blow it. Figure it ain't stealing if it's all made by animotes anyway. Take whatever you need."

I thanked him and he left.

There were bags for Fitz and me, and I found fitting thermals in no time. Opening life-sized visuals of Fitz, I grabbed a few things for him as well.

My alarm buzzed, ten minutes until the meeting. I jogged back to my sleeping quarters and threw the clothes on my mat before heading out. On my way to the meeting, I dropped Fitz's off too.

The door was closing as I got there, Fitz sliding into a seat.

I burst in. "Sorry I'm late! I was talking to Henk and lost track of time."

"No worries, Raek." Lilia beamed like she owned Hrun's presidential chair. "Now we're all here, let's get started. As you know, Hrun passed away. His heart wasn't as sound as it seemed. It's a huge loss for all of us. He was a good friend, too." She paused, swallowing hard. "But we can't let his passing hold back the work he dedicated his life to. He wouldn't want that. We owe him that much, *at least*."

She'd have made a brilliant actress.

When it was clear no one had anything to add, she continued. "That is why I wanted you to come today, Raek, and you, Lyam." She nodded at both of us. "We need to discuss the future of the Initiative, and your role in it. You've heard what I had to say at the meeting the last time the Council convened. What are your thoughts?"

Didn't expect that. Um... "Well, it depends. I'm not keen on being a figurehead or spurring a rebellion," I said. "Don't get me wrong, I want animotes better off. We deserve a heck of a lot better than we're getting. We're third class citizens at best. That's not right. But war?" I looked around. "Is that our *only* option?"

"What would you have us do?" Ganla snapped. "We lose ground, rights, and people every day. This can't continue forever."

"What Ganla's trying to say, Raek," Lilia chimed in, "is our options are limited. We can fight, we can try the diplomatic route, or we can wait... there isn't another option. And *waiting* our way to victory isn't going to work. The government and elites don't even acknowledge us. They think they have us right where they want us, and, in a lot of ways, they're not wrong." She paused, a grim expression on her pretty face.

"Can we at least agree on that so far?" Lilia added.

Several heads nodded.

"For the political route, we need power. We need to *force* them to negotiate with us. If they don't take us serious, it won't work. That's where you come in, Raek." She smiled at me. "You're unique, something they can't take away from us. You're the possibility of reuniting humanity, or at least bringing animotes and cynetics together. Imagine the power we could wield. We'd be seventy percent of the population. We could rewrite the rules and build a fairer world. Isn't that worth fighting for?" She looked at me. "Isn't that worth dying for?"

Of course it was. Did she think me a coward? "I'd give my life for that. But what if we fail? What if the towns rebel and we're not ready?" Was I the only one worried about that? "What if the DNS break 'em before the rebellion begins? I grew up in the woods, spent my days camping, hiking, and in nature. And if you light a fire and it doesn't catch just right, it sputters and dies. But if you time it, you get a branch-burner of a bonfire. It's about timing and coordination. See what I'm saying?" Maybe a camping metaphor was a bad idea for city folk.

Fitz locked eyes with Lilia. "How sure are we about these simulations? Oddsmakers are calling it *very* different."

"We've run the numbers, Lyam," Lilia said in a calm voice, her seething eyes betraying her true frustration. She looked at me and her face softened. "That's a good analogy, Raek. Not perfect, but good enough."

I wanted to make this work. "How could we guarantee success? What would we need?" The excitement was pulling me in. What if we could pull this off?

"Success is *never* guaranteed," Paer replied. "We have to play the best hand we're dealt."

"But what about stacking the deck in our favor?" Fitz said. "What if we waited a couple of months, got teams in place, and coordinated with the towns and local militias. We'd stand a much better chance."

"Unless things leaked. And things always leak. Accidents happen. You of *all* people should know, Lyam!" Lilia replied icily.

"Careful what you say next." Fitz growled.

"I am the president of the Initiative, Lyam!" Her voice skyrocketed. "Remember that when you speak to me and dare to—"

"Enough!" Paer slammed her fist on the table. "Both of you are acting like children. We have work to do."

"I'm sorry, Agtha, Lyam," Lilia snapped. "It has been decided. It's time. We prepare for war, we must. We all know it. It's time to act." She stared around the room, daring anyone to question her.

Fitz's lip curled into a scowl. "You're making a mistake, Lilia."

Lilia's temper flared. "Lyam, I am allowing you into this meeting! You're not a Council member. You abandoned us all those years ago. I won't fault you, but the fact remains. Now, Raek." She turned back to me, voice softening again. "Do you understand the situation better now? You want to help us, right?"

I think so... I nodded.

"Good, that's great!" She gave me an encouraging nod. "We have been preparing for years. Truth be told we never expected *this*, but we've always had contingency plans in place, and agents prepared to spread the message. We'll spend a few days planning and coordinating like you said, to burn everywhere at once. That's what it'll take to succeed, and I don't plan to sleep or rest until we do." Her eyes blazed. "Now, Raek Mekorian, do I have your support? Will you be our champion? Will you help us?"

"I will. On one condition," I added. "I want to be involved in the strategy and planning and I want Fitz—whatever you want to call him —to be in charge of the final operation."

She stared at me for some time, her face an impenetrable stare. I held her gaze until she looked around the table. There were brief nods of assent.

"It's settled," Lilia said. "We prepare for war. I want each of you in touch with your local cells by the end of the day with updates and next steps. We will meet again tomorrow at 8:00 a.m. to go over progress and finalize things."

There were nods all around.

25

DIRTY LAUNDRY

After the meeting ended, the Council split. Fitz, Lilia, Mico, and I ended up heading to grab food. I was exhausted and starving after seven straight hours of planning. We'd lost track of time.

When we got to the mess, the place was deserted. The trays made it obvious why: meatloaf and brussel sprouts. I cringed but was hungry enough not to care.

We all sat, and, despite earlier arguments, things felt cordial, friendly almost. It was nice for a change, and Mico told me about how he'd traveled with his parents serving a wealthy emulate family. He'd visited Old Europe's cities and had stories from his parents and grandparents about London, Paris, and Rome, before they'd been reduced to a shadow of their former selves.

I'd never visited Zone Three, never thought about it. It wasn't an option growing up. Animotes like us didn't travel, *certainly* not overseas. Mom always said, "be happy to have food on the table. Many weren't so fortunate." Yet, it must be so cool. To see how people lived before the Fall, before modernity and the divergence would be fascinating.

Mico promised if we made it through this alive, he'd bring me.

Somehow conversation shifted to Nazi Germany and the similarities to today. Next to me, Lilia mentioned a woman.

Fitz tensed, his shoulders stiffening. Something was up. But what? I tried to focus on what they were saying but Mico was going on about something to do with the Stasi. Why'd he have to be so loud?

"What's this have to do with her?" Fitz's nostrils flared as his voice rose.

"You know full well, Lyam," Lilia whispered. Why was she whispering? "You're resisting because of what happened to *her*. You don't want to lose the boy too." She noticed my gaze and I looked away, but not before she realized I'd been paying attention.

"That was quite a meal wasn't it, Raek?" She gave me a strained smile. "I think I need to walk that off. Lyam, care to join me?" She gave him an insistent look.

"I could use a little exercise."

"Perfect." Lilia rose. "Mico, tell Raek that story about Lyam and the pirates, you know the one. I'm sure he'd enjoy that, and Lyam won't be here to protest." She elbowed Fitz flirtily, but it seemed forced, mechanical. "See you two in the morning."

"We'll talk later, Raek," Fitz said. "Make sure you're staying on top of your studies and doing your homework."

Was that a code? Was *homework* getting ready to leave? I'd done that. But plans had changed. Maybe he was tired, or maybe it was Lilia. She was attractive. Did Fitz have *other* things in mind? That devil.

"So the pirates..." Mico waved his hands to signal an epic adventure. "This must have been fifteen, no twenty, years ago..."

My attention was slipping. It might be a great story, but something gnawed at the back of my mind. What was it?

They'd been talking about Fitz's wife. They'd been comparing her and me, and they'd left. Fitz wasn't interested in bedding Lilia. This was personal. They didn't want *me* to hear. Why?

I had to lose Mico and find out. I wouldn't have another chance to discover what happened to her. But how to escape? The bathroom could work.

"One second, Mico." I scrunched my face and grimaced. "I'll be back. Something I ate, *ugh*." I rubbed my stomach. "I gotta go!" Jumping up, I waddle ran toward the bathroom. Once out of sight, I switched directions, following Lilia's earthy perfume. I was back in business.

Rounding the corner, I heard voices and snuck down the hallway.

"He's a boy, Lilia."

"We need him, Lyam, and you know it!" Lilia hissed. "You are too stubborn and scared to see it."

"Scared?"

"Yes, scared," she said. "You lost Kira. You weren't fast enough and your plan failed. It made you cynical. It made you *weak*," she said. "You lost the fire to see this through."

"Don't tell me what I did or didn't lose, Lilia!" he retorted, his voice hammering steel, slashing and angry and building to a roar.

"So why are you trying to stop this?"

"I'm not trying to stop it, only slow it. We need to control—"

"And if *they* realize he's here?" she spat. "If they place troops in the towns? Or if he turns on us?"

"He won't turn on us," Fitz answered, proud anger in his voice. "Raek's one of us, he's wolfish through and through."

That made me smile.

"I know what you're planning!" Lilia replied, her voice triumphant. "You must think I'm an idiot."

She knew? That took Fitz aback. "What, what do you mean?" His voice wavered.

"Don't play dumb. You planned to escape and take the boy. Cut the crap, Lyam. The nurse told me, Darthie. She overheard everything. You thought you were so smart, so clever." She laughed a mocking cackle.

"Lilia, I don't know what you're—Ah!" A groan. "What was that? Ahhh!"

"That was your heart. Neat Russian invention in the forties, trigger-released Potassium Chloride. I put it in your coffee at dinner. *Completely* undetectable. Elevated heart rate, eventual cardiac arrest.

Sorry, Lyam, but I can't let you ruin everything we've worked for." A poisonous venom lathered her normally polished voice.

Cardiac arrest?

Thud. Was that a body hitting the floor? This wasn't happening...

That heartless bitch.

Fitz coughed. A gasping choke, a rough groan. Silence.

No...

Shit. I had to run, to get out of here. But Fitz, if I could help... I paused, frozen and took a step toward them. What if he was alive?

A door creaked open. Footsteps.

"What should we do with him, ma'am?" a nasally voice I didn't recognize asked.

"Take him away. Make the body disappear. Somewhere in the city, a lake, the woods... I don't care. I don't want him found, *ever!*"

"Yes, ma'am. We're on it." Two sets of footsteps hurried my way.

Stomach churning, I retreated, searching. There was a door to my left. I took it. What if they found me? They'd kill me. Like they killed Fitz. It was all my fault.

Tears fell as my hands trembled. It was locked.

SmartCore controlling my breathing, I hurried to the next door. Locked too. Crap.

The footsteps were getting close, maybe fifty meters around the corner. "Glad you brought the cart, boss," the nasally voice droned.

"No one thinks twice about dirty laundry," a hard voice rasped. "Even if they did, who'd want to look inside?"

They stopped talking. Thirty meters.

Two more doors a ways down. I darted, twisting the handle. Yes! It was open. I crept in as they rounded the corner, closing it as they came into sight.

Don't move, don't breathe. If they heard anything...

They passed and I exhaled.

Wait, I'd hadn't checked the room. I turned.

Shit! Someone was sleeping on the mat. She was still out. My hand shot to the handle but she made a noise. Crap. I froze.

If she screamed, they'd come back. Or worse, Lilia.

Her pulse was rising, she was stirring. I had a minute, *tops*.

Twisting the knob, I inched into the hall. It was empty. Phew.

I sprinted, mind racing. Where could I go? Lilia knew I'd leave. She'd be watching for me. Regardless what I'd said at the meeting, she wouldn't trust me. She'd force me to stay if she had to. She'd killed him.

My room would be guarded, Fitz's too.

That left one option, the storage room. When I got there, it was open and I slid in, locking the door behind me. I turned on the light and his face flashed before my eyes. He was gone... forever. My body shook as I dug into the pile for something warm and durable. He'd want me to stay focused, to survive. Who knew when I'd have another chance.

We must be out in the country, away from prying eyes. I'd lie low in the woods somewhere and figure out a plan. I didn't have anyone to turn to. The government wanted me dead, the rebels weren't much better.

Would I really never see him again? My heart throbbed. Totally alone...

But I could survive on my own. Mom raised me well to be a lone wolf. I smiled despite my pain. She'd be proud, wherever she was. At least I hoped she would.

I put on black biopoly pants, a stretchy fabric, a rugged mix of man-made and natural fibers that were tear resistant, form-fitting, and, most important, warm. My fur would help, but if I was out there when the worst of winter hit... Preparation was the key to survival. Vynce taught me that; Fitz too.

A dark evoshirt caught my eye. It would stop a knife, and be plenty warm. What about a pack or anything else? I found the one I'd seen earlier.

It'd be great to have a weapon, but I hadn't seen any earlier. There was a door next to this one, another unmarked one. If there was a second lost and found, that's where you'd put it.

Couldn't hurt to check. I'd been here all of two minutes. I *should* have time.

Turning off the light, I unlocked the door. My thermals didn't work through the walls, infrared either, so I couldn't detect anything.

Here goes nothing. Opening the door, I peered out. Nothing. I scurried to the next door, but it was locked. Shoot. Guess you wouldn't want weapons walking away.

Could I break it? Maybe. But would it be too loud?

The hallway was empty. It should be fine.

It was 22:06 and there weren't many people about. I flexed a fist and visualized the interior of the big metal door. What did I remember from construction class?

The reinforced bones in my hand were ten times the normal human limit. Would that be enough? Hope so... I swung, and the handle exploded from the doorframe with a dull metal *ping* that echoed a few seconds before dissipating.

The door opened, and inside was a myriad of machines and tools, everything imaginable. From smartbands and solar ovens to Smart-Bulbs and dot point speakers, most too heavy or impractical to bring.

In the corner, hunting knives. Despite humanity's hundreds of thousands of years, the need for blades and sharp objects had never gone away. Probably never would, even with the claws. I grabbed two.

Hooking the larger and more versatile to my belt, I slipped the smaller red into my boot. My just-in-case knife, as Vynce said.

Pushing him and the pains of home to the back of my mind, I looked around. It'd been fifty-nine seconds. I had to hurry. Lilia would be rounding up a search party.

One last check. Nothing useful.

I tightened the tough black straps on my bag and turned off the lights. The door was quiet, so I snuck out. No one in sight. Heading for the entrance, voices. I wasn't going to make it.

"You heard what Lilia said, no one goes in or out without her okay. Council decided to boost security after the meeting, all the Council members being here and all."

"But I was supposed to meet Lysa by the pond," a voice protested.

"Take it up with Lilia," Ashlo replied. "Just following orders, kid."

I backtracked, thinking. There was no other way in or out of the building. Zedda had mentioned as much when she'd shown me around, hadn't she? Still, something nagged at the back of my mind, something Fitz always said, "Always have a backup plan."

No way the headquarters of the entire Initiative wouldn't have an escape plan, right? But where? No one had shown me. An underground passage? A lot of these warehouses used to have storage rooms back when they'd produced goods for ten billion instead of one, right? Basements were perfect.

But what about the roof? Even if for no other reason than surveillance. Two secret exits, a fifty-fifty chance? Made sense. The roof at least, I could find, maybe. There were only so many possible entrances, unlike a basement.

I rushed for the stairs, checking over my shoulder at least five times. No one would be training this time of night, not with all the science on disrupted sleep cycles and performance.

Upstairs was quiet, the halls empty. Where would you hide an escape? Corners? If I was an architect, I'd put stairs in the corner or along a wall. Spacewise it made the most sense.

I darted left but after a few steps, I realized it was all wrong. There were sleeping quarters everywhere. The hallway was devoted to cubicle rooms. That wouldn't work. Roof access must be on the other side, in the fitness area. If it existed at all...

A commotion downstairs. I ran to the big black door but didn't see anything out of the ordinary. The gym was deserted, graveyard still. Corners, walls. On the far side were the bathrooms, men to the left, women to the right. Men's room first. A bunch of urinals, some multi-sized toilets and showers, nothing exciting. It was weird they had separate bathrooms; maybe Caen was more conservative.

Exiting, I headed for the girl's side. For some reason it felt awkward and I hesitated until the gym door creaked open, voices filling the air.

"In here," a male voice said. "You take the free weights. I'll search cardio."

Hurry. Sneaking into the ladies room, I left the lights off. At least, they weren't motion activated. Must be saving money. The bathroom was weird, the shape wasn't even. It wasn't symmetric with the guys' side. At first, I thought it was the urinals, but behind the furthest stall was a solid metal door. This *had* to be it. It made sense too. If you wanted a semi-secret escape, what better place to hide it than a woman's bathroom?

I tried the handle. Of course, it was locked. Shit.

If I broke this one, they'd hear me. For some reason, I remembered a trick Pavel had shown me, some spy film deal, maybe Bond. Without lockpicks, he'd used a small knife to unhook a door latch. It was worth a try.

The hunters yelled to each other. "Nobody over here, you see anything?"

"Same here. This is absurd! Why are we doing this again?"

"Lilia said they'd found a rat, a double agent, tip from one of the towns. They were going to confront the guy but he disappeared."

I grabbed the blade and turned it in my hand, ignoring them. It was crimson with a white cross. Maybe religious, or maybe lucky. I could use some luck.

Their footsteps were getting closer.

Extra attachments folded into the knife's frame. I picked the first, scissors. Crap! Not helpful.

The second was a nail file, but it was too fat.

On the third, I struck gold. A skinny blade. I jammed it in the thin gap between the door and frame and jiggled. Something moved, but I had no idea what I was doing. I kept jiggling, but it was too late, the footsteps were getting closer.

The blade caught the jamb and I pushed the door open, slipping through and closing it as footsteps entered the echoey bathroom. Someone was checking the stalls. *Slam.*

Slam.

Slam.

They paused at mine. It was unlocked. If she tried the handle...

"All clear!" a female voice shouted.

"Same here!" he responded.

She turned and left, whistling as she walked back into the gym.

I closed my eyes, slumping to the floor, a burning breath escaping my lips. That was way too freaking close.

Behind me, spiral stairs led upward. I'd done it. There was a roof! I climbed to the hatch. It was locked, but I popped it open and an icy cold breeze blew over me, sending a chill down my spine. I smiled anyway.

Hopping onto the roof, I closed the hatch. Didn't want to create a draft. They couldn't know I'd escaped.

Wait, where was I? Shit!

I'd miscalculated.

26

ABOVE AND BELOW

The roof was a modest space, gray, dark, and dreary with heating and cooling arrays covering most of it. Several ancient smoke-stacks lined one side and what appeared to be a generator. Not much else. No way down.

We weren't in the middle of the country. This was no rural town or village. We were smack in the middle of an industrial park surrounded by at least a dozen abandoned warehouses, skyscrapers dotting the horizon. We were in *Caen*, the center of everything.

I had to find a way down. But how? My stomach seesawed and I was still a full meter from the edge. We were three stories up, only three stories... Jaw clenched, I lowered my heart rate.

Get a grip, Raek. How'd I survive before cybernetics? And how had doctors added nanoSTEMs—the all-important biomechanical cells—to my body in the first place? Was I an IVF baby? Or maybe a secret experiment... Who knows.

Stop procrastinating!

At the far side of the roof, I swore. This was a terrible idea. While the warehouse might be three stories, it had high ceilings. We were twenty or thirty meters up, not the usual ten. Shoot.

On the third side, I got lucky. There was a lightning rod half a meter from the ledge, similar ones dotting the other abandoned buildings in the distance.

That could work. But somehow, I had to climb down. All. Thirty. Meters.

My stomach pirouetted the second I looked down. What are you waiting for?

I clenched the metal pole. It was cold, wet, and slick, just my luck. Testing my grip, I found I could hold it well. Swinging my legs over the side, I held my breath, squeezing with all my might. Why'd it have to be heights?

Climbing was surprisingly easy. When I reached the bottom, I jumped down.

The place was weird. Concrete and faded gray cement as far as the eye could see. The industrial park was empty. Speaking of, I needed to move. If anyone saw me—the Initiative, the DNS, even a nosy Nelly—they'd be suspicious.

I ran. My connection kicked in thirty meters from the building. I didn't have much time. They might have a perimeter guard or remote sensors.

My SmartCore pinged coordinates. I was on the southwest side of the city, Caen City Industrial Complex 4, three kilometers from downtown, but six from the outskirts.

I sprinted away from downtown and toward the edge of the city. Twice, lights illuminated the area and I jumped behind recyclers. The first was kids joy riding, techno blasting as tires squealed around tight corners.

The second was a closer call. A cruiser flew around the corner, sirens blaring. I dove behind the green composter before their headlights hit me. Where were they going? Did it have something to do with me?

Soon, it became more residential. Everything was new. Mansions everywhere, pristine lawns and flashy electric cars further distancing themselves from the two-room hovel I'd grown up in.

Once I was a solid two kilometers from the base, I relaxed. I'd made it, fingers crossed. Slowing, I opened the map again. Walking would be less conspicuous. I checked the news, both the elite web and our animote access portal.

Nothing interesting until the last site, my picture plastered at the bottom right.

WARNING - Armed and Dangerous

Interesting.

Raek Mekorian is considered armed and extremely dangerous. A wolfish criminal attacked and killed four innocent cynetic officers last weekend and has been sighted in and around the Greater Caen Area. If you see this individual, be sure to geotag your position and ping the DNS. We're monitoring all major channels, comms systems, and media, and have teams on standby. Be vigilant and report any suspicious behavior to your local DNS precinct.

There was a video of my escape, pictures of the dead officers appearing alongside their families.

That didn't help. I had to disappear. I missed Fitz...

"First things first," as Mom said, I needed a new look.

At the end of the street was a drain cover. If there was anywhere I could disappear and have time to think, it was the sewers. Prying the top, I peered down. Nothing, thermal or infrared either.

I hopped in, replaced the lid, and scurried down the ladder. Somehow, my nose downregulated. Jumping off the rickety ladder, I landed in a puddle. Ugh, gross! It reeked. I reduced the sensitivity further, and after a moment, could breathe again.

Which way? The tunnel continued on forever both ways. While the tech above ground had been modernized, invisible infrastructure was always the last thing to change. No sensors or cameras. Thank you budget cuts.

Wading out of the freezing water, I found a dry elevated path above the sludge.

I had to shave. Pulling the knife from my boot, I paused. I'd never cut my own hair before. After what I'd been through though, should be a breeze.

Balancing the hunting blade on a thin horizontal pipe like a mirror, I knelt, checking my reflection. I looked like hell. Gritting my teeth, I pulled the edge of the smaller knife along my scalp. It was less awful than I'd expected, easier too.

I was getting the hang—"Ahh!" A small cut opened on my skull, blood dripping down my cheek.

Dang, I'd gotten cocky. Jumping to the lower platform, I dunked my head in the icy, disgusting stream and swore. Anything to survive. I had to rely on myself now.

When the bleeding stopped, I tried again, slower this time. It took forever, but after three more dunks and a couple scrapes, it was done. I hardly recognized myself in the knife's reflection. I was bald, totally bald. Ugh...

Would it be enough?

It was one-thirty in the morning and I was exhausted. But I couldn't sleep, not yet. I needed a plan. Needed to meditate. I needed one of those miracle moments, a stroke of genius. Fitz was dead. It was just me now.

Focus.

My breath slowed as I drifted deeper into my subconscious. Concentrating, I let my mind wander and explore my SmartCore. It didn't work. Nothing happened. Two hours later, I opened my eyes, frustrated, discouraged, and empty-handed. I was scared and confused as ever.

Drained, I slumped on the graffitied wall with a sigh. What was I going to do?

* * *

Wait, what was Fitz saying? I couldn't make out his voice over the roar. He was talking to Lilia, a serious look on his face. His eyes were slits. Why was he with Lilia?

She yelled something my brain didn't process. What was happening? Was this VR? Not again. Lilia walked to Fitz and kissed him, a hard, passionate one. His eyes widened, shock turning to grinning desire. He put his arms around her waist and pulled her closer.

My senses seemed fine, it wasn't VR. But what was the roar? Was it raining?

A waterfall rushed over the side and into the abyss. It was beautiful, Fitz and his lover kissing on the edge of nature, the edge of the world. The view was breathtaking, flecks of water reflecting misty rainbows across the chasm.

Lilia sprang, pushing him. Fitz stumbled backward, tripped, and fell over the edge.

'No!' I darted forward, but it was too late. He tumbled faster and faster in the torrent of gravity and rushing water. 'Fitz!' I shouted. I couldn't lose him, not again.

As he was about to smash the rocks below, his voice boomed, 'Memorize it! Memorize it. Mem—' His final words cut off as he slammed into the rocks.

An explosion of light and noise engulfed everything.

I leapt as my eyes flew open. That was it. I knew *what* I had to do.

27

A WALK IN THE PARK

I sat for a long time putting it together in my head. Fitz had prepared for this. He'd known he was in danger.

Lars, 1104b Heartlow Drive. He'd had me memorize it.

That was all I had. *That* was all I needed. Why didn't I think of it earlier?

Within seconds, I had a map of the area. It was seven kilometers from here and I needed to get there, somehow.

Excited, I sprang from the frigid, musty floor and slammed my head on the low ceiling. Oww.

It was 5:15 a.m. but it didn't matter. Energy coursed through me. I had a plan!

Thank you, Fitz. You clever bastard, you.

Now, how to get there?

Tunnels? It would be easier and safer. No maps though, and I could get lost. I was claustrophobic as it was and headed for the ladder. Let's get out of here. Climbing, I shook mucky water from my boots and slid out once the coast was clear.

Setting off at a fast jog, I pretended to be exercising. No one faults a runner.

Things got busier four kilometers from Heartlow, trams and

scooters zipping commuters to work. So many people. Why were they all hurrying?

Back home, things were simpler. Work began at dawn, or when it must. There was no rush to an office. Everyone worked from home—or close enough to be called that—at least compared to this city. And trams and scooters... I could walk from one side of town to the other in under ten minutes. Caen stretched on forever.

After a while, I saw the rhythm to the madness. The energy was electric as I walked the streets. I kept my head down to avoid being noticed.

Turns out, I didn't have to worry about that. They were all so busy with themselves, they didn't spare me a glance. The trams were filled with vacant eyed cynetics browsing the web, some enhancers, too, with projected screens or high end SmartGlasses. If you didn't know better, you'd think they were equal. Looks could be deceiving.

A large furry woman passed me with her eyes downcast. So, there were other animotes here. Soon, more: chimpish, wolfish, elephantish... everything. Most wore faded factory uniforms or overalls, their heads down. Was this how animotes in the cities lived? Everyone seemed depressed. We'd heard the cities were better off. Could it be *this* bad, *this* far from the truth? I had to find out.

After a few blocks, animotes disappeared. Must have been a housing project, or maybe they all commuted. Or was it zoning? Maybe we were only allowed in certain areas, or at certain times. I had to find out. The last thing I needed was being reported for entering an animote-free zone.

Closer to Heartlow and downtown, the buildings were huge and growing taller. There was a marked improvement in the quality of the shops and attire of the folks too—a whole new level of affluence. *So rich you don't bother to flaunt it.* Many here wore the bands Kelep's father sold, wore them like it was nothing.

This would take getting used to.

Five minutes later, 1104 Heartlow.

It was a modest building, at least by Caen standards, built after the Fall, constructed of bioidentical net zero polymers (BNZPs). We'd learned about departiclization in manufacturing, the basics at least, and why it was mandated. We'd come too close to climate-driven disaster once already.

I approached the brown five-story building, unsure what to do. Lars didn't own the entire building, did he?

At the crimson door, a voice asked, "Who are you here to see?"

I didn't see anyone. "Um, Lars. He lives at 1104b."

"You mean Mr. Avery?"

"Yes, Lars Avery." So, Avery was it? "I'm here to see Mr. Avery."

"Mr. Avery isn't here. He left for work at 6:00 this morning. Can I take a message?"

"Do you know when he'll be back?" I asked.

"Mr. Avery usually comes home after 17:00."

"Oh, thanks for your help."

"My pleasure."

A second later, they asked, "Who are you here to see?"

"I told you. I'm here to see Mr. Avery."

"Mr. Avery isn't here. He left for work at 6:00 this morning. Can I take a message?"

Huh? "Are you a chatbot?" I'd heard about these.

It repeated itself.

"Please tell Mr. Avery, his striped friend said I should come and he could help me."

The voice confirmed my message. "Is that all?"

I nodded.

"Is that all?" it asked again. Duh, only voice commands.

"Yes."

"Goodbye."

I hurried away before the sequence restarted. They used chatbots? Made sense. Automate simple jobs but never *ever* touch true AI.

It was 7:05, ten hours to kill. What could I find on Mr. Avery? It couldn't hurt to do some digging.

Walking the now less crowded sidewalk, the zones thing hit me. What if the DNS picked me up in the wrong part of town? I searched as I went.

What I found was disheartening to say the least. Animotes were restricted to certain areas of the city, not the nice parts. Downtown was off limits and so was the governmental district.

The outskirts were fine, the industrial areas and poorer south and west sections too. But for a city of five hundred thousand, it wasn't much.

I opened a history of the city. Throughout the Fall, Caen dodged the worst of it. 'Where most areas suffered eighty plus percent death tolls, Caen had banded together.' So, the government whitewashed its earliest years too, explaining away confiscating old American heavy weaponry to force their powerful coalition. To be fair, they'd restored peace and prosperity... for some.

But this wasn't new to me.

Passing a park, I lay down. I was exhausted and others were sprawled in the grass. There was a sign, *Animotes Allowed*. Here at least, I'd blend in and be safe.

Most of the animotes were emaciated, a meal or two from death's doorstep. These must be *the homeless ones* we'd heard about. I'd always assumed that was a legend, something Mom preached to scare us from drugs and VR. She wasn't kidding? I swallowed hard.

Imagine living here—cold, hungry, and alone day after day. How could anyone let this happen? How could so many ignore them?

Laying on the cold, hard grass, I closed my eyes, feeling powerless and feigning sleep while draping my old shirt over my face.

If anyone recognized me, I was screwed.

I found a history of cybernetics and the voice inside my head began.

After speeding through humanity's many experiments, I zipped to the early 2030s.

'...there were two competing technologies poised to transform everything: genetic engineering and mechatronic cybernetics. Both were promising, attracting top scientists, researchers, and funding to build beings of the future.'

'Cybernetics was viewed, at least until 2033, as the lesser of the two transhumanist paths. Around 2030, before the spread of the

Bioplague, a few breakthroughs changed everything. Chief among these, the invention and successful introduction of nanoSTEM cells— nanoscale biomachinery, which, when implanted into in vitro embryos, could be integrated with various cell clusters. These became the basis of modern cynetic enhancement, allowing doctors to design ever greater functionality.

'As cybernetics progressed, doctors found ways to pass bioreplicating nanoSTEMs from parent to child, which made breeding cybernetic individuals—later called cynetics—incompatible with biological humans...'

I must have dozed off because the next thing I knew, something pulled at my head, rubbing the zipper against my scruff.

One of the homeless guys had my backpack with his one good arm and gritted his teeth. He looked feral.

"Back off, dude!" I growled.

He scampered away, in no shape for a fight and interested in an easier target, deformed arm limp at his side. I took a deep breath. What had happened to these people?

Back home, you could leave your doors open all day. Everyone knew and trusted one another. There was no need to steal. If someone was hungry or needed help, the community got them on their feet.

Except Neurowebbers... There was nothing you could do for addicts. At a certain point, they were lost, reality less interesting than what some well-paid, immoral game designer or experience engineer could envision. They were the sad ones, the lost souls. But that was life. At the moment, it wasn't my problem. I had to survive.

It was 15:12. Mr. Avery—whoever he was—would be home in two hours. Who was he?

Turns out, there were a lot of Lars Averys. I tried to narrow the search and cross-checked his address. Even searched Lyam Harding.

There were tons of articles on Fitz. He was described as a radical, a terrorist, a dangerous criminal, and implicated in dozens of attacks, bombings, even four assassinations. Good work, Fitz.

Ten years ago, he vanished. Nothing: no articles, no pictures. He was a ghost.

I smiled to myself, missing him already, even though I'd hardly known the guy.

A siren blared. What the—?

My connection had been getting weaker and weaker. It took a second to click. Search triggers. There must be a search trigger on *'Lyam Harding.'* This had all the signs. Run!

Killing my connection, I cleared my history, heading for the nearest busy intersection.

According to my research it wasn't rush hour. Animotes worked from 7:00 to 19:00 and elites, 7:00 to 12:00. Still, there were a fair number of people about and I slid into the crowd, bodies enveloping me as sirens intensified.

While I was probably safe, I kept walking to be sure, often changing direction and sticking with the largest group.

After ten minutes checking my periphery, I felt better. It was stupid to research Fitz without proper privacy protocols. Had the GDR hacked those too? Heck, maybe they designed them to monitor dissidents.

Plenty of people vanished every year. It was all rumors, but I'd believed it. I'd have to be more careful.

After killing time, I headed back, excited, nervous, and starving.

I got there a few minutes to five and waited on the doorstep, the destitution I'd witnessed invading my thoughts.

Several minutes later, a tall wiry man with a black button-up and matching wool hat turned onto the path.

Lars?

He had large, sharp eyes with pitch black pupils and a gaze that took everything in. A warm face, boyish grin, and close cropped brown hair made him seem trustworthy. Maybe...

"Did stripes send you?" he whispered as he got closer.

"What? Yes, yeah. He—"

"Shhh! Follow me. We'll talk."

The door opened as he approached, and he led me inside. Strange fellow. I hopped up, hurrying into the dated building.

We didn't speak until he'd unlocked his door—all three locks—and peered around. We were in an old, rundown living room: TV and couch in the far corner, facing away from the connected kitchen. A small wooden table, matching fabbed chairs, and a surprising amount of counter space. Not so different from home, other than the mess, clothes, cups and bowls everywhere.

We were alone.

He locked the contraption and said, "Sorry about that. You can never be too careful. I got your message. How's Lyam?"

Oh... "He's dead," I said through gritted teeth. "Murdered."

Lars' eyes flashed. "Dead, what do you mean dead? How? What happened?"

Wait a sec... "How do you know Fitz, I mean Lyam?"

"We go way back, Lyam and I. What's your name, kid?"

"Raj," I answered automatically.

"Okay, Raj. I can tell you're scared and don't trust me. That is fine, good actually. So, Lyam's dead?"

I nodded.

His eyes flared pain. "I met Lyam thirty years ago. Fought together in the early days, but he probably told you that." He looked at me closer. "Are you his son?"

I shook my head. I wish. "He was my teacher."

"I see. Anyways, we got into some mischief, Lyam and I. Caused the GDR a few headaches. Bombings, assassinations, the usual." He smiled to himself. "He must have told you about The Brooks."

He hadn't and I said nothing.

His eyes widened. "Oh wow... I was there when his wife died. She was a lovely woman, Kira, brilliant fighter and strategist too. We were running an op, nothing special, but something happened. Dozens of agents swarmed us from three sides. Were five of us mind you, me, Lyam, Agtha, Yuri, and Kira. We retreated, getting off a few shots to slow them." He sighed.

"We turned the corner and should have gone left. That was the plan, but Agtha turned right. She made a mistake. We realized after a few seconds, but it cost us, Lyam especially. Kira was bringing up the rear and took one in the back. She was dead before she hit the ground, never stood a chance." He shook his head, mouth set in a hard line as he told me about dragging his friend to safety, tears soaking Lyam's face. "We made it but Lyam lost *everything*. That was ten years ago. Haven't seen him since."

So, that's what happened to him. "That's why he is how he is?"

Avery nodded. "By the way, kid, call me Lars." He held out a hand.

"I'm Raek."

"Clever," Lars laughed. "Lyam must have done a number on you." Turning serious, he added, "So, what happened? How can I help?"

I told him everything and by the end, collapsed on his small couch, spent.

"You look like you could use some coffee, kid. Hungry?"

Yes! I nodded weakly.

"I'll fix eggs. You rest a bit, you've been through a lot by the sound of it."

A sad, mirthless laugh escaped me. "Thanks. Didn't know where else to turn." I had no one.

"So cynetic, huh? And you're wolfish." He raised an eyebrow. "Must have been some crazy science experiment or love triangle. And the Initiative's after you too, think you're their savior or something?"

I rolled my eyes. "Pretty much."

"Well dang, kid, certainly know how to get yourself into trouble. I like you." He grinned. "Don't worry, tomorrow's my day off. We'll figure this out. Couch is all yours. Any friend of Lyam's, well... make yourself at home."

"You have no idea how much—"

He cut me off. "You don't have to say anything, kid. I mean it. Lyam saved my life more times than I can count. I got your back. Now, let's eat."

28

COOKS AND BOOKS

We went to bed after dinner. I was exhausted and Lars left me alone, saying something about working on the situation. Whatever that meant. He closed his door and my head hit the pillow less than a minute later.

The delicious nutty aroma of fresh coffee woke me. I'd have swore he ground and roasted the beans himself, it smelled that fresh.

"Thought you could use a pick me up." He handed me a steaming mug. "We've got a big day ahead of us."

I took the cup, rich flavors energizing me. "You read my mind."

"I was thinking about what you said last night. There aren't a lot of great options to be honest, but we'll make something work." A pause. "Way I see it, kid, you got four options. First, confront Lilia and the Council, plead your case, and try to get them to turn on her. While it's suspicious Hrun died of a heart attack and Lyam disappeared a day later, there's no proof. It's your word against hers, and well, she's their president..."

And a liar too. "I know."

"Plus, for all they know, Lyam disappeared again. He did once, what's to say he wouldn't again? So that's out, at least for now. Option two, stay with me and hide out in Caen."

He gestured to the small apartment, tiny kitchen and carpeted living room.

"It's workable, but to be honest, you're on the news once a day and this is the *most* policed city in the world. I'd rather get you out of here. Option three, escape to a town somewhere. Locals might even protect you cause you're one of them. Or they may go for the huge reward and turn you in. That's a chance we'd have to take."

Would they really do that, turn a fellow animote in?

Lars shook his head. "Those first three options are garbage, too dangerous, but I wanted to outline *all* the options. Things might change."

He sipped his coffee before continuing. "Option four, roughing it, get out of the city and live in the woods for a bit. I could come with you if you want, that'd be up to you. From what you've said, you're comfortable outdoors. May be our best option."

I'd been thinking the same thing. "Then what?"

He shrugged. "It's a temporary solution to buy us time and see what happens. With the GDR and the Initiative both rushing thanks to you, things are bound to change fast. And with what you told me about the Initiative's willingness to go to war, we shouldn't have to wait long." He paused to let that sink in. "In a month or two, things could look different. If they push for war or the towns revolt, the Initiative could be dependent on you. You might be able to make demands, maybe even to lead." His eyes twinkled. "You know the story of Jesus?"

The hairy religious guy? "Sort of." What's he got to do with anything?

"For thousands of years, people looked to the heavens for answers, prayed to gods—or god, depending on your era—for guidance, survival, sex... anything. Jesus is the father of Christianity, a religion that reigned for thousands of years. Story was, he was the son of God, the *chosen* one to lead humanity to salvation, and people united around that." He shrugged. "Something inside draws us to charisma, to power, to hope. Today our people have nothing: no freedom, no future. You could be that hope." He smiled.

"You think I should be a prophet? Pretend to be a gift from god or something?" Was he serious?

"No, no," Lars said. "That was a metaphor. This isn't about religion, it's about unifying hope. If you channel that, and step in at the right moment, you could turn the tide of history."

"That's what the Initiative wanted, for me to inspire the people to rise up and revolt. Fitz said we weren't ready."

"Bet you he was right, too." Lars shook his head, smiling. "Lyam— Fitz as you knew him—was the sharpest military mind I knew. He's right, that's what I'm saying. It isn't only the message, it's also timing. And you have to survive long enough. Get it?"

I nodded.

"How much combat training do you have? Lyam teach you anything?"

I wish. "We didn't have time."

"That's priority one once we're out of here," he said. 'You need to learn to fight. You're fast and strong, you've got enhancements. You need training to take advantage of that. The best in the world are in Zone Three. I have contacts over there, people who run combat academies and monasteries. We just need to get there."

Zone Three? "That's far."

He grinned. "They won't expect it, either of them. Besides, GDR's weaker there. Their honor culture and long history make Asians some of my favorite people, and those least like to submit to foreign rule." He pursed his lips. "Flying is out of the question, too much paperwork and security. Plus I don't have *that* kind of legal money." He shook his head. "A ship's our best bet, either as stowaways or joining a crew. I'll put out feelers and see what comes back."

"You think I should run?" I asked.

A nod. "I need to go get stuff ready for the trip and talk to some people. I'll be back. Need anything?"

"When do we leave? How can I help?"

"Depends what I find. I'll be back tonight." He stood, grabbed his jacket, and strode to the door. As he was about to leave, he turned. "Stay here, kid. There's food in the fridge, leftovers. Feel

free to make something. I've got books in my room you might
find interesting. Take a look if you're bored. I'll be back before
19:00."

He left, and once again, I was alone with my thoughts, which
drifted to Fitz. He'd died protecting me. And as stupid as it was, he'd
felt a bit like a father to me. I missed him.

And Mom, and Vynce, and Elly... I missed them all. But I had to
make it through this. If I didn't, their deaths would be for nothing.

I'd do what I had to, like Mom raised me.

Didn't Lars mention books? Could be a nice distraction, anything
to escape feeling and the reality of the situation. After finishing my
coffee and cleaning like Mom drilled, I headed to the bedroom.

Lars was a bachelor all right: bed unmade, clothes and socks
covering the carpeted floor, and a distinct sweaty musk permeating the
place. The far corner had a small wooden desk and an impressive
bookshelf. So many non-governmental books... there must have been
twenty *real, physical* books. These weren't outdated Ministry of Education ones either. No one read real books anymore, but Lars had books
on history, science, space. Even fiction near the bottom. Where to
begin?

Opening the cover of *The Rise of Immortality*, I scanned the faded
table of contents. It looked good.

1. *A History of Man*
2. *A History of Medicine*
3. *The Birth of Modern Agriculture*
4. *The Human Genome Project*
5. *Transhumanism*
6. *Biological Immortality*
7. *Mechanical Immortality*
8. *Virtual Immortality*
9. *The Birth of Emulates*
10. *Immortality at Last?*
11. *A New Chapter*

It was written around 2060 or so, when scientists cracked the code on the human brain and virtually emulating consciousness.

While the chapters on biological and mechanical immortality were familiar, I was clueless about the emulate origin story. How brain-fields could be transferable to new semi-organic surrogate bodies was beyond me. Sounded like magic.

The early experiments sounded horrible: from plugging physical hard drives to invasive personality destroying scans, the earliest tests were done on political prisoners, like the first animote trials.

In 2051 some European scientist figured out probablistic mapping. Progress exploded after that, a huge surrogate market before it was banned and taken over by the government. Playing god was danger-ous, as the world had seen.

Today, no one knew how many bodies there were, or where they were stored. The book mentioned "repositories"—the brain-fields storage facilities known only by the upper echelons of the emulate GDR where emulates rebooted. Like a respawn location.

My stomach grumbled.

It was fascinating, if a bit technical. For sure banned. I'd never heard any of this, at least not in any detail. The author must have published under a pen name, or be dead.

But one thing didn't make sense. How'd the GDR function? If your coworkers lived forever and wouldn't share the secret with you or your kids... there must be bad blood, right?

Too bad the book was outdated, no mention of more recent events or politics. Could have been helpful.

Food time. Grabbing a random book, I headed for the kitchen, poured another cup of fantastic coffee, and opened the fridge. Wow, he had food... Maybe Lars wasn't your typical bachelor.

Yes, ribs! It had been ages since I'd eaten something wild. I found a pan in the cupboard, put it on the burner, and poured some synthoil.

This was all new to me, Elly usually cooked when Mom couldn't. But how hard could it be?

As the pan was heating up, I grabbed a chair and opened the book, *Man's Fall From Heaven*. Interesting. Was this like that Jesus stuff?

A burning stench hit me. What was that?

Crap, the burner. I must have lost track of time. Dropping the book, I sprang to my feet, coughing. The room was filled with noxious fumes and it was hard to breathe.

Shit. Running the pan under cold water didn't help as burning black curdled through the apartment. This wasn't working.

And the building would have smoke detectors. What if the fire department came? They'd be on the lookout for anything suspicious. Running to the detector, I ripped it from the wall but the numbers on the screen kept skyrocketing.

It screamed a high-pitched mechanical beep as I hurried to the window, struggling with the old fashioned lock. It shattered, but at least the street was empty.

Winding up, I heaved the beeping detector as far as I could. It fell with a metallic crash, exploding in a violent *thud* as thousands of tiny pieces scattered the pavement.

Phew. That was close.

The fire alarm sounded.

29

GRABBING A LIFT

I couldn't stay here. I had to get out, ASAP. But if they investigated and no one was here, they'd be suspicious. They'd swab DNA. If they did, they'd get a match.

The officers that had drugged me must have taken a sample. If I was in their database, I'd be screwed. Lars too.

I had to warn him. How? He hadn't left a note.

Stay calm. Hustling around the apartment, I searched for *any* way to contact him. There had to be something.

A stack of envelopes on the counter. I flicked through, skimming. One caught my eye.

United Comms Co. The GDR's telecom and media company was too lazy and bureaucratic to digitize their comms. I tore it open. A bill.

Dear Mr. Avery,

Come on... The back had account information. BINGO!

I memorized it and ran to the couch, grabbing my bag and hurrying to the fridge to stuff all the food I could fit.

Outside, sirens wailed over the blaring alarm. A kilometer or two at most.

Decision time... Staying was too risky. I had to get out of here and get ahold of Lars.

Racing downstairs, there was a back entrance. I took it and was in luck. The shabby lot was empty except for several busted scooters.

Trucks sped to the building, tires screeching as I ran, jumping fences.

Once I was two blocks away, I slowed and merged with other pedestrians, trying to act normal. They'd do a DNA swab and ID me in no time. DNS would be there minutes later.

Hurry.

I opened Lars' information from the telecom, careful to keep my eyes down like the other animotes. It had his username name: *@lars-mars*, and I called him. No answer.

Again, nothing. I sent him a voice message, avoiding any trigger words and told him what happened. As long as he was okay, I'd hear from him soon.

We had to leave the city. Schedules for every lev train and pool ride leaving the city entered my field view. Some headed east, a few west. Either could work and I filed them away for later, sharing the plans with Lars.

Two police cruisers whizzed past, sirens screaming. Shoot. No breaking stories, *yet*. That was good at least. The longer the World News Network (WNN) took, the more time we had.

A notification. It was Lars calling.

'Got your message, kid. Shit! Where are you?'

'Sending my location now.' I transmitted GPS coordinates and a map snap of my position.

'Okay. I found a boat. It's leaving from a port south of Fiern two days from now.'

Two days? All the way out west... 'Can we make it?'

'We're going to have to. I got the lev times you sent. Thanks. Our best bet is hitching a ride on the noon train to Mile High to put some distance between us and the capital.'

'But that's thirty-five minutes from now!'

'We need to hurry. They might shutdown the city when they realize it's you. We need to be out of here.'

'Where do we meet?' I asked.

'Lockerbie Station. It's three kilometers northeast of you. Sending details. Meet me at the coffee shop across the street. Find a hat or a pair of sunglasses, something to blend in. Steal one if you have to.'

Steal? 'Okay.' My heart hammered, but I was up to it. 'I'll be there.'

'And if I don't show, Raek, assume something happened. Get yourself on that lev, hide in the freight section. It should be fully automated. Go to Taub port, two hours south of Fiern. Ask for JJ and tell him Birdman sent you. I gotta go, kid. Good luck.'

I wished him the same, switched off, and ran harder. So this was what a real fox hunt felt like... Time to throw caution to the winds.

A squad car approached as I rounded the corner. The rest of the street empty, except me. A store was open and I slipped in.

It was one of those retro urban clothing stores. Colorful sneakers and jerseys, posters plastering the ceilings, old school hip hop shaking the building from the massive sound system by the counter.

"How's it hanging?" the store owner said with a smile.

"Just looking." I hurried toward the back.

"Let me know if you need anything, brother," he replied in a strange accent.

He was an animote of some kind, long black hair braided in twisted snakes down his back. He turned and busied himself with a box by the credit scanner, humming.

The cruiser passed a minute later. Phew.

"Thanks, man, maybe another time." I headed for the door.

"We be here, me brother, if you be needing something."

I wasn't hip hop savvy enough to have a clue what he meant.

A black cap with odd markings hung by the door. Without breaking stride, I slid it off the display and under my shirt. Was I really stealing this hat?

I slipped out, the owner humming away.

After sprinting a block, I tried on the hat. It fit well, covering my eyes and face. A quick adjustment, and I was off

I'd come back one day and pay that guy.

A notification flashed. I pulled it up. A breaking story.

'Authorities confirmed the animote wanted for killing four cynetic officers last weekend has been staying with this man, Lars Avery. Fire-fighters investigating reports of smoke and a potential fire at 1104 Heartlow, reported Mr. Avery's room unresponsive after several attempts to notify the occupant. Upon entry, EMTs and local law enforcement took genetic samples. DNA matching the murderer, Raek Mekorian, was found at the scene. Citizens are encouraged to stay vigilant and report suspicious activity or sightings of either Raek Mekorian or Lars Avery to their local DNS precinct.

Clicking off, I pinged Lars the news. I'd set an alert on my name and he might not have thought to do the same.

Two minutes later, he called. 'I saw. Doesn't change anything. Be careful,' he added.

'I'll be there in twelve minutes.'

'Good. I'm organizing some last minute things. I'll be there soon.'

After the stress of the morning, the rest of the way was uneventful until the station. It was crawling with cops. Not good.

I messaged Lars. *Anywhere else we could get on?*

Incoming call. 'Kid, you here?'

'Yeah.'

'Good. Head west. See the gray and blue tower? Meet me at the entrance. Hurry!' His voice was loud and strained. It was 11:53. We had seven minutes.

I sprinted for my life. Lars had sounded worried and he'd been unflappable to this point. Did he have a plan?

Four minutes later, the entrance. There was a whistle.

"Over here!" Lars knelt behind a bush, pretending to tie his shoes. "You made it."

"What's the plan?" My voice felt fine. Weird, I wasn't out of breath despite sprinting for thirty minutes.

"We jump it," he said matter-of-factly, surveying the tracks from all possible angles.

"Wh, what? What do you mean *jump it?*"

"It's simple. As the train goes by, we run alongside and hop on. We'll pull ourselves up, sneak into the freight compartment, and we're golden."

"You're kidding, right?" Jumping onto a moving train?

"Wish I was." He shook his head, calm despite what we were about to attempt. "It's our only option. Besides, trains don't pick up real speed until they're a kilometer outside the metro area. Follow me, kid." We ducked a wire fence, hopped a crumbling concrete wall, and moved toward the edge. "Don't touch the track. You'll be fried." Lovely.

"Also," he added, "the train's visual detection system can't see us. If it does, it'll alert security or turn around. We have to wait until the engine passes before we pop up."

Pop up? "What?"

He pulled me behind a breaker. "Here it comes! They're silent until they get going. Electric engines and magnetic levitation."

Sure enough, the bulleted monstrosity hurtled toward us with scarce a whine.

Where'd Lars want us to grab on to? There weren't *any* openings.

"Take these and hold tight." He handed me a pair of fifteen-centimeter poles. "They're maggrips. Jump and squeeze the handle as soon as it hits the train. That'll activate the electromagnets and should be strong enough to support you. *Don't* stop squeezing! Anything below a rough handshake and the EM coils deactivate... Loosen your grip *slightly* to climb or reposition the handle."

"On my count," he said, his eyes set in slits. "Three, two, one!"

He took off and I hurried after him, squeezing the handles like my life depended on it, which in a lot of ways, it did. He took a forty-five-degree angle toward the train, correcting as he closed and narrowing the gap as the train flew by.

It was pulling away from us, too fast... He jumped. "Holy shit!"

Time slowed as his body flew through the air, arms flailing. He slammed into the side and the handles slid for a second. Somehow, the grips held and despite penduluming from side to side, he stabilized.

I leapt a second later, terrified and wired like never before. My arms braced for impact, felt the wind, and adjusted as I flew. The hum of crickets, the beating of my heart, the vibration of the train—everything in an instant as I inched across the chasm.

Flexing my hands as the handles struck, my legs slammed into the train below. Squeezing harder, I forced myself upward and before I knew it, was atop the train, lying next to Lars in a daze.

"Good work, kid." A shocked, boyish grin blanketed his stunned face. "I can't believe it worked."

"We need to get inside," I said. "I researched the train. Compartments fifteen through fifty-nine are freight, the two external doors are at thirty and fifty. We're close to forty-five. That makes backward our best bet."

"Good work, kid, but you didn't know what train we'd be on. When'd you look this up?"

"Just now."

His eyes widened. "What? That was three seconds at most."

Was it? It felt like ages. "I don't know. It doesn't matter now. Let's move before there's a tunnel."

I crawled backward, holding on for dear life, and he followed. We were doing a hundred at this point, and accelerating, even blurring past. At fifty, I went over the edge and flipped onto the grated platform entrance. Solid ground, thank you.

Of course, the huge metal door was locked.

Lars messed with the handle while I researched train specs. He was smart enough not to touch the keypad or fingerprint sensor.

After twenty minutes, I had it. "Every lev comes hardcoded with one of four predetermined passcodes. Must not be too worried about theft…"

Glossing over the details, I said, "Someone found a bug but the company was too lazy to fix it. Never even noticed the post. Four options, but we only get three tries before it triggers the alarm. So, we have two tries, a fifty-fifty chance. If we don't get it with the first two, we're out here for the trip and jump when we get closer."

"What are the codes?"

I reopened the post. "9927, 1430, 1173 and 5158."

"Nine-nine-two-seven," Lars repeated, punching in the code. A red light flashed on the touchscreen pad. "Crap, nothing."

"Wait, wait. Let me think!" Is there anything we're missing?

"We're lucky," Lars said. "It's three hours with no stops. It's the boonies between here and Mile High."

"Let's try one more." What could it hurt?

"You do it, kid. My luck's worn out."

"Like mine's better? Remember the week I've had." I smiled despite myself and typed in *5158*.

Ding. The keypad flashed green this time. It worked! Laughing, I opened the door and Lars clapped me on the back.

Inside was a spartan interior, basic holding docks lined with rows of biorecycled boxes, each sporting micro scanner codes on all sides. Some had logos too, massive State-Owned Enterprises (SOEs) like United Comms Co, United Energy, United Digital Industries, WNN and the World Bank. A few smaller corporations as well: The Everything Store, Europa Auto and RP1, leading legal producer of VR headsets and content worldwide.

We could steal stuff for the poor towns... but we had bigger fish to fry.

Sitting in the corner, Lars told me about his childhood as the son of a poor urban family. His schools were filthy and his parents worked from 7:00 to 19:00 Monday to Saturday in a VR factory, one week vacation a year. His mom died of heat stroke one summer. The factory owner wasn't willing to pay for air conditioning. Life sucked after that, and his dad struggled to put food on the table. Sounded rough. How could someone who'd been through so much be so happy, or at least content? Was it a facade?

The story turned violent: riots, police dogs, tasers. Lars' neighbor was killed in a protest, crushed by a tank. Most protesters were rounded up and shot. GDR couldn't risk news of the riots spreading. Only thirty years ago and I'd never heard about it. It was erased from history.

"One day they came for Dad," Lars said in a hushed voice. "Three troopers kicked down the door, said he was guilty of treason. I was under the bed, hiding. He'd sent me when he heard the knock, knew it wasn't safe. Dad went without a fight, wanted them out of our apartment. He wanted to protect me." His eyes glistened and he swallowed hard. "I could have saved him. I should have saved him." Tears covered the strong man's face and he looked away, embarrassed.

I put my arm around him—the big guy I'd met not two days earlier —without saying a word. I understood, I'd failed too. Every animote had a similar story, *everyone*. We sat for a while and I lost track of time. Eventually, Lars dozed off and I stood, stretching. I had to think.

Mom and Vynce popped into my head. What had happened to them? And Elly and Merie... There was Professor Ivey, tied to a chair, her face decimated. Even in Caen, the homeless animotes and pseudo-slaves. The world was cruel and broken.

My thoughts shifted to the Initiative. I pictured Fitz and Lars and Paer fighting the government, Fitz's wife being gunned down. The burning hate in Lilia's eyes, the pain in Fitz's.

Every resistance fighter must have a similar story, something that pushed them over the edge. So much pain and suffering. Who was I to deny all that? Who was I to hold them back? I could change things, couldn't I? Or at least try. I had to. I had to do something. It wasn't fate, it was more than that. Purpose, maybe?

No more running. No more hiding. No more! I'd do *whatever* it takes.

It was time!

30

PRACTICE AND PURPOSE

W hen Lars awoke, I told him we had to go back. "We're not going to Zone Three." I stared him down and dared him to challenge me. "This is my fight, whether I like it or not."

"We're going, kid. This better not be about me." He shook his head. "You're not dying for me, I won't have *that* on my hands."

"This isn't about you! Heck, this isn't even about me. It's about all of us. Ending suffering. My mind's set, there's *nothing* you can do to change it." I softened my voice. It's not like I was angry with him. It was the world. "I can't ask you to come with me, it wouldn't be fair."

He smiled and rolled his eyes. "You're funny, kid. I'm coming with you. You know that, right? So, what's the plan?"

I smiled despite myself, couldn't help it. Knew I liked this guy. "We're on this until Mile High. You said you could teach me to fight, and military strategy."

"I don't have contacts in Mile High anymore. You need to find us a place."

"On it." I opened a connection, focusing.

Lars tackled me into a headlock.

"What are you doing?" I gagged.

"Training," he replied. "You're not safe, now or ever! You always have to be alert, even multi-tasking."

"Easy for you to say," I grumbled. "You're not searching for a cabin in the woods." I spun my hips and flipped him off me.

He reversed grip, pinning my back and slapped me. "Focus."

"I am, damn it."

"Restart that sequence," he said. "This time, deactivate your cybernetics. I want to fight on the same level. Your technique needs work, and your speed and strength let you compensate, but slow your development."

It took five minutes, but, after playing around, I managed to disable my enhancements while retaining my connection and augmented visuals.

We drilled another hour, Lars always besting me and making us repeat the situation. When we were finished, I was drenched, dead tired, and ready to collapse.

I reactivated my system, and my body came to life again. Phew...

Lars massaged his leg, groaning. "Find a place?"

I had, and sent him details.

He grabbed a fancy black band and strapped it to his wrist. A virtual screen appeared with Lars' operating system.

Within forty seconds, he had the rental open and activated a strange portal. Several encryption and geo-altering protocols later, a banking interface. He had 12,108 units of some currency I'd never heard of, and counted a month's rent, eighty-eight of them.

A motion of his pinkie, and the funds were in the seller's account. "Housing's taken care of."

"What was that?" I leaned closer as he closed it and cleared his history.

"That old thing?" he said. "That's TOR4, fourth iteration of the dark web." He must have seen my confusion. "So governments and corporations can't spy on you, where people that don't want to be found transact in goods and services that aren't exactly legal."

Cool. "The GDR allows that?"

"Of course not. It's illegal. Problem is, it's open-source and run by thousands of volunteers worldwide. Started as a government project but today it's used by the Initiative, hackers and other dissidents to avoid detection."

"Never heard of it."

He grinned. "I'll show you later, now's not the time."

I pulled up GPS; he was right. "We're about five hundred kilometers out. We should get ready. Grab your stuff."

On the platform, the train jolted, slowing at an impossible rate. Within thirty seconds, we were down to forty kilometers per hour. It felt fast, but wouldn't get slower until we reached the city center.

At a small hill overlooking the city, we dove, tumbling hard and rolling but none the worse for wear.

After brushing ourselves off, Lars told me about an old military base east of the city he'd bombed back in the day. "Met a girl too. Spent some time here. She had a little crazy in her!" His longing eyes were far off. "Don't know what happened to Gema. Think she moved back east." He shook his head with a sigh.

Another news story broke as we reached Bear Creek Lake Park, a DNS raid in Broag. 'Two officers were killed in addition to thirty-five rebels,' said the obnoxious Peter Gruy. 'Police took another ten into custody and will be interrogating and prosecuting to the fullest extent of the law as outlined in the Anti-Terror and Espionage Act of 2069.'

I clicked off and told Lars.

"Hope they're still on a need to know basis," he said. That made two of us.

It got nicer and nicer as we got closer, and when we reached the park, I knew it was perfect. Wild and free. We hadn't seen a person in ages.

The smell of pine trees and needles, nearby maple, and fresh snow brought me back to better times. This was my element.

Even Lars peered at the sky, watching birds soar, and took a deep breath. "You forget how beautiful it all is sometimes, living in the city I mean. Out here, I could get used to this."

We followed the GPS to the cabin and found it after a bit of meandering. It was hidden in a clearing off the beaten path and looked like an old rangers' cabin: tiny and rustic, even a *real brick* chimney.

Climbing rickety stairs, Lars grabbed his band and scanned the red door's metallic sensor. The system verified and unlocked.

Inside was nothing special, a basic log cabin with several biofabbed additions off the main living area. Small and cozy, with a bearskin covering the floor. For some reason—maybe the worn couch and general open layout—it reminded me of home. I activated the fire while Lars unpacked, surveying the surroundings.

Taking remote sensors like Fitz had had, he trudged to the door. "I'll be back, kid. Pick a bed."

The first bedroom was cramped, three meters by three, with a window in the far right for afternoon sunlight which spilled through frosted glass, illuminating the wooden bed. A knitted blanket lay folded, a wolf on a sharp outcrop of rock. Talk about a sign. I tossed my bag on the bed. This was perfect.

After relieving myself in the cramped toilet, I checked the kitchen. It wasn't much. Oven, stove, and not a whole lot else. Outside was a firepit, and I was looking forward to hunting.

Putting away what little food we had left, I realized Lars wasn't back. Odd.

If I had free time, I should research the GDR. If we were going to fight and win, I had to know my enemy. I knew the basics, but not much behind the scenes. It had always been a colossal, faceless organization, the Global Democratic Republic. Its five leaders were known as the Board: the Ministers of Security, Commerce, Education, Infrastructure, and Intelligence, and, together, they decided the actions of the entire government.

Three emulates and two cynetics, and not an enhancer or animote in sight. The Minister of Security was Calter Fury, a cynetic who'd risen through military and DNS hierarchy to become the government's chief enforcer, earning a ruthless reputation of upholding justice to the fullest extent of the law, often exceeding it.

He was the most hated man in the world, at least among animotes —despite being loved by elites—thanks to increasing military and police presence in the towns and cracking down on anything viewed as free thought or counterculture.

Next was Minister of Commerce, Jean Gileu, who'd built a thriving biotech business commercializing many of the technologies and genetic patents of today's enhancers. He'd entered politics, become one of the first emulates, and later gained control of most surrogate factories. Prick shut them down to prevent others from joining the club.

Lin Zu was the new kid on the Board, responsible for the future workforce. Citing the need for disparity, she poured resources and energy into already thriving elite schools, cutting funding to ours.

Her election had turned the tide in favor of the emulates, who now controlled the Board three-to-two over their cynetic rivals. In reality, they got along, but there was an ever-present tension.

The door opened. Lars stomped in and snow fell from his jacket and pants as he kicked his boots on the mat.

"There you are!" I exclaimed. "Did you get lost? Took you long enough."

"What are you talking about, kid? It's been what, three, maybe five minutes..."

"Five minutes, as if... it's been—" I checked my OS. "Four minutes thirty-seven seconds." No way. My jaw dropped. "Wow, feels way longer." I told him what I'd found.

"Interesting," he said when I finished. "All that in five minutes? Plus you stole the good room." He raised an eyebrow. "Sure you didn't learn this in school?"

I shook my head.

Lars nodded, considering. "You might have paralleosis," he said at last. He must have sensed my uneasiness because he added, "It's not bad, it's great actually, a rare ability. Only a fraction of cynetics have paralleosis, the ability to process multiple streams of information at once, like overclocking your processor. Your brain and hardware run at superhuman levels thanks to nanoSTEM integration with your brain's neural architecture, but paralleosis is a special mutation. Your biomechanical brain can hyper parallel process."

Say what?

"If I'm not mistaken," he said, "your brain reads and understands multiple things at once. You're reading two, three, as many as five or ten sentences at once. That's how you read all that in three minutes." He stared. "Ever noticed anything like this before?"

Um, no... "I like reading but was never what you'd call fast."

"Interesting. Okay, kid, I want you to read something and summarize it for me. You know Nelson Mandela?"

"Never heard of him."

"Tell me what you find, not word for word, but a summary of the important points. In your own words." He walked into the kitchen and turned on the cheap coffee maker.

I followed him.

"Mandela was one of the most important and influential people in human history. He was a nonviolent, anti-apartheid leader and politician in South Africa before being imprisoned for twenty-seven years on trumped-up political charges. Later, he was freed and became President of South Africa, tackling racism while trying to unify the racial differences in the country, which were enormous." I rattled off other achievements and such. "Seems like a cool guy."

"You got all that just now?" He sounded skeptical. "You didn't learn about him in school?"

"Are you kidding?" I laughed. "They'd never teach us about insurgencies or fighting oppression. That's their worst nightmare."

"Fair point. I guess you have the mutation. Not sure what we do with that..." After checking the coffee maker—which was only half done—he told me about the tracks he'd spotted. There was a ton of game to be had.

But I wasn't interested in hunting right now, I wanted to fight. He'd kicked my butt and I had a ton to learn.

"So, when do we start?" I asked.

He chuckled. "Patience, Raek, patience. There's only so much this old body can handle. There's a lot we need to work on. In fact, most is mental, not physical. If you have to fight, you've already failed," he added in a serious tone. "Our goal is to avoid combat or make victory inevitable. Do you follow?"

I nodded.

"The most important rule of politics and war is to anticipate your opponent. If you know what they'll do before they do it, you gain the upper hand. The second rule, be unpredictable. That's how we accomplished so much with such small numbers. We planned, attacked, and escaped, all while minimizing risk. We knew where their men would be, where they were weakest, and how they'd respond."

"Let's see about coffee." He grabbed two mugs from the drawer. "You need experience. Short of that, we can run simulations of what could happen, what could go wrong. For instance, let's say the DNS found out we were in this cabin. What would they do?"

I shrugged. "How would I know?"

He stared at me, not blinking.

"Well," I said after a moment, "they'd send a few VTOLs, at least a patrol. Maybe even a platoon. They'd want to get here as fast as possible, so they'd contact the nearest military base."

"Where's that?"

Shoot. "I, I don't know."

"You need to know!" he snapped. "Your life depends on it. They could be breathing down our necks in five minutes. We *have* to be ready. Why VTOLs?"

"Speed. It comes down to speed. They don't want us to get away again."

He smiled. "How many would they send?"

"Depends on the number of men."

"Yeah, but how many *would* they send?" he insisted.

"A couple in case something went wrong. And they've tried and failed numerous times. At least four, one on each side to box us in."

"Now you're getting it, kid. What would their orders be?"

"Could be shoot to kill, could be capture if possible. Hard to tell."

His face hardened. "Would you bet your life on that?"

Good point.

"Assume they'll kill on sight. You're better safe than sorry."

He was right.

We spent two hours outlining possible scenarios and how we'd react. When we finished, I was gassed. We'd forgotten all about the coffee.

"That is good for now, kid. Good work. We'll cover more tomorrow. See you at sun up." He walked to his room, leaving me to contemplate everything.

31

LEARNING TO HUNT

I couldn't sleep. The prospect of war—of real combat—terrified me. A drone shooting up our cabin had never entered my mind. It gave me goosebumps. The awesome and destructive power of a bomb, a bomb meant for *me*. I was overreacting. They couldn't know we were here, could they? Still, knowing what a motivated enemy could do and how we were helpless, made you think.

I opened the door and Lars was waiting for me. He handed me a mug. "Drink up and take a piss, we've got a busy day."

We met outside two minutes later. Sparring. He'd etched a three-meter circle in the snow inside another fifty percent larger one.

He pointed. "We'll practice takedowns and close quarter fighting. You need to be efficient with your movements. Want to attack or defend?"

"I'll attack."

"Okay, you defend." Lars grinned. "I'll try to take you down. Defense is more important anyway," he added with a smirk.

Thirty seconds later, I dusted myself off. He'd taken me down and choked me out with near inhuman speed. Lars was a better, more experienced fighter than I was, but that was no reason to quit. I was gonna win this time, damn it. I don't care what it takes.

"Again," Lars said.

This time I'd switch it up, keep him guessing. He saw through my deception, feinted, and swept my feet from under me, pouncing before I'd hit the snowy ground. Ugh.

"Remember what we talked about. It's mental, not physical. You need to read your opponent, know what they'll do before they do it."

I'm trying... Whatever that means.

We must have drilled takedowns and defenses for two hours. I was getting into it and excited for the next when he said, "Your turn."

The tables turned, I was ready to try what I'd learned. And I wanted a little revenge to wipe that smug grin from his face.

Another two hours, another string of embarrassing losses. At least I got better, making mistakes and correcting them every round. I hadn't won yet, but by the time Lars said, "I'm hungry, let's eat," I felt much more confident.

Walking back to the cabin, he patted me on the shoulder. "Don't beat yourself up. You did well for a beginner. Toward the end, you started to get the hang of it. You're no Bruce Lee," he added with a playful smile. "But you did well."

Inside, the fridge was an empty wasteland and I offered to hunt.

Lars thought it was a good idea. "While you're out there, think about Caen. By the time you're back, I want three options to conquer or destroy the city and an analysis of each. We'll talk about them when you're back. Sound good?"

"Yeah." I turned to leave. Let's see—

"And, Raek," Lars added. "Be careful, kid. I'm starting to like you. Can't say that about most people." He smiled. "Good luck."

Slipping out the door, my mind raced. Three ways to capture Caen —that was tough. I wanted to wow him, and was formulating a plan when there was a flutter of snow. The pine tree ahead shook, powder falling from its tall, bare branches.

What was that? I hadn't heard anything and switched to thermals to survey the area. Nothing. I was about to continue when I glimpsed an osprey overhead, reminding me of the drone.

If the GDR could bomb us, couldn't we bomb them? Caen was a

stationary target. Sure, it'd be hard, there'd be missile defense systems everywhere. But a well-placed, well-timed, aerial bomb might be able to take out the Board.

I thought about the drill last night. Then what? What would happen if we took out the Board? Mhm... Chaos, maybe?

If politicians saw a power void, they'd want in, like a hunter shooting the alpha male. With the leader gone, wolves descended into violence, each fighting for alpha status and the mating rights that went with it.

That could work. The Initiative could come in and crush the headless beast. Yes! One idea down.

Checking a map of the park to get a sense of where I might find game, I noticed the name again, Bear Creek Lake. Ironic. An hour, and no bear tracks. So much for a namesake. Oh, it was winter... The fuzzy killers were hibernating, hiding in caves, and living off stores of fat. Like a sleeper cell.

What about a double agent? If we could place someone close to the higher-ups in the Board, we might get somewhere. A bomb at their monthly meeting?

Two down, one to go.

I was getting into it when the wind changed, and the fur on the back of my neck stood.

It took a few minutes before I realized what the wolf in me already knew. There were elk nearby, at least one. Two, maybe three kilometers north. Jogging, I kept my eyes open, straining my ears.

Over the small hill was a magnificent view of the park. Light shimmered off the frosty overcoat. Movement. Sure enough, there they were at the base of the hill. Not a kilometer from where I stood were a small group of elk, four in total. Three adults and a young calf.

Moving into the treeline, I made my way toward them. The wind remained constant, allowing me to get within a hundred meters without startling them.

Hadn't Fitz said the stunner could do fifty meters?

Five agonizing minutes of silent crawling, chest and elbows screaming in protest, my range finder told me I was close enough.

Lining up the calf's meaty side flank, my stomach growled and something spooked the elk. The adults raised their heads in alarm and ran. I fired, but not before the baby took a frightened half step toward its mother.

My shot missed centimeters from the calf's backside. Spinning, I aimed at the fleeing calf but my next went wide too. Damn!

Jumping, I darted after them across the frozen turf. They were less than a hundred meters ahead of me and I pushed hard. That lasted another five minutes until, exhausted from my three-kilometer dead-sprint, I collapsed. I was fast, but the elk were faster.

I never stood a chance but hadn't wanted to give up. I wasn't a quitter. And yet, I'd failed. Loafing back toward the cabin, I took a different route. Maybe I'd get lucky.

I didn't. As the cabin came into sight, I remembered Caen. I didn't want to disappoint Lars, but try though I might, my brain was spent. Two failures for the price of one...

Stepping into the cabin, it hit me. Of course, the elk.

Lars offered a jester's wave. "The mighty hunter returns. How goes it, kid?"

"Crappy. I didn't catch anything."

"Here, have some coffee." The excited fire faded from his voice. "You look cold."

I grabbed the cup. At least it was warm, and he didn't say anything about my failure. "I know how we could fight the GDR and win."

"Ohh?" he said with a disbelieving smile. "And what's the great Sun Tzu propose?"

"What? Sun Tzu who?"

"The ancient Chinese military strategist," Lars replied. "It's not important. You were saying..."

"Oh, yeah! The government is like a pack of rabid wolves. They have their alphas—the Board—and everyone else." I explained the concept.

When I finished, he said, "Good reasoning. But how?"

"Targeted drone strike. We find out when the Board meets and bomb 'em." Drone strikes were impossible for us to prevent, and the

GDR must have defense systems, but it might be possible with enough planning.

"I like it. It's a good first effort."

A good first effort... that's it? "The second's a variation, an under-cover agent, like hibernating. If we get someone into the Board's inner circle—or even the Parliamentary Building—we could sneak a bomb into a meeting, or shoot them outright."

"Also a good idea." He didn't look impressed. "It will take time and be risky though. We'll talk about it later. And the third option?"

"We run." I waited for him to take the bait. He would...

"We run?" He raised an eyebrow.

I told him about the elk. "I kept running, kept chasing. I wanted to win. We could do the same, bait their forces into the open, get them to chase us and hit 'em with a surprise attack. We could turn the tables if they think we're desperate enough."

He grinned. "Now *that's* interesting! A few potential pitfalls..."

We went on like this the rest of the afternoon and well into the evening, talking through situations and scenarios. Lars always played devil's advocate, asking "why not?", "what if...", "did you consider...?"

By the end, we'd had enough and needed to relax. Plus Lars' stomach grumbled.

I winced. "I'll go hunting at dawn and get something this time."

"Don't worry, kid. Shit happens. I'm not as practiced as you at skipping meals. Food's easier to come by in the cities and I've gotten soft. This is good for me." He forced a weak smile.

"When did you move to Caen?"

"Long time ago, kid. Came for work; that was the cover at least. In reality, to be closer to the Initiative and the GDR. Keep your friends close and enemies closer. Anyways, got a job with the city, civil engineer's apprentice."

He'd been responsible for optimizing transit systems and told me about how bad it had been post Green Energy transition. They'd exported Caen's successful models to other cities. "Did that for ten years before I got bored. I've worked a lot of jobs since."

At least, Lars was more talkative than Fitz. Still, I missed Fitz. "Why'd you leave the Initiative?"

"Same as Lyam, I'd guess. I'd had enough. I was tired of fighting and things not changing. Guess I got lazy too."

I didn't know how to respond, so instead, I said the real thing that had been bothering me. "What if we fail? What if I fail?"

"What do you mean?" he asked.

"What if it comes to war and the government wins? What if they crush the rebels? What then?"

He shrugged. "What about it?"

"All those people. All that suffering, all for nothing..."

"If we fail, we fail," he said in a matter-of-fact tone. "But how bad would that be? If we fail, *nothing* changes, but if we do nothing, *nothing* changes anyway, right?"

I opened my mouth and closed it. "Oh, I never thought about it like that."

Lars chuckled. "It's like playing with house money. The worst case scenario is basically the world today. What have we got to lose?"

Good point. "But wouldn't it set the Resistance back?"

"Sure, but that's life. And life's a war, not a battle." He shook his head. "Doesn't matter how many times you get hit or how often you fall, kid. Only thing that counts is getting back up. But let's sleep," he said with a yawn. "We got a big day ahead of us."

"We do?"

"Everyday's a big day. Plus you better catch something or I might have to eat you." He rubbed his stomach with a playful smile.

I laughed, and we both headed to our rooms, exhausted.

The next two weeks flew by. We hit our stride, sparring in the mornings and strategizing in the evenings, little variation to our days. I was getting the hang of grappling, and Lars showed me more sophisticated takedowns. He'd never trained a cynetic before, but said I picked up BJJ much faster than he'd expected. After I won several fights, he switched to striking.

In my spare time, he had me read *The Art of War*, Machiavelli, and other military books. He showed me manipulation classics too: *How to*

Win Friends and Influence People, Influence, the *48 Laws of Power.* Lars had access to everything through TOR4, and I could read a book or two a night.

It started to be fun. I could get used to this.

If only it would last...

32

ARSON

We were sparring and I swung Lars into a choke. I was getting ready to finish it when a notification flashed. Opening it to the side, I squeezed, locking in.

'Breaking News. A small animote town a few hours outside Itany is no more. I'm Richad Daks reporting live from Kiag, home of the notorious terrorist and criminal Raek Mekorian, which burned to the ground last night. As you can see,' he panned to the surroundings.

I released Lars, falling to the ground. My arms fell to my sides.

'There is nothing left,' the reporter continued. 'An entire town, *erased* from the map, and there don't appear to be survivors.'

No survivors? A shiver shot through me. Everyone...

'The cause of the fire is unknown, it's unclear why there wasn't more effort to fight it,' Daks droned on as his words blurred in my mind. 'Investigators on scene... ...multiple fires at once... arson... ...glad this wasn't our home... ...linked to Raek Mekorian? Did he destroy his hometown? All this and more. Until next time—'

Shivering spasms shot through me as I closed it. "They're dead. They are all dead."

"What are you talking about, kid?" Lars knelt and put his hand on my shoulder. "Who's dead? What happened?"

"My town, my home, all of them... they're gone!" How was this possible? "No survivors." Burned alive... "They're *all* dead, someone killed 'em. They're saying I did it."

"Why would they think—Wait, *no* survivors?"

"The reporter said it, he said it, damn it!" I yelled. "He said maybe I set the fire or maybe they deserved it."

"The whole town?" Lars bit his lip. "Doesn't seem possible."

"I know. But that's what they said..."

"Hold on a sec, kid. There are three possibilities: the DNS burned your town to teach you a lesson, they did it to lure you there or it isn't real and they are trying to trick you into going anyway. Either way, they want to mess with your head."

"Well, it's working." I curled my arms around my knees, rocking back and forth. Toras, Pavel, Mikey...

"We're done for the day. I want you to meditate. Go inside, now! Sit on the floor and relax. We will talk later. You aren't thinking straight."

"I'm going to kill 'em," I managed through gritted teeth. "I'm going to kill *every last one!*" I crumpled into his arms, choking back tears. "They are all dead. My family, my friends, everyone... It's my fault."

"Come on, kid." He led me into the cabin, helping me sit. "Breath, just breathe. I'll be outside if you need me. You'll be okay."

He was right, I knew he was. But damn it, screw meditating. I didn't want to feel *okay!* How could I? I didn't deserve to... This wasn't just about me though, I couldn't afford to be selfish.

Deep breath, another. My breathing slowed and the pain, the world, *everything* faded away. When I opened my eyes, the sun was setting, darkness encroaching the wild land. I heard Lars outside and smelled a tantalizing meaty aroma. I opened the door.

"Welcome to the world of the living, kid."

"How long was I in there?"

"About six hours." He turned the meat. "I checked on you a few times, but you were so focused and peaceful, I didn't want to disturb you."

"Smells good. Elk?"

He nodded, worry lines creasing his face. "How you feeling?"

"Better, a lot better. Thanks. Wait, I need to check something." I connected to the animote and elite webs and fired anonymous, multi-factor encrypted messages to everyone I knew back home.

Are you okay? Saw the news. Reply to this, don't say anything you wouldn't want them to read. -R

People would know, but it was cryptic enough to avoid detection.

Next, I posted to several radical forums about the fire. Was it real?

Finding Zedda's old contact info, I sent her a message. She'd told me things she'd never told anyone else. There was something about her, I knew I could trust her.

Sorry about leaving. Will be back. Fitz was murdered. Don't tell Council. -R.

When I finished, I told Lars what I'd done.

"Good. Don't say anything about us or where we are." He lifted the slabs of meat from the spit and set them on small wooden plates from the kitchen. "Let's eat. Remind me after about TOR4."

It was incredible, one of the best meals of my life. Something about a bloody piece of meat relaxed me. Life felt simpler.

When we finished, I said, "So, TOR4?"

"Yeah." Lars reached into his bag and attached his band. "So, TOR4's peer-to-peer, not controlled by any company or government. Perfect for our purposes. For instance, let's see if this fire is real." His fingers flew through the air.

"Here we go." Images appeared. A thread of comments. The schoolyard, the market, my favorite restaurant... all of it charred black, lying in ruin. "Says it's real, kid," he murmured.

"So, they are all dead..." Wow... "Don't worry," I added. "I'm not going to say we have to go there. That's what they want. I won't play into their hands, won't give 'em the satisfaction."

"Good. I was a little worried."

"We can pretend though, what if we tricked the DNS into thinking we are coming? Could we use that to our advantage?"

"Maybe." He raised an eyebrow. "What'd you have in mind?"

I outlined the beginnings of a plan.

"That could work," he said when I finished. "It will take a little help, but that might just work."

33

FRIENDS AND ENEMIES

The next few days flew by: training, planning, sleeping… that was it. It was brutal, but the simple monastic life was what I needed.

One morning, I awoke to Paer's voice outside my door. What was she doing here? Jumping from bed, I opened my door, conscious of my scruffy beard and messy hair. I hadn't shaved in weeks.

Lars was talking to a hologram in the corner. "Agtha," he said, voice tense, "I need to know the Initiative's readiness for war. And this *needs* to be off the record."

"You know I can't do that, Lars. It's against protocol."

"Screw protocol!" he snapped. "After all we've been through together. I need you to do this for me."

"You sound like Lyam, you know that?" she said in a voice she'd only used with Fitz. "Have you heard from him by the way?" she added in a more serious tone. "Bugger shows up after how many years and disappears again."

"He was murdered, Ag."

"What?" She froze. "What are you talking about?"

"Lyam was murdered. By Lilia."

"Shit! Why would Lilia… wait, how do you know?"

"She was afraid he'd protest the fighting," I cut in.

"Is that Raek? Is he there now?"

"Yes." Lars flicked his wrist, and my image appeared.

I told her everything.

"Wait, Hrun?" Her jaw dropped. "Are you saying he was murdered too?"

"Why do you think I ran?" I snapped. "I saw her and Fitz fighting and heard his heart stop. She laughed about it!"

"Shit!" Her nostrils flared in a mask of rage. "I knew Lilia was extreme, but never thought she'd do something like this."

"So, Agtha," Lars interrupted, "what are the Initiative and the Council planning? We saw the Broag sting. Odds are DNS is closing in on other cells as we speak."

"The Council's been arguing since it happened. We're prepping soldiers. It won't work though. We have some citizen support, but not enough." She shook her head. "If fighting starts soon, we'll be crushed. We need more time, and more men." She sighed. "You were our only hope, kid, and you disappeared."

"What if I came back?"

"Are you coming back?" Her eyes brightened. "When?"

"I said *what if.*"

"With you, we could get more towns and militias onboard so the fighting started more places at once and spread faster. There's no guarantee, but we'd have a chance."

A chance... I could live with that.

"Look, Agtha," Lars said, tone hardening, "nothing we say here leaves this conversation, understood?"

"You know I can't—"

"Cut the crap. You need us and can't afford to do anything else. Are you in or not?"

She was, and we explained what we had in mind.

"That could buy us a few days, maybe a week. When?"

"Today, now," Lars said. "There's no time to waste. Can you make it happen?"

She nodded. "I'll manage. I'll have to call in some favors and keep certain people in the dark, but it is doable."

Good. "And then, part two," I began. Paer listened as I outlined the big picture, Lars jumping in as needed. "There's one thing," I added. "Lilia. I want Lilia and I need your help. Deal?"

"Deal, kid. I like the spunk. Give me until the end of the day to get things sorted. I'll send you an update tonight."

"Sounds good, Ag, you're a doll."

"Oh, shut up, Lars, you old dodger, you." She killed the call, leaving us to look at one another.

34

ZOOM ZOOM

The next days were a blur of planning and prep.

We got data from Paer—the readiness and placement of Initiative's troops, transports and various heavy weaponry—and tried to construct realistic scenarios for success. It wasn't promising.

She also shared intel on the army and DNS, anything the Initiative had deemed valuable enough to record. It was a mess of information, overwhelming and near impossible to find patterns or weaknesses in. The GDR seemed to be on top of everything.

Details on the towns and local militias arrived the third day. At last count, eight percent were expected to take up arms, sixty-five percent below what sims said were needed. It looked bad, but nothing was unwinnable, right? I *had* to keep telling myself that. There had to be something, there *had* to be.

I looked into the Board members' backgrounds again for any weaknesses. Nothing. Same with the military and DNS leaders. They had flawless records, or whitewashed backgrounds.

At last, the day came to leave. We still had no idea how to pull this off, but first, we had to get to Caen.

We left the cabin for the final time in silence, feet heavy with all that happened here. My time with Lars had molded me, and I'd never be the same.

When we were an hour from where we'd jumped off the train, he turned to me, eyes pained. "How'd Lyam die?" He must have been wanting to ask for ages.

"Like a hero," I said as goosebumps coated my furry, recently muscled arms. "He was trying to protect me, to keep me safe from Lilia, and out of harm's way."

Lars grimaced. "Lyam was my friend, probably my best friend," he added in a soft voice. "We had a falling out after Kira." He let out a forlorn sigh. "I never forgave myself. I'm sure he didn't either. He came to see me that night, before he died. Said he might need my help, said he was sorry." Lars took a deep breath.

I didn't know what to say, let alone feel, so I said nothing.

"Let's go get those bastards," he said after a moment, the glint back in his eyes.

I opened my mouth but a message from Paer interrupted. *Things are set here, kids. Be home for dinner. Turkey is in the oven.* "Paer says everything's ready. I'm going to spring the Kiag trap."

Opening prewritten messages, I double-checked everything. I dummy-pinged a server near Kiag, sent the messages, and I killed the connection.

We're getting ready to head home, I shot back to Paer and gave Lars the thumbs-up. "All set."

The walk to the train and ride to Caen was uneventful. We got onto the lev and snuck into the compartment without incident. It wasn't until it slowed we realized something was wrong.

Lars noticed it first, a tiny green light above the door. "Where did that come—"

The door sprung open and two glaring security guards stepped in, blasters drawn.

The first was a lean ugly fellow, 160 centimeters or so, with light curly hair, ears too big for his head, and a familiar rabbitish jitteriness. "What have we here?" he said to his partner. "Looks like a couple of stowaways."

"Hands where we can see them, both of you!" his partner snapped. He was enormous, rippling with muscle, and had the striped patterning of tigerish ancestry. His beard was impressive too, spreading from his mean black eyes to edges of his square jaw.

Both held eyes of poison, no love lost for the two of us, despite being animotes themselves.

"Search them," the big guy muttered. My fingers twitched but it was too risky, he was aiming at Lars.

"It's your turn to search them," his partner whined.

"I said search them, Joey!"

"Okay, boss." He moved forward, grabbed our bags, and checked our arms and legs. The whole time, the big guy's blaster never strayed from Lars' head.

"They're clean, boss," Joey said after an invasive search. "Although there's blasters in the bags."

"What you waiting for?" the mountain replied. "Cuff them. And what're the blasters for, eh?"

"One second," I said. What would Fitz do? I peered past them and waved at the door. "Johnny?"

Both guards turned for a fraction and my blasters hit them before they'd realized I'd fired. Sorry guys... They crumpled in a pool of blood and guts, charred organ matter spraying the walls and boxes.

"Time to go." Grabbing our bags, I sprinted for the compartment door.

We burst through and three more guards appeared, blasters pointed at the floor. I shot two and Lars hit the third, but not before he yelled, "Captain, this is Waters, I—"

He never got the rest out, but the captain must have heard the blast.

"Run!" I shouted.

Lars slammed the outside door open and stared out. The landscape raced past. We were going close to seventy kilometers per hour, way too fast to jump. We might not have a choice.

An alarm sounded, blaring through the train. Shit.

35

TUCK AND ROLL

L ess than fifteen kilometers to the city center and things didn't look good.

A VTOL took off, and for the first time, Lars looked worried. "We're going to have to jump."

His unenhanced body wouldn't stand a chance. "No way. I might be okay, but you wouldn't."

"Jump, Raek, now! Either that or I'm going first. We can't afford to lose you."

And I can't afford to lose you. Wait, what was that? "A small pond, look." I pointed. "Four kilometers, we can make it."

"Fine. But you're jumping, either way, kid, even if it's too far for me."

What choice did we have? I nodded as a realization hit me. We had to torch the place. The DNS couldn't find DNA samples or they'd realize I wasn't in Kiag.

Hurrying into the train, I went to work on the crates. There had to be something explosive. After busting several boxes, I knew it wouldn't work. Hundreds of solar cells and microturbines, but no freaking batteries or fuel cells.

We were running out of time. United Digital was a no go.

Come on, one last shot.

Cracking open The Everything Store box, I knew we were in business. It was full of Amazon Elite Vodka. Slamming the case of a hundred or so bottles, alcohol gushing about my feet, I noticed another packing label: *Olive Oil.*

Perfect. I smashed a fortune's worth of cases and waded to the doorway.

The pond was almost on us. Aiming, I fired and the booze caught fire. Two hundred fifty meters, closing fast. Here goes nothing. "You ready?" I asked.

He grabbed my shoulders and forced me toward the edge. It was getting hot. "You're jumping! I'm old and washed up. The Resistance needs you."

Not a chance. I couldn't lose another friend, not like this.

As we argued, a *BOOM*. The main crate of vodka had ignited, engulfing the boxes around it. The heat became unbearable, burning stench of oil searing my nose as we reached the pond. It was too far to jump, at least four meters. It wasn't going to work.

A flame exploded through the door and Lars yelled, "Now, kid!"

I sprinted, and as I was about to clear the edge, I grabbed him, pushing off with everything I had. The look on his face was priceless, pure anger and rabid fear, eyes wide, mouth open in a wordless scream. Straining my muscles and tendons to their max, I willed myself further as sounds of the VTOL broke the crackle. Five kilometers now.

We soared through the air but wouldn't make it. Rotating my hips and timing it with the ground beneath us, my shoulder and hip thudded first, taking the brunt of the blow.

I threw my arms over Lars' head and pulled his body into mine as we smash-rolled along, splashing into the freezing water. Seconds later, we came to a stop: soaked, sore, and shivering—but alive.

"You okay?" I asked as we crawled out.

"Thanks to you, yes. That was some stunt. Shoot, kid, are you okay?"

"I'm fine." I scratched my head. "What's wrong?"

"Your face—"

My hand was drenched in blood. "Are you bleeding?"

"That's your head, Raek!" He touched my cheek. "Are you okay? There's a massive gash down the side of your face."

Putting my hand to my cheek, I felt sticky warmth on my icy fingers. "I'm fine. We need to get out of here." Something wasn't right... "Is it me or did the VTOL stop?"

"I don't hear it either," Lars replied. "Maybe they boarded the train."

"Hopefully the fire slows 'em down. Either way, let's go." I sprinted for the treeline, Lars hurrying to catch up.

When he did, he said, "Wow, you are fine. I need to get me some of those cybernetics. Could use a new bod too."

"Maybe they'll make an exception," I said sarcastically after sending a cryptic message to Paer about the change of plans.

"If they find something, our plan's toast," Lars said as I finished.

"We'll see," I said, sounding more confident than I felt, and reminding myself of Fitz. "That's why we have a backup plan. You taught me that."

"Using my own words against me. I'll have to be—"

A VTOL took off, cutting him short. "They must have finished searching the train. Hurry."

We made it in the nick of time, a VTOL zipping overhead thirty seconds after we hit the treeline. It followed the lev track westward as we continued through the wood, thankful for the cover.

Thirty minutes later, two more *buzzed* by, one headed west, another, north. They were widening the search. At least they hadn't narrowed in on the wood, yet.

Paer called five minutes later to confirm, worried about a trap. We reassured her and asked for updates.

Everything was going according to plan. A local team with backup from Caen was prepping the Kiag mission, and Lilia and the other members of the Council had no idea what would happen next.

The hike to Eagle Creek was beautiful and relaxing. It snowed some, crystals pirouetting through the air, blanketing us and our surroundings in a soft glowing gleam. Caen was stunning this time of year.

And the snow covered our tracks, too, which helped me breathe easier.

It was a snowglobe moment, the kind you'd like to capture, store away and relive again and again.

36

SMELL THE ORGANS

A gtha arrived an hour after we did, calling as she got closer. Despite knowing she was coming, we tensed as her wheels screeched around the corner and cleared the treeline. Hitting the brakes, she made eye contact and threw open the doors. "Get in. Now!" she added, when we didn't move fast enough.

There were pressure cooker bags under her eyes like she hadn't slept for days, and her hair—always perfect despite her spartan existence—was a tousled mess.

Lars smiled. "Agtha, it's great to see you. It's been too long."

"We have to move!" she snapped. "You know how many back alleys and dirt roads I had to take to get here? Cops everywhere, tons of VTOLs searching the skies. You boys sure know how to make an entrance. How were the woods?"

"Kid picks things up fast," Lars replied. "Turns out he's got paralleosis, the super-cynetic speed reading thing."

"Good, we're going to need it," she said, white-knuckling the wheel while Lars embarrassed me, bragging about what I'd been reading.

Once Lars relented, she said, "Council's meeting tomorrow at noon. That's when we should do it."

"Can you sneak us in?" Lars asked.

"Can I beat you in a fight blindfolded, Lars?" Her eyes twinkled in the rearview. "It's good to see you, you old fart."

So, she was human after all.

"You've gotten old after all these years," Lars said with a grin. "Wanted to make sure you still had it."

Paer swore. "We got company. Get in the back, in the boxes. Now!"

In the trunk were two boxes labeled *Hearts* and *Organs*. The tops were open.

I hopped the divider and scrambled in. Lars fell over a second later, squeezing to fit his long body as the car slowed to a crawl.

"Pretty tight in here, Agtha. Could have used bigger boxes," Lars remarked.

"Have you put on weight, Lars?" she whispered. "Quiet, twenty meters. Stopping now."

An electric whirr. "Everything okay, officer?"

"What are you doing out here?" a gruff voice replied.

"I'm picking up a shipment from my brother-in-law," Paer answered.

"A shipment of what?" the voice snapped.

"Deer," Paer said. "Hunts whitetails and gets me to lug the kills back to the city. Lazy git. I get to keep some of the meat though, so it works out. But the bastard gave me organs this time."

"Where's he hunt?" the other officer asked. "He got a permit?"

"He alternates between parks west and north of the city, the ones he could get permits for." She sighed. "South and east are reserved for elites, that's where all the best game is, he says."

"We're going to need to inspect your vehicle, ma'am. Please step out and turn off the engine."

Crap. Not good.

"Sure thing, officers. You fellas hunt?" Come on, Paer, let's see some smooth talking.

"Nah," said the first. "Wife's against it for some reason."

"Same here. Open your trunk."

My breath caught. This was about to get ugly. I tried to position myself for a clean shot but it was too cramped. My muscles tensed. We'd be sitting ducks.

"You officers like organs: hearts, tongues, testicles, that kind of thing? That's all Frankie gave me this time, cheap bastard! Imagine, my poor sister, living with that scum of a man! I'd be happy to give you boys a couple *testes* or tongues if I could get on my way. Got a work shift at 18:00 and can't afford to be late *again*. Boss'll kill me. You know how it is."

Testes… she was laying it on thick.

"Look, lady, you seem okay. But we gotta check. Can't risk our jobs either."

Damn.

"No worries, gentlemen. Pinch your noses. Bags aren't sealed," she added.

"Wait a sec, wait a sec. Jeorg, look. Says here Hearts and Organs. If we open this, we got to report it. That's *a lot* of paperwork. Our kids are at their grandparents'. I got things planned for the wife. Show her *my* organs, if you know what I mean. Let's leave it."

"I don't know," Jeorg said. "I need this job but…" he hesitated.

I held my breath. Everything was riding on this.

"You know what, fine, but you owe me, Tak. Anyone asks, this was *your* idea."

"Yeah, yeah. It was my idea. Let's get you to a bar somewhere and find you a nice piece too."

"Sure you don't want to *smell*, I mean see the organs?" Paer asked.

I almost laughed. Paer had never eaten organs a day in her chimpish life. But she did have a sense of humor…

"We're good, lady. Get out of here. Drive safe. And this never happened!" he added.

"What never happened?" she asked.

They laughed, and we heard the crunch of boots. Phew. Paer hopped in, closed the door and started the engine. That was close.

"Stay down until I tell you otherwise," Paer said, her dominant self again.

"The testicles bit was brilliant, Agtha, no man wants to—"

"Shut up, Lars!" she snapped. "There might be listening devices. We'll talk later."

We drove in silence another hour, pulling off the road twice as VTOLs raced by until the car skidded to a stop. "We're here."

A *thunk* as Paer opened the trunk. Ugh. We twisted out as my muscles and joints strained in protest. At last, my jellied feet touched solid ground. Wait. "Where are we?"

"An abandoned area of the industrial park a kilometer from base," she replied.

Huh? I gave her a funny look.

"I wanted time to talk things over without people breathing down our necks," she said. "There's a tunnel that connects the two buildings, used to be owned by the same company. Leave at 22:00 tonight. It takes ten minutes to walk, and I'll meet you on the other side. I'll show you."

She took us into the building's semi-finished basement. In the far corner was an iron trapdoor, shiny circular handle protruding from the left side.

"It's unlocked. Follow this, you can't miss it." She glanced at her band. "Shoot, I need to go. I'm sparring Ashlo at 15:30. I'll disable the sensors in the tunnel for tonight. See you, 22:10, *sharp*. Don't be late!" She turned and vanished.

We killed time discussing the plan for the thousandth time, it never hurt. Once we felt ready, talk turned to the impending war. Still nothing we could exploit. We needed something soon and were running out of time, but Lars said to, "Relax and put my head to it."

It came down to the Board, it had to. But how to kill the alphas? I'd tried everything I could think of. "Any ideas?"

"Have you tried TOR4?" he asked.

"You're right." How'd I forget that? As I opened a profile on Gregori Schwarz, he swung his leg toward me and I spun him into a triangle choke.

"Schwarz keeps a low profile," I said. "Studied advanced computer

systems and architectures while serving with distinction in the DNS."
Impressive.

Lars tapped my arm, and I released him. "Operated in hot zones
early in his career. After that, he disappeared until being elected to the
Board twenty-five years ago. Oh, and he went emulate."

"This is getting too easy for you, isn't it?" Lars said in mock frustration, dusting himself off. "Turn off the enhancements and let's practice striking."

They were, and I said as much, so we stopped sparring.

"Last one's Priya Patel," I said. "Minister of Infrastructure, a
cynetic. Built her fortune in city planning and transportation. Her old
startup accounts for eighty percent of housing and transport in the
major fifty cities."

"Kids?"

Maybe on TOR4. How'd I not think of that?

"Nothing on Lin Zu, the consummate politician. Works a ton, no
life. Although there are pictures of her flying a VTOL. Maybe a
hobby."

"And Jean Gileu's married, has a husband. Don't see any kids, and
can't find much on the husband. Wait, here's something on the Security guy though, Calter. Oh, snap. He's got a son."

A picture materialized: Thorn. "That's where I recognized him! It's
the eyes."

"What eyes?" Lars asked. "What are you talking about?"

"Remember the DNS guys who arrested us, shipped Fitz and I to
Caen? There was one guy, the leader, Thorn. There was something evil
about him, inhuman. Hated-filled black eyes that sucked hope and
happiness from your soul. When I saw Calter's picture, it clicked.
Calter has a son, Thorn."

"That means…" Things were going a mile a minute. He must be
dying for revenge.

"Think he's in Kiag?" Lars asked, as if reading my mind.

"Actually, yeah." Thorn could be our leverage over Calter. "So, we
ambush the surprise attack, grab Thorn, and send a spoofed message
to his dad for help. If we make it something embarrassing, Calter

would come alone. He wouldn't want others finding out. Then we grab him." Was that the key to everything?

"And we can torture or simhack the information out of him if we have to," Lars added. "We'll have—"

"No!" I snapped, louder than intended. The pain I'd been through still haunted me. "No torture, not even VR. If we do, we're as bad as them." No... A calming breath. "I'll get him to tell us, I've got a plan!"

"How the heck you going to do that?" Lars raised an eyebrow. "Without torturing him?"

I explained what I had in mind.

"Well, I'll be damned," he said at last. "We've got our plan."

Time flew by and before we knew it, it was ten minutes to ten.

Lars opened the trapdoor. It was pitch black, and steep but I activated my infrareds. "Looks good from here. I'll go first."

Lars grimaced. "Be my guest, kid. I always hated tunnels and small spaces."

We dropped in, feet clattering on concrete, and I led the way, Lars' hands on my shoulders to avoid getting separated. Imagine how dark this was for him. I'd forgotten life before cybernetics and had no desire to go back.

Near the end of the tunnel, a muffled voice. "What are you doing, Agtha? It's a bit late to be out and about, isn't it?"

"Oh, Lilia, I didn't see you. I needed a little fresh air, that's all."

"You've been off lately. Is everything okay?"

"I'm fine," Paer said, a little too fast. "It's been crazy the last few days is all."

"I know what's up, Agtha. Don't think you can fool me."

I froze. No...

How could Lilia know?

37
———

GODS AND GODDESSES

"You do?" Paer croaked. A hint of doubt crept into her always confident voice.

"Of course I do." Shit.

"Look, Lilia—" Paer began.

"No, I get it. If you ever want to talk about it, let me know."

"What?"

A pause. "You had a thing for Lyam, didn't you?" Lilia said. "You always wanted him, and he came back. But then he up and left again."

"You knew?"

Phew, that was close.

"Your secret's safe with me," Lilia said in a conspiratorial whisper. "Did you talk before he left? Did he tell you where they were headed?"

"No!" Paer snapped. "Old geezer disappeared without saying anything. Bastard."

"I'm so sorry, Agtha. If I can ever help, say the word."

"Thanks, Lilia."

"That's what friends are for. I have to go, big day tomorrow, with the vote and all. See ya." Lilia's footsteps echoed in the distance.

A few minutes later, Agtha opened the hidden passage with a furtive glance. "Hurry."

We snuck through the corridors and were to a room five minutes later. She slid the door open, pushed us through and poked her head in. "Keep this locked, don't leave. That was a close call earlier. I need to go before anyone sees me. Noon tomorrow, be ten minutes late. Don't knock."

She spun, closing the door, and left us standing there, dumb-founded, tired, and amped all at once. Talk about a day.

I meditated for a bit while Lars opted for sleep. How he could sleep at a time like *this*? My head swirled with thoughts, memories, plans; a sea of adrenaline and danger. Focus, Raek.

After meditating, I still couldn't sleep. Too much to do, too much to worry about. Procrastinating, I found a history of mythology online. Why not? The whole concept of deities was absurd, but they'd played a critical role in shaping humanity. Why? It made no sense.

Still, I remembered what Lars said about being a charismatic Jesus. Yeah right. It was preposterous, ethically and factually wrong. But what made rational people so susceptible to the supernatural? Why had every culture before the Fall worshipped some strange god or another?

What was it?

I spent thirty minutes trying to figure it out. From the newer Christianity, Islam, and Hinduism, to the older, more exciting Norse legends, Greek gods, and Egyptian pharaohs... there were hundreds, the stories fascinating.

As my eyes closed, I sensed a trend. They were all tales, from half-god Hercules' heroic feats to Jesus turning water to wine; from rain dances to witch hunts and human sacrifice... they were all the same: bedtime stories, passed down and intentionally—or accidentally—altered for effect.

Storytelling 101: hyperbole, propaganda, iteration. Nothing had changed. That's how the GDR controlled so many with little to no violence.

The story was *everything*.

That was big. No idea how... but I couldn't let it go for some reason.

My dreams were dominated by gods and goddesses, war, violence, fire... Heavens and earth ripped apart, restored, and ripped open again.

Strands of DNA circled the planet, and the world became a sea of numbers and letters. Shaking, it morphed, letters becoming words, a story. I could write that story.

Fear surged as I struggled. Something was holding me down.

"Calm down, kid," Lars said. "Everything's okay."

My eyes blinked open. Lars?

"It's okay, kid. You're safe."

"What? Where am I? What happened?"

"We're at Initiative headquarters, Raek. In Caen. Remember?"

Maybe... Something like a memory floated, waiting to be redis-covered.

"But the world, the planet, the war... what happened?" My voice was jagged.

"It was a dream, kid, just a dream."

My SmartCore showed a heart rate of 162 bpm. "It was so real."

"Just a dream," Lars repeated. "Want to talk about it?"

"I'm good." I didn't want to relive it. "So, two hours until the meeting." Please change the subject...

He nodded. "You ready?"

I was.

We headed out at noon, silent. Along the way, I was anxious, checking corners and over our shoulder. This was no man's land.

We reached the Council room at 12:07 without incident and paused, looking at each other.

His face was etched in granite resolve. "Know what you're going to say?"

"I guess we'll find out." I opened the door and stepped in.

38

BLOODY MARINARA

The room was just as I remembered it, dull and outdated, but with an air of power. Around the table sat the six Council members, Lilia still occupying Hrun's old seat.

"As I was saying—" she began before recognition dawned. Her eyes flared a second. "Raek, you're back. We were so worried. Is Lyam here?"

"Shut up, Lilia!" I snapped. "Don't you dare say his name."

"Raek, is everything okay?" She looked concerned, her voice placating.

"Cut the crap. I know you murdered him, murdered your own friend because he got in the way. I was there!" I yelled. "I heard it. I heard *everything!*"

"What are you talking about, Raek? You must have gone through—"

"Quiet, Lilia!" Paer cut in. "Let the boy speak."

"So, you're in on this too?" Lilia glared at Paer. "Is this a coup?"

"What are you saying, boy?" Mico's unsure eyes bounced between us.

"I'm saying Lilia and two of her cronies killed your friend Lyam, administered some nanodrug with Potassium Chloride. It gave him a heart attack! I heard the whole thing." I stared at her, seething. "I think she did the same with Hrun."

Something felt wrong. I couldn't place it, but something was *off*. Lilia's hand twitched. What could it be? Gun, itch, unconscious tick, call for help... I tensed.

"Raek, why would I do something like that?" Her voice had taken on a honeyed innocence.

"Power!" I growled. "Power and control. That's been—"

The door behind us burst open.

I reacted, diving. Small spherical projectiles bounced in as I tackled Lars. They exploded and I brought my blaster to bear, shockwaves rippling the room.

My shots missed, blasts of light whizzing past me. The intruders had opened fire.

Most of the Council had been thrown to the floor. Blood dripped from Lars' forehead and my ears rang. Was he okay?

Rolling, I dodged shots streaking toward me. A flash. Lilia sprinted past and the traitors disappeared into the hallway.

Jumping up, I checked Lars. He'd live. The rest were okay too, just dazed.

I darted out the door. She wasn't getting away, not again. Hurried footsteps ahead.

Rounding the corner, someone sprang. Skirting the knife and their blaster, my claws tore at his throat as two more appeared, lobbing lethal micronades my way.

I shot the first from the air and kicked the second away. Explosions engulfed the hallway, smoke billowing, as alarms rang.

Dashing through the soot, I fired twice. They crumpled before they knew what hit them. Where was Lilia?

At the main entrance, the ground in front of me erupted. Dodging behind the barrier, Lilia screamed, "Don't make me do it, Raek!"

Do what?

I peered out, ducking as two more blasts hurtled past. Lilia stood across the expanse, arm wrapped around Fenni's delicate throat. Fenni's eyes bulged in inhuman fear.

Another glance. Lilia had shifted her gun to a stammering Fenni's head. "Lilia, I, I don't understand. What—"

"Shut up, you gossiping, good for nothing skank!" Lilia's eyes raged. "This is all your fault!"

"Lilia, let's talk about this!" I stepped from behind the wall.

"You ruined everything!" she spat. "Not a step closer. Don't! I'll do it."

Would she? I put my hands up. "Let her go. You don't have to do this." If I could lure her into a false sense of security... How long it would take to shoot her? This wasn't Fenni's fault. "We can do this, together, you and me. We can overthrow the government, make things right." She was nodding.

I took a step forward and she stiffened, hatred shattering her calm. "One more step and I'll blow her brains out!"

Fenni whimpered, pants darkening as her bowels released. Shit, Lilia wasn't kidding.

Shifting my body, I took a step back and lined up the shot. I had it. Deep breath. One chance. Fenni couldn't die too.

Three, two—Lilia fired. Nooo... Fenni collapsed, blood spraying everywhere as I fired twice and Lilia leveled her blaster.

Lilia's shot went wide, but mine rang true, launching her into the air. She smashed the wall behind her with a crimson *thud*.

I sprinted over.

Poor Fenni. She hadn't stood a chance, head blown off before I could react. Why had I hesitated?

"You bastard!" Lilia's eyes were unfocused, breath coming in short, sporadic bursts as she grabbed the gaping hole in her chest. "You, you —" A fit of hoarse coughing sent spasms through her body as blood drained out of her, pooling on the floor.

I stepped closer, and she raised a determined hand. Against all odds, she'd held on to her blaster. "You!" she whispered in a quiet scream as her eyes locked onto mine.

Her gun twitched but I fired first, finishing the job.

"That's for Fitz, bitch!"

Lilia slumped to the floor, unrecognizable, upper part of her face and torso gone.

Feet clattered. Paer, Zedda, and Obowe appeared, gasping. Several more popped out of neighboring hallways yelling and crying. They had no idea what was going on.

"Order!" Paer roared. "Order!" She got things under control before it got out of hand.

Everyone was breathing hard. They walked to Fenni, then to Lilia. No point checking either.

Paer turned to the small crowd that had gathered. "Everything's okay. Trust me!"

They looked from Lilia to me to Paer, and back again, eyes wide. No one said anything.

"Someone get maintenance to clean this!" Zedda said. "What happened?" she added in a softer tone, curious.

"Lars? Is, is he okay?" I stammered. I couldn't lose him too.

Zedda nodded.

Phew. "Come on. Let's go back to the Council room. We should talk about this in private."

After a quick chat with maintenance, we trudged back. It was a long and somber slog.

Ganla jumped to her feet when we arrived but sat on Paer's cue, eyes narrowed and blaster on her lap.

Lars had stopped bleeding and gave me a questioning look. "Fast thinking there, kid. You must have had a good teacher." He laughed, wheezing in pain as he did.

"Raek, Lars," Obowe said. "What is this?"

"Let the kid explain," Lars said. "Raek, tell them about Lilia. Tell them what you told me."

I told them everything despite the suspicious eyes and furrowed brows, and left nothing out. I told them about running away, finding Lars, escaping the city, even the cabin in the woods. By the end, they were shocked.

Everyone was silent for a good minute to digest what had happened and what I'd said. After a while, Paer spoke up, "They've been brainstorming ways we can maybe win this war. We had to keep you in the dark. I am sorry. We couldn't risk Lilia discovering what we were up to."

I explained the wolf pack concept of cutting off the head to kill the serpent, and outlined what we'd planned in Kiag.

Last, I brought up their original vision of me as a figurehead. "It sucks, but I think we have to. I don't see any other way." We'd exaggerate and hyperbolize as needed.

"I'll only do it one condition," I added when I'd finished. "We publicize everything once this is over. Including the fact that I'm not some deity or higher power, just an ordinary guy. And I won't rule if we win the war! I don't want that kind of responsibility or to be tempted with *that* kind of power. We create a true democracy, one person, one vote, with *no one* in this room eligible to run." No ulterior motives. "Those are my conditions. Do you accept? We can leave the room while you talk it over."

"That won't be necessary," Paer said.

Her fellow Council members nodded in agreement.

"Good," I answered. The room was dead silent. "Then, as of this moment, we are officially at war!"

39

GAME ON

"We need to get you out there, Raek," Paer said. "Get people united around hope. If we want a revolution we stand a chance at winning, they need a leader." Did I really agree to this? "Lars, you're a wizard with words and manipulation. Want to be in charge of that?"

"It'd be my pleasure, Ag," Lars replied with a devious grin. "So, dark web press releases, videos, articles, animote and elite web... maybe a speech or two—oh, and TOR4. Am I missing anything?"

No one said anything.

"Raek." Lars looked at me like I was the only one in the room. "You sure you're okay with this? Talking about what happened... It humanizes you, shows your dedication. But it's up to you, kid."

They all looked at me, and I wondered again—not for the first time—how some sixteen-year-old wolfish kid from some middle of nowhere town got so far out of his depth. This was going to be harder than I thought, *a lot* harder. I stifled a protest, there was too much at stake.

"I'm in," I said at last.

"So, this is all well and good," Ganla remarked, "but have we figured out the most important part: how to take out the Board?"

"We don't have to decide now," Paer said to avoid a frustrating downward spiral. "We have until Operation Kiag to finalize things. After that, timing is everything."

The meeting ended and a dent in the wall caught my eye. If those had been micronades instead of flashbangs earlier, we'd all be dead. I pushed the thought away as Lars, Zedda, and Obowe roped me into dinner. As long as it wasn't loaf, again...

It was off hours when we got to the mess. The place was quiet, Anti singing away as he prepared a tantalizing meatball marinara. It wasn't ready.

The half-empty metal serving trays were filled with bacon, eggs, and sausage—the staples of a happy, healthy, breakfast. I loaded up, Lars too, and we snagged coffee and an empty table in the corner.

"So, Hrun was murdered?" Zedda murmured at last in a pained voice. "He pretty much adopted me after my parents died."

I put my arm around her. "Fitz and I thought so." Wait, my hand was on her shoulder. No! I pulled it away, mortified. Did she know I liked her?

"So, how do we pull this off?" I said to keep things positive and divert attention. She hadn't noticed, right? "It's what they'd have wanted. They gave their lives to the fight and they wouldn't want us wasting time and energy mourning. There's *always* a solution if you find it, that's what Fitz always said. "

Zedda sighed. "Beats me."

"I am a fighter, not a planner," Obowe said. "Give me an opponent, and I will smash them with honor, but tactics were never my strong suit." His huge shoulders slumped.

"Lars, Obowe, what would Fitz—I mean Lyam—have said? What would he do?"

"He'd think of everything. We'd brainstorm for hours," Lars began, a distant look in his eyes. "We'd come up with plans and shoot the other's down, finding flaws until it was perfect. I focused on details, he preferred big picture." He paused. "Stripes would say 'don't think about Board members, think about the Board as a whole. Don't think about individual battles, think about the war.' We worked well like that."

Could you be more vague? "We've thought about the Board, looked into 'em a ton. There isn't much to go on."

"Have you seen our files?" Zedda asked. "We have dossiers on each. It's not much, but maybe you overlooked something," she added with a hopeful smile. "Give me a second." She tapped her smartband.

A screen appeared above the table and we moved our plates aside. "Here's what we got. Feel free." She made a four sign and passed out copies. We each grabbed a digital version, and I added mine to my SmartCore.

Skimming, I flipped through.

"Okay," I said a minute later. "This is stuff we already knew."

Obowe's jaw dropped. "You read it all?"

Lars chuckled and told him about the paralleosis.

Obowe raised an eyebrow. "A genius."

"Not exactly," I murmured, face burning. "I read a little faster than normal, that's all."

"A *little* faster!" Lars snorted to rub it in. "Raek went from Brazilian Jiu-jitsu novice to besting me—a world class grappler with thirty years experience—in four weeks." He elbowed my ribs. "He's too humble."

"Whatever." I brushed off the compliment. "This is stuff we know. Five Board members, three emulates, two cynetics. Here's the voting history for the last five years. Voted to increase numbers of DNS in towns, rejected a proposal for a thousand new emulates, authorized additional resources in the Broag sting, increased World Bank's interest rate half a percent in 2096 and a couple smaller things. They agree on most things, but there's a twenty percent higher incidence between emulates and cynetics with their fellow subspecies."

"Wait!" Zedda snapped her fingers. "Did you say *twenty percent* higher? Seems high." She raised an eyebrow. "Trouble in paradise?"

"You're right!" I skimmed back, mind racing. My wolfish instincts were on the hunt, senses intensifying. "There might be something here." How'd I miss that?

"They're jealous," Obowe replied matter-of-factly. "Who would not want to live forever without fear of death? How many cynetics have you alone killed, Raek?" he added, eyes proud.

"You've got a point," Lars said. "Emulates... no one likes emulates, except maybe emulates, and probably not even them."

"Zedda, Obowe, you guys came up with the idea, you tell the others," I said. If I'd learned anything from Lars' leadership books, it was credit where credit was due.

Brief smiles crossed their faces and Lars gave me an approving look.

My alarm *buzzed*. "Wow, time flies. We need to go!" I headed for more coffee. The last few days had been brutal. "Anybody else?"

They shook their heads and I poured.

Another notification. *Breaking news*. I opened the feed.

The camera panned to black-clad officers storming a nondescript gray building. 'Authorities in Estovo raided another terrorist cell. The group—members of the animote terror alliance known as The Resistance—are implicated in the bombings of two elite hospitals in Zone Three, killing fifteen people, and the murder of several prominent journalists who'd written an anti-rebel story earlier this week. Sources within the DNS tell me we had credible evidence they were planning larger maternity ward bombings throughout the city.'

I slammed my fist on the wooden table and coffee spilled everywhere. Zedda jumped.

"Did we order an attack on a maternity ward?" I snapped.

"What? What are you talking about?" Obowe's face was blank confusion.

"The news, the cell in Estovo. A hit on a hospital?" I stared icily at each in turn.

"What do you mean?" Zedda tilted her head. "We don't have a cell in Estovo..."

"Are you positive?" My eyes never left hers. I *had* to be sure. "It's all over the news."

"That's bullshit!" she swore. "We don't even have a team in Estovo." We don't? "We've been trying for years. Area's a DNS stronghold."

"So it's a lie?" I said.

"I know nothing of this," Obowe replied. "We are not responsible. A hospital, Raek? Have we no honor?" He gave me a look that spoke volumes.

"I'm sorry." I felt my face flush. "I don't know what to believe anymore."

"That's the point," Lars said, calm and professional as always. "To turn the public against us. Can you prove it? Can you prove it wasn't us?"

Obowe grumbled. "If we published a list of our bases… which we cannot."

"There has to be a way!" I said. Think. "If we show the lie for what it is. That'd be huge." But how?

"And if it was Raek who broadcast it, the half animote, half cynetic…" Lars grinned. "His reputation would take off."

I grimaced. It was bad enough as it was… But he could be onto something. "Has it happened before?"

"It's not the first time," Zedda remarked

"Not good enough." I shook my head. "We need specifics: times, dates, facts. We need a rock solid case."

Lars thought Agtha would know.

I pinged her as we hustled to the Council room, small groups hanging about, discussing the carnage. They stared as we stormed by, our echoing footsteps the sole challenge to the awkward void of Lilia's demise.

Paer flew in as we sat, gliding to her seat. "What is it?" she said in a hopeful voice. "I came as fast as I could."

I opened the news story, activated the room's holo and projected it for everyone. "This!" I explained what we were thinking.

When I finished, she said. "That wasn't us. I don't know how we prove it, at least this time, but I can think of eight or nine other instances. You're saying we go public?" She looked skeptical.

Lars took over and outlined our reasoning. We needed public support to win this war.

"You cheeky bastard. That could work," she said as he finished and the others filed in. It looked like we were in business.

The meeting flew by, a flurry of action and debate, prep and strategy. When we called it quits five hours later, I was pretty happy with the progress. There were a few things to sort out, but on the whole, things were moving.

But was it fast enough?

40

HIDE AND SEEK

I turned to answer Lars to find I was alone on the cold hard floor of my two by three room, lying on the cheap micro pad. Did I dream that?

It didn't matter. It would work, I knew it.

Almost six a.m. No point trying to sleep. Let's see where my feet took me.

The hallways were dark as I exited my cubicle, reddish glow enveloping everything.

The emulates were the key, they always were. Despite being five percent of the population, they were the ones with true power and influence, the ones we all despised.

It must be strange to be immortal, to not fear dying. I'd never thought about it. With a backed up brain-field, you do anything, like a Get Out of Jail Free card. Were they more prone to risk?

Paer? "You're awake?" I asked as she walked toward me.

"I always get up early. Gives me time to train and think. You?"

"Couldn't sleep. Had an idea and had to work it out."

She raised a dark eyebrow. "Want to tell me about it?"

"The emulates are the key to everything. They control three-fifths of the Board and the majority of the Lower Government."

Her brow furrowed.

"We've been thinking about assassinating the Board," I said, "to cripple their leadership and leave the GDR in chaos. What if we killed their immortality instead? Could destroying the brain-field banks have the same effect?"

"I'll be honest, it isn't something we've considered."

"Really? Why not?"

She shrugged. "Too far-fetched I guess. Wouldn't know where to begin."

"But you think it could work?" I asked.

"Maybe... if we pulled off the other parts, I mean. But how do we find the storage locations? Those are their brain-fields—their everything—they must be *incredibly* well protected and hidden."

I shook my head. "I'm not so sure. I don't think you can have both. You can't be both well hidden, and well protected. Protection means people and weapons, right? And those people talk, or show up in stats. Makes 'em hard to hide."

"Fair point."

"The emulates don't want others to know, especially the cynetics," I added. "So the locations have to be secret. They're hidden, so they can't be well protected. And what emulate would work guard duty? So, it must be animotes or enhancers working there. They probably wouldn't want enhancers. Might figure out what they're guarding and have the political power to do something about it."

"So we look for that in the data," she finished, understanding at last what I meant.

Bingo! "We do that, hit the possible locations. Heck, it could be a single facility or two. Would make 'em easier to hide. If we do that and destroy the brain-field backups, the world changes overnight. *If* we defeat the GDR at the same time, we've got our revolution." I couldn't help but grin.

"I'm impressed," she said. "You were just a boy when you first came here—a strong boy who'd gone through hell and back, sure—but a boy nonetheless. You've grown, Raek. The plan has legs." She put her hand on my shoulder in the first real sentimentality I'd seen from her.

I nodded, not sure what to say. "Thanks," I said at last, not trusting myself to say more. Coming from Paer, it meant a lot after all I'd been through. She left not long after.

Three hours to kill before the Council meeting, I had to think. Our data on GDR forces was disappointing, old and sporadic. We wouldn't get what we needed. And we couldn't miss a *single* brain-field facility or they'd recover. It had to be a total reset of the playing field.

How could we get that intel? That was *the* question.

Calter came to mind. He was the Minister of Security and while he was cynetic, if anyone knew exact troop deployments and military facility locations, it *had* to be him.

That was it! That's how we'd use Thorn.

Operation Kiag had taken on new significance. If we could capture Thorn, we could blackmail his dad... That could work.

We could get the intel.

41

I BELIEVE I CAN FLY

E xcited, I got to the Council meeting early and read the Mandela biography Lars had given me. He was fascinating. If only I could be more like him...

The door opened, and Zedda entered. She looked beautiful.

"You're early." I minimized the book from view, nervous. Why was it *always* like this with girls?

She smiled, running her hand through her hair. "Needed some time to think. You?"

"Same. Had a few books to read."

"How you doing with everything? Being the *chosen one* and all?" She laughed but it didn't quite reach her eyes.

Ugh. "To be honest, it's weird."

"Well, I for one, am glad you're back. We all are." She turned to the door as her cheeks brightened. "Was pretty hopeless for a while."

"What will you do when this is all over?" I asked, to change the subject. Was I trying to get to know her better? Why?

She shrugged. "I don't know. Never thought about it."

"Think about it." A flirty smile tickled my lips. What was I doing? "What would you do?"

"I'd like to do something, I don't know, something meaningful. Something I loved that also helped others."

"Like what?" She was pretty. But there was no future for us, her, chimpish and me, wolfish...

She smiled, cheeks reddening further. "I've always loved animals, being outdoors too. As a girl, I'd bring critters home all the time. Mom hated it, but Dad found it fun. I'd make little homes for them: mice and crickets and ants, everything in a little glass globe in our room."

"Sounds fun."

"It was, until one day they were gone. I asked Dad what happened. Apparently Reggie—that's what I called my mouse, a gray little guy with chalky whiskers and the cutest smile—had eaten all of them. They were all dead. The next day, Mom left the door open to air out. When I came home from school, a cat had knocked over the container and was dragging Reggie out the window. Reggie's screams were horrible. I never wanted pets after that."

Jeez. What do you say to that? "How old were you?" I asked after an uncomfortable silence, wanting to put my arm around her but not sure if I should.

"Nine," she answered. "I learned that day, some species don't belong together, they don't play nice. I also learned I should be the cat. Life's better as a hunter."

Stunned, I opened my mouth to say something—anything—but the door opened. Obowe and Ganla shuffled in, and Mico followed seconds later. Before long, everyone was seated around the table.

Shaken from Zedda's story, I stood, taking charge, highlighting progress since last night and the new plan to capture Thorn as thoughts of Zedda clouded my clarity. Paer thought it was doable, if our guys knew who to look for, but there were no pictures of Thorn anywhere.

She had a point.

"I'll go," I said. "I'm the only one who can identify him, and besides, it's me he's after. Plus, I know the area."

"I'm coming with you!" Zedda blurted out, concern filling her eyes for the briefest of seconds. "You'll need backup." Damn it, she was stubborn.

"Bring Henk and Ashlo too," Paer added. "They both fly so you can take a VTOL."

I threw up my hands. "We have to keep things small. Too many people will attract attention." And flying... Oh, crap... flying? "Won't we be detected?"

"Not if we stay low," Lars remarked. "The Earth's magnetic fields block out anything below twenty meters. And you'll have to make room for one more because I'm coming too," he added with a grin. "I've come too far to let you die on me now."

"It's settled," Paer said. "You'll meet our team on site. They'll help with logistics and firepower. You have three days. We can't wait any longer."

Zedda went to find Henk and Ashlo, and in no time, things were set. We grabbed our gear, a few goodies from storage, and set off.

Someone had sent for a VTOL, and it had been delivered from the underground bunker a few kilometers away. It was a work of art despite its age. Flying... My stomach was in knots.

It's *only* twenty meters, it's only twenty meters.

The five of us scrunched through small hatch-like doors and took our seats. Inside, it was bigger than it seemed. Bucket seating for eight, black pods bolted to the floor and ceiling, extra harnesses.

Up front, Henk and Ashlo sat in the miniature cockpit which seemed too basic. A couple knobs and gauges, a single joystick and a few screens. Was that all? Did Henk know what he was doing?

Engines revved and we lifted off, shooting up. My stomach flipped. After five seconds, we were level with the roof. *A lot* higher than I'd expected. What had I gotten myself into?

Henk laughed. "Here we go, kids."

I clenched the armrest as we accelerated, and something touched my hand. I jumped.

"Raek, it's okay. It's me." Zedda took my hand. I was glad it was dark. "We'll be fine. First time?" she asked in a hushed voice.

"Yeah. I like having my feet on the ground," I said as coolly as I could.

She squeezed my hand.

"We'll get there around one a.m.," Lars announced after we'd been flying a while. "Raek, spoof a server somewhere you know well. We need Thorn to *know* where to find us."

I knew the perfect place, where I'd found Elly's body. The Black Forest.

The rest of the journey went without a hitch. As we got closer, I got butterflies. I was going home... but it'd been wiped off the map. And it was *my* fault.

"We should land there." I pointed. "Gives us plenty of time and it should be safe."

We landed, piled out of the aircraft, grabbed our gear, and suited up.

As we were getting ready to leave, the moment I'd been dreading. "Henk, you should stay here with the VTOL. We might need backup or a quick getaway."

He adjusted his vest and gave me a dismissive look. "Not happening. I'm coming with you!"

"We need you here, Henk," Lars added. "If something happens or we catch Thorn we'll need *you* to save our asses."

I knew which levers to pull, but would it work? "If anything, this is more dangerous. You're alone, *you* won't have backup." I put my hand on his shoulder. "We need you, buddy, we need you."

He gritted his teeth, glaring at me. "Fine," he growled after a long pause. "I'll do it. But you call if anything happens, *anything*! Got it?"

I nodded.

"Now that's sorted, let's get a move on, boys, before the sun's up," Zedda grumbled.

I gave her a smile, glad to have her along, as we took off into the night.

42

THE POUNCE

We made good progress considering how cold, dark, and snowy it was, covering four kilometers an hour as we hurried through my old stomping ground. I led the way, a mini lamp on my pack to guide the others.

Memories came flooding back.

The pond where I'd kissed Saley Smith two summers earlier, before the GDR tripled their rent, evicting her family and breaking my heart. Our Star Wars logship Vynce, Toras, and I had ridden in search of better, more equal worlds.

So many reminders, so much had passed; they were gone.

As we got closer, we all stiffened. We'd heard the horror stories of Resistance rendezvous. Young, trigger-happy soldiers meeting other terrified rebels was a recipe for disaster. Add guns and the possibility of betrayal or being intercepted by the DNS, and it was no wonder there were accidental shootings.

I pinged Commander Nim.

He replied seconds later, *Affirmative soldier.*

Good. We should be—movement in the trees to our right. What was that?

Whoosh.

I dove and rolled for cover. Zedda and Ashlo hit the deck as well, leveling their blasters. Lars just stood there, laughing.

"It's an owl, kids. Be careful, it might *hoot* you to death." He chuckled.

Talk about jitters. I rose, dusting snow from my pants, blushing. We were all on edge.

Zedda strode toward the treeline as Ashlo covered her.

"It's all clear!" She turned, lowering her weapon. "It was just—"

The words died as something pounced, flattening pines, and knocking her to the side. A massive paw flashed and sent her careening through the air.

The beast charged.

It was huge, some sick cross between a bear and tiger, a vicious pointed snout, murderous eyes. and jaws to crush a truck.

Ashlo got off a shot but missed, misjudging its speed. I aimed, firing twice, catching the behemoth in the side. It didn't flinch.

Shit. My team couldn't see what was happening. Their goggles weren't on and only I had night vision and infrared.

It leapt at Lars, whose blaster was out but didn't see it coming.

My third shot hit the rippling foreleg but it didn't react. I rushed it, desperate to reach it before it mauled Lars.

Lars fired again, but it was too close and he missed, blowing a hole clean through a pine tree to the side.

"What is that thing?" Ashlo yelled, securing goggles to his head alongside Zedda, who was lying there, unconscious, maybe dying... My sensors said her heart was beating, but *barely*. Hurry. Was she okay? I couldn't lose her.

My SmartCore analyzed the monster in a split second. Five hundred kilos, three meters in length. How could something so big move so fast?

Scans showed a weak underbelly and jugular area. Judging from the blasts earlier, the skin and fur must be tougher than they appeared. A gun wouldn't cut it, but I had to save Lars.

Not another friend, not after Fitz.

We collided midair before it hit Lars, my shoulder crashing into it, fist connecting with its right eye. The force knocked the brute to the side, missing Lars by a hair's breadth.

A sickening roar as paw whirled toward my unprotected head. I blocked it, muscles straining. Shit, I had to finish this fast, or we were all dead.

"I don't have a clean shot!" Ashlo screamed.

"Don't worry about me, check Zedda!" I yelled as another blow flung me through the air. "Cover me, Lars."

Rolling, I sprang onto the creature's back, locking my legs around its huge neck and yanked, leveraging all my strength to choke it.

The thing roared, flailing and pounding me into the icy ground. My body spasmed, absorbing the blow through my spine as it rammed me over and over. I held on for dear life, focusing on everything our people had suffered. The violence, the hatred, the abuse—even Elly and Fitz... channeling all of it. It wouldn't be enough.

Burning rushed through my veins and muscles. I was losing consciousness but I held on. I *had* to.

A *ROAR*, a gasp. *Crash*. The creature convulsed and toppled off me, rolling enough to let me scoot away.

Exhausted, I collapsed, not moving, not speaking, not even daring to hope. I was done, completely, utterly done.

Lars appeared in slow motion.

"Rrraaeeeekkkk," he garbled. "Aaaarrreee yyoou ookay?"

"Six claws," I whispered, giddy. "It had six claws."

"What? Are you okay, kid?" He looked worried as the world came into focus. For the life of me, couldn't figure out why.

"That was it." Uncontrollable laughter, head spinning. "The beast, the six-clawed beast," Tears of laughter and sadness danced down my face. Wait, Zedda! "Where is she? Is she okay?"

"She's fine, big guy," Ashlo replied. "She's waking up, took a hit to the head."

Phew. "I think I like her. I feel *funny*."

"You killed a freaking bear. With your hands!" Ashlo shook his head in disbelief. "Most badass thing I've ever seen."

Lars smiled. "Let's get a few pictures and a video of this thing. It will make great marketing material."

I groaned, both in pain and at the prospect of pictures. "Do whatever you want. I'm going to check on Zedda." I stood, unsteady, and made my way to where she sat.

"You okay?" I knelt next to her.

"Me? I'm fine," she said. "Just a scratch."

I touched her cheek. "This looks like more than a scratch." My finger traced the massive cut on her face.

"I'll be fine." She looked away. "How are you? You okay?"

"I've been better," I said. "I'll survive. Ready to try and get up?"

She nodded, and I helped her to her feet. "I'm good, *really*," she protested. "We need to get going."

She was right. We couldn't afford to be late. "We're leaving."

We set off, walking hard to make up lost time.

43

A GIRL

The rest of the hike was easy, nothing but the shadowy landscape until the sun rose, shedding light on the mysterious, black-and-white world. I pinged Nim. We'd be there soon.

Fifteen minutes later, we reached the small clearing. A group huddled on the far side around a roaring campfire, five pitched green tents to one side; the predetermined signal everything was clear.

"Commander Nim!" I shouted as we headed over.

Two figures emerged and walked toward us.

We stopped halfway from the trees' edge and waited.

The fellow to the left was short and built, boulder shoulders and ruthless arms straining his compact frame. He had the close crop of old war films, camouflaged fatigues, and a rifle over his shoulder, hunting knife at his side. Must be Nim.

His companion, a female of average height and obvious canine ancestry had a friendly face and a wild, fiery glint in her eyes. Dressed in fatigues, she favored a blaster at the hip and wore a bloodstained cap

"I'm Nim." She offered a hand. "This is my Lieutenant, Don. "We're glad you made it." She eyed us. "We've been briefed by Agtha and know the plan, but wanted to hear it from you before we finalize the team."

"Good." I covered the basics, but left out the reason for the kidnapping. The fewer people that knew, the better.

"Where are they holed up?" Lars asked when I was done.

"Bout three-k's east of here," Don replied. "Three-quarters of a kilometer from the original server ping."

"By the way, why'd you choose *that,* of all places?" Nim remarked. "Tactically it isn't great."

"I know the area. It's a *long* story." I didn't want to elaborate.

"No worries," Don said. "Our boys can handle it."

"How many? And how many do we have?" I added on second thought, scanning the camp.

"At least fifty or more," Nim said. "We've got eleven."

Dang.

"And there's probably more than one group," Don added. "At least that's how I'd do it."

"Fifty?" Ashlo whistled. *"Fifty?"*

"Have you searched for other groups?" Lars asked.

"Yes and no," replied Nim. "We did the best we could, but we didn't want to alert them either."

"Let's assume there's more than one." I looked at Nim and Don. "If you were the DNS, how would you run this op? Lars, anything to add?"

"Three teams," the soldiers said without hesitation. "Corner 'em with a triangle and surround 'em if doable. If not, have more than enough bodies to cover the perimeter and take out the target. VTOLs for backup."

Lars agreed.

"So it's simple," I said. "Divide and conquer."

Nim's brow furrowed. "What do you mean? If anything, the situation is reversed."

I shook my head. "We're outgunned and have to win through misdirection. If they're three-quarters of a kilometer from the initial site, odds are, the other two teams are too, but on opposite sides. You said a triangle?"

They nodded.

"We need to separate 'em, spoof three locations at once and isolate each group further. We only need to find Thorn, grab him, and make a clean getaway."

"How does ten-to-one odds help us?" Don said flatly.

"You hunt?" I asked.

He looked lost.

"Ever chase something farther than you should, something you knew you'd never catch but you'd committed so much you didn't want to give up?"

Don nodded, brow furrowing.

"We do the same here, spread 'em thinner by pinging locations that are close to, but separate enough, from one another. They go from fifty to twenty-five to twelve, etc... as they split each time. It'll be chaos as each subunit splinters off, chasing an invisible enemy. And they'll be motivated by huge rewards and promotions."

Don was nodding, Lars and Nim as well.

I played out what I'd been thinking as we dissected the plan, covering our bases and getaway. We'd go at dawn.

Out of the corner of my eye, Zedda crumpled, and my heart jumped. I rushed over but Nim beat me there.

Ashlo, Lars, and Don turned to the treeline, drawing blasters.

"What happened?" Ashlo yelled.

Shit. "I don't know." She *had* to be okay.

Nim checked her pulse. "She's breathing."

I grabbed Zedda's hand too and couldn't let go. "I think she fainted. Probably the blow to the head."

"What happened?" Nim asked.

I told her.

"We need to get her back to camp!" The commander sprang into action, and we hightailed it across the clearing, past bewildered, fatigue-clad rebels polishing weapons by the campfire.

"In here." Nim pulled aside a drab green curtain to reveal a well-stocked med tent.

In seconds, she slid a few flimsy white drawers out before finding what she was looking for. Pouring several gelatinous pills, she grabbed a bowl, a small spoon and crushed the golden capsules, stirring them into a goopy, rancid liquid that smelled like rotting fish guts.

"Have her take this." She handed me the bowl. "Her brain's seventy percent fat, these will help blunt the swelling. The six to twelve hours after head trauma are critical to prevent brain damage."

Brain damage? "Are you sure?"

"Do it now! We don't have time."

I opened Zedda's mouth and worked the bowl into a pourable position as Nim hooked an IV drip into Zedda's arm.

This seemed all wrong. What if this made it worse? "You've done this before?" I asked.

"Yeah. I'm a doctor actually. Have to pay bills somehow." She popped the transparent bag onto a metal hook and twisted the plastic knob. "I'm giving her some vitamins, minerals, and antioxidants to kickstart her system. These will help."

Despite my cybernetics, my hands shook. Nim must have noticed.

"It's nothing that could hurt her," she added. "It'll help her recover faster, maybe a full recovery."

Only maybe? "How long?"

"Depends on her. I'm sorry, can't say. There's a chance she doesn't recover." She winced. "We'll do the best we can."

She might not...

"I know what you're thinking, Raek," she said. "We can't call off this mission, not for a girl, *even* if she's special to you."

How'd she know?

"It's obvious the way you look at her, kid," Nim added. "But we have more important things at stake."

"Damn it!" She was right. I slammed my fist on the table to mask the burning pain inside. "We go at dawn."

"One of my best men will be here with her," Nim said, but I was already halfway out the flap.

44

SEEK AND HIDE

The next few hours passed in a painful blur. Why was I so worried about her?

"Raek, you ready?" It was Lars. He pulled me up from the log I'd been moping on behind an abandoned tent. "It will be fine. We've got to go."

"I'm ready. Thanks."

Lars nodded his understanding, not needing to say anything.

When we rejoined the group, I realized I'd let my team down. I couldn't let pain or emotions cripple me, not now. They were risking their lives for this. They were counting on me.

Stepping onto a small crate, I looked around. "Everyone ready?"

A weak chorus of "yeas" and "yeses."

"I said, everyone ready?" I yelled in what I hoped was motivational anger. "We've got between fifty and a hundred fifty bastards in those woods. Our job's to capture one man, Thorn Fury. It might seem trivial, but trust me, this monster might be the key to the entire war." I let that sink in.

"Have you been beaten down by the GDR, seen your family and friends subjected to unspeakable humiliation, violence, and hate? I have. My sister was murdered by those *pigs*. My family disappeared too. They've taken *everything* from me, including my town. It's our time to hit back. So, again, who the hell's with me?"

This time, a roar.

"That's more like it! You know what to do. Go do it."

"Nice speech," Nim said under her breath as we got underway.

"Thanks," I whispered. "I'm back."

"I know. She'll be okay, kid." A smile crossed her thick lips. "Let's go get him."

On the edge of a small clearing a kilometer from the spot, Nim stopped and raised her fist. The squad froze, snapping into position and leveling blasters, turning to cover all sides.

I fired off preprogrammed web access requests, spoofing the first server. A new wave would trigger every two minutes. By eleven minutes, we'd have their platoons reduced to sections of three or four, and spread over close to five square kilometers... at least that was the plan.

"It's started," I said to no one in particular. "Ashlo, get Henk on standby."

"Roger that."

"Spread out, folks!" Nim yelled. "Like we drilled it."

The soldiers jumped into action, running in their respective directions over logs and branches, sweeping disturbed snow to cover their tracks and find cover for the inevitable shootout. It was still dark.

The next sequence went as Lars and I took up positions behind a pair of ancient oaks.

We waited, wordless, as the area brightened. It was going to be a beautiful day, one filled with blood. Henk better be ready.

A small *crack* and rustle of leaves... seconds later, snow crunched. Footsteps.

I alerted Nim, straining my eyes and ears. A few hundred meters.

There it was again, and again. Again.

Soldiers appeared, guns drawn as they marched in staggered formation, trigger fingers ready. They were masked in helmets and goggles, chests covered in armor. This was going to get ugly. And there were at least twenty. Jeez.

"Listen, ladies," Thorn's icy voice rippled through the night. I'd never forget *that* voice. The burning hatred sent cold chills through me, a distinct evil. "Stay sharp. They're out there. They wouldn't pull this stunt otherwise. There's some objective. They're trying to spread us out. They can't be dumb enough to think they can win, which leaves one thing, retrieval. Kid probably left something behind."

I hadn't thought of that.

"What if there's no one there, sir?" a timid voice asked. "What if it's a goose chase?"

"Then you're getting paid good money to play hide-n-seek, soldier. You got a problem?"

"No, sir, it's just—"

"Good!" Thorn snapped. "Anyone else have something stupid to add?"

No one said anything. "Now in case you forgot," Thorn said, "this kid's important. The Board's anxious to meet him, even if it's in a body bag. You ladies want to be the sorry lot that let the Board down?" He sneered.

Shhh... Any noise at all would spell disaster. We'd guessed Thorn's route but dangerously underestimated his force. We were outnumbered at least three-to-one.

Nim messaged me. *That him?*

Yeah.

Copy that. Wait for a better opportunity. Too close to retreat, she shot back.

We'd been sitting for thirty minutes, not fifty meters from Thorn's thirty-or-so—at this point relaxed—men, when one rose.

"Gotta take a piss," he said to his buddy.

I froze. Crap. Was this guy's bladder going to get us killed?

He ambled to the side, whistling as he unzipped his black cargo pants. He was a tall shaggy guy, goggles around his neck, paint under his eyes, a high powered blaster on his back. Typical special forces.

If Thorn's squad was special forces, we weren't outnumbered, we were screwed.

A splash shattered the silence, slowing to a drizzle. The zing of a zipper. He turned to leave.

That was close...

Two steps, he jumped. "Crap. There's a footprint here!"

"What'd you say?" Thorn yelled. Oh no...

Someone fired, catching the pisser in the torso.

The clearing erupted.

45

CAPTURE THE FLAG

W e opened fire on Thorn's men.
To his credit, he shouted, "It's a trap! They've got us surrounded. Take cover. Hit them, boys!"

People screamed and soldiers moaned as smoke filled the clearing, trees tumbling.

"Go!" Thorn ordered. His men charged Nim and several other rebels, and despite taking heavy fire, hammered through our stretched lines.

Our soldiers broke ranks, chasing them through thick pines and picking off Thorn's men. I aimed and fired, catching one square in the chest and jumping to my feet as Thorn's men stopped retreating and dropped into a surprise defense. The seamless maneuver fooled many of Nim's inexperienced fighters who were cut to shreds in the ensuing crossfire.

Who was winning? It seemed like us, until that last exchange.

'Nim, status report?' No response.

We were getting killed up there now. Our guys needed help, something. Lars and I must have had the same idea, because we raced off to flank them.

There was heavy fire up front where Thorn's remaining men had dug in, but overall, it was dying down. Smoke billowed everywhere and fires raged. Most of our men were down.

Still nothing from Nim, not a good sign.

Rounding the cluster of trees, we found the rear of Thorn's guard. "On three," I whispered.

We charged, and his first shot took out one guy. I got two more, and we were in.

Soldiers hunkered everywhere, focused on the frontline. Time slowed. In one fluid motion, I dodged an incoming blast and got off four shots before they realized anything.

Hitting the ground rolling, I shot another woman as she raised her weapon. My claws slashed the heel of a cynetic next to me and I shot him as he fell.

Thorn appeared and leveled his arm before turning and running.

Wait, what? Were we winning?

Thorn... crap! I sprang to my feet and went after him, pinging Henk. 'We need you, now!' Disabling my safety restraints—didn't know I could do that—I sprinted faster, tendons screaming. He wasn't getting away, not this time. That bastard.

A hundred meters. Faster. Come on. My heart rate skyrocketed.

He must be heading for backup. I couldn't let him, but killing him would ruin everything. I set my blaster to stun and fired.

It went wide but slowed him a tad. That could work. As I tore through the trees, I opened fire. None of my first three connected, but each altered his path.

The fourth caught him in the back and he toppled. Yes! We got him! It was over.

'Henk, I have Thorn. Do you copy?'

'En route to your location.'

I closed the gap in seconds, but it was too late. Thorn was on his feet and firing. What the—?

"You should have finished me when you had the chance," he spat. The tree next to me exploded. "My armor isn't the shit *you* filth use. At least a blaster might have injured me. You're a dead man."

Would have been good to know. I needed him alive. Could I take him?

I dodged behind a tree. "Too bad! I thought you were man enough to fight me. Guess I was wrong."

"Man enough to fight you?" He laughed. "Please, kid. I lead the most badass warriors in history. You're can't play mind games with me."

"I thought you were man enough to fight without blasters—hand to hand—like real men used to. By the way, what'd your father say when you showed up empty-handed?" I pressed. "I'm sure Calter wasn't very welcoming, was he?"

Come on, take the bait. Take the bait.

"This has nothing to do with my him!" Thorn snapped, a new venom to his voice. "You want a fistfight, *fine*. It's your funeral."

He strode from behind a large maple, vicious eyes engulfing me, relaxed.

I walked toward him. Could I trust him to fight fair?

"So, we meet again." He smiled. "How were the docs? Did you enjoy that?"

I still had nightmares. The sim had nearly broken me. "Piece of cake. Like this will be," I added with a smirk.

His eyes narrowed and he shot toward me, fist slamming my chin before I could react and sending me stumbling.

"This will be easier than I thought," he said. "I'm going to enjoy this."

I grimaced, assuming a defensive posture.

He came again with a complicated series of punches. I dodged all but the last, which did damage. He grinned, foot rocketing toward my face. Deflecting it, I countered with a weak jab.

He laughed. "You hit like a girl."

Thorn landed two painful body blows and I staggered. "At least you'll die on your feet, kid. No more mistakes. I'm not bringing you anywhere this time." His right foot trainwrecked my ribs and I fell hard. Was he human?

"Get up, boy. Aren't you man enough?"

I was in trouble. Despite my training, he was a *much* better striker. He laughed as I pulled myself to my feet.

The ground was my one chance. Lars had taught me well. Would it be enough?

He swung and I swept his leg, sending him crashing to the frozen earth, an amazed expression on his face. I was on him at once.

A quick elbow to the face and I had him. He squirmed and struggled, but I twisted my legs locked around his neck and squeezed. I had to put him out.

He strained, smashing me, but I held firm. As he was about to pass out, his hand swung. I blasted it off seconds before he lined up the shot. Screaming, his other arm arced toward me. I shot that off as well, blood drenching my shirt as he passed out.

'Henk, come in. Anyone! I have Thorn and need a sedative ASAP!'

Nothing. I slung him over my shoulder and ran.

It took two minutes to reach the aftermath of the chaos. Bodies everywhere. Lars was tending to one of them.

"Lars!" I yelled. "I got him. Where's Nim? Where's Don? I need sedatives, now!"

"Nim's dead. Don's over there." Lars pointed.

Sprinting, I yelled, "Don, sedatives! Do you have any?"

"What?" He saw Thorn. "You got him?"

I nodded.

"This is all I got." He pulled a small dropper from his pocket. "Nim had the rest but well, the vials exploded when she did…" He handed me the syringe.

Nim's dead? No… "I'm sorry about Nim." Grabbing the syringe, I jabbed Thorn's arm, pressing the plunger. The liquid disappeared. "How long will it last?"

"Four or five hours for a normal human. Cynetics might be stronger though. We should re-up in two."

I noticed carnage for the first time. Holy crap. "How many dead? Injured?"

"Five dead, four wounded." Don's face was a confused mask of anger, professionalism, and pain.

Lars came over, eyes downtrodden. "Ashlo didn't make it."

What? My head spun. "Guys, I'm sorry. It was my plan and—"

"Don't be stupid, kid!" Don snapped. "It was a great plan. Sometimes, shit happens. We knew what we signed up for. You got your guy, so let's get the hell out of here and win this war before his friends come looking."

The VTOL appeared over the treeline and I signaled Henk. He landed, and we loaded the wounded the second the skids hit.

"Dang!" Henk murmured when he saw the bodies. "What happened?"

"Later," I said with a look that silenced him. "We need to get out of here." If he knew what happened to Ashlo, he might not be able to fly. How was I going to break it to him?

As if on cue, blaster fire slammed our craft. Lights on the dash flashed.

"Move, move!" Don roared.

Another VTOL took off.

We jumped in and Henk lifted off as a ragtag crew burst from trees, opening fire as we gained altitude. Henk avoided all but two shots before zooming off.

"We need to grab Zedda, more sedatives, and get out of here," I said.

Henk grinned. "She seems to be fine, keep your fingers crossed." A look of horrified realization came over him, eyes widening as he asked the question I'd been dreading. "Wait, where's Ashlo?"

I swallowed hard. "I'm sorry, Henk. He, he didn't make it, buddy."

"Damn it!" Henk smashed the dashboard. Again. "Damn it, damn it, damn it! That stupid, blubbering idiot. I should have been there."

Poor guy... "Henk, we'd all be dead if you'd come." I put my hand on his shaking shoulder. "They had an army coming down on us. You saved us and made the mission a success."

Henk's empty eyes fell. "But still, I mean... damn!"

"Without Ashlo we'd have lost that fight," Lars chimed in. "He was a hero, took one to the chest so we could overrun their position. He died a true warrior, Henk, how he'd have wanted."

Henk's eyes glistened, but he batted them away. "Two minutes," he said in a clipped voice. "Get ready."

"Don, where should we bring you and your men?" I asked.

"We have transport at camp, more than enough to carry the wounded. We'll be fine. Get your girl and bring this bastard to Caen. Make it worth it," he added with a soldier's resolve.

I gave him my word, and wouldn't let him down.

We landed and I ran off while Lars and Don loaded the injured into waiting off-roaders.

Zedda... When I got to the med station, she was awake and sitting. She wanted to know what happened.

"Long story. I'll tell you on the way. We got him. You okay to walk?" I asked, my voice softening.

"I think so."

"Good." Or was she playing tough, like usual? "Any idea where the sedatives are?"

She shook her head. At least her eyes seemed focused.

Together, we ripped open shelves and drawers as I ran a quick web search for various sedatives and tranquilizers. Within two minutes, Zedda found Etorphine, a synthetic opioid that induced long periods of unconsciousness and catatonic states. Perfect.

Grabbing all of it, we hurried to the VTOL. I kept a close eye on Zedda in case her legs faltered.

"There you two are!" Lars yelled. "We need to go."

We said our goodbyes and good lucks, and soon Henk took off. "Everybody stay buckled this time," he said. "We might have company."

I shot another dose of Etorpine into the makeshift IV someone had inserted into Thorn's arm, and collapsed into my seat.

After sending messages to Paer and the rest of the Council, I turned to check on Zedda. She was fast asleep. Sleep, that'd be nice. There was too much to do.

I closed my eyes, that would make it easier to focus.

46

THE STORY

Paer was there to greet us as we climbed out. "I'm sorry about Ashlo," she said as Henk shuffled off, giving him a brief hug. "Good work, guys. Ready for the Council?"

Lars grabbed coffee while I carried Zedda to her room, and laid her to rest on the cushioned mat. She looked so helpless lying there. I wrapped a blanket tight around her, and left with mixed feelings. Five minutes later, we all sat in the Council room, except Zedda.

It was early and everyone nursed coffee and tea while I briefed them on everything. Lars stepped in here and there as needed.

When we finished, Obowe said, "Great work, both of you. It is too bad about Ashlo and Nim, but this fight is bigger than any of us. Lars, the promo stuff?"

"We're ready." He twinkled with creative chaos. "Raek and I are filming after this."

We were?

Talk turned to next steps, and Paer said, "We've got people working on Thorn's SmartCore. They'll have access to his system within the hour. We won't get everything, but should be able to fake a message to his father."

Mico nodded. "So, official story is Thorn got captured and—"

"What if we flipped the script?" I cut in. "What if, instead of trying to capture Calter, we got him to come to us?"

Lars raised an eyebrow. "How? Why?"

"The same way we get him to share the intel; jealousy and a thirst for power. What if we pretend Thorn met someone—a scientist or something, someone who can complete the emulation process—who's willing to do it for Calter and Thorn in exchange for immunity and a position of power?"

I paused but no one said anything. "Calter would want to meet. It's what he's wanted for decades, immortality. And he can't risk *anyone* finding out, especially not other members of the Board."

Paer raised an eyebrow. "And once we meet, then what?"

"We tell him we're planning to destroy the brain-field backups and end immortality for emulates. It won't be what he expected, but it's what he wants. If he can't live forever, no one should, right? That's comparative psychology 101."

Lars was nodding. "You crafty bugger. I love it!"

A rare smile creased Paer's lips. "Any objections?"

No one said anything. "Get on it, Raek, after you get that speech filmed."

Oh, great...

"On it, Ag," Lars said. "Come on, kid. We've got work to do."

Lars and I stood and left after one last sip of harsh coffee.

On our third try, we found an empty room and set up shop. It was small and whitewashed with a two-person table in the middle. It would have to do.

"Here's some notes I made." Lars touched his band and a virtual screen appeared, a list of twenty or thirty bullet points.

"You want me to say all that?" That'd take ages.

He shook his head. "Not everything. They're suggestions. You decide what to include. " He gestured to the wall and seven lit up. "These are the most important."

- *First ever cynetic-animote hybrid*
- *Raised in poor town of Kiag, later torched by the DNS*

- *Sister assaulted and murdered by cynetics*
- *If interspecies breeding is possible, so too is unity/equality*
- *The GDR lied about Initiative attacks - cite examples*
- *Fight, not for revenge, but for equality. To build a better world*
- *Rise up, help us win*

My stomach twisted. "I don't know if I can do this."

"Course you can. I heard that speech in Kiag." He patted my shoulder. "You're a natural."

"That was a spur of the moment thing, I didn't think."

"We'll practice without recording," he countered. "Sound good?"

No. "I'm ready, ready as I'll ever be at least."

He gave me a countdown and nodded.

"Hello, my name's Raek Mekorian. I've been called a terrorist, a murderer; I'm here to set the record straight." And I did, even demoing my blaster, which I thought was a good touch. "I'm a freak, I'm a hybrid... but I'm also hope, hope for our people, hope for equality... freedom and unity for all."

I talked about Elly, the horrific attacks, and hammered home every injustice.

"They do it because they fear us. They fear the power of a unified animote army. They. Fear. Us!" I slammed my fist on the table. "They should. We outnumber 'em and we are strong. We fight for our future, for equality, for our children and our children's children. We fight for a better world. So, who is with me?"

"And, cut," Lars said.

Wait, cut? "What? That was a test run..."

"Are you kidding?" He laughed. "That was brilliant. Of course I was recording. I don't think we'll need a take two," he added.

"Oh... You should've told me." At least it was over.

"And ruin *that*." He shook his head, smiling. "We have enough to do as it is. If you'll excuse me, I have some editing and special effects to work on. And you have a message to write."

And I would, right after a quick lunch. When I got to the dining hall, Zedda and Henk were on the far side with empty plates.

After grabbing the one thing left, eggs, I headed over.

"Hey, guys," I said. Turning to Henk, I added, "I'm sorry about Ashlo." I sat, giving him what I hoped was an encouraging smile.

"Thanks, Raek, it's okay."

"Feeling better, Zedda?" I asked, unable to hold eye contact.

"I'm fine," she replied, looking her usual self again. "I can't believe you guys went after him without me."

"A lot of good you would have done unconscious." Henk glowered at his plate. "At least *I* should have been there."

I sighed. "We all did the best we could. We got him! We lost friends and family along the way, but we got him. Speaking of, where are they holding him? I'm supposed to talk to the techs."

"I'll take you," Henk volunteered. "Will give me something else to think about."

"Thanks, let me finish this." I shoveled the scrambled eggs before remembering Zedda. "Ohhh." My face flushed a guilty smile. It wasn't the coolest of looks.

She laughed, and two minutes later, we were off. "He's in the underground cells," Henk explained. "Used to be storage, but we retrofitted several of them. This way."

He led me to an unmarked panel built into the slab wall and typed a code on the mini touchscreen display. A thick metal door swung open, revealing a small spiral staircase twisting downward.

We descended and heard country blues emanating from an open door. "That you, Raek? Come in."

Thorn was sprawled on gurney in the center of the featureless holding cell, arms, legs, and chest bound to the bed with Teflon nanoties, sensors tattooing his body with marks. "We got your cynetic right here," the woman standing over him said. "Been working on his SmartCore since he arrived."

She was mid sixties I'd guess, with smart, focused eyes, a pointed nose, and a trace of blonde whiskers on her lip. Was there some weasel in her? I didn't dare to ask. They didn't have the best reputation.

"You got access?" I asked.

"Sort of. We got into his SC's social matrix, ie. how his brain, and yours, store and categorize everyone you've ever met." She must have noticed our blank stares and cut to the point, "The messaging will work. The rest will take weeks to decrypt. Never heard of this much security at the SC level."

Whatever that means.

She analogized it to the cliché oldies, a hero disarming a bomb in a race against time. "Some SmartCores have similar protections, frying everything. Or external alerts..."

Still clueless, I said, "But it'll work?"

"Yeah, sure. Use this." She grabbed two screens by the wall and handed me one.

I rotated the input field to make it easier to use.

"Put your message here," she said. "Let me know when you're ready."

"And this will send as if it was him? There's no *possible* way the receiver could know?" A slip-up would ruin everything.

She nodded, and I entered *Calter Fury* in the recipient field

His name appeared alongside a stream of images, videos and user-names. Could my SmartCore do that? I'd look later.

After choosing the Minister, I got to the message. To the side was a past history tab. I scrolled their previous correspondences to get a feel for the relationship.

Okay, it all made sense now... Thorn overcompensated to make up for problems with his dad. There was an undercurrent of tension throughout, poor guy wanted to impress Calter. Needed recognition but never got it. The minister seemed cold and controlling, even downright cruel. I'd rather be a bastard... Focus.

I started typing.

Dear Father,

I have the best news. I know I should be in Kiag waiting for the half-breed, but I came across an opportunity too good to pass up, one you've sought for ages.

In Itany, I met one of the original scientists on the emulation project. He created and managed the first backups and surrogate brain-field transfers before

the ban. He's been on the run ever since and undergone several reconstructive surgeries to avoid detection.

Anyways, one of the idiots who couldn't keep his mouth shut mentioned I was your son. I was furious, but later the scientist, Alexei, approached me about a deal. He wanted immunity, a new life, and high ranking position in exchange for emulating the two of us.

At first, I didn't believe him. Seemed too good to be true. I threatened to kill him if he didn't confess, but he said again, he was telling the truth. Said I could do what I liked because he was backed up. I believe him.

I stayed in the city and sent my men onward, telling them not to report me missing. Secrecy is critical. Now, Alexei and I are traveling to Caen under the guise of a father and son trading company.

I waited to send this until getting closer. We don't want Intel getting a whiff of what's happening. Reply as soon as you can.

Your son,

Thorn

I read the message twice more, and sent it, fingers crossed.

Closing the screens, I turned to Henk and... I blushed. "This is embarrassing. I never got your name."

"I'm Ania." She held out a petite hand. "Pleasure to meet you."

"The pleasure's all mine. If you'll excuse me, I need to see the Council. Can you ping me if we get a response?"

"Sure." Her fingers danced through the air. "What's your username?"

I gave it.

"Now you'll get an alert if we get a response. Anything else?"

"No, that's great," I said. "Thanks, Ania. By the way, no one's allowed in this cell until you hear from me or the Council." I paused. How do I say this... "That includes you guys. Sorry."

Both nodded without a word and Ania locked the door as we left. We went our separate ways.

On the spiral staircase, a notification. That was fast.

I opened it.

47

THE BOY WHO CRIED WOLF

The livestream started, fires everywhere.

'Leed Goralich reporting from Kiag, what's left of it. You may remember Raek Mekorian, the wolfish terrorist who murdered four officers in the capital a while back and torched his hometown, Kiag. It appears he's struck again.'

The image panned to an overhead of the Black Forest, bluish green smoke billowing from the smoldering inferno. 'Chemfires are raging, destroying more and more *animote* land, farms, and livestock in the process. We at the WNN and GDR feel for citizens affected and beg anyone with information to report it to the DNS. Leed Goralich signing off, stay safe.'

Clenching my fists, I felt lightheaded. They'd destroyed everything I'd ever loved, and now the forest—my one true home... Those bastards.

I raced to where I'd left Lars, ignoring the calls and waves as I passed, everything burning red. This couldn't go on. I wouldn't let it.

Bursting through the flimsy door, I snapped, "Lars! Is it ready?"

He turned, a curious expression on his face. "Oh, kid, you're back?"

"Is it ready or not?" I showed him the clip.

"Almost."

"Add this." I improvised a response to the fire and footage. "Now, show it to me, the whole thing."

"I need more—"

"Show it to me!"

He flipped a few screens, dragged several frames and let out a pleased sigh. "That should do it. Here."

A holo of me appeared, dramatic music in the background.

When it was finished, I was impressed. "Good work. Now publish it! Everywhere."

"We need to figure out—"

"I said publish it. Spread it like the fire that leveled my town. We have those bastards in a lie. We don't have time to screw around."

His hands flew. "Done. Should hit the major elite and animote webs, forums, message boards and social sites at once. All major alt news outlets. We're on TOR4, other darknet channels, and there's holo and video options for any tech stack." His eyes twinkled.

"Thanks, Lars."

A notification came. Another, and another... soon, a torrent. "It's happening!" I exclaimed. That was fast.

A new message popped up.

What the—? It was from Ania. Oh, wow. That was even faster.

I grabbed Lars. "Come on!"

Three minutes later, we were at Thorn's cell, and Ania unlocked it. "That was quick."

"Open it here." I created a screen outside her view.

Our conversation materialized. Holy crap. He answered!

Lars and I were silent as we read.

Thorn,

Interesting.

Good work.

Where and when?

- CF

"He has a way with words," Lars said sardonically.

You got that right. You should see his other messages. "I'll set up an emergency Council meeting. Ania, can you lock the room. We'll be back in thirty minutes or less."

Once we were out of earshot, I asked, "What do you think?"

"He's a tough father, that's what I think."

"Dang it, Lars. You know what I mean."

"We need to pick the right location and pray there's no secret code between the two. Our best bet is somewhere deserted."

Everyone was there when we arrived and updates went quick. "So, where do we do this?" I asked. "Any suggestions?"

After some debate, we settled on an abandoned factory north of the city. We were banking on the fact he'd come alone, not wanting to reveal the possibility of emulation to any but his closest circle, in other words, himself.

And tonight, not too late. We couldn't give him time to think things over. We'd have a small force of six, and I'd talk to him myself. The others ran off while Lars and I hurried back.

Dear Father,

It's good to hear from you.

The sooner, the better. Let's meet at the old Apple warehouse, north of the city. You know the one—abandoned since the company went under.

Eight p.m.? It's late enough to avoid attention but not too late to attract suspicion.

Wear a blue shirt with black pants if everything's fine, otherwise, we'll assume you've been followed.

Walk in the door on the East side. We'll be waiting.

Your son,

Thorn

We both read it once more, and I hit send.

Seconds later, a reply.

Sounds good.

- CF

We looked at each other. There was no turning back.

48

VIRAL

We got there early for recon, assuming Calter would do the same.

Paer came, as did Henk, Zedda, Lars, and Obowe, who would play the scientist, until we revealed the true plan. Zedda would cover us from above while Paer and Henk guarded the East entrance. Lars would circle the remaining doorways.

It was 17:00. Three hours to kill.

After an eternity, an electric *whirr*. Wheels skidded to a halt and piano music faded. This was it.

He was an hour early. Gravel crunched as footsteps crept toward the doorway. He stopped.

What if he messaged Thorn again? How did I not think of that?

After a minute, the footsteps continued. Phew. A door creaked open and thudded shut.

"Thorn," he said in a soft, firm voice. "Where are you?"

Calter stepped from the recessed doorway onto the immense fulfillment center floor, boots *clacking*, athletic frame tense. Dark malevolent eyes took it all in as if readying himself for war, looking every bit the dangerous predator he was. "Thorn, if this is a game!"

"Don't shoot, Calter." I moved from behind a small wall, hands in the air. "My name's Raek Mekorian. You've been chasing me for weeks. I want to talk."

His hand shot up, aiming at me.

"Don't," I said. "We have you surrounded." Zedda, Henk and Paer appeared.

"We don't want a fight, this isn't a kidnapping." I added. "We're here to talk."

"Where's the scientist? Where's my son?" His voice rose, eyes narrowing. He hadn't lowered his blaster.

"Thorn's safe. We've got him sedated in a secure location."

"Where is he?" Fury snapped.

I had to be careful, his blaster was pointed right at me. One false move... "I know you hate emulates, you've always envied them. We all do. Their immortality and disproportionate power, talk about a corrupt system. We want the same thing, you and I. You want power and I want to end the emulates reign, to make us equal."

"What are you saying?" His eyes were wary but interested.

"We're going to destroy the brain-fields. All of 'em." I let that sink in, smiling. "We're going to turn emulates into ordinary people. Level the playing field."

"So, there's no scientist, no one to perform the emulation?" His jaw twitched.

I shook my head.

"It's impossible!" he growled. "Don't think I haven't tried. Their facilities are hidden."

Lars stepped forward. "We found a way."

"Who is this?" Calter spat, blaster still pointed at my head.

"Part of our organization," I cut in. "We need your military deployment data, information on all locations with less than ten or twenty guards."

A mirthless laugh. "I'm not giving you that."

"Only the ones with all animote guards," I said. "Emulates wouldn't want cynetics or enhancers at the facility, might figure out what they were guarding."

His brow furrowed. "I'm listening."

I explained the compromise between secrecy and protection. "It'll be well hidden as opposed to well guarded."

"So you can figure out where they are," he finished.

I nodded. "We don't care what happens afterward, or who takes power. We figure it will be *you* in all honesty." I paused, knowing that was his ultimate goal. "The emulates will be in disarray, and they'll be mortal again. They'll piss away their power."

His eyes were gleaming now.

"If you're willing to guarantee basic rights for animotes, we're willing to help. Are you in?"

He sneered arrogance. "What do I need you lot for? You gave me what I needed."

"Deniability! You'll have someone to blame and no repercussions. Think about it."

"I want my son back! How do I know I can trust you?"

"How do we know we can trust you, Calter?" I said. "We can't, and neither can you. But we both want the same thing. We have a common enemy. It's up to you."

He turned to leave.

"Well?" Lars yelled after him.

"You'll have your intel, tomorrow. I want my son!" he added. "I'll send you details." With that, he swept into the cold night, humming one of Bach's more insidious pieces, a freezing gust of wind chilling our bones in the eerie silence as the door clattered shut.

No one spoke. We were a third of the way back when Zedda broke the silence. "That was easier than we expected."

"I was thinking the same thing," Lars said.

"Did you see the way he looked at me?" I asked. "Disdain. Mutual admiration too, though. He knew we'd bested him and his son, and respected that, almost as much as he hated us. For him, this is personal. Something must have happened with the emulates."

The question was, what?

"If you can't beat 'em, join 'em," Henk said. "And if you can't join 'em, crush 'em. It's human nature."

Which was also what screwed us in the first place.

"Either way, we need teams on high alert," Paer said. "The attacks *have* to be simultaneous. If they have advance warning, they'll move the backups," she said with an uncharacteristic worry.

"Or worse yet," I said, "create more. Can you coordinate?" I asked her.

"Guys, we might have a problem," Henk said. A moment later, "Oh shit!"

"INCOMING, INCOMING," the VTOL blared. "BRACE FOR IMPACT."

49

FALLING GLASS

"Henk, what's going!" Zedda yelled. "Shut up, shut up!" The VTOL pitched forward, dropping. "Behind us!" Henk yelled.

A missile streaked toward us. Another flash two hundred meters back, another.

Zedda grabbed my hand. I squeezed back.

"Must have been following us," Henk said. "This is gonna be tight!"

The craft slammed left, rocketing toward the east of the city as we dove again. "It's right on us!"

"Don't head back to base!" I snapped. That's what Calter wanted, but his guy got jumpy.

"INCOMING, INCOMING. BRACE FOR IMPACT."

"Hold on!" Henk white knuckled the controls as we shot through two tall buildings. The missile smashed a brick behemoth to our right. We shot out, five meters up and doing two hundred as we zipped over sparse traffic.

"I can't shake him," Henk said.

"Emergency landing?" Paer's voice was tense.

Henk shook his head. "Too dangerous. They'd shoot—"

"INCOMING, INCOMING. BRACE FOR IMPACT."

We missed the enclosed skyway by meters and it erupted in a sea of glittering glass, fragments showering the street below.

The other VTOL blasted through the falling glass and pirouetted upward. He was good.

"Don't we have *any* weapons?" Lars asked.

Henk shook his head, eyes fixed on the bridge ahead.

There was no other way. She'd die otherwise, they all would. "Can you open the doors?" I asked through gritted teeth. "I might be able to—"

"No!" Zedda grabbed my arm. "It's too dangerous."

"What choice do we have? Henk, do it!" I ordered.

He did, and the black butterfly doors folded inward. I unhooked my belt and pushed Zedda to safety as icy wind shot in. She glared from the rear but said nothing.

The aircraft jerked and I grabbed a harness, feet slamming as I righted myself. My stomach was in knots. *Soooo* high!

"INCOMING, INCOMING. BRACE FOR IMPACT."

Another missile rocketed toward us. I fired twice but Henk swerved, diving again. The missile zinged past, locking on a car and annihilating the street below. Windows shattered and a pair of scooters burst into flame.

I fired again, missing badly. It was impossible to aim.

"Hold us level, Henk!" I said.

"Sure, if you want him to hit us," Henk retorted.

Three more shots. Nothing. This wasn't working. I swore under my breath. "I need you to drop me off."

"What?" Henk yelled. "You're crazy."

"Over there! See that building. If you can get me there, I'll jump and be able to shoot."

"Raek!" Zedda gasped.

"Do it!" I snapped. Before I lost my nerve.

We ripped around a corner, leveling. The military ship had fallen back. "Ready?" Henk asked. "Sure about this?"

No... I clenched my fists, stomach already skydiving. "Yeah!"

"Ten seconds!" We shot up and floored it for the tower. "Three, two, one. Now!" Henk screamed.

I leaped. There was *no* building.

I wasn't going to make it.

50

THREADING THE NEEDLE

I came in backward, tumbling. Momentum slammed me into the concrete, flipping me twice, and hammering my head, stopping inches from the edge. Holy shit.

The VTOL rushed toward me but I couldn't get off a shot. It was too fast, and stars flickered across my vision. I couldn't lock on.

The two raced through the air. Henk turned and dove but his pursuer was equally skilled.

Henk called. 'We're coming. Get ready!'

The ship sped around City Hall, cornering the impressive three-story building at unbelievable speed. Another missile fired. Henk gunned it. So did his pursuer.

Two hundred fifty meters. Here we go.

Four seconds later, they rushed past. I aimed. One chance.

Time slowed as I focused, locked on, and fired. A direct hit slammed into the side. Yes!

Wait, nothing happened... The VTOL kept flying.

'Henk? It didn't work.'

'Shit, armor!' He swore again, hurtling away. 'We're screwed.'

No. 'Do it again! I've got a plan.' They weren't going to die because of me, not them too.

Less than a minute later, they streaked toward me. 'He's out of missiles at least,' Henk said. The other craft fired. 'Damn!'

Crouching behind the lip of the building, I waited. He couldn't see me. This wouldn't work if he remembered where the first shot came from.

'Slow down, Henk! One hundred or less.'

Lars laughed in the background. 'Crazy bastard. He's gonna…'

Wait. For. It.

Jumping, I screamed as it raced toward me. I fired.

I was right, the window of the VTOL had been open. My blast caught the pilot in the chest. Blood spattered everywhere. Did it work? Tumbling, I didn't know until the VTOL veered off course, smashing into a building.

Yes! I did it.

SLAM.

Everything went black.

51

A WHISPER

My eyes fluttered open as we landed. Dazed, I squinted, exhausted. It was 21:45.

"Raek!" Zedda reached over and touched my face. "Are you okay?"

"I'm fine. The VTOL, did we…"

Lars nodded, a proud look in his eyes. "Thanks to you."

My head was throbbing, and I shook it to clear it. "So, everyone's okay?" They all stared at me in the cramped craft like they'd seen a ghost. Had something happened?

Henk laughed, shaking his head. "You're crazy, Raek."

"Calter?" I asked. "Was it all for nothing?"

Lars shrugged. "Looks like it. We should have seen it coming."

I didn't say anything, it was my fault. We had nothing to show for it and were back to square one.

The doors opened, and Paer said, "I don't know about you all, but I'm off to bed."

Soon, they went their separate ways but Zedda grabbed my sleeve. "Shhh, there's something I wanted to show you," she whispered.

"Wha—"

"Shh. Follow me," she said. "We can't talk here." She grabbed my hand and led me along the hallway, finger to her lips.

"Zedda, what's going on?" She was scaring me. Why did we need to be quiet?

She held her finger to her lips again.

"A traitor, a spy, a—"

She put her hand over my mouth and pushed me through an open door.

"Fine, we're alone. What? What's going on?" My heart thundered.

She closed the door and locked it, body pressing against mine. "Zedda?"

"Shhh." A light kiss on my lips. "I never thanked you for saving my life, Raek."

Oh... "You don't have to—"

"I want to." Her lips embraced mine as hips rubbed across my leg, her chest pushing into me. My breath came faster and faster.

Was this really happening? "Are you sure—"

"Shut up, Raek." She laughed. "You're cute and I like you, but sometimes you talk too much. Just feel it, just be."

Something triggered in me, something primal. I let go and instincts took over. Wild wolfish blood ran through me, desires unleashed. And it's not like we could get pregnant...

It could have been five minutes or five hours... time ceased, unlike anything I've ever felt: raw, pure, *real*. When it was over, we collapsed into each other's arms, asleep the moment our heads touched the floor.

Later that night, I awoke to her soft eyes on my face. "Zedda?"

"I was watching you sleep. There's something about you."

"Such as?" I knew the feeling but wanted to see her squirm. She couldn't put it into words, and soon, talk turned to my sister, my family. "I let them down. They're all dead because of me, because I lied." I shivered as the brutal truth escaped my lips, and she pulled me tight.

"It'll be okay, Raek. It's not your fault." I couldn't fight back the tears, but she never let me go. I must have fallen asleep.

When morning came and I was still in her arms, I couldn't help but smile. I could get used to this.

She was asleep and I didn't want to bother her. It was four a.m. but I was wide awake. I'd go to the mess and bring her coffee. She'd wake in an hour or two. For some reason, I'd needed less and less sleep after my nanoSTEMs activated.

Obowe was in the mess when I got there. Was he such an early riser?

I walked over. "How's it going?"

"There you are, Raek. I was hoping you'd be soon. We got the troop deployment data."

No way... "Really?"

"Looks like we had it last night when we got back. The tech didn't check Thorn until this morning. Have a look." He replicated his display and handed it to me.

Studying the chart, I skimmed. "The animote-only bases?"

He nodded. "There are four with four guards or less. The rest have *at least* eight."

Interesting. "So, odds are it's those four?"

He shrugged. "I hope so. If it is all twenty-five... We cannot hit that many."

"Meilo, Rhoda, Dever, and North Wal," I read off. "Zones One and Two and two in Zone Three. Makes sense, spread the risk, especially from natural disaster." I pulled up information on each.

"They're all near small cities of less than twenty thousand, an average of five hundred meters above and at least ten kilometers from water. These might be it. It makes sense. These could be our backups."

He nodded. "It fits."

Two hours later, we were all back in the Council room.

The early birds among us had seen the data and been brainstorming for hours when Zedda walked in, a blissful smile on her warm face. A knowing grin between us as we all settled in.

Paer briefed everyone, and handed over to Obowe and I.

I highlighted the rows of the chart corresponding to Meilo, Rhoda, Dever, and North Wal, and summarized everything.

"Any way to verify any of this?" Ganla asked. "Or at least troop numbers? It could be a trap."

I know. That'd been worrying me all morning. What if we sent teams and Calter had played us?

"We're sending scouts," I said. "Here's the limited satellite imagery we have." The screens changed to reveal four sets of overhead snapshots. "The pictures are grainy and the locations are well hidden, but there's one thing that makes us almost certain it's what we're looking for. See this." I pointed to a red and white circle. "These are VTOL landing pads. Most smaller facilities don't have 'em but *all* four suspected sites do. Makes sense. Emulates want a quick reboot, and to get back to civilization. They don't want to be stuck in the mountains or riding ground transit."

"And scouts?" Zedda asked.

"If we could use drones, we'd have visuals in six hours," Paer remarked. "But these bases, while secret, probably pack some major security and surveillance. We're sending locals disguised as backpackers to get close enough to report back. Should have the last updates by 16:00 tomorrow."

I resumed where Paer had left off. "We've notified local commanders and leaders of the situation. We need to act soon. The day after tomorrow, we set things in motion: attack the sites, trigger the riots, and launch primary attacks at five a.m. to catch them off guard." I took a deep breath. "Any questions?"

Mico nodded. "What do the simulations show?"

"We stopped going off sims a long time ago," Paer said. "Too many variables. We have a shot, it might be a small one, but we can pull it off. Let's focus on that, people!"

She gave a rundown on best case scenarios while I excused myself to run to the bathroom.

It was happening. I couldn't believe it.

When I got back, Lars had a holo playing in the center of the room. I realized what they were watching.

"You're not going to believe this, kid, a hundred million views since yesterday!" he burst out.

I froze in the doorway. "A hundred million?" I murmured once my mouth was working again.

"One. Hundred. Million." Lars laughed. "The GDR must be shitting themselves. It's been blowing up. They've delisted it 253 times but people are reuploading. The numbers keep rising and rising. You're famous, kid."

"I don't want to be famous," I said. "I want this to work. I could care less what people think about me."

"You might not care," Paer replied. "But they sure do." She pointed to the skyrocketing view counter.

I rolled my eyes. "Let's get back to business! There's a lot to—"

"No!" Zedda retorted, staring me down. "This is important. This is what we needed, what we hoped for. You need to do another. People need to know what to do. It's what we wanted. It's what *you* wanted." She gave me a hard look. "We need people to fight. They need you."

"She's right," Lars added. "We need another video for when the attacks start, to coordinate this thing."

Of course, they were right. "Fine. What do I need to do?"

Filming wasn't as easy this time. The day passed in a blur, one painful take after another until Lars was satisfied. If that wasn't bad enough, the mess was a bombardment of people. *Everyone* knew my name and wanted to talk. It was *way* too much.

52

UNCHARTED TERRITORY

The next day was a whirlwind; people coming and going, plans finalized, scrapped, and remade, scouts confirming locations. It was a rollercoaster for everyone.

Ganla and Zedda came to blows over a press release and Mico had a queasy stomach all day. Then there was Obowe. He'd risen in a strong honor culture, killing his first lion at twelve and his first cop at sixteen. When he'd turned fifteen, he'd undergone the right of passage every boy in his clan did, a brutal week alone in the jungles of Zone Four amongst nature's toughest predators. He'd emerged a week later, a fully fledged man, a warrior through and through, built for battle, wise in his ways, and with the untempered pride of his people. He was devastated there weren't any emulate facilities in Zone Four. His people "deserved the chance to prove themselves."

He called the various tribes and rebel alliances all day to drum up support, twenty or thirty in total: loud, defiant and often slamming his fist to emphasize a point.

There was a passionate beauty in the way he spoke, in the way his deep voice begged, pleaded, and challenged local leaders to take up arms. "Will Africa contribute nothing?" he'd boom. "Will our children and our children's children hear tales of foreigners freeing Africans from the shackles of history? Our people need you. Will *you* stand by and do nothing, or will you fight?"

Always some variation of that. And it worked. Our numbers kept rising. From hoping for ten-to-fifteen percent of Zone Two towns yesterday, to now, close to seventy-five percent committed, Obowe single-handedly united the towns and tribesmen in a way none before him ever could.

As he left the room to take another call, I stood and pointed to the door. "I need *that* level of conviction from you. Obowe's done thirty calls today, spoken with leaders of every major town in Zone Four and quintupled our support. Tomorrow, two weeks from now, two years... will we regret not trying *everything* in our power? I for one, won't take that risk. I'm guessing none of you will either."

They were all nodding. Lars even gave me a thumbs-up.

"Tomorrow, I'll be joining the rebels in the attack on the capital," I said. "Lars, I need you there filming. If I have to be their warrior hero, so be it, but I won't let my people die in the streets while I do nothing! If I can inspire others to join the cause, all the better."

"I'll be there, kid," Lars replied with a grim determination.

"The rest of you," I said. "What do you need help with? Lars and I can make calls or help with coffee, *anything* to make this happen. Are you with me?"

A brief smile touched Paer's lips. "Yes, we are. Get to work, folks!"

A newfound fire blazed in their eyes as we separated, long nights ahead of us.

After a few hours with Lars and later Paer, I had to see Zedda. I snuck out under the guise of hunger, and headed to her room.

The halls were crowded this time of night, but with my hood, I slipped through with relative anonymity. Reaching her door, I paused. What if she didn't want me? What if it was a one-time thing... the heat of the moment?

Should I be here? Who was I to assume? At last, I knocked, albeit timidly.

"One second!" She opened the door, looking surprised. "Oh, Raek." Her face lit up.

"I wanted to see you so we could talk. Now a good time?" I asked in a quiet voice.

"Now's perfect." Her eyes gleamed with a devilish intensity as she grabbed my shirt and yanked me in.

I'd wanted to talk about us, about the future, about what might happen tomorrow. That didn't happen. Instead, we found comfort, desire, and more in each other's arms.

Time flew and stopped, ceased to exist at all.

After, I grabbed my shirt and slipped it over my head. "I wanted to talk about us. What is this, this thing between us?"

"Let's just get through the next couple days," she said with a crushing nonchalance. "There's enough to think about and do without any distractions. This," she gestured between us, "who knows what *this* is." Our eyes locked. "I like you, Raek. But let's not complicate things yet, at least until the fighting's over," she added. "Deal?"

"Deal." I tried to sound more enthusiastic than I felt. It wasn't easy. This was uncharted territory for me. The wait and see, *laissez-faire-ness* was killing me. And she meant something to me, a lot, actually.

But she was right, now wasn't the time.

53

RISE AND SHINE

M y SmartCore woke me at 4:00 a.m. to get ready and I snuck out, snatching a glimpse of Zedda's sleeping form as I did. She was beautiful and caring, even in sleep. A vibrant energy and vitality emanated from her, an infectious optimism and go-get-it attitude I loved. Irresistible. Smiling to myself, I slid out the door.

"Finally up?" Paer asked.

What? I stopped dead. "What are you doing?"

"Come on, kid. I may be old but I'm not *that* old. I can recognize love, especially the young, crazy kind."

Crap. "Don't tell the others."

"Your secret is safe with me, but I'd be surprised if most didn't know. Enough about your love life, we have more important things to discuss. The teams are in position, ready to attack on our signal. Backup's ten kilometers out in case they fail. Do you have the announcement ready?"

Um... "The what?"

"Lars thought it would be good for people to hear it from you that we'd destroyed the brain-field backups. Explain why it mattered and why we did it."

This was the first I was hearing about it. "Did he now?"

"Well, you had a busy night, didn't you?" she added with a smirk. "Find him, get that done."

I blushed. "What about local militias?"

"You were right. We doubled, and in some cases tripled, support in the major regions thanks to the calls. It's huge. Is it enough though, that's the question."

Lars called.

'On my way.' I hung up before he could reply. "Gotta go," I apologized, running for the stairs.

"Where have you been?" Lars snapped as I flung open the door. "We need to get this done." He was pacing, screens arrayed around the room, bags under his hypercaffeinated red eyes.

"Sorry." I looked away. "Fell asleep early."

He rolled his eyes but rather than pry, talked about what he had in mind. Fifteen minutes later, we had our recording. "This will have to do," he said. "We don't have time to try again."

Five minutes later, the Council room. "Attacks start in twenty-five minutes," Paer said. "Anything else, folks?"

Wow, twenty-five minutes.

We shook our heads.

Paer flipped a switch on the table, and four separate holograms appeared, two men and two women, all in fatigues.

'Can you hear me?' Paer asked.

'Yes.''Roger that.' 'Loud and clear.' 'Yes ma'am.' They responded in a blur of voices.

'You have the green light. Start the assault. Permission to use any force necessary. Provide updates every ten minutes when possible. We need to know where we stand.'

'Affirmative,' they answered in unison before signing off. One by one they disappeared, leaving us on the edge of our seats.

"And so it begins," Lars murmured.

"We need to go." I stood, nervous adrenaline coursing through me.

Zedda rose. "I'm going with you!"

I fought to keep my face a mask. "Don't they need you here?" It was too dangerous.

"Not a chance." She gave me a *don't even think about it* scorcher. "I'll be there watching your back."

So freaking stubborn. Damn, I loved that about her.

"Holos all set, Lars?" I asked.

He nodded. "Ania has everything. She'll help Agtha upload when the time comes."

"Are we missing anything?" I looked around. There was always something.

Obowe shook his head. "It is time we play our cards. Go, we will be here. Good luck and give them hell."

"We will," I promised.

54
STREET PARADE

We arrived downtown thirty minutes later, in time for the start of the action. A crowd gathered on the marble steps of the Justice Building, thousands of individuals of every shape, size and color lining the streets, carrying pitchforks and blasters, audio amplifiers, and even a few old powder rifles.

It was a sight to behold—stripes and scales and fur—animotes of every age and walk of life, here to fight and die for their future. It gave me goosebumps.

Further up the road was a DNS barricade, an unending wall of black-clad soldiers. VTOLs hovered overhead, news crews and air force ships vying for space and to control crowds.

It was way more than I expected. There had to be a few hundred thousand on the streets, twenty to forty percent of the capital. The energy was electrifying, both terrible and awe-inspiring at once.

A voice burst through. "THIS IS THE DEPARTMENT OF NATIONAL SECURITY. RETURN TO YOUR HOMES AT ONCE. YOU ARE IN DIRECT VIOLATION OF GOVERNMENTAL DECREE SEVENTY-SEVEN SECTION SIX. BE ADVISED, WE ARE AUTHORIZED TO USE FORCE IF NECESSARY. RETURN TO YOUR HOMES IMMEDIATELY."

A *BOOM* shook the streets. Hundreds of amplifiers came to life, voices joining in a crackle. Song erupted. "WE AIN'T GONNA TAKE IT, NO, WE AIN'T GONNA TAKE IT. WE'RE AIN'T GONNA TAKE IT ANYMORE!"

The music got louder and louder, and my heart shook, deep bass rocking my very core. When it couldn't get louder, it faded and my voice echoed *everywhere*. The video from two days ago reverberated through the streets, silencing everyone. People froze. What was happening?

A *buzz* enveloped the crowd as people stomped their feet, chanting. "Down with the GDR. Down with the GDR. DOWN WITH THE GDR."

I joined in as the cheers eclipsed even the heart-stopping music earlier, tension building. This was it. The moment was magical. The emotion, overpowering.

BANG.

Someone fired. Shit.

Shots filled the air; tens, hundreds, soon thousands... The police had opened fire.

People scattered, regrouped, and charged the black-clad soldiers and cops. Objects hurtled through the air. Explosions everywhere. The building to our right erupted in flame. Cars and scooters went up in smoke. Around us, screaming animotes collapsed.

This wasn't how it was supposed to go.

A massive rev stopped my heart. What was that? To the left, a huge military transport barreled toward us; it must have housed a hundred men. No... I opened my mouth to shout when another appeared behind us, boxing us in.

Zedda grabbed my arm, pointing. A third rocketed toward the crowd from the right. They weren't boxing us in, they were mowing us down like bowling pins. How could they? Dozens were crushed by oncoming vehicles as fear jolted the crowd. It had gone from a fight to a slaughter in seconds. Their VTOLs opened fire, high caliber blasts ripping three meter wide holes in our ranks.

What had I done? Blood everywhere.

Targeting the closest transport, I laid down heavy fire and hit the driver. The truck careened into a wall in an explosion of glass and concrete. Lars and Zedda battled a VTOL to my left as a bearish man with an anti-aircraft gun was blown apart not twenty meters away. That could have been her...

Sprinting toward the onslaught, I fired. My first shots missed as the vehicle bulldozed bodies, picking up steam. The fifth shot got him, but it was too late... speeding for a huge crowd. There'd be hundreds of fatalities.

I hurdled a boy throwing rocks at the oncoming behemoth, and lost it. Not him too, he was just a child. Slamming the rig, a shock-wave rippled through me and the truck launched into the air, landing five meters from the screaming boy.

"Go!" I yelled. "Get out of here!" He ran, and made it three steps before he was blown apart by an airborne blast. No! I could have—a soldier fired, but I shot him.

To my left, Henk stood over the wreckage of the last transport, firing like mad. Zedda was right; he was an animal in combat.

Speaking of Zedda, where was she? Was she okay? My heart pounded. What about Lars?

A message from Paer: *Two locations down.*

What? Oh, yeah, the brain-fields.

An endless supply of soldiers piled into the fray, and from the east, the roar of more VTOLs. We were getting murdered.

Something slammed into me and I spun, ducking as I leveled my blaster. Holy shit, Lars!

"There you are!" he yelled over the chaos. "I almost killed you. We're getting massacred."

"I know! Have you seen Zedda?"

"No, but we need to push back one of those columns or we're all dead—" Something streaked toward us and I tackled him. The ground we'd been standing on exploded in a plume.

"Follow me!" I darted down a side street, away from the action. Could we flank them, like Thorn's men? We had to.

Lars seized my arm. "Are you running away?"

What? "No." We passed a zombie-filled VR den, turned, and burst onto the main thoroughfare behind the advancing column.

Switching to automatic, I opened fire. The first line of soldiers whose backs were to us were cut down instantly. We didn't let up, not even pausing to aim as wave after wave collapsed to the bloody pavement.

In twenty seconds, their column of several thousand had been reduced to a third. As they countered, rebels charged. It was the *perfect* accidental two-pronged attack.

Within minutes, all lay dead or dying.

A cheer from our supporters, the first moral victory of the one-sided battle. Somehow, I couldn't bring myself to cheer death. They'd chosen sides, but that didn't mean I had to like it.

Paer called. 'We got trouble!'

55

VISITORS

'The Dever team called, they haven't located the brain-field banks,' Paer said.

A lucky shot whizzed past as we ran for cover. 'What's the problem?'

'It's Calter,' she hissed.

'What?' Despite the carnage, my heart stopped. What about him?

'He's there, with a special forces strike team no less.'

I froze. 'But the first two facilities were destroyed?'

'Yeah,' she said.

'Patch me through to Dever.'

'One sec.'

A second voice crystalized, clean cut face to my right. 'Rogers here.'

'Rogers, this is Raek Mekorian. What's your status?'

'We captured the facility, sir!' he barked. 'But we've haven't found any storage banks, sir.'

'Paer, did the other teams find the brain banks?' I asked.

'Nothing labeled brain-fields or emulations, but they found matching neural hookups at both locations. Sending images now.'

An alien-looking image materialized, a metallic halo crown covered in spaced dents, tentacled black wires winding downward to a silver harness with another metallic halo.

Where had I seen that? Think.

An explosion shook the alleyway as it hit me. Lars' book, *The Rise of Immortality*. I accessed my saved memories. A picture in Chapter 9 depicted an eerily similar setup captioned *Earliest Attempts at Emulation*.

That had to be it. I told Rogers and Paer, but they hadn't found anything like it in Dever.

'You *have* to find that brain-field bank,' Paer cut in. 'Everything is riding on that.'

All our best laid plans... 'How long until Calter's forces breach the base?' I asked.

'Hold on. We hacked the cams.' Several images materialized— fifteen in total—showing the fortress: walls, perimeter, everything.

'You getting this?' Rogers asked.

We were, but Lars wrenched me behind a recycler, and shoved a hand over my mouth. "Shhh!" He held his finger to his lips, and pointed to a wave of soldiers marching down the street, backup for their fallen comrades.

'Shit!' Rogers yelled. 'Hangar alarm is going off. Smalls, get over here!'

A huge soldier ran to him and saluted. 'Reporting for duty, sir!'

'Smalls,' Rogers said. 'I need you and Drog to check that, ASAP!'

Our entire plan hung in the balance and I couldn't do a thing about it.

The hanger appeared, a forklift racing toward an abandoned VTOL, a guard at the wheel.

They missed a guard. 'He's trying to save the backups!' I yelled.

'Smalls, Drog, come in!' Rogers squawked. 'We got company. There's another guard in the hanger driving a forklift to save the brain-fields. Their reinforcements breached the base. Shoot! Doors two and four are compromised as well!'

We were losing. This couldn't be happening.

This was Calter's chance at immortality—and deniability—and he was taking it. I'd miscalculated...

Two figures sprinted into the hanger as the forklift was in the process of loading the VTOL. They opened fire. A few shots hit home but nothing happened.

The hanger doors blew off their hinges, daylight poured in along with black-clad figures. The soldiers concentrated their fire on Smalls and Drog as the VTOL's engines purred.

This was it...

Calter appeared on another screen, eyes twinkling and smug as he tapped out Mozart with one hand, holding the other to his ear.

Now what? 'It's okay, Rogers,' I said.' You did your best—' A cry cut me off.

Rogers dashed through the facility, carrying something, headed for the hanger. What the—?

'What are you doing, soldier?' Paer yelled.

The object in his hand was about the size of a brick, not quite rectangular, an almost doughy shape. What? No, it couldn't be... A bomb.

'Rogers, no!' I bellowed.

Into the hanger he sprinted, soldiers everywhere. No one noticed until it was too late.

'Rogers!' I screamed. Don't do this. Not you too.

'I'm sorry!' He yelled, diving toward the motionless VTOL. 'Freedom!' His voice reverberated through the cavernous hanger as his finger pressed the detonator.

Nothing happened.

56

MAKING IT RAIN

H e exploded in a ball of light, shockwave pulsing the hanger, incinerating everything, before the camera konked. A high-pitched static ringing.

'Paer?' I said in a shocked stupor.

'I'm here,' she answered in a hushed voice.

We'd sent those soldiers to their fate. After a full minute of silence, I asked how things were going.

It wasn't looking good. 'Their air support is killing us,' she said.

'How soon until the fourth facility's breached?' That's all we needed. Once that was done, there was no stopping it.

An officer passing our alley noticed us and opened fire. We ran.

'They keep sending reinforcements!' I yelled to Paer as we raced down the alley. 'Do we have *any* backup?'

No, and no. And it was an hour until team three arrived on site.

We rounded the corner as a large contingent of protesters charged the Parliamentary steps, flinging homemade bombs and spraying the building with blaster fire.

Four nearby VTOLs turned, concentrating their fiery carnage on those rushing the stairs. Concrete and marble spewed as groups of rebels were cremated in an instant.

An anti-aircraft gun from somewhere in the crowd took out the closest bird. Within seconds, the man holding it—and everyone unlucky enough to be within four meters—had been reduced to ashes.

Our guys didn't stand a chance. I targeted the nearest VTOL, cycling my blaster settings. After the flying fiasco, I'd done some research. While VTOLs were resistant to blaster fire, their instruments were highly sensitive and relied on precision maneuvering. Small errors or losses of power could be catastrophic.

And catastrophic was *just* what I needed. Would it be enough?

Selecting stun mode, I locked on and fired twice as the ground to my right imploded. Bingo.

The engine stalled midair and the VTOL plummeted. Less than twenty meters from impact, it roared to life. Crap, pilot must have rebooted. I fired again. The engine froze and resumed its fall, exploding as it bounced off an empty fountain and took out half the World Bank.

The other pilots pulled back. They'd seen their friend's fates and wanted no part.

A cheer went up from the rebels, even as a micronade clunked at my feet.

Oh crap.

Zedda.

It exploded, launching me into the air.

57

HEAVEN AND HELL

S omething wasn't right. I'd died, and gone to hell, that was the only explanation.

But hell wasn't real. There was no right and wrong, no good and evil...

Yet, *here* I was. This was no dream. It wasn't VR either. Everything was real, and somehow, ethereal.

The world was happening around me, like I'd become something *else*.

Bodies everywhere, butchery beyond imagination. Raw horror. Everything reeked of death. It was ALL my fault!

But who'd won? I needed to know. I headed toward the worst of it but stopped dead. Henk was sprawled on the frozen earth, coughing blood.

'Henk? There you are. Can you hear me?'

"Help!" he cried. "Can anyone hear me? Is anyone there?"

'Henk, it's me.' I reached to pick him up. 'I got you budd—' The words died on my lips. Where were my hands? My arms? My body was gone.

No No No! Was I dead? Was I a ghost? Or something...

I ran—or glided, I guess—away as fast I could. I was going to be sick.

'Can anyone hear me?' I screamed. 'Help, help!' What was happening?

Farther, faster; bodies and blood and death as far as the eye could see.

The scene changed. I was somewhere else, yet time stood still. A sign, *Itany*. Here too: death, destruction, suffering.

'What is this place?' I yelled in a wordless scream. 'What do you want from me?'

Suddenly, back in Caen, a small side street. Zedda's bloody face alongside a headless man. What was she doing here? I ran to where she lay. Her chest and torso were gone, nothing left. No, this couldn't be happening. Tears came as I threw back my head and wailed. She was all I'd had left, and she was gone.

'Why are you crying, son?' a voice behind me asked. 'We all lose loved ones, you of all people should know that.'

It sounded like, but it *couldn't* be.

Fitz? I turned. Sure enough, it was him, his presence at least. I felt it.

'You're here?' I whispered. 'How?'

'Yes, son, I am. World's worst afterlife, isn't it? I was expecting tropical beaches, beautiful ladies, fine wines… Oh well, what are you going to do?' He smiled.

'You're dead too?'

'Don't worry about that, worry about you. You managed to screw things pretty good. I'm gone for what, two months, and you and Lars start all kinds of trouble.'

'We thought we'd win,' I mumbled, ashamed. 'We thought we were ready.'

'This is winning?' he asked, sarcastic even in death.

'So we lost?' After all that...

'Does it matter?' he said. 'Look around. This isn't winning or losing, this is ending. There's an old song I like. You might not know it. "Nobody wins when everyone's losing. It's like one step forward and two steps back..." Forget it, I can't sing. You get the point.'

I nodded, or at least meant to. 'It's too late now.'

'It's never too late. We're having this conversation, aren't we?' he quipped. 'Think about it, son. I need to go, my time is running short.'

But wasn't this infinite? 'Wait!' I protested. 'Wait, I need to ask you—"

He disappeared as a sharp pain seared my chest.

This was it.

58

TRIPS AND SHIPS

I came to in a big white room, bright lights piercing my eyes. Ugh. I coughed as pain shot through my chest.

Where was I? What happened?

My hands! There they were, attached to my arms. I had fingers too, but couldn't move them, my arms either. Everything was numb. Was this hell? Torture after purgatory?

A noise caught my attention. A floating screen above me, numbers flashing, and what looked like a heartbeat. Another loud beep. Was this a hospital? Where were Dr. P and Dr. R?

Zedda burst in. She hadn't died too, had she? Please no. I passed out.

Bits and pieces of what they were saying flooded in.

"Are you sure his brain,"

"...a high explosive."

"lucky to be alive..."

"Should we wake him?"

My head spun, vision blurring as my eyes opened. "Howw lonngg haavve I beeeenn outtt?" I slurred. "WWWWhat happpeeened?"

"Raek, are you okay?" Zedda sprang from the chair and ran to me. "Thank goodness. Can you hear me?"

Zedda... what was I supposed to remember? "I'mmm ffinee. Ddddooesss myyy voiccce sssounnddd funnnnnnyyyy tttttoo youuu?"

A door opened, and Lars swooped in, followed by a nurse in a white gown and goggles.

"You made it, kid." Lars smiled. "We were worried there."

"Where am I? What happened? Did we win? Wait..." Something on the edge of my awareness, something big. What? "Am I alive? Where's Fitz?"

"What?" They looked at each other, bewildered.

"You are *very* much alive," the nurse cut in. "My name's Nurse Jannie, and you're back at headquarters. I can't believe you're awake. A micronade from two meters... you're lucky to be alive." She shook her head. "Never seen anything like it."

"I died!" I gasped. "I was dead. My body was gone. I talked to Fitz. There were bodies everywhere." My voice rose as I recounted what happened, including finding Zedda's body.

"It's okay, Raek," Zedda squeezed my hand as she wiped a tear. "Everything's fine, you're here." I was so glad she was too.

"Could be the sedative," Jannie remarked. "I put you on an IV the moment you got back. You were quite banged up. Didn't think you'd survive, to be honest."

"But if I didn't die, if none of that was real, what happened?"

"Well, things were going bad and got worse," Lars said. "I got you out of there and hid your body in a dumpster, but the DNS realized you were gone. We were sitting ducks without air support." He paused. "Around 10:00 a.m., the last facility fell. We'd done it, but we were down to a few thousand. There were four or five times as many soldiers," he added.

A few thousand... the streets must be littered with bodies. I'd sent all of them to their deaths...

"The video played on the Everything Store sign," Zedda said. "The fighting stopped after thirty seconds. When you said the backups had been destroyed, a hush went through the crowd. Everyone froze. The world stopped. You were closer, Lars, you tell him."

"Soldiers threw down their weapons and bolted. What started as one or two turned into a torrent. Soon, hundreds were dropping their guns, running for their lives. Several officers opened fire on the deserters but it didn't stem the flow. We were dumbstruck. Clashes broke out amongst the GDR as cynetics, emulates, and enhancers shot anyone not in their regiment. A holy war ignited."

"Paer ordered us to stand down," Zedda said. "We retreated amidst the madness."

An exhale. Had I been holding my breath? I was terrified of ruining the moment. "Then what?"

"That's it," Lars answered. "It's 13:00 now."

Was that possible? "I need to get out of here!"

"Out of the question, young man!" the nurse barked. "I have to monitor you overnight. Too many possible complications. Your heart rate hasn't stabilized, hormone levels are out of whack, and you've sustained damage in—"

I sat up. "Sorry, Ms. Jannie, wasn't it? I'm leaving, whether you like it or not! I *need* to see the Council. Give me a booster or something to help me recover faster. I'll sign a waiver, or we can pretend I escaped. There's too much at stake."

She shook her head. "I know hardheadedness when I see it. Don't make me regret this." She unhooked the sensors. "No strenuous activity, meetings are fine. You two!" she snapped at Lars and Zedda. "Make sure he doesn't do anything stupid. He has to stay off his feet a couple days."

She set up remote monitoring to track my vitals and checked biometrics before grabbing a translucent vial. "In fifteen minutes, once this IV's done, you're good to go. Okay?"

"Sounds great," Lars said before I could object. When she left, Lars added, "I couldn't say everything while she was here. Here's the latest." He shared a series of files, the casualty numbers staggering.

My IV beeped. Finally!

Pulling the needle from my arm, I stood, and my legs crumbled, head woozy. Lars and Zedda grabbed me by the shoulders and helped me to a wheelchair. It was old school, not even electric, but it would get the job done. I started to push, but Zedda took over, gliding me across the polished floor.

"Thanks," I whispered once Lars was out of earshot.

She grinned. "No worries. Thanks for saving our necks back there."

Again, I was lost for words. What could I say?

Five minutes later, the War Room. The air shook with pent up energy, crumpled cups, and half-empty coffee mugs scattered about.

"Any updates?" I asked.

"The web's exploding with news and controversy," Ganla said. "The GDR instituted martial law in several cities and we've captured five others. It's unbelievable, more than we ever expected. Racial gang warfare at its worst."

"Members of the government have fled," Lars added. "Nothing's been heard from the Board—with the exception of our friend Calter—since 11:00 a.m. this morning. Reports say Gileu and Zu retreated to private palaces in the mountains, and many more are thinking about it."

A knock on the door. It slammed open without waiting for a response. A boy hurried in, hands on his knees. "Check the WNN! Ania sent me, said you had to see this."

In seconds, the simulcast was up. A dim, cramped room, a well-dressed man slumped in a chair. What the—?

'What you're seeing is live!' a voice cut in. 'This is Richad Daks, and the following feed is our beloved Minister of Intelligence, Gregori Schwarz. Wait, his captor's coming back.'

A black door at the back of the room opened, a tall masked intruder entering with a wave to the camera. 'If you are just tuning in,' Daks continued, 'Minister Schwarz has been abducted by a yet unidentified group, and is being held against his will.'

The creep turned to the camera, smiling. 'Wondering why Gregori Schwarz is sitting here, hogtied like the criminal he is? Ask Minister Schwarz, this is nothing new for him, except *being* in the chair, that is. Our "great minister" has overseen the torture and execution of countless dissidents and political prisoners over the years. You don't become an emulate-class Board member without ruffling a few feathers, do you Gregori?' He smacked the bound man hard across the cheek.

Schwarz's black eyes glinted as he spat. 'Take your hands off me. You'll regret this. I'll make you beg for death.' His powerful body shook but the chair was bolted to the floor.

'I'm sure you would,' the mysterious figure replied. 'But here you are. And your brain-field's gone. No reboot *this* time.' He laughed, grabbing a knife from the counter. Schwarz squirmed.

'How's it feel to be mortal, to be vulnerable?' his captor taunted. 'You've personally killed at least two dozen animotes and enhancers, even a handful of cynetics. And that's not counting the thousands of executions you've ordered. Gregori Schwarz, how do you plead to the charges put forth by the people's court?' the masked man hissed, mouth inches from the Schwarz' ear.

'What? Charges...? You're insane! Untie me, you—'

'Wrong answer,' the vigilante cackled. 'The people's court hereby finds you guilty of murder, torture, and harm to the nth degree, and sentences you to die for your sins. Any last words?' He twirled the cleaver between his fingers.

'Holy hell!' Richad Daks swore. 'I think he's going to...'

Schwarz went white, quivering. 'You can't do this, you can't. I'm a Minister of the Board, a representative of the GDR! Tears fell as the blade swung, piercing his neck and thudding into the wall.

This wasn't happening...

'Justice. Is. Served!' The vigilante's gavel fist hammered the table. 'Let them pay for their crimes.'

The video ended.

59

POWER

There were a slew of simulcast murders after that. Despite curfews, battles raged into the night, roaming gangs seeking outlets for decades of hatred and resentment.

Tension—brewing on all sides—continued to boil over.

By the end of day two, the death toll surpassed eight million, another twenty-to-fifty million suffering mild to severe injuries. And that didn't include Neurowebbers.

Most cities lost power for a while, and many VR inhabitants died instantly, feeble medkit-sustained bodies not designed for extended power loss. A hundred fifty million more lives extinguished overnight.

It was sickening. What had we done? What had I done? How'd I let this happen?

I couldn't sleep that night, the next either. Widespread violence haunted my dreams. Reports of cities burning, full-scale bombings, at least a dozen high profile assassinations. This *had* to stop or we'd tear ourselves apart and enter a new dark age; that's what history suggested.

The one bright spot—if you could call it a bright spot—was we were winning, at least by the numbers. The majority of casualties were enhancers and cynetics. There'd been a lot of emulates killed the first day too, but their numbers were small and their importance so diminished, mobs lost interest. This was about power now, revenge and power.

Simulations showed we'd control the government in three-to-five days with a lion's share majority: sixty-four percent. It would continue to rise. So why did I feel empty inside? We'd been fighting for this—dreamed of this—for decades... freedom, liberation. Why'd it feel so wrong?

And why couldn't I sleep?

I should meditate. I needed clarity, needed direction. Clearing my head might help.

Sitting against the wall, I closed my eyes and focused on my breathing. My thoughts swarmed, a tsunami of doubts and fears and whatifs threatening to capsize me. I resisted. It died down, became a stream, a trickle, and dried to nothingness. Images of pain and violence appeared. Eventually, they stopped bothering me.

Once my mind was clear, I opened my eyes to a renewed sense of calm and purpose. I knew what to do. The question was, could I pull it off?

It was 2:21 in the morning. No one was up, but this couldn't wait, so, I rehearsed what I had to say. Once I felt ready as ever, I turned to the camera. Was I making a big mistake? Was I about to do *this*?

"Hello everyone, my name's Raek Mekorian. The last few days I've been called everything from a hero to a villain, terrorist, messiah... Whatever your thoughts, I'm here to apologize for the war and suffering that's befallen our civilization. And I say *civilization*, because we're all one people—one humanity—united in our collective history.

"Our world's collapsing before our eyes. Wholesale destruction on an unprecedented scale... and at our own hands. I propose a truce, a meeting of the minds of *all* subspecies—animote and cynetic, enhancer and emulate—to decide our future. We can't go on like this," I continued, citing stats and forecasts of how bad things could get.

This had to work. It had to.

"Clearer heads must prevail. How many more brothers and sisters, mothers and fathers, friends and loved ones, must we sacrifice to this mindless struggle? We're all human, we're all equal. We are one!"

It felt right. I hit publish.

60

A BIG TABLE

B ANG. BANG. BANG. "Kid, are you there? Raek? Get up!"
I sat up from the mat on my floor as Lars shouted, "Open up! What were you thinking?"

I staggered to the hammering door. "What?"

"The video... Did you do *that* last night? The Council's freaking out." His eyes narrowed, an angry expression creasing his face. "What were you thinking?"

"I did what needed to be done."

He shook his head and sighed. "Let's go, kid. They're waiting downstairs. I brought coffee." He handed me a mug.

Three minutes later, we were outside the War Room. Lars grabbed my shoulder. "I can't protect you in there, what you did... You crossed the line."

I nodded, not saying anything, and pushed open the door.

The War Room froze as we entered.

"Raek," Paer said at once. "Do you know what your video has done?"

"Probably what I intended. Stopped the fighting and made people question what they're fighting for?"

"We had the GDR right where we wanted them!" Ganla snapped.

"You've seen the numbers, we were growing stronger every day."

"We weren't growing stronger, we were getting weaker," I said. "Proportionally stronger, sure, but millions were dying for *no* reason!"

Ganla's fiery eyes flashed. "If we want to defeat the enemy, we have to crush them. We can't afford to show weak—"

"That's your problem!" I cut in. "There is no enemy. We are *all* people here."

"Raek," Mico replied, "you know what Ganla means. For animotes to gain power and take our rightful seat at the head of the table—"

Damn it. "You don't get it, do you? That mentality is what created this mess in the first place. It won't fix it! This isn't about propping up animotes, it's about equality. It's about *lasting* peace." Hadn't they heard of Mandela? What would Fitz say?

Ganla's face contorted. "How can you speak of peace and equality after all that's happened?"

"Revenge and retribution always leads to more bloodshed." I shook my head. "Look at World War II, we all had *that* in history class!"

"Raek," Paer said. "This isn't about revenge, not yet. It's about military strategy. The fact is, you compromised the advantage we had. A truce gives the other side time to regroup, and maybe unify. If that happens, we're back where we started."

Oh... "I didn't think about that. But we need to end the bloodshed for all our sakes."

"You're just a boy!" Ganla said. "What do you know about—"

Just a boy? I slammed my fist on the table. "How dare you? Who planned to target brain-fields and figured out the locations? Who captured Thorn and tricked Calter? Who nearly died yesterday? Just a boy..." I scoffed. "How dare you?"

"Raek's right," Lars said. "He has *at least* as much right as any to a seat at this table. We owe him. Let's not forget who made the videos and is our rallying cry," he added.

Thank you, Lars. I knew I could count on you.

"What do you propose?" Paer eye's bore into me, silencing Ganla with an icy stare.

"Negotiations," I replied. "We send delegates from all subspecies to hash out a new governance system, propose non-binding decrees and open 'em to public vote. If two-thirds approve, it becomes law."

"And if we don't like the results?" Paer countered.

"We accept the consequences, like everyone else. We have to negotiate in good faith if we want others to." Talk turned to what an ideal system would look like, and we agreed, a direct democracy with a higher governing body.

Lars was skeptical. "You think emulates and cynetics would agree; going from elite to average overnight?"

We knew the other side's weaknesses, didn't we? "Think about it," I said. "If you'd beaten down animotes your entire life, what would you fear most?" I paused. "Trading places... They'll be happy we aren't out for blood. And we'll bring that up." No one said we have to play *totally* fair. "As long as they feel they're getting an honest deal."

In the end, a vote: five-to-two in favor. It felt like a win, but at the same time, meant we'd be having more meetings. Lovely...

It took two days for other groups to agree to a ceasefire. The delay cost another million lives, and the cynetics, of course, were last to cave, recognizing their position of power. Even they couldn't fight the public outcry forever.

Once the fighting fizzled out, we'd lost 144 million in four days. And that wasn't including the Neuroweb junkies... Humanity was on the brink, again.

It was decided Paer, Obowe, and I would go as the animote representatives. The agreements were non-binding, and people would have to ratify them, but I felt an enormous responsibility. What if I screwed up?

Before I knew it, the talks were upon us. I couldn't sleep. Even spending the night with Zedda didn't help. *Everything* was riding on this.

I awoke at 6:30, ruined, like I'd been beaten for days with a club. Struggling to my feet, muscles sore and brain foggy, I thought through these past months—the suffering and hardships at the hands of the GDR, Elly, my family. Everything...

And Zedda... Lying there, she was the picture of peaceful serenity.

Why'd she make me feel like this? And even after hours and hours sharing everything with one another, she was a mystery.

But I had a job to do. People were relying on me. I *needed* coffee.

Obowe was in the mess when I got there, nursing a steaming cup of caffeinated goodness. "Ready, Raek?"

"Ready as I'll ever be. Have you seen—" The door opened and the wiry woman stepped in. "Speak of the devil."

"Good, you two are up," Paer commented. "Ready?"

"Waiting on you, Agtha," Obowe said in what could have been a joke, but his face was more of a blank stare. You never could tell with him.

"Let's get lids and go," Paer said after her first sip. "We're better early than late."

We chit-chatted on the way to the entrance and I was reminded of that day Zedda first brought Fitz and I here. So much had happened. Was it about to come to a close?

A short VTOL ride and we were outside the great library. The building was majestic, an air of power and purpose that grabbed me. The white marble arches and massive stone staircase had the historic feel of ancient Rome, ascending the Library of Alexandria. This was the center of the known world, the bastion of science and reason, and of humanity's progress. There weren't many left... Would it be enough?

Powder white snow coated the treetops and sidewalks, giving an ethereal feel to the whole experience. We were the only ones here, no screaming protesters or advocacy groups. We'd agreed to a three block perimeter to protect the proceedings. At least for now, it was working.

At the top of the steps, I gazed out at the city. Not two weeks ago, bloodshed engulfed these streets. Hundreds of thousands dead, buildings incinerated, bodies littering the frozen earth. Today, all was calm and quiet.

The contrast was eerie.

The door opened as we approached, and we stepped through oak-paneled double doors. Holy cow: level upon level of books, manuscripts, digital files, all manner of statues, photography, and art. It was as if Michelangelo met da Vinci, Jobs, and Einstein in the epitome of man's creativity and progress.

Obowe elbowed me. Shoot, we'd arrived. At the embossed wooden table in the center of the main level sat a small group that appeared to be enhancers.

Two tall men sat rigid in high-backed chairs, observing us as we approached. One had short blond hair, the beginnings of a beard, and blue eyes that invited confidence. His sturdy neighbor sported a bomber jacket, buzzcut, and enough gritty facial hair to display dominance as a male. He whispered to the woman to his right, a drop dead brunette with deep brown eyes, high cheekbones, and an air of intelligence. She was stunning, irresistible actually, holding me transfixed. I thought of Zedda and felt ashamed.

Paer broke the ice. "Looks like we're not the first ones here."

"Pleasure to meet you." The blond man pushed back his chair and stood, colleagues following suit.

The enhancers had wanted to get the lay of the land as well. We both wanted to ensure we weren't walking into an ambush.

Pleasantries completed, Obowe circled the table arranging microcams to prevent any funny business. As he sat, the Library doors opened and sunlight streamed in. The cynetics and emulates had arrived together. Interesting.

The two parties marched wordlessly toward us. Calter led the way for the cynetics, staring me down. He knew he'd been played and hadn't seen it coming. It'd be interesting to see how things played out. I doubted his fellow delegates knew. He wasn't the type to disclose anything. Maybe we could use that...

The emulates followed at a distance with an unmistakable tension. The Minister of Commerce, Jean Gileu, and I locked eyes, death stares burning into me. Where was Lin Zu?

After strained introductions, they too set up recording gear.

No one said anything.

I stood. "I'm glad you all came." The faces around the table were impossible to gauge. "We have to put a stop to the violence. We've all lost friends and family, and if the fighting continues... This isn't about winning or losing or avenging past crimes. This is about moving past those to an equal world of prosperity for all."

Obowe nodded, encouraged, and two of the others did likewise. The rest seemed unconvinced, angry, or fearful. This wouldn't be easy.

"I don't have an agenda," I continued. "These are preliminary talks. Everything needs to be ratified by the people. I've said enough. I want to let anyone with something to say to take the stage." I sat.

Jean Gileu burst to his feet, glaring at me. "In these discussions, let's not forget the actions and ramifications of the actions your people have committed. You've killed me, murdered my husband, and our two children. Our brain-fields were backed up, you ruined that, stole that from emulates everywhere. So let's not sit here and pretend you animotes are so high and mighty," he added. "You've murdered millions and act as if you're a savior."

I recoiled.

"And," the longhaired oddball to Jean's right added, "millions have died at your hands and millions more will before this is over. You caused *all* of it! You are the greatest mass murderer mankind has ever known!" He snarled.

Mass murderer, me? How could he—

"If we're honest," the beautiful enhancer piped up. I couldn't remember her name—Iyanna, I think—I'd been distracted. "The GDR treated our animote cousins like filth for decades. We're guilty as well. We let it happen. It was just a matter of time."

"We're not here to assign blame!" I cut in. "It doesn't matter who is at fault. We all are. But, things are broken and need fixing."

We went back and forth for hours, arguing minute details, politics, and, of course, blaming everyone but ourselves. Politicians...

At noon we broke for lunch, famished. It'd been a slog of a morning. Each group headed to find food and discuss the morning's developments.

Obowe and Paer were frustrated with the lack of progress. The emulates weren't happy with any way forward. Cynetics saw power as their probable future. Neither seemed willing to compromise. The chasm between felt insurmountable, and growing.

After a quick lunch, it was time to head back. As before, trust but verify. We all double checked recording equipment before starting. The afternoon session passed much the same as the morning, and by 19:00, I was sick of the whole thing. A day of arguments, and *nothing* to show for it.

Back at headquarters, we had more meetings in the War Room. Ugh.

I found Zedda afterwards, needing to be close to her tonight, to share my innermost thoughts and fears. Later, we made love. I told her about being called a mass murderer, about the blame and hate I felt, even my fears for us.

What if we failed, if I failed? Could I live in a world where my children were second class citizens at best?

A tear touched her eye as a happy smile enveloped her.

"What's wrong?" My heart skipped a beat. Was it something I said?

"Oh, it's nothing, Raek." She wiped a tear, staring at me in the dim light. "I was going to wait until this was all over." She smiled, blinking away uncharacteristic tears. "Raek, I'm pregnant!" she blurted out. "I'm pregnant." She laughed, smiling and crying all at once.

"I'm pregnant."

61

DREAM TEAM

We fell asleep in each other's arms, talking late into the night about the baby, the future, our life together. It was the scariest, happiest moment of my life. I was so ecstatic, I missed the obvious question...

You're going to be a dad, Raek. Over and over, that permeated my dreams in a cloud of contentment. But my last dream—the most vivid of all—was dark and mysterious, a storm beyond the horizon. It was coming.

I awoke with a start as my last sleep cycle ended. The room was empty. *Zedda?* Where was she? And why was my pulse pounding? Maybe she'd gotten hungry, or something happened. There was a message: *Emergency Meeting.* I hurried off.

The enhancers had proposed an alliance to discuss collaboration. Our goals were aligned and it was more or less what we'd expected. We'd meet for lunch to talk details.

Lars was worried for some reason. "Something doesn't feel right. My gut says something's off."

"If we were going to get anywhere," I said, "there has to be trust and compromise on all sides. Are we too afraid to make the first move?"

No one had a good response, and we agreed to see what they had to say.

What could it hurt?

62

A FRIENDLY ENCOUNTER

A VTOL whisked us off before I had the chance to talk to Zedda. I was going to be a dad. Wow! Talk about mixed emotions... Maybe it was the cybernetics. How else could we have a child together? A chimpish and a wolfish... Yet somehow, miraculously, we'd gotten pregnant. If we could, maybe others could as well. Happy goosebumps everywhere.

Focus, Raek. What was Priya saying?

"We've always structured government with the best and brightest to optimize outcomes for all. And cynetics have the upper hand. Our SmartCores, subprocesses, and constant connectivity lead to better, more informed decisions. Doesn't it make sense we'd want the most talented among us to lead?"

"If you are *implying*," Paer said, "we or our enhancer and emulate friends are less intelligent or qualified, you'll be hard pressed to make a convincing case. How do you explain a bunch of uneducated brutes bringing your well-equipped military to its knees with so little resources? Seems like flawed reasoning..." Her eyes flashed, daring Priya to object.

"While there are certain areas of intelligence—" Priya began.

"Cut the bullshit!" Paer exclaimed. "Animotes have the worst schools, least funding, and intentional systemic bias. If there's an achievement gap, it's primarily—if not *solely*—due to circumstance. Take a kid with nothing, parents unable to put food on the table, and decades old material, and you get what we have today: a factory to produce factory workers. If that isn't rigged, I don't know what is!"

We went round and round for hours, never reaching consensus, but had broached the topic of voting when it came time to break. We were getting hangry. Food might help.

As we went separate ways, I got a message from Calter. How had he found my anonymous username? Creepy.

Stay behind for five minutes. - CF

"I'll meet you guys in five." Paer and Obowe left, and I strode to the legacy shelves—eighteenth century American lit—and grabbed a book. Calter sidled up two minutes later, standing uncomfortably close.

"What?" I asked. This wasn't at all what I'd expected.

"I got Thorn back!" he said. "What happened to his hands?"

"He tried to shoot me. I only disabled him. You're welcome."

"You'll pay for that!" he barked. "I'll make you suffer, you pathetic excuse for a human. Stay out of my way."

He put his hand on my shoulder, and I spun, dropping him to the floor. "Don't you ever lay hands on me again," I breathed, blaster pointed at his face.

He snarled, sizing me up.

"Don't!" I said. "I'm not your enemy but I won't be pushed around either. You pull a stunt like that again, you'll regret it. Did you want anything else?" I added. "Or are we done here?"

"We're done. You'll regret this, kid."

I walked out of the Library without bothering to look back or help him to his feet. Prick.

On the way to lunch, I was rattled more than I cared to admit. It'd been the two of us. If it was a trap, I'd have been screwed. What was I thinking?

I had to tell the others. Wait, did I? If I told them, they'd worry. The last thing I needed was the Council restricting my movements.

Things were claustrophobic enough as it was. I'd play this one close to the vest.

Lunch with the enhancers went well, but there was an undercurrent of tension throughout. They were enthusiastic yet hesitant, and wanted to avoid being left out of the political hierarchy. With such a large animote population, they worried they'd be relegated over time. And it made sense.

Zill was pushy on the subject, several heated discussions about the need for protections. We never reached a formal consensus but all felt it was a success, and agreed to meet tomorrow to continue the dialogue.

On the way out, Iyanna pulled me aside. "Raek," she said in a hushed voice. "There are things you should know. You shouldn't—"

"What?" I asked, a little loud.

Zill turned, and gave her a look that froze her. His glare told me more than words ever could. Something was off.

"I was asking Raek about the fighting," she murmured in response to Zill's chilling look. "Must have been terrifying. I couldn't have done it."

"It was all instincts, to be honest," I added, continuing our would-be conversation. "I got lucky."

Zill shook his head in disgust. "Come on, Iyanna. We need to talk."

She walked away, giving me a faint nod. Zill didn't notice. What was that?

As we separated and walked back, I told the others.

"You're overthinking things," Obowe said. "We're all a little paranoid right now."

Despite their reassurances, I couldn't shake the feeling.

Something was off, very off.

THE TALK

The afternoon session was more of the same, and before I knew it, we headed home. Lars rode shotgun in the VTOL that picked us up. He waved, shooting an evil glance at Calter and the cynetics as he did, receiving daggers in return.

He laughed as we hopped in, patting me on the back. The doors closed and his face hardened. "I don't trust them," he grumbled. "Not after last time." He took a gray connectivity sensor from his pack like Fitz had had.

I rolled my eyes. "Really—"

BEEP.

Lars raised an eyebrow. "Someone was tracking you. Take it off." He motioned to my shirt. Calter, it had to be...

I slipped off my shirt and handed it to him. He opened the window and tossed it with a scowl before running the scanner along my arms and legs once more. Nothing.

"Agtha, Kamau." After a quick inspection, we were deemed clean and landed not long after.

I'd let Calter get close and we'd almost paid for it with our lives.

FLUSHING

The night was a whirlwind of meetings and endless caffeine. By the time we retired to our rooms—tired and weary beyond reason—it was 1:00 a.m. Zedda and I were drained and dropped like flies, out in seconds, desire the furthest thing from our minds.

A terrible dream woke me around four a.m. Something had happened to Zedda. I gave her arm a light shake.

She groaned. "What?"

I told her about the dream, and we spent the few remaining hours just talking, enjoying each other's company.

"You'd have loved the farm, Raek. I wish you could have seen it, met Ryian and Tem too. We invented tons of games. Smartband sim fights were always popular. Even Mom and Dad played, before she got sick..." Zedda took a deep breath and I gave her hand an encouraging squeeze.

"My brothers enlisted once they were eighteen. It was just me, Mom, and Dad after that. That was okay for a while, but one day, Mom came down with something. Doctors couldn't help, said rest and drink lots of fluid. As if we weren't doing *that*." She scowled. "We couldn't afford any testing and nothing helped."

Her back and shoulders were taut as elkhide. I rubbed them, but she didn't seem to notice.

"We moved to Dearth. Docs said we needed an elite hospital. Like that would ever happen. Dad tried, but they turned us away at the door. He fought and begged and pleaded but it didn't matter. Soon, we were homeless. Mom got weaker and weaker." She swallowed hard.

"One day, we got a message from Paer; Ryian and Tem were killed in an ambush. That broke Mom and Dad. She died the next day. He didn't make it a week..." Tears formed as she closed her eyes. I wiped them and took her into my arms, holding her tight. It was the most natural thing in the world. After a long, quiet while, she stopped shaking.

"I've never told anyone," she whispered.

My alarm buzzed at 6:00 and I snuck out to meet Paer and Obowe. We were the only ones up, and headed out at 8:00.

I couldn't stop thinking about Zedda, about all this. Was it a boy or a girl? Either way, they'd grow up in a better world. They had to. I'd die for that.

The morning went well. The cynetics—Calter in particular—were less aggressive and hostile than usual. Weird, but I'd take it.

At noon, we separated for lunch and met the enhancers.

Something wasn't right when we got there. And Iyanna was more reserved than last time, only speaking twice. Zill and Deane must have given her a tongue lashing.

She excused herself for the lady's room. That was my chance. I started to stand, but Zill rose and went to the men's room. Was he guarding her? I stifled a laugh. Stop being paranoid.

The bison was great, but progress stalled. Before long, it was time to leave. I hadn't gotten to talk to her. The enhancers stayed behind, something about a team meeting.

The weather was nice, a crisp sunny day and we were the first ones back. Odd, we were a minute late.

Man, I had to pee! I hurried to the bathroom while Obowe and Paer reviewed notes.

I was halfway through when the building shook, an earthquake tearing through the library. My feet shook as urine spilled everywhere, soaking my shoes. What the hell? Had an air amplifier blown? I squeaked to the door.

The center of the library—where we'd been not two hours earlier—was charred black, burns lining the marble floor and ceilings. Books and shelves flew, scattered across the floor and several small fires raged.

Was that a bomb? At the talks? Impossible. The library door burst open. Armed soldiers rushed in.

"Spread out!" A deep male voice yelled. "Make sure they don't get away!"

Holy crap. My brain kicked into high gear. Someone assassinated Paer and Obowe. They'd meant to kill all the delegates and were here to finish the job. Run.

I slipped back into the bathroom. The windows above each of the stalls didn't open.

Hopping onto the toilet, I slammed my fist through the glass. Shards flew as I ripped at broken pieces. Had they heard?

Hurry.

Once there was enough clearance, I leapt onto the stall walls, scurried through the jagged opening, and dropped to the pavement.

The coast was clear. Sprinting like my life depended on it, I weaved through empty winding streets and alleys, putting as much distance between myself and the library as possible.

After three blocks, it hit me. Yesterday... Iyanna had been trying to tell me. She'd *known*. How?

I sent a high priority message to the Council. It didn't work. Lars or Zedda either. No signal.

Something was jamming comms. Had to be the military, or the DNS. No one else had that kind of tech.

I *had* to get back to headquarters—out of this dead zone at least—to warn the others. They'd united against us. The elites were still trying to 'win.' And Obowe and Paer were dead...

A news story flashed. I had a signal.

'There's been an unclaimed terrorist attack at the Subspecies

Talks!' a newscaster exclaimed. 'Reports indicate a bomb exploded in the Library of Caen prior to afternoon sessions claiming the lives of animote leaders and known terrorists Raek Mekorian, Agtha Paer and Kamau Obowe. They seem to have arrived early. Luckily, no other representatives were harmed.' He paused, shaking his head.

'This loss is made all the more tragic as it was probably perpetrated by animote radicals unhappy with their more peace-minded leaders and again highlights the importance of the GDR to keep citizens safe. No doubt the talks will stall as animotes persist in violence, violating the ceasefire *they* themselves proposed. Perhaps rearchitecting our government and society to include such radicals is, at best, an iffy proposition. This is Gad Iaad from WNN signing off.'

Bullshit.

Despite everything, the GDR was shoving propaganda down people's throats—anything to remain in power. Anything.

Lars called. 'Raek, you there? You okay? We got your message.'

'It's a lie, all a big cover up!' I said. 'Paer and Obowe are dead. I was in the bathroom—'

'Where are you?'

I transmitted my encrypted location. They'd be here in thirty minutes.

There was one thing going for me. The explosion would make it hard to identify bodies. The GDR—at least what was left of it—wouldn't know I'd survived.

But who was calling the shots? *That* was the question. The Board wasn't some all-powerful, unified force anymore. It had been pounded to its core and cracked under pressure. Someone or some group must be in charge, someone with enough power and influence to pull off an attack like this. But who?

A cruiser raced by, sirens blaring. The third so far.

I needed a disguise, to disappear. Passing a boarded up electronics shop and seedy VR cafe, I slipped into the first open door with clothes. The place was empty and I hit the men's section.

Grabbing a gray sweatshirt, I snuck into the dressing cubicles. Perfect. I'd lie low and kill time, as long as they hadn't tracked me...

But who'd organized the attack, and what should we do about it?

All the usual suspects came to mind. Calter? He had the military connections to make something like this happen, and plenty of reasons to hate me. The more I thought about it, the less it made sense. We'd been the only ones back. This must go deeper, it had to. *Everyone* knew to arrive late. They were *all* co-conspirators.

That terrified me. I was a salty steak and too many glasses of water from being confetti. This was an act of war, a stealthy, brilliant act of war designed for deniability.

But what was the point? We'd keep fighting and become a larger and larger majority. It didn't make sense. It had short term appeal, but wasn't sustainable. If anything, I was pushing for a more moderate, fair system for all. I'd gone on multiple streams and said...

No... That was it, it *had* to be.

The attacks weren't meant for the animote leadership... they were meant for me.

65

DELIVERY

*Z*edda messaged me, *We'll be outside in two minutes. Hurry.*
   I crept out of the dressing room and through the store. The attendant was at the checkout, plugged into some gaming rig. Waving, I walked to the door.

A small white delivery van headed my way. I zoomed in. Zedda was at the wheel. It'd be so good to see her after all this.

Several scooters shot from an alley as the van neared, all six sporting dark helmets, visors and black studded jackets. That was the last thing we needed, more looting and a fight.

I held my breath as the van skidded to a stop. The first rider, a tall blond, hopped off his scooter, and leveled a blaster at Zedda. Others followed suit and cut off any potential escape.

Why'd it have to be Zedda? "You don't want to do this," I said in a low voice.

The blond glared. "This has nothing to do with you, kid." Turning to Zedda, he said, "This doesn't have to be hard, darling. We need the van."

"Not going to happen!" I retorted.

"Six-to-one, maybe six-to-two." The leader laughed and leveled his blaster. "It's gonna happen."

Zedda reached under the dash and the ringleader snapped, "Hold it, missy!" He motioned with his blaster at Zedda. Two riders inched forward, guns trained.

"Last chance," I said, fighting to keep the fear from my voice. What if they hurt Zedda? The baby?

He laughed again.

I raised both hands, targeting the goons nearest Zedda and fired twice before anyone blinked. Twisting, I nailed the fat one with a head-shot, dove and shot a fourth in the chest.

The two remaining gang members reacted, firing.

Zedda hit the fifth guy with the van. A loud *crunch,* and she reversed to be sure. I dropped the leader with a shot to the knees, but couldn't bring myself to kill him. If I did, I'd be as bad as them.

"Get in the car!" Zedda yelled as he collapsed. The side door flew open. I jumped in as a red truck hurdled around the corner. Not good.

Zedda floored it and the old van exploded down the street, away from the approaching truck.

Lars was in the back seat. "You made it, kid. We were worried for a while there."

"Worried?" Henk commented. "Zedda was more than a little—"

"Shut up, Henk!" Zedda replied, a happy flush to her face. She'd been crying. "Are you okay? You scared me."

"I'm fine. But Paer and Obowe." I swallowed. "They didn't make it." I explained what I'd realized.

When I finished, Lars said, "Makes sense. You're the biggest threat to the political order, both as a rebel and a politician. Last thing they want is a free and open election. You'd win in a landslide."

"I don't want that though!" I said. "They could have asked." More blood on my hands...

"They saw you as a threat and wanted to neutralize you first." Lars paused. "Plus, with you out of the way, if it did go back to war, the 'rallying cry' would be dead. Would kill morale."

No one said anything and the enormity of the situation hit me. As we turned into the parking lot, a notification appeared. What if I just ignored it? I couldn't.

'This is Viktor Maelne reporting on the situation in Faelig where large numbers of armed cynetics are taking the city by force. It appears the deteriorating Subspecies Talks and violation of the ceasefire is leading some to take things into their own hands.'

The screen changed, images of dead tigerish and dying wolfish filling my view. 'Animote forces in the city have responded, but seem to be fighting a losing battle. Will the violence spread to other cities and regions as peace slips away? This is Viktor Maelne —oh, wait! I'm getting updates within the last hour, similar conflicts have erupted in Hiazen and Taub. Things are heating up and we'll have it all for you on the World News Network. Until next time.'

"Fighting started in Faelig, Hiazen, and Taub again," I said. "They're claiming we violated the truce. Faelig's fallen and others may be on their way." I let that sink in.

"If we don't act now, we could be in trouble," Lars said.

He was right. "But what about the talks, diplomacy?" We weren't getting anywhere... I slammed the door harder than I'd intended, the window shattering.

"The time may have passed." His face was set in a grim line. "If we wait too long, it could be unwinnable." Damn it.

Five minutes later, what was left of us were assembled in the War Room. We'd been briefed, and, in short order, decided to denounce the claims while gearing up for war. We'd see how people reacted and respond accordingly.

Lars and I ran off to record another video.

Once that was done and uploaded, I collapsed onto the floor, glad for a moment to myself.

That lasted all of two seconds before the alarms sounded.

66

NO TIME TO WASTE

S irens echoed through the halls as people flew everywhere. It was chaos.

I bumped into Drue. "What's happening?"

"No idea!" he yelled. "I've never heard the alarms. I think we need to evacuate."

"Are you sure? To where?"

He shook his head. "I have no idea."

Zedda's voice crackled over the air speaker. "ATTENTION, ATTENTION. OUR SPIES IN THE DNS ALERTED US: POLICE ARE INBOUND ON OUR LOCATION. WE HAVE TEN MINUTES MAX. DESTROY ANY CLASSIFIED DATA OR COMMS. GRAB ANY BELONGINGS OR WEAPONS YOU CAN CARRY OR CAN'T LIVE WITHOUT, AND GET OUT OF HERE. EMERGENCY ESCAPE PLANS BEING PROJECTED ONTO THE BUILDING AS WE SPEAK. FOLLOW THE HIGHLIGHTED PATHS." The walls lit up as virtual screens appeared, identifying exits. Green arrows materialized at our feet.

"FOLLOW YOUR TEAM LEADER TO YOUR RESPECTIVE SAFE HOUSE. THERE SHOULD BE VEHICLES AND TRANSPORT FOR EVERYONE. GO."

The place exploded into action. Despite everything, there was an order to the madness.

Someone yanked my sleeve. "Come on, kid!" Lars yelled over the roar. "We need to go. Forget your stuff." Turning, he pulled me toward the illuminated exit.

"How did they—"

"Not now!" he yelled.

We slammed into a wall of people at the blinking exit. The door was too small and there weren't enough vehicles outside.

I altered my voice to inhuman levels and shouted, "If you are waiting for a ride, wait outside! You're holding up the rest of us! We'll be trapped!"

The line shuffled forward and we made it through, but we were in trouble. It had been two minutes. If the DNS arrived early, or cars and VTOLs didn't appear fast, we were sitting ducks in the slushy parking lot.

Two cars had been loaded since we'd made it outside, nowhere near enough. Thirty of us stood here, shaking.

"How many rendezvous points are there?" I asked the crowd.

"Three!" someone cried.

So, at least a hundred hadn't escaped yet. It had been five minutes.

Lars grabbed my elbow and dragged me forward. "You can't wait here, kid. We have to get you out first."

First? "What? No!" I pushed him off me. "We need to get everyone—"

"No, Raek!" Lars barked, smacking me. "There isn't time. We need you, more than me. More than anyone."

I was about to protest when my SmartCore alerted me to sub-auditory sounds coming in, restoring normal hearing.

An electric *whirr*. My heart stopped. "VTOLs inbound. At least three of 'em. Southeast." I pointed but didn't see anything yet.

A truck pulled up, three parked VTOLs on it. People piled in. Zedda's head bobbed onto the steps, surrounded by bodies. Soon, the first two were full and took off.

When it was apparent we wouldn't fit in the third, Lars raised his blaster and fired.

"I'm sorry!" he shouted. "Raek needs to be on that VTOL. He's the best chance we have, the only one who can unite us, and possibly the other subspecies."

Even as I resisted, people parted to let us pass. No... We got to the door and Lars pushed me aboard. I turned but he shoved me again. "Go, kid."

"What? Aren't you coming?" Everyone stared.

"It will be faster with less weight." As he said it, others on the ship rose and climbed off.

"No!" I tried to stop them. Not them too. "Stay, it'll be fine."

They slipped past, smiling as they raised their fists. Only the pilot and I remained.

"All set?" he asked.

No! All these people...Where was the next VTOL?

Lars nodded, his eyes resolute.

Goosebumps wracked my icy skin as the VTOL took off.

The approaching craft were less than two minutes out from the sound of it. I peered out as we raced away, close to the ground to avoid detection. I had to be sure they got away.

A minute later, a massive explosion. Another, another. A dark cloud plumed over the buildings and treetops. No... they were early. The pilot dropped and landed in a small patch of pine. "It's not safe to fly further," he said. "They'll have dozens of VTOLs en route. We might be spotted. This ship's built for speed, not combat. We're seven kilometers out. Should be good until nightfall and we'll head to the safehouse."

I stared at him, wordless. What could I say? "They all died, didn't they?" He'd put me before him, sacrificed himself. Closing my eyes, tears came. "They all got off and died, all because of *me*."

The pilot spun and ripped off his helmet. He must have been twenty-five, a strong furry jawline and the sinewy arms of a chimpish. Without a word, he lifted my chin and looked me in the eyes. "They didn't die *because* of you, they died *for* you! They gave their lives for something bigger than themselves. I'd have done the same if you could've flown this thing. We hit nine hundred kilometers per hour in under a minute. That's unheard of! A full load would be 400-600, tops. DNS will cordon off every square meter they can. With twelve people in this bird—heck, with a third of that—we wouldn't have made it. Sure as sin, they'd find us. Yeah, they might of died, but they chose to and they'd do it again." He gave me a sobering look. "Don't let them down!"

I couldn't help picturing Lars as the missiles struck, of all the time we'd spent together. And now, he was gone. Guilt stabbed my stomach. "Where do we go?"

He told me the plan while we covered the craft with camo fabric. I didn't hear any of it, I was in shock. Once finished, we climbed in and talked a bit.

His name was Janek Liilisky, and he'd been with the Initiative three years, but this was his first real action. He'd had two brothers, Aleks and Iger, both pilots. Both died in Caen. At least his parents hadn't lived to see that, dying years earlier during a work inspection.

After a while, we fell into silence. He fell asleep, snoring, while I replayed things in my head. How'd they find us?

The delivery van, it had to be. The DNS pieced it together and traced the van to base. Jeez, we'd parked at base... We'd been in such a hurry, we'd forgotten protocol. I'd spared that bastard gang leader and he'd tipped them off.

My fault... More tears. Lars and everyone else, all dead, because of me.

Positive thoughts: what are you going to do about it?

I messaged Zedda and heard back at once. At least she was okay!

A third of our people had gotten out. Ganla too, but they weren't sure about Mico or Lars. I told her Lars didn't make it but couldn't bring myself to say more.

The silver lining—if you could call it that—was the VTOLs had destroyed everything. In their rush, the DNS had squandered their one chance to dissect our networks. Calter would be furious.

And again, they didn't know I'd survived. They weren't learning from their mistakes. I filed that away for later.

When I awoke, we were flying low over the faded landscape. The sun had set hours ago, and ominous shadows blanketed the world, the occasional snowflake floating in the wind.

Janek must have noticed me. "Two minutes."

We cleared the treeline and a small red barn rose in the distance. A minute later, we landed in front. Three solid guys pulled open sliding doors and Janek maneuvered forward, landing on pallets next to the other two craft.

Zedda was there, and I swallowed a pained gasp. I hadn't realized how worried I'd been.

She ran, kicking snow, and threw her arms around me, kissing me hard. Once we separated, she turned to Janek and pecked him on the cheek. "Thanks for getting him out."

Janek stiffened, blushing.

"Raek, come on." Zedda pulled my hand. "There's a lot going on."

A rowdy crowd gathered in the dining room of the farmhouse, clustered around two rustic wooden tables. There were maps out, food everywhere, and a chaotic buzz of purpose. These people wanted revenge.

Walking into the country style kitchen, someone clapped me on the back. "We were worried, Raek," Henk said with a grim smile. "Didn't know if..."

He left the question hanging.

"You must be starving." Zedda pointed to the counter. "Grab food and follow me. Ganla's upstairs in the study. We can talk there."

The counters were cluttered with nuts and dried meat, things designed to last. Contorting guilt filled my gut, along with burning anger. I'd make them pay for what they'd done.

"Over here, Raek!" Zedda yelled as I ascended the rickety stairs.

The door at the end of the hall was ajar. Inside, seated around the antique iron table, were Zedda, Ganla, and someone I didn't recognize.

"Raek, this is Caell, he owns the safehouse and manages the farm for the Initiative," Ganla explained. "We're glad you made it. We were worried."

I ignored Caell, cutting to the chase, not bothering with niceties. "So, what's happening? They tracked the van. I figured that much. We messed up. What's happened since? How many people got out? Who'd we lose? Anything else?"

Ganla told me, but it was nothing new. Sixty-five of our hundred strong had died, and it was my fault.

"You saw the news," Ganla added. "They are milking it for all it's worth."

I shook my head, confused, taking in the dim, cozy space for the first time.

"Yeah." Zedda rolled her eyes. "I've never seen this much coverage of a raid. They're saying they won the war. Many speculate the library bombing was an excuse for us to carry out larger-scale attacks."

Those freaking liars. Somehow, I stayed calm, fists hard as iron.

"Don't forget Couve and Ghrail," Caell added. "Both broke into widespread fighting and are in the process of falling to the cynetics."

"The cynetics?" I eyed the thin man. He had bland features and strong hands to match his farmer's tan, only his whiskers notable, a wispy blond mustache in stark contrast to his thick auburn hair.

"The cynetic factions within the DNS have unified and are pushing for total cynetic control," Ganla said. "We think Calter's behind it."

Of course he is… I paused, taking it all in.

"We can't wait any longer," I said at last. "Notify everyone you can contact. As of this moment, we're officially at war!"

67

A LITTLE RELAXATION

Between calls, coffee, and chaos, no one slept much. The farmhouse was electric, fifteen-odd folks firing on all cylinders to make our people ready.

When the rooster crowed, a sigh went up from the troops splayed across couches and countertops. It was rough, but we'd done it. By mid-morning, we were ready, at least as ready as we'd be. The main bases had been notified and we'd begun the next stages of our blitzkrieg.

We'd renounce the ceasefire and launch assaults on several tier one and tier two cities that morning. Not Caen, that would come later. We didn't have enough support with the losses we'd suffered.

Timing would be everything.

I'd filmed several videos that night condemning the violation of the truce and the growing violence in Couve, Ghrail, and the six other cities in full-blown anarchy. Animotes had to rise up again.

At noon, we released the videos and kicked off the attacks. Lhalas was the first to fall, and I couldn't help but think of Fitz. A deep throbbing. Who'd he wanted me to meet? Why?

Lhalas was a huge win for us, a megacity of two million inhabitants. According to reports, there were homeless animotes everywhere in the cold ex-Canadian metropolis, the abandoned subway in particular. When word was released, animotes flooded the streets by the thousands, like rats emerging from a sewer.

Local GDR officials and military personnel never prepared for anything like this. That morning, hundreds of thousands poured out of the underground and clawed, tooth and nail, literally, to victory.

The next several days, a similar pattern emerged in several tier one cities. And while we captured Maste, Willon, and Broag, VTOLs carpet bombed dozens of animote towns and villages, killing tens of thousands and injuring many more. The GDR wanted us to choose, freedom or your families.

They didn't stop there.

Most cities had strict zoning laws and pilots wasted little time decimating animote neighborhoods in an effort to eradicate us—pest control at its most inhumane.

The fighting deteriorated and death tolls skyrocketed as each side doubled down. In theory, that was okay, at least in the short term. If there was an end in sight... But there wasn't. Neither side was making progress in the bloody, WWI-like slog.

I didn't know what to do.

By the fourth day, I was despondent. By the fifth, borderline depressed. We'd been so close before it all came crashing down.

"I'm going out," I announced to no one in particular. Zedda and Henk were slumped on the couch but said nothing as I slipped out the door.

A deep breath on the porch. Another. The picturesque beauty amplified the numb bleakness inside me. What was the point? Millions more would die anyways.

Walking padded snowy trails, I soaked it all in as a hawk soared in ever-expanding circles. He must be hunting too, if only it was *that* easy.

I stumbled through a large snowdrift and reached a frozen pond. It had been ages since I'd skated. Wouldn't that be nice?

A flash. What was that, by those trees? A blur... It was a doe, blood trickling down her fleecy side. Even at a hundred meters, the gory scrapes along her left flank were obvious, ripped raw. By what? Was that a thornbush?

She kicked and let out a high-pitched wail. The thorns tightened as she squirmed.

We had plenty of food at the house so I didn't want to kill her if I didn't have to. A quick stun and she collapsed. I hurried over, claws making fast work of the thorny vines ensnaring her scrawny torso. Once she was free, I rubbed her wounds to stimulate blood flow and dragged her from the entanglement.

How'd she get so tangled? Must have brushed a thorn and panicked.

Wait, that was it! We didn't need to win the war, per se.

We just had to sever the *thorn*. Calter...

68

HELLO AGAIN

Sprinting back to the farmhouse, I called Ania to go over a few things. I had Calter's username, only he had enough power to make things happen. We called him.

'Calter?' I said as soon as he answered.

'Who is this?' He sounded wary.

I turned on video, keeping my surroundings out of the picture.

'What do you want?' he spat, glinting eyes betraying his curiosity. His background shifted from an oak-paneled masterpiece of an office, grand piano in the background to a bland white wall.

'I want to meet,' I answered. 'Just the two of us. I know you planted the bomb, coordinated all of it. If it weren't for a lucky break, we wouldn't be having this conversation.'

'What do you want?' he said again, face unreadable.

'The fighting's gone on long enough. You aren't going to win and you know it. And neither will we, at least not for a while. This'll go on for weeks, months maybe. We'll destroy everything we worked so hard to rebuild since the Fall. You can't want that...'

He narrowed his eyes further. 'What are you saying?'

'Who's controlling the government, the military, the police? I'm guessing it's you. You have the power to end this, *only* you. But you'll want some guarantees for the future, right?'

'I'm listening.' He tried to look bored but his lips twitched. It wasn't working.

'All I'm saying is," I continued, "we can make things work for you. A position in our government? Done. Beautiful mansions by the ocean, the mountains, wherever? Not a problem. We can make you disappear and give you a new identity. Anything you want. We need to end this. It'll be better for everyone. If it takes some spoils, that's worth it. Think about it.'

He paused and my heart stopped. Would he fall for it?

'Why should I trust you?' he said at last.

I shrugged, fighting to stay calm. 'Do you have a choice? Whether it's ten days or ten years, eventually, we'll be an inevitable majority. So, do you go down a war criminal and pull a Hitler as we're arresting you, or do you start a new life with a clean slate? It's that simple. You don't have to decide now,' I added before he could say no. 'Call me tomorrow.'

He smirked. 'You have no idea, do you?'

'What?' Something in his voice terrified me. He knew something I didn't. But what?

The line went dead.

"Did we get a trace?" I turned to Ania.

She grinned. "We got him. I got his location and history too. I'm guessing he's at work, so that won't help us. The history could be interesting though."

Was this was the break we needed?

"Give me a few hours!" Ania eyes locked on her screens, voice accelerating. "A normal GDR account would be near impossible to hack, but looks like he's drunk on power, not taking basic precautions. I can't promise anything," she added. "But we might find something."

"Great work, Ania!" I clapped her on the back. "Want some coffee or anything?"

She was already gone, the rest of the world disappearing under an impenetrable veil of focus. "Nevermind," I said to myself as Zedda and I left to give her space.

* * *

W e were upstairs, analyzing Zone Three when there was a scream.

"Yesss!"

I rushed down to make sure everything was okay. Ania had a huge smile and was pumping her fist. "I got him. We got him!" She noticed us. "Guys, come here."

We took the remaining steps two at a time and piled onto the sofa. A few others came to see what the commotion was about.

"We planted a virus disguised as a distorted-pixel in your video feed, Raek," she began. "Calter's AV programs didn't catch it. By cross-referencing his search history with old GPS check-ins before a security patch and some picture and video files, I used a probabilistic distance matrix to—"

"In English please," I cut in. The farmhouse was silent, collective breaths held. This could be it.

"Oh... We found him, where he lives. And it looks like he has a regular mistress; photos of two different women on his personal server, some homemade adult stuff." She smirked. "He's cheating on his second wife. Was this what you were looking for?" she asked with a timid smile.

"This is better!" Grabbing her shoulders, I pulled her into an unexpected hug. "Change of plans, guys. We found him, we found Calter. That's where we should focus!"

"But there's no proof he was behind the attacks," Ganla replied, sounding skeptical.

"It doesn't matter," I said. "This is our chance to cut the head off the snake. If we capture him, we'll have access to all their secrets and be able to manipulate the DNS at will. None of 'em would question a direct order from him. He's the most powerful person on the planet right now. And if his security's any indication, Ania could spoof messages to their troops."

After talking it over, we agreed the mistress' house would be the place to take him. His own home would be impenetrable, with security cams, drones, guards, and more. If he was cheating on his wife though, he wouldn't want to make that public knowledge.

Her apartment would be easier to stake out and raid if it came to it.

According to Ania's analysis, he visited his mistress twice a week. For a man fixated on security and control, he made himself an easy target. I guess power will do that to you. Everyone's invincible, until they're not.

Now was Fury's time to fall.

69

PERFECT TIMING

We kept eyes on the place for the next two days to no avail. Something, or someone, was keeping him busy. By the fourth day, I was worried. Did they have a falling out? Had his system found the intrusion? Or maybe a more beautiful mistress...

Whatever the reason, those four days were miserable. Every day, there were dozens of stories on what the WNN had taken to calling World War IV. Tens of millions were slaughtered as fighting outpaced even the brutal first days of the conflict. The footage was horrifying; bodies strewn everywhere, a jumble of arms and legs and decomposing corpses.

The GDR seized control of several megacities while exterminating dozens of towns, and our forces captured nine tier one and tier two cities. Overall, it felt even, each side delivering crushing blow after crushing blow on a daily basis; heavyweight boxers ruining each other's future with every swing.

And Calter still hadn't called back. My plan had failed. Morale was bad and worsening. I couldn't blame them.

Wednesday, Zedda and I went for a walk. It had been ages since we'd had a moment alone, months of constant crab cooking pressure... and it was only four days.

"How are you feeling?" she asked when we reached the pond.

I sighed. Only she knew how I was *really* doing, that the optimistic facade was a front to motivate the troops. My insides were dying.

She took my hand and placed it on her belly. She wasn't showing, but I knew. That was the one ray of hope in all this, the one thing keeping me going. "He's here for you, Raek. We're here for you." We both thought it was a boy, but hadn't had the chance to see a doctor, or run a test. A son, wow. My son... What would he be like? Was I ready?

"What about you? How are you—"

A call came in. Crap, was it Calter?

It wasn't. One of the undercovers watching the mistress' apartment was on the line. Someone matching Calter's description had pulled up in a high-end Volvo with tinted windows and hurried into the building.

Zedda and I ran back to the farmhouse.

The kid—Baker was his name—had managed a quick snapshot of the suspect. I got it seconds later.

'That's him! That's Fury!' This was it. 'Good work, Baker. We'll have a team onsite in two minutes. Stay put, watch the door. Once they enter the building, get out of there. Find somewhere safe to hide, but keep your eyes out.'

'Yes, sir!' Baker stood straighter. 'Thank you, sir. It's an honor.'

I ignored the sir comment and made the call. We had a team of five ready round the clock.

'It's on!' I said as soon as the call connected, the entire farmhouse gathered around me, listening. 'He entered the building.'

'Roger that!' the leader replied in a Georgia twang. 'En route now.'

'Call when you have him. We'll send backup.'

'On it. Over and out.' He signed off.

This was either going to be ingenious or an absolute disaster. "How soon can we have a second team onsite?" I asked.

"Ten minutes," Zedda said without hesitation.

"Do it! We should be fine, but just in case."

She made the call.

But what was I doing here? I needed to be there. Since retreating to the farmhouse, it had killed me sending others into harm's way. It was one thing when my life was on the line, but from the safety and comfort of the safehouse, it felt wrong.

Screw it! "Get me a VTOL!" I said.

Zedda grabbed my arm to stop me. "But, Raek, you—"

"I'll explain later." I pushed past, hurrying to the barn, calling Henk as I ran.

'Hey, Henk, I need a ride.'

We were airborne two minutes later. It would take eight to get there, minutes after the second team arrived. A call came in on the approach. That was quick. Was it really that easy? I patched it through the farmhouse so they could savor the moment, muting them before answering.

'Hello?' I said.

A long pause, and what sounded like Beethoven in the background. Beethoven? I tensed. 'Did you think *five* would be enough?' a voice hissed.

No... I closed my eyes. It was Calter. 'Surely you didn't fall for the oldest one in the book? An unsecured comms line.' He laughed.

My head spun. This wasn't happening. 'What do you want, Calter?' I spat.

'A meeting. Just you and me,' he added in an innocent voice.

'Are they alive?' I asked. Had I condemned more innocent people? If I could keep him talking...

'Of course,' he said in a low, sarcastic voice. 'Well, two of them, and barely.'

'Let me talk to 'em. I need proof.' The fur on the back of my neck tingled.

Henk looked at me, worried. *Three minutes,* he mouthed.

'Raek, it's me Zedric,' a voice coughed. 'He's—' *Thud.*

'Zedric's out again, that should do for proof. If not, here's, what's your name, boy?'

'Frankis, Frankis Caol,' a voice whimpered.

'Ah, yes, Frankis.' Another *slam.* 'Frankis and Zedric are alive. I can't say the same for the other three, or the kid on the corner. It was pathetic.' He laughed again, freezing me. 'Their deaths are on your hands, boy. Tonight, 23:00. I'll send you coordinates twenty minutes beforehand. Come alone or these two die!'

'Wait!' One minute until our backup arrived. Would they be in time?

The call ended, the connection to the farmhouse unmuting.

The room was silent.

They'd heard everything.

70

CONFETTI

'What's the status of team two?' I asked, voice wavering. 'One minute to target,' Ganla replied.

'Connect me.'

She did.

'Raek here,' I said as the call connected, our VTOL descending.

'We're here, sir. It's Michaels. Entering the building now.'

'Wait!' I shouted. 'Wait for me. Calter took out team one. Has anyone else come or gone?'

'Negative. Got here two minutes ago and secured the perimeter,' he added, reading my mind.

A door slammed. 'Move, move!' another voice yelled.

The ground raced to meet us. Twenty meters, ten. We hit the pavement hard, doors flying open. I jumped out, smelling blood as Henk messed with controls.

'Prepare for breach in three, two—'

BOOM!

An explosion rocked the building, flinging me back. Debris showered from a gaping hole on the fourth floor, a deluge of brick and wood and concrete plummeting toward me.

I dove into the entrance as a support beam slammed into the

street. The implosion launched chunks of concrete into the air, reverberating through the building, and echoing down the streets.

'Come in, Michaels. Come in!'

Nothing. Five seconds later, again. I was already halfway up, taking the steps three at a time. 'Michaels!' I screamed.

No response. No...

Hitting the fourth floor landing, I launched myself into the corner and leveled my blasters. The view was breathtaking, the entire wall decimated by the blast. Jumping broken glass, I hurried into the apartment and checked each room.

First room, all clear.

A call from Henk. Not now.

Where are you, Calter?

I kicked down the second door and spun, firing twice as a precaution. Other than Bikkins and Todd—both covered in blood and missing half their torsos—it was empty as well.

Judging by the size of the building, there were two more rooms. My heart pounded, everything in slow motion as I cleared the third room.

One to go.

I darted in, blasters leveled.

71

A WORK OF ART

I didn't believe in god, but this man exceeded even the most sadistic of demons.

The posh well-lit bedroom looked straight out of Dante's *Inferno,* a bloody mosaic covering the king sized bed where a beautiful pale woman lay lifeless. Her throat was slit, a gory kitchen knife to one side. There was blood everywhere; rich crimson splattering the milky carpet below, and a bloodstained message on the walls: *You did this. This is ALL your fault!*

I bent, retching. It was more than I could take.

Backing out of the room, I called Henk. The smell was putrid, burnt flesh and blood-soaked fibers mixing with the explosive exhaust fumes.

After a quick check of the apartment revealed nothing else, I stumbled out the door and downstairs, ears ringing. Ten more dead. Waves of guilt.

"Really?" he asked in disgusted disbelief.

I nodded, unable to speak and climbed in.

He stifled a grimace and took off. We were sixty seconds from being debris ourselves.

Henk took us through some crazy maneuvers on the ride back. We were worried about tails, but twenty minutes later, we were back at the farmhouse without incident.

Zedda and Caell ran to meet us. Without speaking, we trudged upstairs, everyone silent, processing what happened.

They'd all be questioning my leadership, questioning my morality, questioning me. And they were right. Who was *I* anyway? Why'd I think I could do this, take on Calter? It was one failure after another. Hopeless, I sank into the chair next to Ganla. No one said anything. The tension was palpable, everything left unsaid. And it was all my fault...

The rest of the afternoon was awful, and Calter had Frankis and Zedric.

Zedda found me not long after. "Wanna talk about it?" she asked, face somber but eyes kind.

I shook my head, but that didn't help. Everything came pouring out. I couldn't help it. Feeling like an impostor, letting Fitz and Lars down, failing as a leader, being a fraud... All my doubts and fears flowed out, wave after hopeless wave.

She said nothing, waiting until I finished before putting her arms around me. "I'm pregnant," she whispered, holding me tight. "I love you, Raek."

Wrapping my arms around her, I held on for dear life. She was the *one* thing grounding me, my rock, and I was crumbling. Tears came and I let them. Rubbing bleary eyes, I murmured, "I love you too!" Staring into her eyes, alone and desperate beyond belief, I knew without a shade of a doubt, it was true.

She smiled, and I felt a bit better. That small gesture, that little reassurance... it meant the world.

Then the call came in. I hurried downstairs. It was time.

72

FOOTSTEPS AND FANS

'Calter?' I said, shell-shocked as we connected.

'The old Colts' stadium. Lucas Oil. You have twenty minutes. Meet me there, *alone*,' he added. 'Southeast corner of the field, what's left of it.'

I mouthed the name to Henk and Ganla before adding, 'You won't get away with this. You're a monster, you—'

The call ended.

"Henk, I need a lift. Old Lucas Oil. Is the VTOL ready?"

"Everything's ready," Zedda said. "But are you sure about this? After what you've been through… You can't do this, not alone."

"I have to!" I snapped. "It's my fault this happened." Why couldn't she see that?

"I'm coming with you!" she burst out. It wasn't a question.

"No you're not," I said, shaking. "I can't—I can't have to worry about something happening to you."

"It's not just you anymore, Raek!" Zedda hissed through gritted teeth. "We have—" she paused, noticing everyone as if for the first time.

Ganla cut in, "She's right, Raek. We can't afford for you to go by yourself. You're our best hope at a peaceful resolution."

"Fine! We can send backup, not by air though," I added. "They need to come from the sides and avoid detection at all costs. Henk can bring me to the wreckage, and I'll walk in on my own. You guys arrange backup. If Calter's going to try something, he'll have the area jammed. We'll need backup comms."

"Or we could track your signal," Ania said. Everyone turned to look at her. "If Raek had a simulcast going out, if his connection died, we'd know he got jammed. If that happens, it's a trap and we rush the place, right?"

"Ania, you're a genius!" I exclaimed.

She blushed, picking her nails, a proud smile on her face.

"Okay. We need to go. I'll simulcast to this address." I sent a link to each of them. "You guys coordinate the backup, a small team. No more than five."

They nodded.

Fifteen minutes later, Henk and I passed over the dark remains of the stadium. It must have been impressive in its day. Today though, most of the walls and seating had collapsed, cracked by Caen's harsh winters and lack of maintenance.

We couldn't see Calter from the air, too much debris and temporary housing littered the place. Plus it was enormous. He could be anywhere. This was nuts, but what choice did I have?

I jumped out as soon as we landed and surveyed the rubble, hurrying off. Eyes open.

Picking my way through the cold, dead landscape, I heightened my senses, heart rate quickening. He could be anywhere. At the edge of the stadium, I headed for a dilapidated entrance to my right. It looked safe enough, but looks could be deceiving.

Inside was a mess. The stadium had been the home to tens of thousands of homeless during the ruthless winters, before the government kicked them out. The ground was covered in wrappers and bottles, all manner of packaging. Most wasn't recyclable. A lot had changed in the last few decades.

From the crumbling stands, I scanned the ghost town in front of me with thermals. A familiar glow illuminated the place, but nothing moving. The place reeked of despair and better times, death too.

Creeping toward the field, I hopped to the bald astroturf and set off for the Southeast corner. Calter *should* be there.

The field was huge, grimy tents and biofabbed huts everywhere; remnants of the displaced strewn like leaves in the wind. Suffering for decades...

Something moved. "Calter?" I yelled. "Zedric? Frankis? You there?"

A stumbling shape emerged and fell to the ground. It was Frankis, arms and legs magcuffed, mouth covered. Calter must be nearby.

A crash behind me. I dove, spinning as I did. Zedric toppled, similarly bound. At least he was alive.

What was happening?

"Calter, you wanted this meeting!" I shouted as I got to my feet, heart pounding, every noise amplified. "I'm alone and unarmed. Show yourself!"

"I did." A figure turned the corner and fired, shattering the silence.

I leapt and the blast incinerated the ground I'd been standing on. Shit. Another hit Zedric in the chest, killing him instantly. Not him too.

I tried messaging the others. No luck. My connection was gone, jammed. Frankis whimpered something unintelligible.

"You don't have to do this, Calter!" I shouted. "You have me, that's what you wanted. Let the boy go!"

A slight movement behind me. I ducked, firing. A scream as a black-clad figure collapsed, army insignia on his fatigues.

Calter had brought a hit squad. How many?

Another rounded the corner, blaster leveled. Somehow, I got off the first shot and dodged his hurried blast. There was an explosion several meters away. I ran as blaster fire filled the air.

My one chance was the maze-like complexity of the area. If Fury had lied and brought men, he'd have more than enough to finish the job. He didn't strike me as someone who left things to chance.

Escape or wait for backup, there was no other way. Would they be fast enough?

The building in front of me collapsed.

Sprinting for cover, I heard footsteps everywhere. Another figure knelt behind a wall. I fired. Two more.

A VTOL took off.

At least Henk was coming, if I could hold out.

Eruptions to my left. They didn't know where I was. Maybe the jammers blocked their comms as well. A VTOL appeared over the northern walls.

Huh? Shouldn't Henk have come from the southwest?

The ship opened fire.

The area to my left detonated, sending chunks of concrete and turf flying. I raced for cover. I had to get to the walls.

Blaster fire behind me caught my attention, missing me by centimeters. Dropping, I started crawling. The VTOL would have thermal imaging. If they saw me, I was a sitting duck.

It turned my way, closing the distance. I wasn't going to make it.

I ran, and the pilot took a few seconds to react before the barrage resumed. That probably saved me.

When I saw the second VTOL, I knew I was done for. Was my hearing damaged? Why hadn't I heard it?

The second closed at a blistering pace as the first raced toward me, guns rattling. He rose higher, lining up the shot. The second ship smashed into it. What the—?

A ball of flame enveloped the pair. They crashed to the earth with a resounding *BOOM* that rocked the night. Henk! He'd sacrificed himself.

Another friend gone... A raging sadness engulfed me. Two shadows materialized to my right, soldiers running to check the pilot. I shot both.

Where was Calter?

Frankis screamed, and I turned back. I had to get him out of here. Sneaking along the outer wall, I backtracked. A soldier looking down his scope lost his throat before he realized what happened.

Another was lying under a tent, muzzle pointed toward Frankis. I thanked my wolfish ancestors as I slipped in for the silent kill.

I'd dispatched nine of Calter's men so far. How many more could there be? And where the heck was my backup? They should have been here by now.

Frankis was up ahead, hanging by a thread. Blood pooled from a wound on his forehead and his right leg was twisted at an unnatural angle. Reminded me of Bruce. He didn't have much time.

A *crunch* of footsteps. I spun, preparing to fire. Something made me hesitate.

It was Henk.

"Henk?" I whispered. "You're alive? You made it? But—"

"Autopilot," Henk said. "Dove out before impact."

"Where are the others?" Were they okay?

"Somewhere in here." He looked around. "I don't—"

A scream. We took off.

73

TOUCH DOWN

W e picked off two more soldiers crossing the shadowy stadium but didn't hear anything, eerie silence resuming. I was worried. Where were they?

We headed toward the other end and were about to turn back when there was another yell, a female voice this time. My heart stopped. Zedda?

I ran harder, safety and stealth the furthest thing from my mind as Henk struggled to keep up. Not my problem. Zedda needed me! There was a volley of blaster fire at midfield.

Someone got hit, falling hard to the ground. My eyes sharpened. It was Calter, he stood over two bodies.

"Calter, you bastard!" I sprang, tackling him. As I flew, time slowed. He turned, raised his hand and fired. I recognized Keff—the lionish I'd met at the farmhouse—a gaping hole in his chest. Next to him, Drue, half his face missing.

Calter fired twice more as we collided, hitting my left foot. My nerves exploded in agony and I disabled them as we thudded to the icy turf. Henk collapsed.

Fury's elbow clobbered my face as we rolled, stunning me—the force inconceivable for a human. I slammed my fist into his gut, coming face to face with a third body. It was Zedda, a bloody chasm in her belly where our child had been.

NO... "Bastard!" Pure agony impaled me, a howling scream escaping my lips as my claws tore at his throat. "Lars, Rogers, Ashlo, Zedda, my whole family... you killed all of them!"

He fought back, throwing punches and kicks, powerful, yet helpless as I pounded him, claws piercing his light body armor. He lifted his hand to fire but I sliced it off. Roaring, he kneed me in the stomach and shoved me away. "Dammit, boy. I'd never hurt Preta."

What? "You knew her?" I slashed for his throat as he tripped over Zedda's lifeless body. Screw the plan, screw the future. Screw *everything*.

He fired as my claws connected, shredding his worthless...wait. What? My fingers slipped, the tips gone, incinerated. I struggled, squeezing his bloody throat with my nubs. My left hand battled his right. I had to kill him.

"Of course I knew her. How do you think you—"

As I choked the life out of him, he tried to roll. I held firm, locking my legs like Lars had shown me. It didn't work either. The leverage was off, my foot a ruined stump.

His injured arm smashed me and he managed to free his throat enough to croak, "Raek, you're my son."

My heart stopped and grip slackened. "What'd you say?" I spat, still crushing his throat. It wasn't possible.

"I'm your father. Your mother, Preta, we met in Itany ages ago."

"I don't believe you!" I shouted, unable to comprehend what he was saying. But he knew her name...

"How do you think you got nanoSTEMs?" He was no longer resisting. "We're more alike than you think, son. I've missed you."

"You're lying." I pressed harder. It couldn't be true, it couldn't...

"Thorn's your brother," he gasped. "Half-brother actually. Why would I lie?"

My grip died as he proceeded to describe Mom, and how they'd met. It all made sense. A bomb detonated inside me, annihilating everything I'd ever known about myself. Him? No... I was going to be sick. Hands failing me, head spinning. "Dad?"

His arm whipped toward me, firing

I dodged, rolling and slashing with my good hand. "We are *nothing* alike!" Tearing at his throat. "Nothing!" Blood erupted as slack-jawed shock registered on his hard face. Nothing...

"You—" He coughed, gasping before crumbling to the ground in a pool of crimson.

I threw his limp body off me and screamed it again in a desperate whisper as poison torched my veins and heart. "We are *nothing* alike."

Zedda. I crawled toward her, every meter, searing agony. I reached her, but it was too late. Our child, our future... splayed across weed-strewn concrete. Taking her beautiful face into my hands, I lost it. Shaking convulsions gripped me. "Zedda!" I gagged, vomiting, writhing pain. "Zedda, No."

But the warmth of her body was already fading, a bluish tint to her perfect lips. She was gone, she was really gone. Pure agony. I sobbed, holding her in my arms as emptiness engulfed me. First Elly, now her. Sopping misery, bleary nothingness.

It was all over. And all for what?

After what felt a million heartless lifetimes, a VTOL approached. It landed twenty meters away and Ganla yelled, "Raek, Raek?"

What was she doing here? What did it matter?

This must have been how Fitz felt when he lost Kira.

I passed out.

74

A SMALL WORLD AFTER ALL

I awoke to the sound of sadistic cheering.

The doors opened, and Ganla and Henk helped me hobble down the steps. Everything was a blur of pain: faces, cheers, clapping —pure agony.

As we entered the farmhouse, I spun. "How can you celebrate at a time like this?" I cried. "We lost people, we lost Zedda! She was preg —" The words caught in my throat. I reached out to grab the nearest person, to shake sense into them and crumpled into a sobbing heap on the snow.

"How could you?" I sputtered. "How could you?"

Henk helped me to my feet and carried me through the door. Everything disappeared.

* * *

Sunlight hit me. Why hadn't I died? Tons of messages and notifications. I ignored all of them. I could care less. I was done. I'd lost everything, EVERYTHING! *Nothing* could change that.

There was a message from Zedda. Crying, I sat up. It almost killed me. Not now, not like *this*.

Swinging my legs out of the old fashioned bed, I stood, keeling over. Pain wracked me as nerves in my stump of a foot exploded.

Struggling, I wrenched myself to my feet, waiting a few moments before dulling the pain. I needed to feel something, anything. At least physical torment I could handle.

There was a wheelchair in the far corner. Someone had prepared for me, the cripple. I stumbled into the chair and wheeled into the hallway.

Everyone froze.

No one knew how to react. It was awful.

"There you are," Caell said with an awkward smile. "We wondered when you'd be up. Hungry?"

Was he kidding? Hungry? Why was he being nice to me? It just highlighted the emptiness inside. How could he—my stomach grumbled.

"Yeah," I said grudgingly. "Thanks."

"We got bacon and eggs," he replied with a forced cheer. "Sound good?"

I shrugged, unable to speak. Whatever.

Henk came over to check on my leg. "It doesn't look half bad." He motioned to my foot. "Thanks for saving me. Would have been in some trouble if it weren't for you."

"It was my fault you were there in the first place. How many made it back?" I added, dreading the answer but needing to know.

"Just us," he said. "We got Calter though," he added, as if *somehow* that made things better. But how could it? And how had Mom fallen for Calter? Was that why I was so wicked?

So many questions left unanswered, dying with him.

"The plan failed!" I snapped. "We needed him alive. Even then..."

A long, awkward silence until Caell interrupted. "Hungry?" He handed me a heaping plate.

I forced myself to eat, downing the tasteless food. Halfway through, I choked on bile and tears came. She was gone, our son too.

Henk excused himself, leaving me to mourn. Sitting in my wheelchair, surrounded by the energetic buzz, I was more alone than ever. What was I going to do?

Ages later, someone tapped my shoulder. "Room for one more?" Ania asked.

I nodded, unable to speak or swallow that last bite.

She sat and put her feeble arm around me. "How you doing?"

I shrugged, not wanting her to know how bad it was.

"I'm sorry about Zedda," she said at last. "I'm sorry about everything."

"It's not your fault." It's mine.

"It's still horrible. I feel bad."

"Thanks," I muttered, voice failing me like I had our unborn child...

"Seen the news?" she asked, saving me yet another gravity well of despair.

I shook my head. What did it matter?

"The military fell apart. You were right, Calter was pulling the strings. The government lost it this time. There are stories of the DNS facing off against the army. And the alliance with the elites has imploded. We've captured a dozen tier one and tier two cities in the last thirty-six hours. Even the WNN's calling for peace."

It barely registered, or maybe it just didn't matter. "Thirty-six hours?" I was out a day and a half?

She nodded. "You didn't know?"

I shook my head. I could care less.

"It could end any day," she continued, her excitement the mirror opposite of the emptiness I felt. "You did it, Raek. We're almost there!"

Ganla appeared. "We didn't want to wake you, figured you needed the sleep. But things have been moving. We might see peace in our day. You can say I told you so," she added with a grim smile.

A hopeless laugh escaped me as the impact of what they were saying reached me. "It's not about right or wrong. I'm glad..." A deep breath, hold it together, Raek... "Glad maybe it was worth it," I finished, choking back tears.

Ganla put her hand on my shoulder. "Ania, can you come with me? Raek needs some time."

The next few days passed much the same, everyone avoiding me and unsure what to say.

One morning, we got the news, the war—if you could call it that— was over. The other sides were tired of the bloodshed and ready to end it at any cost. Celebration and high-fiving all around. It was sickening.

In the middle of it, I wheeled to the door, unable to stand their joy and happiness. Rolling along the breezy winter trails, I thought about all I'd lost, everything that had happened. Elly, my town, Fitz and his murder. Being on the run, meeting Lars, sparring. The time Zedda rescued us, making love, our future. The son my monster of a father robbed us of.

So much, both incredibly good and incredibly bad. The world would never be the same. Neither would I. And somehow, it would continue on. It couldn't just end.

At the fork in the path were the first signs of spring, an oak sapling sprouting tiny green buds through the cold, dead earth, emerging from a hard winter for the seasonal cycle of growth and repair.

A wolf howled in the distance.

Something about the rawness of the moment gave me comfort. I don't know why. Zedda would have liked it; the beauty of nature and of simple wonders always made her smile. I should check her message. If a tree could fight for its life, defying all odds through the worst of winter, so could I.

Her face materialized and my heart skipped a beat.

'Raek,' Zedda began, her face so beautiful. 'I realized there's a chance we might not see each other again, that something could happen tonight. I didn't have time to tell you everything I feel, everything I wanted to say.' She paused.

'Raek Mekorian, I love you, and my future is with you! I didn't want to distract you earlier. But there are no guarantees. In case anything happens, I wanted you to know. And,' she added with a smile that took my breath away, 'You're going to do great things. The world demands it of you. It needs you. I don't know if we'll be together, if that's what fate has in store.' She took a deep breath.

'You're the smartest, strongest person I've ever met, remember that. Remember it when times are hard. You're capable of much more than you know. Don't limit yourself.' She smiled and turned as if someone was coming. 'I need to go, Raek, it's time. Before I do, one more thing: When this is all over, if it ever ends, you're the type of leader I'd follow. You're the type of person that could unify us. Don't change, don't back down. Do it for all of us, do it for me. Love and stuff. See you soon.'

Transmission ended.

No. That couldn't be it. There *had* to be more. I replayed the message twice, but that was it. She was gone...

I sank to the frozen ground and sat there for a long time, eyes closed. "Do it for all of us, do it for me." Her dying wish reverberated through me. Unify mankind?

It was too much to ask.

But she'd asked it, damn it, with her last immortalized breath. There was no un-hearing that. And who was I to deny her? I couldn't let her down. My fists clenched as her impossible mission engulfed me. That was it. That's what I'd do. I had to.

Haunted memories and burning pain spurred me as I rose from the ashes around me.

I'd do it for her. I'd do it for all of them.

I headed back to the farmhouse.

It was time to get to work.

To be continued...

AUTHOR'S NOTE: PLEASE READ!

GET FREE ADVANCE COPIES OF MY UPCOMING BOOKS

Building a relationship with my readers is the best part about writing. I hope you enjoyed Cynetic Wolf and continue to read my books. Raek's adventures will continue, I promise.

I occasionally send newsletters with details on new releases, exclusive offers and discounts, and free copies of my books for early beta readers.

And if you sign up to the mailing list, I'll send you:

1. Free copies of my upcoming books to review.
2. Dozens of hours of interviews with leading biotech researchers like the director of the Human Genome Project, the lead science advisor to the Jurassic Park series, the world's foremost expert on longevity and anti-aging science... plus tons more.
3. Polls on future book titles, cover designs, character names, and more...

You can access everything, be the first to read and review my future books **for free,** and get tons of BONUS hours of content by signing up at mattwardwrites.com/bonuses.

Enjoy this book? You can make a big difference!

Reviews are the most powerful tool in my arsenal when it comes to getting attention for my books. Much as I'd like to, I don't have the finances of a New York publisher. I can't take out expensive newspaper ads or plaster subway stations, *yet*.

But I have something even more powerful and effective, something publishers would kill for.

You guys! A committed, loyal bunch of readers.

If you enjoyed this book, a positive review would be greatly appreciated as it affords me the opportunity to focus more of my energy on my writing and helps persuade others to read my work (it can be as short as you like). Just visit the link below and click: *Write a customer review* at mattwardwrites.com/wolf

Reviews are enormously helpful when it comes to Amazon's rankings and allowing more readers to find my books. And I personally read each and every one!

And don't forget to join my newsletter and FREE advance beta reader team to get exclusive early copies of my upcoming books and more at: mattwardwrites.com/beta

Thank you for taking the time. I hope it's been more than worth your while.

Cheers,

Matt Ward

mattwardwrites.com

ABOUT THE AUTHOR

 Matt Ward is an author, entrepreneur, host of the Disruptors.FM tech podcast, and the #24 ranked futurist worldwide. His work focuses on the intersection of exponential technologies and the ethical issues confronting humanity in the 21st century, as do his novels, which are inspired by the cutting-edge scientists he interviews on his show. Today, Matt writes fast-paced science fiction, fantasy, and speculative fiction technothrillers with a dystopian bent on the question: what does it mean to be human?

You can find Matt online at mattwardwrites.com. Or, you can connect with Matt on Twitter: @mattwardwrites, on Facebook: facebook.com/MattWardBooks, or Instagram: @mattwardwrites, or email him at matt@mattwardwrites.com if you'd like to say hey.

ALSO BY MATT WARD

Raek's Adventure Continues in Wolfish:

Order Wolfish Today!

His impossible hybrid rebellion crushed the immortal government. But then, his wife died, and his unborn son, both at the hands of his all-powerful father.

Now a cripple, Raek must rise once more to fulfill his wife's dying wish: to unify the splintered species of humanity... Even the cyborgs and fallen immortals push for war, revenge, and the absolute decimation of the once subservient hybrids.

Unimaginable destruction amidst a veneer of peace, until a mysterious figure from Raek's past emerges once more.

Overnight, Raek's world is obliterated. Politics, power, betrayal... a new world order? There's a war coming for humanity's future, one with murder, massacre, and intrigue. An awful game, yet all that stands between tyranny and total destruction is a seventeen-year-old wolfish warrior with built-in blasters, and a dying promise he dare not break.

Welcome to 2097, the beginning of the end, or of something much greater. Only time will tell.

Grab Wolfish today if a fast-paced coming of age technothriller of dark twists and unexpected turns to keep you up at night sounds downright dystopian, and awesome!

Join my newsletter to never miss a thing: mattwardwrites.com

DEATH DONOR

Would you sell your life to save another?

Special forces vet, Samantha Jones, is a lowly bodyguard for Ethan Anderson, the biotech billionaire who revolutionized life extension. But at least she's got a job, unlike most, and won't have to sell her organs to support her family. Sure, they're poor, but she's got death insurance and a roof over her head. Life is livable...

But then Sam's daughter is kidnapped and sold for parts. Overnight, her life (and belief in the system) shatters. When the rich bastards get off scot-free, Sam's weak husband commits suicide, and the ex-assassin snaps.

Someone is going to pay.

The question: how to kill the heartless elites that use the poor like livestock and whose security rivals the president? And then there's the senator fighting to abolish life extension, the trillion-dollar corporate standoff, and bloody protests in the streets as conditions deteriorate. Things are about to get ugly.

Death Donor is a speculative fiction technothriller by renowned futurist and sci-fi author, Matt Ward, that features espionage, political drama, and fast-paced adventure in the dark dystopian world of synthetic biology. If you like Michael Crichton, Daniel Suarez, or Neal Stephenson, or loved dystopian classics: the Handmaid's Tale, Brave New World, and Ready Player One, you'll love this page-turning science fiction thriller.

Buy Death Donor today for an action-packed techno thriller... right up to its shocking conclusion.

* * *

Neanderthal King: Imagine Game of Thrones, but with Neanderthals

It's 1107, and the once-great Neanderthal empire is no more, laid waste by the dark Sapien king, Isaac, the same bastard who slaughtered the Thal queen's young heirs. A brutal reversal of medieval power forged in blood and fueled by Sap ingenuity.

But one babe escaped the mad king's wrath.

Raised the son of a simple Thal herder, Maralek's a rough lad with the ferocious pride and temper of his ruined people, a scorn for rules and rulers, and less than a little creativity in his thick skull. In a word, your average Neanderthal.

And life's livable, until King Isaac resumes his bloodthirsty crusade, and Maralek's forced into slaving shackles. Then, a rowdy caravan, a mysterious gypsy, a whispered prophecy… A whirlwind of devastation and war as his master is murdered, his fate unwoven, and his world ripped asunder in an epic battle to end all.

For permission requests or ordering information including quantity sales, contact the publisher, at the address below, or via email: matt@mattwardwrites.com or visit mattwardwrites.com

ISBN: 978-1-7345922-0-7 (Paperback)

ISBN: 978-1-7345922-1-4 (eBook)

ISBN: 978-1-7345922-2-1 (Audioboook)

Any references to historical events, real people, or real places are used fictitiously. Names, characters, and places are products of the author's imagination.

Printed in the United States of America

First edition 2020.

Myrmani LLC

300 Viewpoint Drive

Peachtree City, GA 30269

mattwardwrites.com